SALINA PUBLIC LIBRARY
1701 9100 212 980 3
W9-CAY-771

THE WEB AND THE STARS

THE WEB AND THE STARS

Book 2 of the Timeweb Chronicles

Brian Herbert

FIVE STAR

An imprint of Thomson Gale, a part of The Thomson Corporation

Detroit • New York • San Francisco • New Haven, Conn. • Waterville, Maine • London

Five Star, an imprint of The Gale Group.

Set in 11 pt. Plantin.

LIBRARY OF CONGRESS CATALOGING-IN-PUBLICATION DATA

Herbert, Brian.
The web and the stars / Brian Herbert. — 1st ed.
p. cm. — (Timeweb chronicles ; bk. 2)
ISBN-13: 978-1-59414-217-8 (alk. paper)
ISBN-10: 1-59414-217-3 (alk. paper)
1. Space warfare—Fiction. 2. Space and time—Fiction. I. Title.
PS3558.E617W43 2007
813′.54—dc22 2007031808

First Edition. First Printing: December 2007.

Published in 2007 in conjunction with Tekno Books and Ed Gorman.

Printed in the United States of America on permanent paper
10 9 8 7 6 5 4 3 2 1

For my loving wife and incredible soul-mate, Jan. Thank you for believing in me wholeheartedly, and for never doubting me when I told you truthfully that I had dedicated *Timeweb* to you, and the printer forgot to include that page. With Book Two in the series, *The Web and the Stars,* I am including that original dedication:

Of all the books I have written, I owe the most to Jan for this one. You are the love of my life and my daily inspiration. Thank you for being so understanding while I spend much of my life in my study, taking fantastic journeys through space and time. You are a blessing beyond words.

Chapter One

A thought can be immortal, even if its creator is not.

—Noah Watanabe

They floated in orbital space, torn fragments of thick, lifeless flesh, drifting apart slowly in bright sunlight. Nearby, the powerful sensor-guns of a pod station waited for the emergence of another podship, in a flash of green light. But it did not happen. Now, following three explosions in a matter of hours . . . obliterating as many podships and all of their passengers . . . an eerie silence prevailed.

Looking through the porthole of a shuttle as it made its way through the carnage, Noah Watanabe felt the deepest sadness in his entire life. To his knowledge, nothing like this had ever before happened in history. He had been responsible for it and felt considerable guilt, but reminded himself that the violence had been necessary to prevent further Mutati attacks, and that podships and their passengers had been dying anyway, each time the shapeshifters used their super-weapon against a merchant prince planet. Entire worlds had been annihilated!

For millions of years the gentle Aopoddae had traversed the galaxy to its farthest reaches and back, making their way through perilous meteor storms, asteroid belts, exploding stars, black holes, and a myriad of other space hazards. The sentient spacecraft had survived all of those dangers, and might have continued to do so for the rest of eternity.

If not for the unfortunate intervention of galactic warfare. . . .

They're shooting podships out of space!

In the millennium that he had been the Eye of the Swarm, the leader of the Parvii race, Woldn had never faced a crisis of this dimension. Now he had to make a quick decision and knew it would be the defining moment of his life, the event that would be remembered for eternity.

He flew from star system to star system and then back again in a matter of moments, accompanied by an entourage of only a few million Parviis, moving with him almost as if they were part of his body. Usually he had many more of his kind with him, linked telepathically, but now he needed solitude and room to think. This small group constituted his royal guard, and now he was performing the Parvii equivalent of pacing, flying back and forth across great distances.

His worries caused him to fly faster. He reached such a speed that he very nearly left the others behind. Just before flying into the heart of a red giant sun, he spun around and returned, speeding past his entourage again, in the other direction.

He knew what had led up to the podship crisis, the Mutati torpedoes that destroyed four merchant prince planets, attacks that stemmed from the long-standing enmity between the Humans and their shapeshifting enemies.

When his guards had finally caught up with him, Woldn had made his difficult, monumental decision. The slender Parvii had slowed in the spiral arm of the galaxy, and come to a dead stop in space. His defenders gathered around.

From there, where no outsider could see him, the powerful Eye of the Swarm communicated his decision to his Parvii minions, sending mental signals so powerful that they reached completely across the galaxy, to every sector.

Effective immediately, without regard to who was at fault for the destruction of the three podships at Canopa, the Parviis would cut off all podship travel to and from Human and Mutati worlds. No notices would be sent; podships would simply no longer go to those places. Throughout the rest of the galaxy, service would continue. Furthermore, all podships presently operating in Human and Mutati sectors were to jettison their passengers and cargoes, and report to a remote region of the galaxy.

He transmitted the telepathic commands, ranging far and wide. In those targeted sectors, the bellies of hundreds of podships opened in-flight and everything tumbled out, sending the unfortunate, unwitting passengers to their instantaneous deaths.

In a matter of hours, Woldn received a troubling report that his messages had not reached every Parvii pilot. He had feared this might happen, since the number of telepathic dead zones in the galaxy had been increasing at an alarming rate, running parallel with the disintegration of Timeweb.

Boarding a podship, the Eye of the Swarm prepared to broadcast from a sectoid chamber directly to pilots in other sectoid chambers, a method that boosted his signal strength. In Woldn's lifetime this had never been necessary, but it was one of the methods his predecessors had employed successfully in times of need. On the downside, it might injure the podship he transmitted from, due to the painful amplification of signal strength. But that was a risk he had to take.

Too much was at stake.

Chapter Two

> In the vast universe, there are always hunters and their prey, either overt or latent. As a corollary, all relationships are only temporary, depending upon circumstances, mutual needs, and the availability of alternate sources of energy to satisfy the basic requirements of the living organisms. Symbiosis is only an illusion, and a potentially dangerous trap for the unwary.
>
> —Master Noah Watanabe

As Tesh clung to the wall of the sectoid chamber at the nucleus of her podship, she guided the vessel along the gently curving strands of a deep-space web. Thinking back to a very special wild pod hunt centuries ago, she recalled her initiation into the ancient process. It had been in one of the darkest and most mysterious sectors of the galaxy, where hardly anything could be seen by the naked eye or instrumentation. But from an intense racial need, or survival-based instinct, Parviis on the hunt were able to see with a powerful inner eye—one that illuminated the fleeing podships as glowing green objects, like luminescent whales in a stygian sea.

She had been with other Parviis flying freely in space, millions and millions of them swarming to capture the feral pods, using neurotoxin stingers on the big, dumb creatures to subdue and train them. Gradually, as the podships were controlled and began to respond to the commands of their handlers, the Parviis cut back on the drugs, and drastically reduced their own numbers . . . until finally one tiny Parvii could control each Aopoddae vessel.

Employing that procedure, Tesh was given command of her first sentient ship. It had been an extraordinary, exhilarating experience, and she came to feel that the captured podship was her very own, like a Human teenager with a pony. At the time she knew the ownership sensation was preposterous, because her people rotated piloting duties, but she couldn't help feeling it. Afterward, in due course, she passed the pod on to one of her comrades and went on to other duties.

Reminiscing now, she sighed and felt a profound, deeply satisfying connection with her people and their collective past. For hundreds of years Tesh had piloted countless other podships, but none had been as special as that first capture; like a first love, none had ever occupied the same place in her heart.

Within a narrow range, each Aopoddae ship had a subtly distinct personality, a slightly different way of responding to her commands. While all podships were similar in appearance, her trained eye could make out slightly different vein patterns on the skins, and with a touch she was able to distinguish varying textures. Inside the green, glowing core of this one, she inhaled deeply and identified barely perceptible musk odors, some of which reminded her of that first pod.

She was thinking how relaxing it was out here, speeding along the faint green web strands, hearing only the faint background hum of the sectoid chamber. Then the podship vibrated and slowed.

Using her linkage to peer through the eyes of the sentient vessel, Tesh saw that the web strand—ahead and behind—was slightly frayed, with tiny filaments fluttering in space, as if dancing on a cosmic breeze. Still vibrating, the vessel proceeded slowly over a rough section, making Tesh uneasy. She'd known the web was deteriorating but had never discovered the reason, and as a pilot she had never experienced anything like this before.

Presently the strand's integrity improved, and the podship accelerated again.

The web was a living organism, and over the eons slight aberrations had appeared in it, sections that were not perfectly symmetrical, but this was different. If she'd been a close confidante of the Eye of the Swarm, as she used to be, she could have asked him about it. Woldn was a storehouse of such information.

Parviis communicated with each other in a variety of ways. When flying in a swarm of only a few million individuals, they could beam thoughts to one another telepathically, and could communicate through speech when in close proximity. They could also transmit messages across great distances of space, from sectoid chamber to sectoid chamber, when piloting podships.

But since bygone times, the most important means by which Parviis remained in contact was through the extrasensory morphic field that extended outward from the Eye of the Swarm, reaching Parviis in all sectors of the galaxy. It was one-way, with only Woldn able to transmit freely across space with it, but for Tesh it had always been a comforting, wordless presence, an ineffable sensation that she was part of a larger organism, linked to the Eye and to every Parvii who had ever lived.

Recently, however, she had felt her connection to the morphic field weakening, and an odd, growing impression that she would one day be completely on her own. She wondered if it had anything to do with this podship she had taken control of without Woldn's approval. She was a podship pilot by profession, but was only authorized to operate one that had been captured by a Parvii swarm, under Woldn's supervision.

This Aopoddae was entirely different, a peculiar vessel that she had struggled against Noah Watanabe to control, and which he had eventually permitted her to operate while he took heroic action in an effort to save humankind.

Noah was unlike any *humanus ordinaire* who had ever lived. He had unfathomable powers, abilities that in some respects went beyond those of the Parviis, and of the Tulyans. He frightened her. She sensed that he could take control of the ship back from her at any moment, by reaching out telepathically and overriding her commands. It would do her no good to turn the podship over to the swarm; Noah could just take it back.

Her earlier experience with Noah had occurred during a hiatus from Tesh's duties as a pilot, an ongoing break that had not been relaxing at all, not with all of the problems in the galaxy, including the terrible war between the merchant princes and the shapeshifters. She hoped Noah was safe, but since their parting she had only heard hearsay about him, that he had been taken into custody by the Doge Lorenzo, despite his selfless bravery.

With respect to the podship she was guiding now, she had never heard of a Parvii taking command of one this way. Tesh knew the situation was a gray ethical area, but perhaps in her unique situation she could make a salvage claim to Woldn, and be awarded long-term control of the vessel. She had never heard of a case exactly like this one, but over the millennia some Parviis had received rewards for extraordinary exploits. She recalled some details of other cases, drawing parallels so that she might argue her case to Woldn.

Besides, what if this particular vessel had been contaminated by Noah's connection with it? It might make sense for her to keep it separate from others in the fleet, to avoid having all of them fall under Noah's strange, potentially dangerous spell.

But a sinking feeling told her this was an unfounded fear, a rationalization of her questing mind to come up with an excuse for keeping the podship.

Inside the green luminescence of the sectoid chamber, the background hum intensified, and she heard the Eye of the Swarm communicating with her over the strands of the podways. Tesh's heart sank. But it was not a message for her alone . . . it was for all Parviis in sectoid chambers around the galaxy, and with it she heard the distant squeal of Woldn's podship, from the extreme pain of the galactic transmission.

The urgent, drastic command of her superior appalled her. Despite the destruction of three podships by merchant prince guns, and the ongoing state of war between Humans and Mutatis, that did not justify Woldn's decision. He was committing murder.

Impulsively, Tesh guided her podship through deep space at high speed, searching the main podways for jettisoned passengers that she might rescue. Time after time she arrived too late, however, and found the horribly damaged, space-frozen bodies and other remnants of victims, from most of the galactic races.

And no survivors.

Trying to maintain her composure, Tesh speculated on Woldn's reasoning, that he wanted to discontinue all space travel immediately in the dangerous regions. Such a terrible way to do it, though. He should have ordered the ships to sectors that were not controlled by Humans or Mutatis, permitting the passengers to disembark safely.

Tesh was already considered something of a malcontent in the collective consciousness of her people. In the past she had voiced her opinions openly to Woldn, often to his annoyance. The last time she had defied him, he'd briefly suspended her privilege to pilot a podship. Something like that could happen again, or worse. But she could not worry about that; the stakes were too high. When she saw him again, she would be even more vociferous . . . no matter the consequences.

Stubbornly, Tesh continued to search the podways for signs of life, taking a few minutes longer. Then she set course toward the distant rendezvous point specified by Woldn, which for Parviis was the most secret, most secure place in the entire galaxy.

Chapter Three

> Send nehrcom messages to the best research and development people on the Hibbil Cluster Worlds, and tell them we need faster-than-light spaceships to replace podships. Such a new invention is a matter of utmost priority. The entire Merchant Prince Alliance depends upon it.
>
> —Private wordcom, Doge del Velli to his Royal Attaché

"Our prisoner was right," the uniformed officer announced. He stood stiffly at the center of the richly appointed office while the old nobleman, Doge Lorenzo del Velli, paced along a window wall.

They were in the Doge's new headquarters on Canopa, established as the capital world of the Merchant Prince Alliance after the Mutatis had destroyed Timian One. Francella Watanabe had leased him the top three floors of her own CorpOne headquarters building—for a steep fee, of course.

"Oh?" Lorenzo said. He paused and faced his subordinate, Captain Sheff Uki. In his tailored military garb the young officer had the appearance of a fashion model, but he was tougher than he looked. He was also irritatingly sycophantic at times.

Off to one side, the Doge's Royal Attaché, Pimyt, looked on sternly. The furry little Hibbil stood motionless, his red-eyed gaze fixed on the officer.

"Well, one-third right, Sire," Uki said. "The lab just gave me a report. One out of the three pods carried a deadly explosive device, with Mutati markings on it. Some sort of mega-bomb, our people are saying, a massively powerful torpedo."

"It might be the technology the Mutatis used to destroy Earth, Mars, Plevin Four, and Timian One," Pimyt suggested. The little alien scowled, scrunching his salt-and-pepper beard.

Lorenzo the Magnificent nodded, said, "I want the remains analyzed from every direction, turned inside out. Maybe we can build our own planet-buster and turn it on the slimy shape-shifters."

"That might be possible," Uki said, "but it would take time. We'd have to ramp up, with only bits of information available right now. There would be a big learning curve."

"What about the other pod stations where we set up sensor-guns? Any useful information there?"

"No reports of activity yet. We're getting a steady stream of nehrcom reports from all seven hundred ninety-two of them, orbiting the same number of worlds. No additional MPA planets have been lost, and no more podships have appeared."

The Doge rubbed his projecting chin. "So, Noah wasn't crazy after all. Thank the stars I moved quickly, instead of turning his recommendation over to the Council of Forty for study. Those noblemen would have set up committees and wasted a lot of time."

The officer flicked something off his own lapel. "You made the intelligent decision, Sire. If you hadn't moved quickly during the crisis, I daresay we would not be having this conversation at all."

"Most insightful of you to say that, Captain Uki."

"With your permission, Sire," Uki said, bowing, "I'd like to be excused, to order the investigation you desire."

Doge Lorenzo nodded.

After Uki left, Pimyt said, "He's too smooth to be an officer. I don't trust the man, so I've arranged to replace him. In my customary fashion."

"Kill him, then. But wait until he completes the assignment."

The Royal Attaché smiled, and thought back. It was not the first time Lorenzo had authorized him to get rid of someone, particularly the sniveling sycophants who were drawn to the Doge like iron particles to a magnet. At times like this, whenever he felt respect for the merchant prince leader, Pimyt almost regretted what was about to happen.

Soon, he and his allies would make their move, and it would reverberate across the galaxy. . . .

Chapter Four

> Nothing is ever as it seems. For each apparent answer there is always another more significant one. This is true at every level of observation and interpretation. Thus, the final answer to any question is never attainable . . . perhaps not even by the Sublime Creator.
>
> —Tulyan Wisdom

For weeks, Acey and Dux had stayed in the Tulyan Visitor's Center. The globular, posh orbiter wasn't a spacetel as they had initially thought, since the Tulyans apparently never charged any of the dignitaries for staying there. According to a waitress that Dux befriended in the gourmet dining room, the place had more than a thousand suites of equal size and quality.

Dignitaries!

The first day they were there, Dux walked around with his chest puffed out, imagining how important he and his cousin were. In the corridors, they saw well-dressed personages of varying galactic races whom they imagined to be ambassadors, noblemen and their ladies, and even kings and queens by their appearances, replete with royal entourages. The gaping boys' imaginations ran to considerable extremes. When the two of them later told stories about this experience, any rational listener would undoubtedly discount their assertions, knowing how insular the Tulyans tended to be. There could not possibly have been so many galactic VIPs present at one time. But Acey and

Dux, while having the good sense to avoid making any contact with the other visitors, had fun imagining who they might be. The boys also enjoyed picking out the various alien races they could identify, and marveling at those they had never seen until now. It only whetted their appetites for traveling more throughout the galaxy.

Acey kept saying he was anxious to leave for more adventures, and he'd been developing all sorts of plans about other star systems he wanted to see, and how he would get there. Every day he expressed his increasing restlessness to Dux, and to Eshaz whenever he looked in on them every few days. The Tulyan was performing important work for the Council of Elders, though he would not provide them with details. Whenever the teenagers asked him why they had to stay there, Eshaz said he felt responsible for their safety, and that he would be able to spend more time with them soon.

Soon.

Even Dux, who enjoyed the Visitor's Center far more than Acey, was growing suspicious of that promise. Eshaz's focus seemed to be elsewhere.

As time passed, Acey went to increasing lengths to avoid the comforts of the orbital center. Seeming to make a game out of it, he not only slept on the carpet instead of the bed; he refused to eat in the gourmet dining room, accepting only leftovers or slightly stale food. In addition, he wouldn't go anywhere near the very tempting amenities of the center, not the pools, spas, game rooms, or performing arts chambers.

At first Dux thought his cousin was going too far, but then he began to understand. The two of them would have to leave soon, and Acey's way of handling the overabundance of luxury was easiest for him. In contrast, Dux fully accepted the fact that their stay would not endure, but he went for the full treatment anyway, to "broaden his life experiences." For him, this made complete sense. So, each day Dux luxuriated in the pools and spas, permitting a beautiful *Jimlat* masseuse to give him treatments. He gorged himself on fine foods, and gained two kilos a day.

One afternoon as he headed for the main performance hall, Dux saw Eshaz approaching, lumbering along the corridor with his heavy strides. "Where is Acey?" the Tulyan asked. His scaly bronze skin glistened. He wore a tan cloak with a circle design on the lapel, which seemed to be his formal attire when working on important matters with the Council.

"Hey, Eshaz," the teenager called out, cheerily. "I don't know. Maybe he's walking on nails somewhere." He spoke of Acey's behavior in a humorous way, then noticed that the big reptilian looked upset about something.

Eshaz wouldn't tell him anything until they located Acey, who was sitting in the back of the main kitchen, eating with the workers. Acey, in a large chair at the head of a long opawood table, had been spinning grand yarns, embellishing stories of his adventures on board a treasure ship, taking his listeners to distant, exotic lands in their imaginations. The workers, all of whom were Tulyan, nodded their heads politely, but did not look that impressed. Acey, not seeming to notice their reactions, rambled on, looking like a child propped up on pillows in the Tulyan chair. He stopped when his cousin and Eshaz entered the room.

Seeing Eshaz, one of the most honored web caretakers, the kitchen helpers all stood and bowed respectfully. Eshaz bowed in return, then led the boys to a private dining room, where he ordered tea. When the beverages were delivered and the doors closed, he peered at the pair through slitted eyes, and said, "You young men are in my safekeeping for the moment. I trust you are being treated well here?"

"Like royalty," Dux said. "I've been using every facility. They make you feel like a prince here."

"That is our custom," Eshaz said. "We are a simple people, but we understand the needs of other races, such as your own."

"When can we leave?" Acey asked. "I know. Soon, soon."

"You are anxious to continue your adventures, I see," Eshaz said. "I can understand that, and I apologize for not being able to spend more time with you. But that will change one day." He hesitated, as if avoiding the annoying word "soon," then said to Acey, "It seems odd for a Human not to enjoy the comforts we offer. Are you ascetic for religious reasons? You follow the Way of Jainuddah, perhaps?"

In a sharp tone, Acey responded, "I'm not sure what you mean, but I don't have any religion. I just do what feels best to me."

"Ah yes, Human viscerality," the Tulyan said, nodding. He paused. Then: "I am saddened to inform you that four merchant prince planets, including the capital world of Timian One, have been destroyed by the Mutatis. As a result, Doge Lorenzo has set up a new base of operations on Canopa, where he is presently engaged in warfare against Noah's Guardians." For security reasons, Eshaz did not tell them exactly how he and the Council of Elders had learned all of this, using their Timeweb connections.

"Timian One is gone?" Dux said. "I can't believe it."

"Along with Plevin Four, Earth, and Mars."

"Mars!" Acey said, leaning forward and accidentally knocking his tea over. "Dux and I saw what was left of it!" Acey sopped up tea with a napkin while relating how they had been aboard a podship that passed by the debris field, and the horrors that the passengers saw.

"We thought a huge meteor must have struck the planet," Dux said.

"No meteor," Eshaz said. "The Mutatis have a terrible

weapon." He went on to tell the boys what he knew about Noah's involvement and the pod-killer sensor-guns he caused to be set up on pod stations orbiting all merchant prince planets, weapons that were designed to blast podships the minute they arrived from space, since they might contain Mutati weapons. Then he added, "Unfortunately, Noah is now a prisoner of the Doge."

"He sacrificed himself for the merchant princes, and that's how they reward him?" Acey said. "What kind of gratitude is that?"

"The ways of your race are most peculiar," Eshaz said. "Despite Noah's bravery, Doge Lorenzo and Francella Watanabe are speaking against him, blaming the cutoff of podship travel on him. They don't provide details or reasons, only the false assertion that it is the fault of Noah and his Guardians, and they will be punished for their misdeeds."

"They're lying!" Acey exclaimed.

"Of course they are," Eshaz said. "It is one of the things Humans do best. The truth is, Noah Watanabe is a most remarkable man, rare among the galactic races."

"We need to get back and help him," Dux said.

"But we cannot get to Canopa anymore," Eshaz said, "or to any other merchant prince planet."

"That puts a crimp in our travel plans," Dux said.

Looking out the window of the private dining room, watching the cosmic mists swirling around the Tulyan Starcloud, Eshaz said, "Podships aren't going to Human or Mutati worlds anymore. After they were attacked at Canopa, the creatures started avoiding potential war zones."

"The podships made that decision?" Dux asked, his eyes open wide. "A boycott?"

Eshaz hesitated, for he knew Parviis controlled the vast majority of podships and must have made the decision themselves.

He just nodded, then pointed to the nearby pod station, in synchronous orbit over the starcloud. "For what it's worth to you, we can still travel throughout the rest of the galaxy."

"I've always suspected that podships are smarter than people say," Dux said, "that they're not really big dumb animals."

"I am not permitted to say much about them outside the Council Chamber. I will tell you this, however, my young friends. The Tulyan people have had a relationship with the Aopoddae going back for more years than you can imagine. In modern times our connection with that race has been much more limited than in the past, but I hope to change that one day."

Deep in thought, trying to imagine what the Tulyan was not telling him, Dux nodded, and gazed out the window of the Visitor's Center. The young man watched a podship leave the pod station. As the spacecraft accelerated, it became a flash of light that shifted from pale to brilliant green, like an emerald comet. Then it was gone, vanishing into the black void of the cosmos.

Chapter Five

As Human beings, we are often not proficient at considering the consequences of our actions. Rather, we plunge forward carelessly, taking the path of least resistance. Short-term pleasure. But for the sake of our children and grandchildren, we need to look farther ahead than the stubby tips of our noses.

—Noah Watanabe, *Eco-Didactics*

With his ears attuned to every noise, Noah heard footsteps. Boots, but he could not recognize the stride, the one foot scuffing. Maybe it was another doctor coming to examine his condition. He hated them for probing him every few hours, taking cell and blood samples, hooking him up to machines.

For three days Noah Watanabe and Anton Glavine had been incarcerated at Max One, believed to be the highest-security prison on Canopa. They were in individual cells on separate floors, preventing the men from communicating with one another. The facility, like the notorious Gaol of Brimrock that had been destroyed with Timian One, fronted a broad canal, and had been built around the same time, during the reign of Lorenzo's father.

To Noah it seemed ancient, with green-and-black grime and mold on the stones, and lingering, unpleasant odors. Max One had an ugly reputation during the decades it had been operating, with stories of tortured and murdered prisoners. His father,

Prince Saito, had always said they were only unsubstantiated rumors, but looking around his own cell and walking the rock-lined corridors whenever he was escorted by guards, Noah sensed that bad things had taken place here, and might be occurring at that very moment.

On the third night he heard voices down the corridor, the authoritative tones of guards and the whimpering pleas of a prisoner, followed by an ugly sounding thump. Then footsteps again, and the dragging of a heavy object, probably a body. The noises receded, leaving Noah with his own troubled thoughts.

The fortresslike building echoed with emptiness. The muscular, red-haired man climbed on top of a chair and looked out a high window at the canal. Through the soft orange glow of electronic containment bars, he saw the lights of the Doge's military encampment on the opposite shore, casting reflections across the water. Even at this late hour, soldiers moved around over there, tending to their various tasks.

Any fears Noah had were diminished by the fact that he now seemed impervious to physical harm. In one of his most optimistic projections, he only had to wait, and eventually he would discover a way to gain his freedom. His enemies could not kill him. Or, he didn't *think* they could. Certainly, every method had not yet been attempted. Not even close. He shuddered at the thought of what the Doge's torturers might do to him, the unspeakable suffering they might inflict on him as they performed cruel tests to see how much he could endure. He might be immortal, but apparently that did not come with invulnerability to physical suffering. He remembered only too well the intense, searing pain of the puissant blast to his chest when his own sister shot him.

Through it all, Noah at least had an avenue of escape into the paranormal realm, and he hoped to perfect that ability enough to endure even the most terrible atrocities that his torturers might visit upon him. Noah was able to break away mentally for a few moments at a time, and sometimes longer, to take what he called "timetrance" excursions into the web. But the ability was erratic and unpredictable.

On an earlier excursion into Timeweb, Noah had been able to remote-pilot podships, one at a time. But when he attempted to do the same thing from the prison cell, his power proved unreliable. Like the tendrils of a plant, his mind would reach out into the cosmos, questing, trying to secure itself to a podship. Sometimes he could do it, though for only a few moments before the living vessel jerked away and fled into space. On other occasions he could not even touch one of the vessels. Such attempts disappointed him, because he thought he'd been making progress at unraveling the mysteries of the alternate dimension. But like a playful lover, Timeweb seemed to withdraw and elude him whenever it felt like it, dancing away and then returning, always enticing him, while remaining out of reach.

If only he could remotely control the podships on a regular basis, even one of them at a time, he might find a way of going after the Mutati torpedo weapons. But previous visions had shown him that there were hundreds of the super-bombs in space, surrounding the Merchant Prince Alliance. Noah would need to make a concerted, methodical effort, and he didn't have anywhere near the capability necessary to accomplish that yet. He also realized that even if he found a way of destroying the super-weapons, that wouldn't solve the underlying problem—the ability of the Mutatis to create more of the devices. He couldn't just treat the symptom of the disease. It went much deeper than that.

Despite Noah's frustrations, his ephemeral sojourns into the mysterious realm gave him something he could look forward to. Curiously, some of the paranormal occurrences, even if they lasted for only a few seconds, seemed to take much longer, like complex dreams that were experienced in an instant. But it was not always that way, judging by his own wristchron, which his jailers had allowed him to keep. Sometimes it was exactly the opposite, as longer trips seemed to pass in an instant, and an hour became five seconds. It was as if Timeweb, the teasing lover, was not allowing him to figure out patterns, not permitting him to exploit it.

Noah steeled himself as he heard the footsteps getting closer, and he vowed to outlive this prison, all of its wardens, and all of its doges. He would find a way to survive and live a full, rewarding life, a contributing life. *Life.* Such an unpredictable force, even in his own case, with his cellular system enhanced.

What did his tormenters want of him this time? Had they thought of some new experiment to conduct, yet another painful intrusion? He took a deep, shuddering breath. They weren't giving him enough time to sleep, but he had already noticed a diminishing need for rest, beginning right after Eshaz connected him to Timeweb and gave him the miraculous cure.

Now a new guard appeared on the other side of the containment field, with his features fogged slightly by a glitch in the electronic barrier. He fiddled with the black field-control box on his waist, cursing the trouble he was having with it.

Finally the energy field fizzled and popped, then went down entirely in a crackle and flash of orange.

Noah sprang into the corridor and tackled the guard before he could grab a weapon, slamming him to the floor. Noah was powerfully built, and had been doing daily exercises in his cell, trying to stay as active and strong as possible. The guard was no match for him. With one punch to the jaw, Noah knocked him unconscious.

Just as he was removing the guard's uniform, however, he heard a noise and reached for the man's gun. Before he could unholster it, a bolt of yellow light knocked the weapon away.

Doge Lorenzo emerged from a side passageway, with half a dozen Red Beret soldiers. One of them fired a stun dart at Noah, hitting him in the shoulder and dropping him hard to the stone floor.

"We've been observing you," Lorenzo said. "Taking bets on what you would do. I won, of course."

Chapter Six

Truly great acts are never transitory.
They last into eternity.

—Master Noah Watanabe

It had been a hard day of supervising digging operations in the deep tunnels of the subterranean Guardian base, and Giovanni Nehr felt the leaden weight of fatigue. He still wore the armored, machinelike shell that had been custom-fitted to his body by his robot companions, but it now had green-and-brown colors, like the uniforms of Noah's Guardians. All of the fighters under Thinker's command sported such colors on their bodies now. Gio remained the only Human directly under the command of the robot leader, although he was beginning to work more closely with other Humans all the time.

Subi Danvar greeted Gio in the main cavern, near one of the makeshift barracks. "You want to grab a beer?" the portly adjutant asked. He grinned. "You're the only 'machine' who will drink with me."

"I was going to take a shower, but what the hell. That can wait, eh?" Gio patted Subi on the back, and they trudged off toward the drinking chamber that the Guardians had named the Brew Room.

The bar inside the dimly lit space was a conversation piece in and of itself. The elongated, silvery shell of a decommissioned

Digger machine sat on huge treads that were now bar seats on two sides, fitted with dirty pillows and mattresses to ease the discomforts that even heavy drinking could not mask. Thinker had devised a mechanized method of serving drinks, with glasses of beer popping out of openings all along the hull of the machine onto little platforms that formed tables in front of each seat.

As the two men climbed on a tread and sat down, Gio felt he was making good progress toward getting close to Danvar, who had taken charge of the Guardians in Noah's absence. Already Gio's strong personality had gained him an important position in charge of ongoing construction activities at the base, and he expected further personal gains. That goal was much easier to achieve now that he had gotten rid of those two troublesome boys, Acey and Dux, by drugging them and dispatching them into space. He smiled, thinking about the confusion they must have felt upon waking up inside a cargo box in some distant star system, and not knowing who did it to them . . . although they must have had some suspicion. No matter, they were far away now and couldn't get back anyway, because podship travel had been shut down.

Just then a squat, female Tulyan entered the chamber. Zigzia was one of the few of her race who worked as a Guardian. Like Eshaz did before his departure, she performed ecological recovery and inspection operations. Now, she went to Subi and spoke to him briefly about an environmental-impact class she was starting for younger Guardians.

While ordering a beer, Gio adjusted his armor so that he was more comfortable. He rested his arm on one of the machine's nonfunctioning drill bits, a rough metal bar wrapped in padded cloth. Subi did the same with the drill bit beside him.

The beer flowed while men and women in Guardian uniforms chattered noisily around them, drinking and telling stories, using alcohol to relieve the stresses inflicted on them by the continuing war against the combined forces of the Doge's Red Berets and the corporate army of Francella Watanabe.

In the midst of that conflict, Noah's Guardian forces had been substantially restored on Canopa, and now amounted to thousands of Human and machine soldiers and equipment. All were housed in an elaborate network of underground burrows and large caverns that had been hollowed out by Digger machines that the Guardians had reclaimed. For the past month they had been raiding both Red Beret and CorpOne storehouses, and had also made a number of successful guerrilla attacks against troop barracks, weapons depots, and other military installations.

"I find it amusing and ironic," Gio said to Subi, "that we inhabit a warren of tunnels and caverns deep underground, with much of it directly beneath Noah's old ecological demonstration compound."

"By design, my friend," Subi said. He finished his fourth beer, then shoved the glass under a tap and watched it refill. "Noah chose this place right under the noses of his enemies, where they would not think to look."

"We lead a dangerous life," Gio said, "though we do have a multifunction scrambler system that masks our heat, sound, and visual signatures."

The adjutant nodded. He had set the system up himself, with Thinker.

Suddenly Subi Danvar felt the hum of machinery, but in a place where he hadn't expected it, in the Digger bar itself. With a series of percussive clicks, the drill-bit armrests retracted and the tread began to move, propelling the entire bar slowly to Subi's right. All along the tread, Guardians cried out and jumped off. Beer spilled.

Subi swore, using the most choice selections in his colorful vocabulary. He jumped up on a platform, then noticed that Gio was walking on top of the moving tread, going against the motion and holding onto his glass of beer.

After traveling a few meters to one side, still a good distance from the cavern wall, the mechanism stopped, and drill bits popped back out, still with their padding.

Calmly, Gio placed his beer on a drinking platform that was directly in front of him now, and sat down again on the tread. Looking over at Subi, he said, "A little musical-bar-stool trick we added," he said. "I suggested it to Thinker, and he thought it was a fine idea, to keep the Guardians alert to anything."

"They look more than alert now," Subi said, resuming his seat beside Gio. "In fact, I'd say they're in an ornery mood."

"Drinks are on me!" Gio said, as he watched people wipe dirt off their uniforms. "Set 'em up."

Actually, none of them had to pay for beers. It was one of the fringe benefits of their dangerous jobs.

Gradually the word got out about what Gio Nehr and the machines had done, and nervous laughter erupted in the Brew Room.

"When will it go on again?" a man shouted, as he climbed back up onto the tread.

"When you least expect it," Gio said.

Beer and hard drinks flowed, while Subi turned the conversation to the one that had grown closest to his heart, the whereabouts and safety of their missing leader, Noah Watanabe.

"I'd like to break him out," the adjutant said, "But we have conflicting reports on where he is."

"I've been on two of the recon missions," Gio said.

"Yeah, I know."

"Thinker got all the data, and doesn't think our chances of finding Master Noah are very good, since there are too many possible holding places for him. This is a very large planet."

"No matter," Subi said. "We'll keep sending out robots and people like you. I promise you, we'll find him no matter how long it takes. Some reports have him in one of the fifteen prisons on Canopa, or in one of the smaller jails, or even underground. I don't think they took him off-planet, not with the cessation of podship travel and the slowness of other means of space travel."

"Sounds like you've analyzed every detail yourself," Gio said.

"I have, and I'll never give up until we find him."

"I know you won't. None of us will. At this very moment, Thinker is undoubtedly assembling all available data on where Noah could be, and running probability programs. Unfortunately, the Master's captors have covered their tracks, and have dispersed many false clues as to his whereabouts."

As the buzz of conversation died down, Gio excused himself and walked wearily out into the main chamber, to the barracks there. Most of the other Guardians did the same, but Subi remained behind, nursing his last glass of dark ale.

Whatever method the Guardians used to rescue Noah, it would have to be a guerrilla strike . . . in and out quickly, like the successful attacks they had been making against Red Beret and CorpOne facilities. The Guardians, even with the inclusion of Thinker's small army, did not have the force necessary to fight their powerful foes any other way. They had to use cunning and subterfuge.

Finally, Subi trudged back out into the main cavern, moving slowly and purposefully through the low illumination. As he climbed the stairs of the barracks, his thoughts drifted back to Giovanni Nehr.

While Subi was impressed by the man's energy and ideas, he was troubled that he could not quite figure him out, could not quite get a comfortable handle on him. At times, Gio could be smooth and erudite, while on other occasions he mixed easily with the lowest ranks, the grunts and trainees. He certainly was an independent sort, with potentially strong leadership qualities. But something troubled Subi about him, something he couldn't quite grasp.

In bed, he lay awake thinking about it. The teenage cousins had not liked Gio, based upon their prior relationship, but so far those details had not surfaced . . . and probably never would, now that they had gone AWOL. Before that he'd asked the boys and Gio for more information, without receiving any satisfactory answers. Acey and Dux had probably gone off to join another treasure ship, or they were on some other space adventure. They were known to have talked about such things on the night before disappearing.

Gradually the calming effects of alcohol sank in, and Noah's loyal adjutant drifted off to sleep.

Chapter Seven

By their very nature, secrets are invariably contained in imperfect vessels that crack and leak, given the right set of circumstances.

—Lorenzo del Velli

On the strangest morning of General Jacopo Nehr's life, he awoke to hear alien voices jabbering inside his bedroom, as if people had seeped through the walls from somewhere outside. But as he sat up and yawned the voices drifted away, and finally fell silent.

Swinging out of bed, he shambled to a bay window, thinking it must have been a dream. Still, the voices had seemed to come from somewhere around here. At a window seat, he pushed a mobile nehrcom transceiver out of the way and sat down to gaze out toward the front walkway of his forested estate.

Rubbing sleep from his eyes, Nehr saw two of his blue-uniformed security men working with a large black dog, doing training exercises. The men did not appear to be concerned about anything, and Jacopo had observed this sort of activity many times before. Nothing seemed out of the ordinary.

A fuzzy, staticky noise near his leg caused him to jerk, before he realized it was the shiny black transceiver he always carried, which he had forgotten to turn off. But it never made that sort of noise, because nehrcom transmissions were always crystal clear, even when made across great distances of space.

Perplexed, he lifted the unit and fiddled with the digiscroll settings. He heard a static pop, followed by voices again, this time unmistakably alien. Jacopo did not understand the rapid-fire words, but felt a sinking sensation. The way he had set up the nehrcom installations around the Merchant Prince Alliance, all under Human control, he should not be hearing anything but Galeng—the common galactic language—and clear signals.

Something was terribly, terribly wrong.

Perspiration formed on his brow as his mind whirled. If aliens had taken over a nehrcom station and figured out how to transmit and receive, the signals should still be clear. It didn't make sense. The system was unproblematic the way he had set it up; it couldn't possibly go out of adjustment. It was either completely on or completely off, and trouble-free either way. Jacopo knew the technology well.

He also knew the security system. As the nehrcom inventor and the appointed Supreme General of the MPA Forces, this information was etched indelibly into his mind.

The secret workings of nehrcom transceivers were protected by internal explosive devices that would go off if anyone scanned or tried to open them. The booby traps were common knowledge, and there had been widely publicized explosions and deaths. They were not ordinary blasts either, because they left absolutely no evidence behind about the original composition of the transceivers. Every piece was left unrecognizable, with even the cellular structures changed. He had devised an extraordinarily clever method of protecting his priceless secret.

Nonetheless, something had gone dreadfully wrong.

Jacopo locked on to the mysterious signal and sent a tracer, bouncing the nehrcom transmission back to its source. A holo-image of one of the galactic sectors popped up from the transceiver, and floated in front of the astonished inventor's eyes.

The signal was coming from one of the Mutati strongholds, the planet of Uhadeen!

Utterly impossible. He rechecked, and rechecked. No doubt of the source, and he found additional transmissions going back and forth between Uhadeen and Paradij, the capital world of the Mutati Kingdom.

But how could that be?

A nehrcom unit could not be moved from its original place of installation, unless one of two people personally deactivated the detonator. No one knew how to do that except him and his daughter Nirella, whom he trusted implicitly. The two of them worked closely together, so he would need to confer with her about this disturbing situation.

Jacopo was developing an intense headache. His clothes were drenched in perspiration. He couldn't stop shaking.

The holo-image shifted as the transceiver tried to pick up a visual of whoever was talking on the other end. Nothing came across, no matter how much he tuned it, just static.

One unmistakable conclusion occurred to him. The Mutatis now had their own version of the system. But how did they accomplish that? They didn't seem to have perfected their version yet, since it was making static sounds. He recalled having had that problem himself early in the development process, and then figuring out the solution.

Another voice came out of the transceiver. This time it was in Galeng, but with a whiny Adurian accent, complaining that the Mutatis had no access to podships anymore, and could no longer launch "Demolio attacks" against merchant prince planets.

Demolio attacks?

Jacopo's pulse was going crazy. His thoughts could not keep up.

Thinking back, struggling desperately to comprehend, Nehr

remembered one unfortunate leak in security two months ago. On that day, Doge Lorenzo's Royal Attaché, Pimyt, marched into Nehr's office and showed him a holo-image of the internal workings of a nehrcom transceiver. Nehr had been startled half to death, but felt immensely relieved when Pimyt promised not to reveal the secret—and ruin him—if Nehr just performed a few innocuous tasks for him. Discreetly, Nehr had launched an investigation to determine the source of the leak, but nothing had turned up.

It was blackmail, to be certain. But the penalty had not seemed too great. Nehr only had to send occasional communiqués—provided by the Hibbil—to all planets in the Merchant Prince Alliance. The messages had been about corporate and military matters, the moving of business assets and war material around.

Nehr had been adhering to their secret agreement. It seemed to be some sort of war-profiteering scheme that Pimyt had come up with, a way of boosting his government salary. Nehr had seen countless examples of greed in the Alliance, and he had learned to look the other way more than once.

As for Pimyt, he was beyond reproach from a security standpoint, having once served as the Regent of the Merchant Prince Alliance, during a brief period when the noblemen could not agree upon the election of a new Doge. If he made some extra money during wartime, that just made him like so many others in the government.

And now, Demolio attacks against merchant prince planets? Nehr would have to discuss the matter with Lorenzo. Perhaps . . . probably . . . it had something to do with the MPA planets that had been destroyed.

But he couldn't discuss any of this with Lorenzo. Pimyt had threatened to ruin him if he revealed their little arrangement to anyone, and the little Hibbil had mentioned the Doge by name.

Beyond that, Pimyt had insisted that Noah come to him first if anything unusual happened involving nehrcom transmissions. This certainly qualified.

Demolio attacks.

Nehr and Lorenzo knew the Mutatis had a terrible planet-buster weapon—was it called a Demolio?—and the Doge had taken steps to block it. Steps that had worked only too well, cutting off all podship travel in Human and Mutati sectors. But should Nehr keep this new information from him? Having made his bargain with Pimyt, Nehr had no choice. If any of this got out, he could be charged with treason, based upon an accusation that he had sold nehrcom secrets to the Mutatis.

He thought of his younger brother, how he had vanished. Could Gio have contacted the Mutatis and told them something about nehrcom technology? No, it wasn't possible. Gio had not been privy to the information, and besides, the two of them were brothers. At times Jacopo wished they had been closer, but it hadn't been in the cards. Now Gio was gone . . . probably killed on one of the destroyed merchant prince planets. So many deaths in this war. So many innocent lives lost.

Nehr cursed at the situation in which he was caught, and shut off the transceiver. The resulting silence held no answers for him.

Chapter Eight

There is great skill in concealing your feelings of antipathy from someone you must deal with on a regular basis.

—Jacopo Nehr, confidential remarks

Throughout the Merchant Prince Alliance—on the seven hundred ninety-two surviving planets—there had been no appearances of podships whatsoever. On every one of those pod stations, sensor-guns were ready to fire, but they remained silent. People expected something to change at any moment, something big to happen. Time went by slowly and painfully for everyone, as if the clock of the universe had a sticky mechanism.

On every planet the citizens felt isolated, that they would never see distant loved ones again, and would never again be able to journey to their favorite places around the galaxy. It was like a cruel, galactic-scale version of an old party game. Wherever a person happened to be when the podships stopped was where they remained, perhaps for the rest of their lives.

When podships first appeared long ago, Humans and other galactic races had been hesitant to trust alien craft that they could not control, especially since they had no idea how they worked and couldn't gain access to their inner workings without causing violent reactions. But as decades and centuries passed, and podships (left to their own devices) kept transporting the various races safely to far destinations, the races had come to trust them. The sentient spacefarers became familiar to everyone, as their regular appearance at pod stations became a fact of life and of the heavens . . . like the sun seeming to rise in the sky each morning.

For a long time there had been talk of improving other space-travel technology, and recently there had been a rumor that Doge Lorenzo was calling for a massive research and development program to do so. Even barring that, it was still possible for people to travel on factory-made ships. But the hydion drive engines transported them so slowly in comparison to podships that it wasn't even worth comparison. It might be decades, if ever, before engineers came up with comparably fast vessels.

At least the Mutatis, with their solar sailers, were even farther behind. That provided some measure of comfort.

And, though Jacopo Nehr could not go directly to Doge Lorenzo with his startling discovery, at the risk of agitating Pimyt, he had decided to take another course of action. One that would not subject him to court martial and execution for hiding important military information during a time of war. As the Supreme General of all merchant prince military units, he had to walk a tightrope.

He was convinced that Doge Lorenzo could not be kept in the dark about this, but there were necessary channels to go through, to protect himself.

With a recording device hidden on his person, Nehr located Pimyt in the Royal Attaché's private exercise room, in the basement of the administration building. It was certainly the most unusual workout facility that Nehr had ever seen, and after passing through security he saw Pimyt on a machine that was a prime example of this.

The furry little Hibbil was on a stretching rack, resembling a torture machine of medieval Earth, except that this one stretched the body sideways, not head to foot, and there was no "victim." Pimyt, connected to straps on the machine, operated the controls with a brass-colored, handheld transmitter.

Nehr knew why. The Royal Attaché was one of a small number of Hibbils who had a chronic disease known as LCS—lateral contraction syndrome. Hibbils had a secondary vestigial spine that was no longer of any use, and in some members of their race, this spine had a tendency to compress in width, drawing other bones inward and causing the body to narrow, sometimes to such dangerous proportions that organs were crushed and death resulted. Some victims survived, but were crippled, no longer able to walk or use their arms.

For LCS sufferers, it was important to go through regular, rigorous physical therapy, as Pimyt did several times a week. It seemed like a primitive way of treating the condition, but reportedly it worked better than drugs or other methods.

When Jacopo Nehr approached Pimyt, the Hibbil was grimacing in pain as the machine pulled him from his left and right sides. His eyes watered.

"I need to talk with you," the general said. "I'm sorry to disturb you, but it's urgent."

"Well, what is it?" Pimyt pressed a button on the transmitter to increase the tension, and the pain.

"It's something the Doge needs to know, and it involves the internal workings of nehrcoms. You cautioned me not to discuss . . . certain things . . . with him, so I thought it best to come to you instead."

"You're not making any sense."

The chisel-featured man cleared his throat. "As you know, I keep a mobile nehrcom transceiver with me at all times. This morning I heard voices on it in an alien language. Tracing the transmission, I found it was going back and forth between the planets of Uhadeen and Paradij, in the Mutati Kingdom."

"What?"

"Toward the end of the transmission I identified an additional voice, speaking Galeng in an Adurian accent."

He brought the shiny black transceiver out of his pocket, and switched on a playback mechanism. Alien voices spoke for several minutes, followed by the Adurian-accented Galeng.

After listening, Pimyt said, "What's the significance of this?"

"There shouldn't be transmissions in the Mutati Kingdom at all, and the Adurian-accented voice is of additional concern. The Adurians are allies of the Mutatis, as you know."

"This is very strange." The Hibbil looked up at him with watery red eyes. "You must be mistaken."

"No mistake. I checked and rechecked. It came from the Mutati Sector."

"They stole some of the units?"

He shook his head. "Not possible, due to the detonators I rigged at every transmitting station. No, the Mutatis must have built their own transceivers. The transmission quality was fuzzy, but clear enough for us to understand what the Adurian said. You heard him. He spoke of the Mutatis no longer being able to employ Demolios—whatever they are—against merchant prince planets, since they could no longer use podships."

Pimyt glared up at him. "Are you accusing me of leaking the technology?"

Nehr's eyes widened in anger. "No, of course not."

"Because if you are, I can still let the details of your nehrcom secret out and ruin you when your business competitors find out how simple the transceivers are and start manufacturing their own."

"Not without piezoelectric emeralds, they won't. Those stones aren't easy to get anymore, not without podship travel."

Pimyt tightened the tension on the stretching machine again, pulling his body even more. He set the control device on a table, and said, "Maybe so, but it would still ruin your reputation as a *genius* inventor." Despite his pain, Pimyt laughed. "The great inventor Jacopo Nehr! A child could have put together what you did. No wonder you concealed the secret for so long."

"A child could not have cut the piezo emeralds with the necessary precision," Nehr huffed.

"Nonetheless, my point is well taken. It is a comparatively simple system, easily understood by a layman."

"Even so, the nehrcom system is one of our critical technologies, a military secret. You don't want to compromise that."

"What difference does it make now, if—as you said—the Mutatis already have it anyway?"

"Look, I don't want to argue with you. I know you're just making your own profits off this war, and that's fine with me. It doesn't mean you aren't a patriot at heart. We're both on the same side with the highest level of security clearance, and we have an understanding between us. As you instructed, I sent your communiqués to all merchant prince planets, and in turn you're protecting my business secrets. The Mutatis must have come up with the system on their own, and they haven't perfected it yet."

Pimyt pursed his lips, thinking. He looked agitated. His dark-eyed gaze darted around the room.

Nehr felt a mixture of fear and rage, and intense loathing for this Hibbil. But he concealed his feelings, not letting the furry little bastard see anything in his expression. Still, the inventor imagined grabbing the control for the stretching machine and torturing Pimyt until he was torn apart.

As Nehr savored the idea, Pimyt grabbed the control unit. "You are wise to come to me," he said. "I will discuss this with Doge Lorenzo, and we will order an investigation immediately. Do you think it could be a defect with your mobile transceiver? Could it have picked up freak radio signals?"

"I don't think so."

"Nonetheless, you will give me your transceiver, since we will need it for the investigation."

"But I am the only one capable of working on the system, along with my daughter, Nirella."

"Don't be absurd. A child could work on nehrcoms, and you know it. I have people I trust to do the work . . . under strict security clearance, of course."

"Uh, well, I don't know if. . . ." He wilted under the Hibbil's red-eyed glare, and added quickly, "All right." Reluctantly, Nehr brought the mobile unit out of his jacket pocket and set it on the table.

Pimyt disconnected himself from the stretching rack and swung his short legs onto the floor. He walked around stiffly, then said, "As a reward and a token of our friendship, General Nehr, I am in a position to obtain additional tax benefits and other cost-saving arrangements for your manufacturing facilities on the Hibbil Cluster Worlds." His face darkened. "I am also in a position to do the opposite, if I wish."

Nehr stared at the floor. "With podship travel cut off, I'm not sure if I'll ever see those tax advantages."

"Then we'll come up with something else."

"I would appreciate that."

Without another word, the Royal Attaché took the nehrcom transceiver and left through a side door. The meeting was over.

When he was alone, Pimyt listened to the Adurian voice on the recording again, confirming his own first impression. It was, without a doubt, VV Uncel, the Adurian Ambassador to the Mutati Kingdom.

He was a friend of Pimyt's . . . but not of the Mutatis. Uncel must have gone to Paradij on business for the clandestine Hib-Adu Coalition, which was working to overthrow both humankind and the shapeshifters, and he'd been stuck there by the podship crisis.

The Hibbil scowled for a moment as he wondered if Jacopo Nehr could upset his carefully laid plans. But the thought passed. Nehr was like an insect trapped in a narrow tube, with only one way to go.

Chapter Nine

We are receiving sporadic reports of nehrcom transmission glitches, of inexplicably weak and even lost transmissions. The problems seem to have nothing to do with our transmitting stations around the galaxy, since service personnel have checked and rechecked every one of them. The failures are few and far between, but remain troubling, since nothing like this has ever occurred in the past. In their first decades of use, nehrcoms earned a reputation for perfect reliability and strong signal quality.

—Confidential internal document, Nehrcom Industries

Early one morning, Noah awoke to the noise of men arguing, in the corridor outside his cell. He tried to see them, but could not get an angle to see more than shadows against a rock wall.

"I received no notification of this," a voice said. "I will have to check with Warden Escobar."

"He won't be in for hours," a man said in a high-pitched, irritated whine. "We can't wait that long, and I have an authorization that supersedes him anyway. Now, open the damned cells!"

"Well, I don't know. . . ."

"Do you want to answer to the Doge's office for your stupidity? They will not be kind to you, and could put you in one of these cells. If you are allowed to live. I am here on a Priority One assignment. Look at the authorization, you fool. If you can read."

"I can read, I can read." Noah heard papers rustling.

"Gad, you're an idiot. The authorization allows me to take any and all prisoners, as needed, for work details. With the cessation of podship travel, there is a shortage of slaves and imported robots to perform menial tasks on Canopa. Thus we are forced to draw work crews from Human and non-Mutati alien prisoners. Do you understand?"

Finally the guard said, "OK, I guess this is in order, but if there's any flak over putting Watanabe on work detail, you're taking it, not me."

"Yeah, yeah."

A loud click ensued, and then a slight dimming of the electronic containment barrier around Noah. The glowing orange bars disappeared.

"All right!" the high-pitched voice said, as the man pounded something metal against a wall. "Everybody out. It's time to go to work!"

The man turned out to be a work crew boss, with a squad of armed guards. They herded Noah and other prisoners out a side entrance. On the paved street, Noah encountered Anton in the midst of the prisoners. Approaching the younger man, Noah saw that he had a bright red mark on one side of his face.

"What happened to you?" Noah asked.

Looking around warily, Anton whispered, "They burned me with a laser on a low setting, threatened to blind me if I didn't confess."

"Confess to what?"

"To trying to assassinate the Doge. I told them that was preposterous. I only followed you to the pod station to make certain Tesh was safe. She was my only concern. I had no idea the Doge or Francella would be there, or that we would be arrested."

"No, of course not." Noah didn't comment, but remembered

noticing signs of Anton's jealousy concerning his own relationship with the pretty young woman who had once been Anton's girlfriend. While Noah had reached an understanding with her over the control of a podship, he'd never had romantic intentions toward her.

"There's something I want to discuss with you," Anton said. "I've been having memory problems, an ability to remember some things, while other details fade away whenever I try to recover them. It's like . . . like my mind is playing tricks on me."

"They tortured you," Noah said angrily.

"Yes, but I started having this problem right after they took us into custody on the pod station. I recall trying to go to sleep in my cell that first night, with thoughts churning in my mind, but my brain wouldn't work, at least not completely. I sensed things slipping away."

"I'm no doctor, but it sounds stress-induced," Noah said.

"We sure have a lot of that," Anton said.

A guard pushed them apart with an electronic prod and shouting threats.

All of the prisoners were loaded on a groundbus, and whisked away to a walled compound just outside the industrial metropolis of Rainbow City. Noah recognized the area. He'd been there many times, under better circumstances. As the gates opened and the bus surged through, he saw a high, round tower ahead, which he knew to be one of the nehrcom transmitting stations for sending high-speed messages across the galaxy.

The work crew spent the rest of the morning performing landscape work and spraying poisons outside the transmitting station. Supposedly, this was to keep insects, small animals and plants away from the highly sensitive facility, which required an almost antiseptic environment. Noah had heard about this procedure, and had always wondered if it was one of many ruses employed by Jacopo Nehr to throw anyone off track who might be trying to figure his transceiver out.

As Noah sprayed a canopa oak, he forgot where he was for a moment and smiled at Jacopo's eccentricities. Now the famous inventor was Supreme General of all Merchant Prince Armed Forces. Noah wondered how he was doing at that, and which planet he had ended up on when the podships stopped.

Preoccupied, Noah didn't notice a black robot watching him intensely. The robot moved closer. . . .

Moments before, Jimu had come out of the nehrcom building, having sent a cross-space message on behalf of the Red Berets. He had no idea what the message was, only that it was high priority. By definition, anything sent by this means fell into that category. Afterward, he paused to watch the work crew around the building.

It was almost midday, with low gray clouds that threatened to dump their moisture on the land.

Thinking he saw a familiar face in the crew of prisoners, Jimu had paused to search his internal data banks. Now he brought up the information: Noah Watanabe, along with a summary of his biography and the charges against him.

The blond, mustachioed man working near him also looked familiar. Moments later, Jimu had his name, Anton Glavine, and all of the particulars on him, including his parentage: Doge Lorenzo del Velli and Francella Watanabe.

Concerned about finding such high-security prisoners on the work crew, Jimu did rapid scans on the others. None of them were anywhere near the caliber of these two.

The robot was deeply concerned. This was important work at the nehrcom station, but he didn't think that such high-priority prisoners should be included in the assignment. It must be some sort of a mistake.

He activated weapons systems on his torso, and took custody of the two men. "You will come with me," he said, in an officious tone.

Three guards approached, weapons drawn. Jimu had the prisoners behind him inside a crackling energy field, a small electronic containment area.

As he argued with the guards, Jimu opened a comlink to his superior officer in the Red Berets, and notified her of what he had discovered. "I thought it best to protect the prisoners, and then ask for instructions," he reported.

While the dedicated, loyal robot awaited further instructions, more guards appeared and surrounded him. None of them were robots, and he knew he had the weapons systems to blast through if necessary. But he maintained his mechanical composure. A standoff.

Twenty minutes passed.

Finally, Jimu's superior officer in the Red Berets appeared, a self-important woman named Meg Kwaid. She marched up to him sternly, followed by half a dozen uniformed soldiers. A tall woman with curly black hair, she smiled and said, "That was quick thinking, Jimu. This will look good in your personnel file."

She ordered Jimu to release the two prisoners, and when he did, she assumed custody over them. "This pair is going back to prison," Kwaid said.

Just before departing, she took a third man into custody . . . the work crew boss who had removed them from the prison in the first place.

"No one told me they were high-value prisoners," the man protested. "I was only ordered to get the work done, and I didn't have the manpower."

His protests were to no avail. The man was put in a cell just down the corridor from Noah Watanabe.

Jimu returned to his own assignment, with his career path enhanced.

Among the Red Berets, Jimu's machines were unusual: they were "breeding machines" that could locate the necessary raw materials and construct replicas of themselves. Since joining the force, Jimu had been supervising the construction of additional fighting units, more than quadrupling the number of machines he originally brought with him from the Inn of the White Sun. All of Jimu's machines serviced themselves, and made their own energy pellets from raw materials, including carbon and mineral deposits.

Now, with the high demand for laborers, he was ordered to increase his production rate, adding a new type of machine—a worker-variant—to the fighting units he had been manufacturing. As with everything he did, Jimu completed this assignment with utmost efficiency. In short order, he had full production lines operational, producing both types of machines.

For this, and for his quick thinking in the Watanabe and Glavine extractions, he was promoted to a fourth-level Red Beret. This gave him access to more of the secret rituals, language, and symbols of the military society. Jimu just memorized them; he didn't really understand why people were so fascinated with such matters.

But Jimu had a continuing problem.

The sentient machines under his command were being mistreated, jeered at and kicked by many of the Red Beret soldiers, especially whenever the Human men drank. Too often, alcohol was thrown at the robots to see if they would short out—a bitter, sticky drink called nopal that the men favored.

Through it all, the machines still remained loyal to their Human masters, and so did Jimu. Their internal programming did not permit them to do otherwise, and they had fail-safe mechanisms to make sure nothing went wrong.

Chapter Ten

What is the highest life form?
What is the lowest?
The answers defy analysis.

—Tulyan Wisdom

In his cell one evening, surrounded by the orange glow of a pattern-changing containment field, Noah had plenty of time to think. The guards had modified the electronic field around him. Instead of traditional bars, now triangles, squares, and other geometric shapes glimmered and danced around him.

In them, he thought he saw images of Humans being blasted away or maimed, with their arms and legs flying off. Since he had performed amazing mental feats himself, it occurred to him that he might be able to focus and catch what he thought were subliminal messages in the containment field, cruel tricks employed by his captors. Noah tried this for a while, but found himself unable to do so.

His thoughts drifted to what kept him busy most of the time when he was alone, envisioning ways he might escape from this dismal cell in Max One. Intermittently he had been able to accomplish this, but only in his mind, where he took fantastic but unpredictable space journeys. And always when he returned from those sojourns into the realm of Timeweb, he was faced with a stark reality, the imprisonment of his body.

As before, the space journeys were like timetrances, and he looked forward to them. They were increasingly unpredictable, though, in that he could never predetermine how long he would remain in the alternate dimension. Sometimes, after only a few moments of mental escape, he felt himself kicked out, dumped back into his cold cell.

One morning Noah lay on his bunk, staring at the ceiling. A spider was working up there, using its legs to spin an elaborate, wheel-shaped web to trap insects. The spider went down the web, working for several moments with one pair of legs, then alternating with others. Then it went back up.

From somewhere, Noah heard a terrible scream. His heart dropped. He hoped it was not Anton. He also prayed that the injury was not too severe. But the scream told him otherwise.

As far as Noah was concerned, the Doge was the worst of all men, not only for his cruelties to prisoners, but for the damage his Merchant Prince Alliance inflicted upon the environment. The ecology of each planet—like the cellular integrity of each prisoner—was a living thing, deserving of respect and care.

Noah became aware of the spider again. It had lowered itself on its drag line and was suspended just overhead, staring at Noah with multi-faceted eyes. Noah saw intelligence there, and perhaps more.

This tiny creature seemed, in many respects, superior to a Human being.

Abruptly, the spider rose on its line and returned to its web. Noah found himself struck by the perfection of the gossamer structure, so uniquely beautiful and astounding in the way it had been spun. He found his mind expanding on its own, spinning into the cosmos and onto the faintly green cosmic webbing that connected the entire galaxy. As if he were a podship himself, he sped along one strand and then another, changing directions rapidly, vaulting himself out into the far, dark reaches of space.

He saw a podship and caught up with it, but he could not gain control of it. He was, however, able to seep inside, and entered the central sectoid chamber. There, he saw a tiny Parvii pilot controlling the creature from a perch on the forward wall of the chamber.

Tesh! he thought, feeling a rush of excitement.

She looked to one side, and then to another, as if sensing his presence.

Noah noticed something different this time, compared with prior occasions when he had journeyed around the cosmos. A faint mist formed where he was, and it took the barely discernible shape of his own body, dressed in the very clothing he had on now. Could she see this? Was it really occurring, or was it only in his imagination?

Drifting closer to her, he dwarfed her with his presence. And he whispered to her, but to his own ears the words were ever so faint, as if coming from far across the cosmos. "I've missed you," he said. "Can you hear me? I'll tell you where I am."

No reaction.

He said it again louder, and this time he added, "Have you been thinking about me, too?"

She looked to each side again, and then turned her entire body and looked around the sectoid chamber.

"You heard me, didn't you?" he said.

A perplexed expression came over her. She looked toward him, but in an unfocused way, as if peering beyond him.

To check her, Noah moved around the chamber, and after a moment's delay each time, her gaze followed his movements. "What do you see?" he asked.

No reply. Obviously, she could not make out the words, and he didn't think she could discern his ghostly mist, either. But she seemed to be sensing something. How far did it go?

On impulse, he floated to her side. Since his physical form

(as he saw it) was much larger than hers, and he wanted to kiss her, he brought his mouth as close to hers as he could and let his lips touch hers. Or seem to.

Instantly, she jerked her head back, then brought a hand to her mouth.

"Who's there?" she demanded.

He kissed her again in the mismatched way, like a hippophant kissing a tiny bird. This time she didn't pull her head back, but left it in position, and even moved toward Noah just a little, as if cooperating in the cosmic contact.

"Noah?" she said as they separated. "Is that you?"

In response, he attempted to kiss her again, but this time she showed no reaction at all. He tried again, but still she didn't respond. "Tesh?" he said. "Did you feel that?"

Abruptly she turned away, and resumed her attention to her piloting task. "I'm going crazy," she said. "That wasn't Noah. It couldn't be."

"But it is me!" he shouted. Now he didn't hear the words at all, not even the faintest sound. And looking down at his misty form, he saw that it was fading, disappearing entirely.

In a fraction of a second, Noah found himself back in the prison cell, wondering what had just occurred.

Chapter Eleven

Never let down your guard, especially in time of war.
—Mutati Saying

The violence had been totally unexpected.

On the grounds of the Bastion at Dij, the Emir Hari'Adab strolled along a flower-lined meadow path, skirting a grove of towering trees. A large white bird flew beside him, alternately soaring upward into the cerulean sky and then back down again, keeping pace with him.

But it was not really a bird. It was a shapeshifter, a female aeromutati with whom he had a special relationship. For the moment, she left him to his troubled thoughts.

In contrast, Hari'Adab was a shapeshifter who moved along the ground, a terramutati like his father the Zultan. As a boy growing up on Paradij, he had always intended to do what was expected of him. Since Zultan Abal Meshdi and Hari's late mother, Queen Essina, had little time for him, the boy had been raised by tutors, always taught the proper way of doing things. In particular, he was taught to show respect for his elders and for the rules of Mutati society that had been laid down by the wise zultans and emirs of countless generations.

In Mutati society, a man kept his word, and that imperative started at an early age, as soon as he could speak and understand the rule of law, and the unwritten code of honor that was passed on from generation to generation by word of mouth. By those standards he had pledged to uphold important traditions, the threads that held together the powerful social fabric of his people.

Throughout his young but eventful life, though, Hari had expressed more than his share of defiance, bordering on rebelliousness. He had steadfastly refused to use an Adurian gyro that his father gave to him, a foreign-made mechanical device that was supposed to help him make better decisions. In the past couple of years it had become very popular in Mutati society, particularly among the young, but Hari didn't trust the Adurians or their inventions. That race, from far across the galaxy and supposedly allied with the Mutatis, had insinuated themselves on Mutati society in a short period of time, bringing in their loud music, garish clothing, noisy groundjets, and a whole host of other products.

It didn't make sense. Hari had been brought up to respect Mutati traditions, but his father had permitted an alien culture to change what it meant to be a shapeshifter, causing Mutati citizens to neglect their own civilization and pay homage to another. It was a terrible shame, in Hari's opinion, and he hoped to reverse it when he became Zultan himself one day. He had no idea when that might occur, or if it would ever occur. His father often expressed his displeasure and his disappointment in him.

It wasn't just a disagreement between the two men over cultural matters. It went much deeper, as Hari had frequently expressed his opposition to the war against the Merchant Prince Alliance. During one argument over this the month before, the Zultan had called him a traitor. A traitor! Hari had been in complete and utter disbelief.

"If that's what you think I am, have me executed," the young Emir had said. "Obviously, I'm not fit to be your successor."

Pausing by a gold-leaf lily pond, Hari saw the white bird soar to the other side of the water and perch in a tree. In his preoccupation, Hari had not noticed that he was being watched. And that he was in great danger.

"Now, now," Abal Meshdi had said. "At least you've expressed your opinions only to me, and have not gone public with them. You have shown respect for your elders, following the time-honored rules in this regard. Contrary to your belief, I do not want you to agree with everything I say or do. That is only in public. I warn you, do not dishonor me in front of others, or it will be the last thing you ever do."

"I understand, Father. But I must be honest with you. I must tell you what I think is best for you and for our great race. Our culture is being watered down by the Adurians, and they constantly urge us to war. Why do we need to listen to them?"

"We were at war with the Humans long before we ever formed an association with the Adurians, and long before we ever brought them in as advisers."

"But without their influence, we might reach a peace accord with the merchant princes. I do not trust that VV Uncel. He is more concerned with his own Adurian people than with ours. I fear he will be our downfall."

"You worry too much, my son."

"You don't worry enough."

"That is all we will discuss of this. Perhaps the next time we talk, you will have grown a little wiser."

The conversation had ended like that, with the elder's condescending remarks, his expressed hope that Hari would eventually fit the mold that he wanted. Privately, Hari called it the "stupidity mold," and he vowed never to pour himself into it.

The two of them had not seen one another since the podship crisis, though that did not cut off contact. They had been talking over the new (though staticky) nehrcom system several times a week, and could visit one another by taking a solar-sailer journey of a little over a month. They were in adjacent solar systems, not that far apart, or Hari would have been completely isolated from him. That might have been preferable in some regards, though he did not want to run from Mutati society; he wanted to influence it and improve it, especially the moral underpinnings.

The bird lifted off from the tree branch and approached him, drifting tentatively. Hari smiled at her, and saw the return sparkle in her eyes, and the softness of her features, a different version of her original countenance. Parais d'Olor was his beloved, the one Mutati he cared more about than any other. She landed near him on a patch of grass and tucked her wings.

He looked away. Now Hari was doing something that was certain to rouse the royal ire of his father if he ever discovered it. The young Emir had a secret life. He was not a traitor, or anything like that. Rather, he was a patriot and only wanted the best for his people. That included the welfare of all three factions of Mutati society—the terramutatis, the aeromutatis, and the hydromutatis. Too often his father favored his own racial subtype over the others, but Hari believed in equality of the three groups.

In the past, both aeromutatis and hydromutatis had ruled Mutati society from the Citadel of Paradij. The legendary palace had been built by an aeromutati zultan, Vancillo the Great. For two centuries, that flying shapeshifter had ruled a peaceful Mutati realm, a period known as the Pax Vancillo . . . until the Terramutati Rebellion. The terramutatis had always been the most aggressive of the three groups, and had favored going back to war against the Humans. Abal Meshdi's great grandfather, Iano Meshdi, had led the revolt, citing infractions committed by Human society against Mutati worlds and the shapeshifter race . . . especially military and economic incursions against

Mutati planets. The old zealot had drawn a line in space, saying he would not permit Human civilization to encroach any farther into Mutati society.

How ironic that Abal Meshdi had drawn no such line with the Adurians, who were obviously an inferior race, with poor military forces and a decadent social structure. Hari didn't understand what his father saw in them. They should be taking advice from Mutatis, not the other way around!

As he continued on the meadow path with flowers all around him sparkling in the sunlight, he hardly noticed the natural beauty. The aeromutati flew beside him again, this shapeshifter that had taken the form of a large white bird. In her way of infinite patience and understanding, Parais d'Olor had tried to converse with him earlier, but she had given up for a time, saying she would wait until his mood lifted.

Parais was the most lovely shapeshifter he had ever seen, though his father would certainly not concur, since the *Holy Writ* required a highborn Mutati to marry within his own racial subtype. (He could have mistresses of the other types, but any resultant pregnancies had to be aborted.) Despite the expectations, Hari had never been attracted to terramutati girls. From the first moment he laid eyes on an airborne female, he'd been fascinated. And when he met Parais, he stopped looking at other girls at all.

In her natural form Parais had the folds of fat, tiny head, and oversized eyes of any Mutati, but instead of arms and legs she had functional wings. She could also metamorphose into any number of flying creatures, such as the one she favored now. Her movements were always graceful, like those of an aerial dancer.

"Come with me, my love," she finally said. "I am a great white gull, with a built-in saddle on my back for you to ride. Let me take you to our favorite beach-by-the-sea."

In no mood for a holiday, Hari shook his head. He did not notice a shadowy creature moving along beside them in the woods, just out of view. . . .

Parais flew toward the woods and fluttered between tall evergreen trees. Moments later, she returned.

"Someone is watching us," she said. "I saw no one, but I know they are there."

He stopped and looked in that direction. "How do you know?"

"I sense it." She tucked her wings and landed beside him.

"But you are not telepathic; you are not a hydromutati . . . a Seatel."

"Nonetheless, I sense something," she said, looking nervously in that direction. "Come with me now. Let me fly you away from here."

Hari was not pleased, and not afraid. "Someone doesn't approve of our relationship," he said. "Just like that time in your village. Is it one of your people again? How did they get past security?"

"I . . . I'm not sure who it is or how he got here. I just think we should go."

"This is my home. I'll be damned if I'll run from my own home!" He marched toward the woods.

She flew beside him. "Don't!" she said. "Please listen to me. At least summon the guards."

"We have a right to life without being spied on, without Mutatis questioning our lifestyle, the choice of whom I wish to love. I've always tried to follow the rules, but I keep finding too many reasons not to. Somewhere along the line, life got in the way, I guess. Now let's see who's spying on us."

Consumed with rage against the intruder, Hari heard her saying something about danger, but he didn't interpret that as physical peril, only as a risk to his reputation, and hers. As he rushed headlong into the woods, he wished he wasn't even a Mutati, that he was a Human instead, and that he had at least crossed over and changed his racial appearance, as Princess Meghina of Siriki had done. She had been widely scorned in Mutati society for doing that, but she had followed her heart. She had shown tremendous courage, and he had always admired her for it.

Just then a loud *pop* rang out, and in the trees Hari saw the distinctive, silvery muzzle flare of a jolong rifle. A projectile whizzed past his head, and ripped a nearby sapling in half. As he ducked, another shot rang out and thunked loudly into a tree.

Hari heard Parais scream behind him.

The Emir did not travel unarmed. He pulled a white handgun out of his tunic, and pressed the top of the handle to activate it. "Did you see who shot at us?" he asked her.

"Mutati. No wings." Parais pointed. "He's on the move. Look!"

Seeing the slight movement of underbrush, Hari set the weapon's seeking mechanism so that it would home in on the heat signature of a Mutati. It was a gun his father had obtained on special order, one that only the elite of their society had.

Hari didn't even have to aim. He just fired in the general direction he wanted, and saw a flash of fire tear through the underbrush. A piercing scream echoed through the woods.

"Get on my back," Parais urged.

The Emir did so, and clung to the bar of the saddle. Parais extended her wings partway and lifted off powerfully through the trees, rising higher and higher until the two of them cleared the treetops. She had taken additional mass from nearby vegetation to become a large bird, but there were limits that she could not exceed in this process. From medical tests, Hari knew that she—like most other Mutatis—could only become large enough to carry one adult shapeshifter on her back, and that any additional mass absorption would be dangerous to her cellular structure and to her life.

Below, he saw his palace guards pour out of the bastion, running toward the woods. He sent them a telebeam message, telling them what had happened, and ordering them to find out who had shot at him.

Parais opened her white wings to full extension and beat them rhythmically, heading west.

"They'll investigate," Hari shouted, raising his voice over the sound of the wind. "Even if the assassin survives and escapes—or if his confederates take the body away—I know I hit him, and he'll leave cellular material behind. With the DNA of every Mutati on file, we'll find out who did it."

"But what if your father sent an assassin after you?" she asked. "Maybe he found out about us." She looked back as she flew, her features profiled against the blue, cloudless sky. Her blond hair flowed like a mane on the back of her neck.

"The Zultan wouldn't kill me for loving an aeromutati, though he might disinherit me for it. He has threatened to kill me if he gets tired of me, but I think it's all bravado. He wouldn't sentence his only heir to death for that."

"What happened, then?"

"Assuming it's not one of your old boyfriends, I'd say the merchant princes activated a sleeper agent. Now, where are you taking me?"

"I told you where I wanted to go . . . and now you're in no position to argue."

An hour later Parais circled over a familiar, isolated stretch of red sand beach, scattered with driftwood. Aquamarine waves lapped gently against the shore.

The lovers had been there many times before, in utmost secrecy.

Chapter Twelve

It is said that twins have a unique, even clairvoyant connection. I have never delved into that realm, at least not to my knowledge. Still, I sense something horrible is going to happen to my brother. In fact, I'm *certain* of it.

—Francella Watanabe

For two decades Francella Watanabe had done her best to forget her son and only child, to set aside the fleeting images she'd had of him as a newborn baby, the dangerous, unintended glimpses she'd stolen before having him removed from her sight and taken away forever.

Now, a burly guard escorted Francella into a side entrance of the prison where her son was incarcerated. She felt leaden, uncertain if she wanted to go through with this. But she kept pace.

In due course, Francella had learned the name given him by his foster parents . . . Anton Glavine . . . along with bits and pieces about what he was doing and where he was. She'd heard he was a member of Noah's interplanetary environmental force, and eventually that Noah and Anton were holed up on the orbital EcoStation. They had fled there after an incident in which her own CorpOne forces—in a joint venture with the Doge's Red Berets—attacked her brother's Ecological Demonstration Project. She'd known her son was on the orbiter but had wanted to destroy it anyway, since her hatred for her brother was so much greater than any love she felt for Anton.

But Lorenzo, upon learning of Anton's whereabouts, had refused to attack the orbiter. Anton was his son, too. What an unfortunate set of circumstances. She had thought for sure that she would kill her brother there, finally cornering him and wiping him out of existence. It had been an infuriating wrinkle in her plans.

Then, in another unexpected twist that followed, she had seen Anton Glavine at the Canopa pod station, where she'd encountered Noah only moments before. She had been trying to kill her brother again, this time by shooting him in the chest . . . but like a demon, Noah had come back from the dead and regenerated his flesh. Damn him! In all the commotion, Anton had been arrested and taken into custody by the Red Berets.

Since that time Francella had been thinking about her son, unable to get his face out of her mind. After all these years, seeing her own child! He'd grown into a fine-looking young man, with features that reminded her of Doge Lorenzo.

Following Anton's arrest, she had obtained a DNA test on him to be certain, and it confirmed his parentage, showing the undeniable genetic markers. Francella had paid to keep the report secret, but apparently no amount of money was enough for that. She should have known that nothing was secret from the Doge, especially when it concerned his own son.

Lorenzo had brought the report to her himself, slapping it down in front of her. It had not changed anything. For months the two of them had assumed Anton was their son based upon available information, and now they knew for sure.

The Doge might even know what she was doing at this very moment, wearing a black cape as she hurried through the dark of the night. If so, he wasn't doing anything to stop her. . . .

The guard pointed down a rock corridor, and allowed Francella to walk through it by herself. As instructed, she halted at the end, and peered through the soft orange glow of the electronic containment field of a cell.

Anton sat in orange illumination, on the edge of his bunk. His blond hair was combed straight back, and he had a bound copy of the quasi-religious *Scienscroll* open on his lap. Looking up at her, he quoted from one of the verses: " 'The night washes men's souls; it is the time of true honesty.' "

She considered the passage, recalling a bygone time when her late mother had read such verses to her and Noah in their childhood, while they sat at her feet. The words sounded familiar.

"I know who you are," Anton said, "and I have no more feelings for you than you have ever shown for me."

During the past two decades, Francella's aides had sent regular support payments for her son, though she had tried to remain detached from him emotionally. But seeing him at the pod station, something had changed, making her want to see him and speak with him.

"I don't blame you for saying that," she responded. Then, unable to deal with her own emotions, she whirled and left.

Chapter Thirteen

> It is the Second Law of Thermodynamics. All things move from structure to waste, from useful energy to energy that is no longer available. Timeweb, the infrastructure of the galaxy, is no exception. It has fallen prey to the dark, degenerative forces of Entropy.
>
> —Report to the Tulyan Council of Elders

Tulyan Starcloud. . . .

Having been ordered to perform timeseeing duties for the Parviis, Eshaz had been conducting sessions in an anteroom of the Council Chamber. Each of these comparatively small enclosures was different from the others, and—if any Tulyan desired more privacy—each anteroom was capable of floating freely in the sky around the inverted dome of the central chamber. At a thought-command, Eshaz could engage or disengage from the dome. In a very real sense this was more a perceived sense of privacy, and an ephemeral one, since at a touch Tulyans could read the thoughts of each other, or of other races. But the private anterooms permitted some Tulyans more mental latitude in their creative and paranormal thinking abilities, a temporary respite from the constant mental linkages around them.

Thus far, over a period of days, Eshaz had been unable to timesee anything, and Woldn had grown increasingly upset. It had been Eshaz's intention from the beginning not to report anything to the Parviis, but he had honestly attempted to time-see anyway, to no avail. He heard the buzzing discontent in the background as he tried to focus, and knew in his heart this would be another failed day.

The sound grew louder. Opening his eyes, Eshaz saw Woldn and his band of tiny, flying Humans hovering in front of him, their buzzing sounds coming through some internal vibration of their bodies, since they had no wings. "We've had enough of this!" Woldn said. "You're faking!"

Eshaz withheld his comments, and his energy. Calmly, he sent a thought-command, and the anteroom floated back into its connecting port on the topside of the Council Chamber. "We shall discuss this with the Elders," he said.

"Oh, we will do that!" Woldn and his entourage sped out of the anteroom the moment the door opened. They were waiting for him, when Eshaz marched purposefully into the large central chamber and faced the Elders.

"Let me begin by saying that I have not been disingenuous," Eshaz said, gazing up at the broad-necked First Elder Kre'n.

She looked at him sternly, then stepped down from the bench. Approaching Eshaz, she touched his scaly bronze skin and closed her eyes.

Eshaz trembled as he felt the mental linkage, the two-way flow of information between them. It was not a complete transference by either of them; barriers still remained. Some were partial, while others were full and complete barricades. This was normal.

All grew silent to Eshaz, except for a faint, rushing inner sound as data flowed back and forth. He tried to calm himself, knowing that more details about how he had healed Noah Watanabe were emerging, beyond what he had already told the Council. Eshaz felt the outward flow of truth, the immensity of what he did to Noah and the web.

He detected Kre'n's probing questions on the subject, that she was not yet getting everything she wanted to know. Even with the skin contact—the truthing touch—she was not learning all of the reasons for Eshaz's momentous and dangerous decision, including the full details of his history with the remarkable Human. Somehow, Eshaz's internal barriers were holding this back, but he would tell her anything she wanted to know if she ever asked him.

But he realized that he was not conscious of all of the reasons himself. Maybe there were subconscious motivations, or other forces at work that he did not understand himself. Despite what he and his people knew about Timeweb, it remained an infinitely mysterious realm, a massive puzzle with only a small number of its pieces showing.

Kre'n withdrew. Then, looking emotionlessly at Woldn as the tiny creature hovered near her, she said, "This timeseer has told you the truth. It is incontrovertible."

Looking deep into Eshaz's eyes, she added, "There, may, however, be a way of opening the pathways of his mind even more, of moving aside whatever may be blocking full revelation. For that, the Council must be alone with him."

Grumbling, Woldn at first refused to leave. His words were loud, despite his diminutive size. "You Tulyans have always been a nuisance, and never deserved to hold dominion over podships. We've taken them away from you, but you still find ways of causing problems, of interfering with our rightful mission in the galaxy."

"Woldn," Kre'n said, "with all due respect to your position, I must point out how . . . undiplomatic . . . your remarks are. Perhaps you would be better served to deal with us through a professional ambassador, instead of personally."

The Eye of the Swarm shouted, "I will hear no more of this!"

In a huff he attempted to leave, but at a signal from Kre'n, the guards blocked his exit, sealing the chamber off. At this he raised a commotion, citing all kinds of treaty violations that were being committed against him.

Calmly, the First Elder returned to her chair, and gazed dispassionately at the angry leader. Like a small cloud of insects, they flew one way and another, attempting to escape. Eshaz saw the twenty Elders unite their thoughts, recognized the little signs of this, the subtle, matching twitches on all of them, the simultaneously blinking sets of eyes, the way their gazes moved as if from the eyes of a single organism. They were in mindlink.

Gradually the Parviis stopped their tirade, and settled down.

"The guards will escort you back to the anteroom," the Council members said, their voices perfectly synchronized. "We will summon you after our private session."

With no choice in the matter, Woldn and his entourage flew away, following guards out a door that was opened for them.

Now Eshaz faced the entire Council of Elders, inside the inverted dome of the Council Chamber, floating in the misty, ethereal sky. Still in mindlink, the wise leaders stared down at him sternly. First Elder Kre'n sat in the center of the arched table. On her left sat the towering Dabiggio, the largest Tulyan Eshaz had ever seen. He did not look well, and had droopy, tired-looking eyes, skin lesions, and reddish patches of skin where the scales fell off.

Eshaz had heard stories of physical problems suffered by Tulyans in recent months, for the first time in their long history. Many were suffering from fatigue, and their missing scales were slow to grow back, if they did at all. Tulyan leaders said that the weakening of Tulyan bodies spelled the approaching end of their immortal lives, and it was somehow tied to the problems with the deteriorating cosmic web.

Dabiggio was the first victim Eshaz had seen first hand. It struck him as curious that the Tulyan Starcloud had not shown any signs of web deterioration in its sector, but its citizens were being impacted first. He assumed that the starcloud would show signs of decay as well, and soon.

Answering their unspoken questions, Eshaz expanded on what Kre'n already knew. He elaborated on how he had healed the Human, Noah Watanabe, by allowing Timeweb nutrients to flow into his dying body . . . and how Noah thereafter gained access to the web through his mind.

Eshaz also described how he met Noah Watanabe years ago, when the Human led a fledgling activist organization with a forgettable name, the Planetbuilders. Eshaz gave him a much better name for the organization that reflected its multi-planet importance: the Guardians. The Tulyan also made a number of operational recommendations and went to work for the organization, as his busy schedule permitted. After that, the Guardians grew in number and in prominence.

"I believe in Noah completely," Eshaz said. "This Human may become the first truly important member of his race, on a galactic scale."

Speaking in unison, the Council said, "Guilt over your Timeweb infraction may have blocked you from timeseeing, weighing heavily on your mind."

Dismayed but not ashamed, Eshaz refused to hang his head. Instead, he looked at his superiors steadily and said, "I never felt guilt over what I did for Noah. I did it for the good of the galaxy . . . to fulfill my sacred caretaking oath. As I told you earlier, he may be the one spoken of in our ancient legends . . . the Savior we have awaited for millions of years."

"We need not remind you," the eerie voices retorted, with more than a hint of irritation, "that no matter the idealistic intentions and efforts of Noah Watanabe, there have never been any great Humans on a galactic scale. Humans are known to be limited by their pettiness, shortsightedness, and proclivity for warfare. They are parochial creatures, lacking in compassion or foresight."

The Elders released their mindlink, and one of them, a smallish male known as Akera, spoke separately. "Nonetheless, we are willing to reserve judgment about Noah. You may be correct about him, though there is no way to tell yet, based upon the limited evidence available."

"I have told you all I know," Eshaz said, "even what is in my heart."

"You are to increase your timeseeing efforts for the Parviis," Kre'n said. "And do not even think about concealing anything from them. It is not only a matter of treaty, but of honor."

"As you wish." Eshaz bowed.

"Afterward, you have our permission to return to Noah's Guardians at the first opportunity," Kre'n said, "as soon as space travel is reopened to Human-controlled worlds."

"We want you to protect the Human," Akera said. "Help break him out of prison if you can, and keep him from causing harm to the fragile environment of Timeweb. We cannot do that from afar."

"It may also be necessary to eliminate him," Dabiggio said. He coughed. "If he proves dangerous."

Eshaz recoiled at the vile thought. He knew little of violence, and could not imagine committing it against anyone, especially not against a man whom he had come to admire so much. But what if he had been wrong about Noah? What if the concerns of the Council proved well-founded?

I am a caretaker of the web, Eshaz reminded himself. *I must do whatever is necessary.*

Having been summoned to return, Woldn and his followers flew back into the chamber like an angry swarm of bees. They were in high fever, flitting around, buzzing in the faces of the much larger Tulyans, but eliciting no physical or verbal response.

"Our timeseer is ready to serve you," the First Elder announced.

"You've cleared the cobwebs out of his head?" Woldn asked.

Eshaz glared at him.

"I have ordered a rendezvous of my people," Woldn said, "and I cannot waste more time here." He flew in front of the Council members. "You have failed in your obligation."

"Then the timeseer will go with you," Kre'n said. "Summon a podship and transport him to your rendezvous point."

"That is out of the question. No outsider is permitted to know where we meet. Now let me out of here!"

"You refuse the services of a timeseer when he is prepared to fulfill his duty?" Kre'n said. "That sounds like a treaty violation to me. Now you must remain here to work through the problem. It has very serious diplomatic consequences, which this Council cannot ignore."

"You're wasting my time!" Woldn shouted.

"You waste your own time by being obstinate," Kre'n insisted. "Can't you conceal the location of your meeting place from Eshaz, blindfolding him, preventing him from seeing?"

"You are all mind readers when you touch us, but we do have ways of concealing something so essential, something so vital to the survival of our race. Very well! The recalcitrant timeseer will come with us."

Woldn summoned a podship. It arrived in a matter of moments, with a distant green flash and a rumble as it entered the atmosphere of the starcloud. The craft made its way to the outside of the Council Chamber, and landed on a flat portion of the top, opposite the inverted dome.

Deep in thought and troubled, Eshaz boarded the vessel. He

had left word for Acey and Dux that he expected to return in a matter of days, but in the chaos around him he knew that might not be possible.

Chapter Fourteen

> Those infernal podships are holding all of us prisoner, leaving our worlds only connected by a thread . . . the nehrcom communication system.
>
> —Doge Lorenzo del Velli

Following the destruction of Timian One and the Palazzo Magnifico, the Doge had relocated to quarters that were suitable to his position. His courtesan wife, Princess Meghina, had her own royal apartments on Canopa—in Rainbow City—and when the podships stopped she found herself stranded there, unable to return to her beloved planet of Siriki. Lorenzo liked having her nearby, and enjoyed the company of Francella as well. But the two women barely tolerated one another, and had always competed for his affections.

His relationship with them was different in so many ways. The Doge maintained Meghina as his favorite courtesan, taking care of all of her expenses and siring children by her, seven daughters so far. The girls were all on Siriki now, but remained in touch with their mother by nehrcom. Lorenzo hardly ever spoke with them himself, or cared to. Though they were financial heirs to him, they could never step into his shoes to rule the Merchant Prince Alliance. The noblemen would never stand for a female doge.

In contrast, while Francella was his lover as well, she was financially independent from Lorenzo, and loathed the very concept of a courtesan, considering such women to be no more than well-dressed harlots who lived off men. No paragon of virtue herself, Francella had borne him a male child out of wedlock, who, while a bastard, might still be accepted by the princes as their doge.

Wishing to maintain his own independence, Lorenzo did not want to live with either of the two women in his life. Even though he had formalized the relationship with Meghina by marrying her, she had—by mutual agreement with him—maintained her status as a courtesan, having relationships with the most famous princes in the realm. And he had his own wandering eye.

With the loss of his palazzo, Lorenzo had taken over a large suite on the top floor of the opulent cliffside villa of the late Prince Saito Watanabe, generously offered to him by Francella, the late tycoon's daughter. The lease fee had been substantial, as part of the deal she made to also let him use the top three floors of offices in her own CorpOne headquarters building. The villa lease included cliffside terraces nearby, where Lorenzo arranged for Meghina to construct a private zoo, featuring exotic breeds. The facility, nearing completion, would be much smaller than the one she had on Siriki, but it would serve to cheer her up, missing her pets and her daughters as she did.

Raiding private and public collections for animals, the Doge was limited to whatever was available on Canopa. But it was a large, wealthy planet, with an extensive selection. He obtained the services of a genetic technician—a "gene-tech"—who located a number of rare humanoids and animals for the new facility. The gene-tech, while an Adurian by birth, had sworn allegiance to the Merchant Prince Alliance, and had passed a thorough loyalty test administered personally by Lorenzo's Royal Attaché, Pimyt.

Despite the fact that the major galactic races could not

interbreed, the gene-tech told Lorenzo it was still possible to obtain interesting combinations within the various genetic families. His Adurian race had special knowledge in the field of biotechnology.

One evening at his villa, Lorenzo met with his military leaders and advisers, who summarized the lack of progress that the forces led by the Doge and Francella were making against Noah's rebellious group. The Guardians seemed to be increasing in number and power, and there had been disturbing reports of robots fighting alongside them.

"Of course we have our own sentient machines," General Jacopo Nehr said, "and they are replicating themselves at a high rate. We should be able to counter anything they throw at us. The tide will turn."

"Our machines are breeding like rabbits," Lorenzo said, "or should I say like robots?" He looked pleased at his witticism.

"Yes, our machine leader Jimu is doing a fine job," Nehr said, "and we will need every one of them." He stood up and paced the room. "The Guardians are clever. We can't figure out where they are or what they will do next. They make guerrilla attacks against our most fortified installations, somehow threading their way through and finding our weaknesses. It is very disturbing."

Lorenzo heard an explosion outside, rocking the furniture and reverberating in his ears. "What the hell?" he yelled, running to a window and looking out. The officers gathered around him. He saw flames in the crescent-shaped dry dock area at the base of the cliff, and quickly figured out what was burning.

"Damn them!" he said. "They got my space yacht!"

Flames rose high over the burning vessel, illuminating other pleasure craft moored by noblemen at the dry dock. He also saw the shadow of an unlit aircraft speeding away from the scene.

As Nehr and the other officers ran to the door, the Doge shouted after them: "Find out who fell asleep on the job and bring them to me! I'll interrogate them personally for this."

"We're on it, Sire," Nehr shouted back. "We'll get whoever's in that aircraft, too."

Lorenzo heard Nehr yelling into a com unit, dispatching grid-copters to take up the chase. Moments later, the Doge saw aircraft flying out over the valley. At least that was going efficiently. Maybe they would capture or destroy the bastards this time. If so, it would be one of the few successes.

Suddenly he whirled to cross the room, and nearly tripped over Pimyt, the Royal Attaché. Lorenzo had forgotten that the little Hibbil was in the room.

"Sorry, Sire," Pimyt said, picking himself up, and wiping a trickle of blood off his own furry gray chin.

"Get me a report on this whole sorry affair," the Doge snapped. He kicked a message cube that had fallen on the floor. The cube struck Pimyt in the chest, an unintended result.

Pimyt's red eyes glowed brightly, like the embers of a fire, and his face contorted in anger.

For a moment, the Doge focused on the burning glare, but was not frightened by it. His aide was just intense, and Lorenzo had always liked that. Abruptly, the eyes softened, and the little alien smiled.

Then Pimyt hurried away.

Too edgy to sleep, the Doge went out in the middle of the night to his in-progress zoo. As he stepped out into the cool air, a dozen of his house guards snapped to attention and accompanied him.

The Adurian gene-tech, KR Disama, was summoned, and hurried out of his small house on the grounds.

Then, beneath bright lights Lorenzo examined animals that

were being kept in temporary cages. One was a dagg-sized creature with high-gloss blue fur and a head on each end.

"Where are its private parts?" Lorenzo wanted to know, for he could not see any.

The gene-tech, a completely hairless homopod with a small head and bulbous eyes, smiled and responded, "It does not have any. Hence, it is, by design, perfectly house-trained."

"But how does it relieve itself?"

"It exudes through its pores, into the air. Fear not, though. The substance dissipates quickly and is completely odorless."

As the animal walked around its cage, Doge Lorenzo could not tell whether it was going forward or backward. Despite everything on his mind, he laughed out loud. For a few minutes, he almost relaxed.

Then he remembered his destroyed yacht, and scowled ferociously.

Chapter Fifteen

The Parvii Fold is the end of the entire galaxy, the place where all known reality drops off into enigma.

—From a Parvii scientific report

Bound for the rendezvous point ordered by the Parvii leader, Tesh piloted her podship through the narrowing, dangerous Asteroid Funnel, at the far end of a magnificent spiral nebula. Linked to the sentience of the living spaceship under her command, she felt the creature's primal fear, its hesitancy to proceed. But as she clung to a wall of the sectoid chamber at the core of the ship, she had the Aopoddae vessel under total control, and it could do nothing to resist her.

All around them, glassy stones hurtled by, glowing luminous white in their passage. She saw it all through the visual organs all over the outer skin of the vessel. Maneuvering carefully to avoid full impact, Tesh felt smaller stones bouncing off the podship, causing the creature's angst to increase. But it flew onward, combining its own abilities with Tesh's as they reacted with split-second precision to select the safest route.

Steering sharply into a gray-green side tunnel that was clear of loose stones, Tesh soon exited into the legendary Parvii Fold, a broad, enclosed region that was bigger than most solar systems. Concealed from the rest of the galaxy, this was the back of beyond, and the sacred breeding zone of the Parvii people. While her race had no homeworld, they did possess this uncommon, highly secure region that few outsiders had ever been permitted to see, or even to know about.

Inside the sunless, worldless fold she saw scores of Parvii swarms—each in its own distinctive formation—and each containing tens of millions of tiny, flying people. The Parvii race did not require oxygen to breathe, or common nutrients for sustenance.

As Tesh guided her podship into the cavernous galactic fold, she saw many other sentient vessels off to one side, an immense basin of the blimp-shaped, sentient creatures tethered together in the airless vacuum. Instead of steering in that direction, however, she headed straight for the central swarm, where she expected to find Woldn. When her ship moved forward, the multitude parted and let her through . . . but hundreds of the strongest pilots boarded the craft with her, and she felt their mental presence monitoring her movements and decisions, preparing themselves to take control of the craft away from her if necessary. She absorbed their thoughts and they absorbed hers.

Just ahead, she made out an elaborate structure floating in space, glowing in multicolors and formed by the living, interlocked bodies of Parviis. This was the magnificent Palace of Woldn, which had been shaped according to his exacting specifications. Docking there and disembarking from the podship, she relinquished control of the craft to one of the other pilots. Keeping her personal magnification system switched off, she remained her normal tiny self.

As she entered the palace, she felt simulated gravity that was formed by a specialized telepathic field. Stepping onto a simulated mosaic floor that was generated by the closely-knit forms of her people, she admired the elegant and intricate new designs they had created by radiating a variety of glowing colors. All around her were Herculean facsimile sculptors and paintings that had been created in the same manner, by the arrangement of living organisms. The large scale of the palace enabled Woldn to entertain visiting dignitaries from the few other races who knew of the existence of Parviis. It was a small list, including the Tulyans, and anytime they brought a visitor in, it was done in a way that blocked all information on the whereabouts of the secret galactic fold.

In Parvii society, the Eye of the Swarm was not a godlike figure, but he was the supreme commander and all-powerful central brain of this ancient galactic race. Like his followers, Woldn was mortal, although he was expected to live longer than normal, from the beneficial strength and energy imparted to him by his followers. For some time he had expressed concern, however, as the average Parvii life span had been dropping precipitously. For millions of galactic years, since the beginning of known time, Parviis could be expected to live for 2,500 or more years, but the average was down to 2,085 now, and continued to fall. He was himself 2,172 years old, and had told his followers he felt the coldness of his mortality fast approaching.

As Tesh entered the glittering central chamber of the palace, she saw the distinctive reptilian outline of a Tulyan in the middle of the large room, with a layer of Parviis all over its body, as if it had been dipped in a batter of them. Only the Tulyan's face was uncovered, and she recognized him as Noah's friend, Eshaz. Tiny Woldn, wearing a silvery robe, was perched on top of his head.

Joining the cluster on the reptilian man's chest, Tesh felt him absorb information from her by the touch of his skin against hers—a physical connection between two races that had coexisted uneasily since time immemorial. Tulyans could read the minds of each other and of other galactic races through direct skin contact, their truthing touch. With respect to these

Parviis, it meant he was absorbing data from them in order to perform timeseeing services for the swarming race.

Even though the two races had never been on friendly terms after Parvii swarms took control of virtually all podships long ago, they did have a long-standing diplomatic arrangement by which a limited number of Tulyans were permitted to journey around the galaxy as podship passengers—the only race that had been limited in its space travel, prior to the recent cessation of podship service to all Human and Mutati worlds.

"Well?" Woldn demanded impatiently. Hands on hips, the diminutive man continued to stand on top of Eshaz's head. "What do you see in our future?"

"Even in the best of circumstances I can see only a short distance into the future, and sometimes not at all," Eshaz said.

"Don't stall me!" Woldn screamed. "This is critically important, damn you! The galaxy is crumbling; our lives are shortening!"

"I see nothing at the moment," Eshaz said hesitantly. "Only layers and layers of darkness. This has never happened before, so I must interpret it. Darkness could mean everything will soon be gone, and nothing will be left. Or it might only refer to you, Woldn, and perhaps to your entire Parvii race."

"Stop lying to me!" Woldn screeched. He stomped a tiny foot on the Tulyan's thick skin.

"I'm not lying! Previously when I was unable to timesee, a wash of brilliant light filled my eyes and mind, without details. This is much different." Tesh thought he sounded nervous, and she felt a slight trembling in his skin.

"Your future is linked to Timeweb," Eshaz said, after a long pause.

"A boilerplate answer," Woldn snapped, "imparting no real or useful information. Stop stalling around or we'll dump you in deep space, with no way to return home."

"That would create a diplomatic incident."

"No matter. We hold the upper hand over your people."

"I am not afraid of any threats," Eshaz said. Gently, he brushed Parviis off his body, and most of them flew a short distance away, like gnats without wings. Woldn, Tesh, and a few others remained on him, but moved to one shoulder, where Eshaz could see them peripherally.

Eshaz went on to say that Timeweb had been deteriorating, and that its troubles seemed to parallel those of the Parvii race, and those of other races around the galaxy, including the Tulyans. "We are an immortal people," he said, "but our immortality is linked to the web and all of its problems. Some of us are feeling aches and pains for the first time, and falling ill."

Woldn fell silent for a long time. Inside the palace, his swarms stopped flying and alighted wherever they were, on their densely grouped companions who were shaped in the architectural components of the structure.

On the way there, Tesh had resolved to express her dissent against Woldn for dumping podship passengers into space, and she wanted to make a salvage claim on the podship. Locking gazes briefly with the Eye of the Swarm, she felt him receive this information telepathically. She would feel better speaking it, but under the circumstances—with a Tulyan present—this would have to do.

But Tesh had momentarily forgotten an important detail, the fact that she was touching the skin of the Tulyan. She felt him absorb information from her, but she remained where she was anyway. Both she and Eshaz were Guardians, and she felt safe with him.

"Guardians," Woldn said, in a sharp and sarcastic tone. He lifted off and flew around angrily. "Both of you have sworn allegiance to the strange Human, Noah Watanabe, haven't you? Eshaz, you continue to deceive me. Is there no honor left in your people? And Tesh, you continue to disappoint me."

Neither of them responded.

"I have decided on punishments for both of you. Tesh, you are banished for the rest of your days. I officially declare you an outcast, never to return to the Parvii Fold or associate with any member of this race. You are to take that unreliable podship with you, and Eshaz as well to avoid a 'diplomatic incident,' as he calls it. I won't transport him, not after his complete failure—whether through deception or ineptitude, it really doesn't matter. As for the podship, we can swarm and take it back whenever we please. There are ways to overcome your hold on it. Now, go!"

The two of them boarded the podship, but as Tesh hovered in the air in front of Eshaz, she had an empty feeling in the pit of her stomach. In the background of her consciousness, she only half heard Eshaz tell her that he had important ecological work to do, and that he urgently needed her assistance in transporting him to the Tulyan Starcloud.

"What?" She hesitated inside the passenger compartment.

He repeated himself.

"For what purpose?" she asked.

"My position is sensitive. I cannot confide in you without permission from the Council of Elders. Do you think a Parvii such as yourself could ever trust a Tulyan? We both work for Noah Watanabe and admire him, so our goals must be similar. At the moment, I'm in a hurry, and I must place myself at your mercy."

"We each have secrets," she said. "Woldn concealed the location of the Parvii Fold from you, one of our racial necessities."

"That is true. I was blindfolded in a sense, unable to determine where we were going. Presumably you would do the same on the return trip."

She nodded.

It occurred to her that he might try to steal her podship at the first opportunity, or might lure her into a Tulyan trap where others did so, but she dismissed the thought. This was a trusted friend of Noah Watanabe, and she did not think he would harm a fellow Guardian. As she hovered in front of Eshaz with a slight buzz, she wondered if the Tulyans and Parviis could ever reconcile their differences. Maybe this would be a step in that direction, even if it involved only two people. She vowed to give it a try.

Behind her, she heard the scorn of the palace full of Parviis, with Woldn's voice rising above the others, and telepathic winds buffeted her. She hurried into the sectoid chamber, and got underway.

Chapter Sixteen

Does my brother think I am a monster, with no feelings? He has never understood me. To be accurate, I have feelings for *him.* I hate him with every fiber of my being.

—Francella Watanabe

"You don't seem to realize it," Francella said, "but I've had a lot on my mind lately." In her black underclothes, she sat on an immense, disheveled bed, beneath a gilded headboard that bore the golden tigerhorse crest of the Doge's royal house.

"And I haven't?" Lorenzo snapped, as he dressed to leave. "Where do you think I'm going now? I have an important military meeting."

"So like a man," she said, "acting like a woman's concerns are nothing. Sometimes you make me feel invisible. Am I no more than a sexual partner to you?"

At her own villa, they were in the large top-floor suite that she had leased to Lorenzo. The morning sunlight was too bright for Francella. At a snap of her fingers, she lowered the automatic shades.

Clearly agitated, Lorenzo had difficulty buttoning his dark-blue tunic. "What is it this time? It's always something, isn't it?"

"Lorenzo," she said, in her firmest tone, "I want you to sit down and listen to me." She only began sentences with his given name when she wanted him to feel like he'd done something wrong.

From their long relationship, he understood the code between them. With a long, annoyed sigh, he sat on the edge of the bed and looked at her, leaving his tunic unbuttoned.

"You've been a bad little boy," she said with a smile, "and I think you need a spanking."

He fought back a smile. "After the meeting, OK? Please hurry and tell me. What do you need?"

Her eyelids fluttered. "Not so much. I just want to know what you're going to do with my troublesome brother."

"You know we've been questioning him, and performing medical tests to find out why he recovered so easily from the wound you gave him. My experts tell me they still have a great deal of work to do."

"I'm his sister, remember? Perhaps I can figure out what your experts cannot. They are taking a long time, too long. Having trouble, aren't they?"

"Well, yes, but Noah is an unprecedented case."

"As his twin, I might have certain insights."

The Doge arched his gray eyebrows. "Don't tell me you have the same ability?"

"No, nothing of the kind. But I do know more about him than anyone else. I grew up with him in the same household. If anyone can get through the barriers he has set up, it is me."

"I'm not sure what you're getting at."

"Let me supervise the research; put me in charge of Noah. As the owner of CorpOne, I have the finest medical laboratories on Canopa, but you haven't even used them. Your investigators seem to be protecting their own turf. But they're not making any progress, and it's time for a change."

"You want to keep Noah's fate in the Watanabe family?"

"You could put it that way."

He scowled. "I find it ironic that you would ask this of me, when you kept me from deciding about the fate of my own son.

For more than twenty years, I didn't even know Anton existed."

"We've already been over that, and it is beside the point." She slid over by him and nibbled at his ear. "Besides, I already apologized for that, many times. Would you like me to do so again?"

He smiled, but looked troubled. "Not now. I have too much on my mind."

"You're not going off to that big important meeting with this unresolved, are you? It will just block your reasoning powers. You need to clear this up first, and then your mind will be clear and sharp for the meeting."

Looking exasperated, he shook his head, but smiled. "All right," he said. "You're in charge of Noah from now on. Make the necessary decisions, and find out how he healed himself from a puissant-gun wound that should have killed him."

"Oh, I will," she said, giving him a kiss on the cheek.

Quickly, the stocky, gray-haired nobleman resumed dressing. "One proviso," he said.

Alarmed, she asked what he meant.

"I'll decide what to do about our son . . . without consulting with you."

"Agreed," she said, not showing any hesitation. Though she felt some belated motherly concern for Anton, Francella didn't have the time or adequate inclination to follow through with it. Another matter was far more important.

She needed to unravel Noah's secrets.

Later that day, Francella sent Noah, under heavy guard, to one of her laboratories to have him analyzed. There, she and her chief scientists met with Dr. Hurk Bichette, who was the newly installed director of CorpOne's Medical Research Division. The doctor had an interesting biography. He had held this position previously, but his career had been interrupted when Guardians kidnapped him and forced him to tend to Noah, who was gravely wounded when the Doge's Red Berets attacked the orbital EcoStation.

Bichette's time with the Guardians had been most peculiar, and intriguing to her. Having resurfaced right after the podship crisis, he told her he recalled being forced to undergo an electronic procedure by a sentient robot in the employ of the Guardians, and afterward his memories had been sketchy. He'd been left with a general knowledge that he'd been with the rebel group and that he had tended to Noah himself, but without important details. He knew that Noah had recovered from his injuries, possibly due to Bichette's own medical skills, but little more.

Most importantly, he had no memory of where he had been with the rebels and where they were hiding now. When he came back to CorpOne, Francella's people performed a battery of lie-detection tests on him, along with stringent loyalty tests, before permitting him to return to her Medical Research Division.

He had passed them all with flying colors. . . .

Noah awoke to find himself on a hover stretcher, looking to one side at a window and a wall. His muscles felt sluggish and heavy, and his eyes became sore whenever he moved them too much. Even so, his thoughts seemed clear, making him wonder if he could vault out of there mentally the moment he felt like doing so. That might be the best sedative for him of all. But he didn't make the attempt, at least not yet, since he wanted to see what they were going to do to him.

For the moment, he didn't see or hear anyone in the room with him, though he heard distant, muffled voices.

He thought of Tesh, and the paranormal kiss he gave her, reaching across the cosmos. Not a real kiss; they'd never had one. Envisioning her classically beautiful face and bright, emerald eyes, he felt a tug of emotion. So unfortunate that the two of them ever had conflicts, but Noah realized now that he was responsible for much of the acrimony himself, since he hadn't wanted to intrude on Anton's romantic interests. But Noah had noticed the way she looked at him, and recalled the secret way he felt for her whenever they were together.

"Ah," Dr. Bichette said in his basso voice, as attendants guided a hover stretcher into the laboratory. Noah realized that he was unable to move, because electronic restraints held him down. "I've been looking forward to this!" The doctor's eyes were filled with wild fascination. Three men in white biocoats and gloves looked on, scientists who were dressed as their superior was.

Noah thought back. This was the first time he had been aware of the doctor since Francella shot Noah in the chest and he recovered afterward miraculously, in only a few remarkable moments.

As Noah listened, Francella filled the director in on the security measures that would be followed. Armed guards would always be present in the laboratory, and for even greater security Noah had been fitted with an electronic restraint system that could be customized for the movements he was permitted to make, and would stun him if he tried to do anything without authorization.

"So," Bichette said, when he finally had a chance to examine Noah, "you claim to be immortal, eh?"

Noah glared up at him. "Let's put it this way. I have no need of your medical services."

With a tight smile, the doctor removed all of Noah's clothing except for his underwear. Then, with Francella looking on, he proceeded to look at the skin on Noah's chest with a high-powered magnifying glass. "Remarkable," he said, looking away from the eyepiece of the instrument. "I see the faintest evidence of a large wound—directly over the heart—but it is completely healed. This is not possible."

Running a scanner over Noah, he next examined the internal organs. "Incredible, incredible," he said. "I don't believe it. They've all regrown. There is evidence of massive new cellular growth."

Going back to the magnifying glass, Bichette continued to go over the skin of Noah's entire body, centimeter by centimeter. At the left ankle, he said he found a very faint line all the way around. "Like an amputation mark," he said.

Noah muttered an insult under his breath, and smiled to himself when he noticed that Francella could not make out the words.

Performing an interior body scan, Bichette exclaimed, "Yes! This entire foot was amputated! Then . . . then . . . it *grew* back. I see new bones, muscles, tissue. This is unbelievable."

"Don't be so dramatic," Noah said. "You cut the foot off yourself, said you had to do it or I would have lost my leg, or my life. You were also there when the foot regrew."

Bichette looked at him blankly.

"He doesn't remember any of that, dear brother," Francella said. "One of your robots zapped his brain."

Not even looking in her direction, Noah considered what must have happened to the doctor. Subi Danvar or Thinker must have instituted a security measure, sometime after the Doge put Noah under arrest.

"Like a lizard," one of the scientists remarked. "This guy grows body parts back like a lizard."

"Yes," Francella said in a wary voice, "but lizards can be killed."

Maybe not this one, Noah thought. And a shudder ran down his spine, as he considered the horrors that this woman might inflict on him.

Chapter Seventeen

Racial extinction is always closer than anyone realizes.

—Parvii Inspiration

The armored man watched as a long silver machine dug a new chamber, throwing dirt and bits of rock around, making so much noise that he had to wear high-decibel ear protection. Giovanni Nehr stood back at a safe distance to avoid the debris cast by the machine, which rolled forward on treads and had spinning drill bits on its body. Soon, new barracks would be constructed here, but not for Humans. As the Digger proceeded, it illuminated the work area in high-powered beams of light.

With the burgeoning number of robots under Guardian command, owing to Thinker's ambitious manufacturing program, additional quarters were needed. Sentient machines could live in tighter quarters than Humans, with their metal bodies stacked higher and packed tighter; they had to be kept somewhere, couldn't be left to wander around the subterranean tunnels and caverns of the compound.

There were also more Humans wearing Guardian uniforms, from Subi's clandestine recruitment program around Canopa. He and Thinker had initiated strict security controls, developing a comprehensive electronic interview method and even a selective memory erasure procedure—such as the one they had used on Dr. Bichette before releasing him. In addition, the two of them had set up an electronic barricade across all tunnel openings, so that no one could pass in or out without setting off alarms.

One of the young female recruits had dated a Guardian, and he had given her an interesting gift, a nearly extinct little alien creature named "Lumey." The amorphous creature, which she afterward took along with her to the underground hideout, had once been Noah's pet—but had been left behind in the rushed escape from EcoStation when the Doge's forces attacked the orbital facility.

As the machine proceeded now, digging deeper and wider, mechanical scoopers and dumpers scurried about, gathering debris and carting it away. They would dispose of it in a series of deep, vertical tunnels that had been dug by rampant machines in the past, when they were the mechanical pests of Canopa. The current debris removal system had been developed by Thinker and Gio. No one knew how they disposed of excess material in the past, but Thinker theorized it might have been in underground fissures and caverns. Occasionally, piles of dirt and rock had been found on the surface of the planet, but only on a remarkably few occasions, considering the extent of excavation that the machines had been doing.

Without warning, the Digger accelerated and increased the speed of its drill bits. It crashed into a wall and began boring through, where it wasn't supposed to go. It made fast progress, creating a new tunnel. Gio ran after the errant machine, with guards behind him and alarm klaxons sounding.

Reaching for his belt, Gio pressed a transmitter, sending an electronic signal to the computers controlling the machine. Abruptly, the Digger shut down all systems, including its lights. For several moments, Gio found himself in darkness, down the escape tunnel the machine had dug.

Then he saw lights coming from behind. Moments later,

Thinker reached him, clanking and whirring. "I was afraid this would happen," the robot said.

"It's a good thing we were ready," Gio said.

Thinker led a robotic team to inspect the Digger. They disassembled the internal workings of the machine's computer. Presently, Thinker went back to Gio and said, "Just as I suspected, it has an override system, so cleverly concealed that we didn't see it before. The unit found a way to supersede your commands, but we had our own ace in the hole."

"I assume you disabled the mechanism?"

"Oh yes. But before we use this Digger again we'll need to reprogram your disabling transmitter and the receiver on the machine."

"The old signal won't stop it next time?"

"Better not try it. There could be more tricks in this Digger, more than we've discovered so far. Even if we successfully disable its present override system, it could have another, and another. We must be on constant alert."

"Why haven't our other two Digger machines done this?"

"Maybe this one is testing us, and somehow they're communicating with one another. They *are* sentient, after all. Maybe they're smarter than we assumed, with hidden intelligence."

"Kind of a game, isn't it?" Gio said, in an edgy tone.

"Not the way I look at it," Thinker said. "Machines are my life."

Subi Danvar, as acting head of the Guardians in Noah's absence, received reports from Giovanni Nehr and from Thinker on the episode with the Digger. He also heard from Gio that he'd grown tired of supervising the necessary construction activities, which kept enlarging with the increasing forces and supplies. The man wanted even more important duties.

Impressed with Gio's ambition and desire to contribute, Subi assigned him to work more closely with the machines that had brought him here and with the newly manufactured robots, to form them all into an efficient fighting force.

"But I have no real military experience," Gio admitted.

"You have an inventive mind, don't you? Doesn't it run in the family?"

"Well, I don't know. I do have a lot of ideas."

"Some of the men said you had ideas about military formations and training. Comments you made over beers."

"Well, that's true."

"They passed a few of your ideas on to me. My boy, if you can think that well when you're drinking, I'd like to see what you can do when you're completely sober."

The two men laughed, and clasped hands to mark the new relationship between them.

A couple of days later, Gio and Thinker reported to Subi that disturbing news had just come in: The best machine fighters—led by Jimu—had left the Inn of the White Sun some time ago and joined the Red Berets. Even worse, they had initiated a large-scale robot manufacturing program, and with access to more raw materials theirs far outpaced the program that Thinker had established for the Guardians.

It was indeed troubling news. After considering the situation for a moment, Subi said, "We need Noah back more than ever. He'd know what to do."

"We've already discussed that," Thinker said, his mechanical voice weary. "From our reconnaissance missions and other reports, I've assembled all available data, and Noah is nowhere to be found. Since his captors have no podships to take him off planet, we know he's on Canopa. Hopefully alive. The Doge's people have set up an elaborate disinformation campaign about his whereabouts, with tens of thousands of Noah sightings reported all over the planet. Too many for us to investigate with our limited resources. We can't mount a rescue effort until we have some idea of where he is. Why, he might not even be in one of their government prisons. In fact, I suspect he isn't."

"That's your analysis, is it?" Subi said.

"It is. Absolutely."

"And didn't you also analyze the Diggers some time ago, without finding their override system?"

"Yes."

"That proves that there are possibilities beyond your intellect. There is a way to find Noah and break him out—I'm convinced of it—and we need to find out what it is."

"You'll never outthink a machine," Gio said, as he listened in.

Ignoring the comment, Subi said, "It must be a perfect plan, against superior forces. Nothing is more important." With that, he stalked away, followed by Thinker, who continued to argue with him. . . .

For days afterward, Gio began to think about this at length. If he could pull off a rescue of Noah, or at least get credit for it, he would be rewarded extremely well. Thinker, however, remained obstinate against sending out any rescue missions until they had more data. He and Subi could frequently be heard in loud exchanges.

Chapter Eighteen

Tulyans call it the "Visitor's Center," a large facility that can accommodate more than thirteen hundred guests at once. And yet, they have used an odd singularity in the title for it, as if the place was only capable of taking one person at a time. They claim to have merely named it that way to make the place seem more personal for each visitor. We suspect that the facility may, in fact, have been built for only one person, and a very important one. Tulyans dismiss our questions about it. On the surface it seems a trivial matter, but we have an idea that it may be one of their secrets.

—Merchant Prince Diplomatic File #T16544

Though Dux had initially enjoyed the luxuries of the Visitor's Center and Acey had steadfastly resisted them, now both of them loathed the place. Acey had begun calling it a "velvet-lined prison," and Dux could not help agreeing.

Worst of all, the teenagers had thought that Eshaz would take them under his wing, but now the big, enigmatic Tulyan had gone off on a mission far across the galaxy. The waitress they'd befriended told them he had gone on a "timeseeing assignment"—whatever that meant—with the leader of the Parvii race. The boys had no idea who Parviis were, and at this point neither of them cared. They just wanted to leave the posh orbiter by any means possible.

The pair would prefer to go to Canopa or another Human-controlled world to volunteer for military service, but could not reach any of them by podship, and all other means of space travel were too slow to be practical. As a result, when added to the bad news about planetary-scale losses, Acey and Dux were no longer their usual outgoing and fun-loving selves. They had, at very young ages, become quite serious.

The Human race was in trouble.

Each day, the boys gazed longingly out at the nearby pod station, a rough gray globular structure that kept pace with the Visitor's Center, orbiting over the starcloud. The two orbital facilities were only a few kilometers apart.

"Too bad we can't get back and help Noah," Acey said.

"Maybe that's not meant for us," Dux said. He brushed his long blond hair out of his eyes. "Gio Nehr is on Canopa, and could cause us a lot of trouble. We'd probably have to kill him, or vice versa. As for me, I'm not sure I want to go that far, not even with him."

"The first step is to get away from here. Agreed?"

"No question about that," Dux said. "But how do we get on the shuttle to reach the pod station?"

A grin split Acey's wide face. "We don't. I found what looks like an emergency evacuation system. A series of passenger launchers—individual, man-sized capsules that shoot into orbital space."

"Show me."

Acey led the way through a narrow servant's passageway. He had timed it perfectly, having watched for the schedules of the employees. The teenagers slipped into a small chamber, and closed a heavy door behind them.

"This is one of the emergency-escape launch rooms," Acey said. "There are hundreds of them around the structure."

Dux surveyed the room and saw a number of clearplex tubes,

each capable of holding a large person, stacked on racks. It didn't take him long to figure out how the system worked, and he saw what appeared to be cannon barrels on the outside wall. "This looks like a circus trick," he said.

"More sophisticated than that, but you're not far off."

Dux felt hesitant. "It looks dangerous."

"Well, if you'd rather stay here and loll around on vacation, that's fine by me. But I have things to do and places to see. All right?"

Again wiping hair out of his eyes, Dux said, "We promised to stay together."

"Exactly my point. You have to go with me, don't you see?"

Shaking his head, Dux stepped toward one of the tubes, and moved it. The container was light. He carried it over to the launcher and slipped it inside, then opened a hatch on one end of the tube and crawled inside. "Now what?" he asked.

He no sooner had the words out when the launcher shot him into space. Dux felt surprise, but more exhilaration. It was like a super ride in an amusement park. In a few moments, he experienced a floating sensation.

Seconds later, Acey followed him out. Then Dux heard Acey's voice over a comlink. "Grab the joystick," he said. "The handle activates directional jets when you move it, taking you in the direction you want to go."

Acey roared past him, heading for the pod station.

But Dux had trouble with the controls, and veered off course. He heard Acey shouting at him over the comline. Finally he figured out the pressure pads and toggles, and made his way toward the pod station.

As the pair arrived and stepped through an airlock onto a platform, they saw no podship present, and no other vessels docked there. Looking back through a viewport, they saw a shuttle take off from the Visitor's Center.

"Not a good sign," Dux said.

"I timed this for the arrival of a podship," Acey said. "While you were swimming and getting massages, I was watching schedules. I thought one would be here now."

"What a time for them to change their schedule."

"Look!" Acey pointed, and jumped up and down with excitement.

Dux felt a surge of hope as he saw the telltale green flash of a podship arriving from deep space.

"Come on! Come on!" Acey said. "Faster!" Looking back, he saw the shuttle enter the pod station first, and make its way toward them.

Unexpectedly, the podship turned and departed without ever going into the pod station. Apparently, something had startled the creature.

The boys didn't even try to get away. Furious, they just waited to be taken into custody.

Chapter Nineteen

> The Human brain is a marvelous, wondrous instrument, with razor-sharp cutting edges that can slice in countless directions. At all times, the user must be careful not to harm himself with such a powerful weapon.
>
> —Noah Watanabe, *Commentary on Captivity*

Noah didn't like the odors inside the CorpOne medical laboratory, the disturbingly strange chemicals he could not identify. His vivid imagination worked against him now, making him wonder what the doctors and other technicians intended to do with those substances, and with the dangerous-looking array of medical instruments he saw in clearplax cases all around him. In the few days he had been housed in the facility, he had not been able to get used to the underlying sense of evil that permeated the place, and he knew he never would.

Early each morning, Dr. Bichette's assistants brought Noah out of his heavily guarded, locked room on the top level and took him down to the laboratory on the main floor, which had an operating theater in its central chamber. The laboratory was metal and plax, gleaming silver and white. Everything was voice-activated. Whenever the doctor wanted a vial or device, he spoke it by name, held his hand out, and waited for the elaborate machinery of the chamber to give it to him. Instantly, conveyors and servos in the ceiling whirred to life, removing items from cases and lowering them to his waiting hand.

From tiers of seats that circled above central operating station, around twenty people looked on, men and women. On previous days, Noah had noticed his detestable twin sister sitting in one of the front-row viewing seats above him, and he had watched her send messages to the medical personnel down on the central floor. This morning, however, she stood beside the doctor at the examination table and glared at her brother while the assistants activated electronic straps over his wrists and ankles to secure him in place.

In response, Noah gazed at her with calculated, loveless disdain.

Under different circumstances he might have been the owner of his father's corporation and all of its operations, including this one. In an odd image, he tried to imagine what it might be like to be himself, strolling into the laboratory, looking at himself on this examination table. But the hardness of the table against his backside, along with the people looking at him like a bug under a microscope, reminded Noah only too harshly that he had no degree of control over the situation. Not in a physical sense, anyway.

But he still had his mind.

In this facility and in the prison before that, Noah had been forced to undergo rigorous medical examinations, with the doctors paying close attention to the healed gun wound in the center of his chest and his regenerated left foot—wounds that showed no easily visible scars or signs of internal injury. He wondered what was on the agenda for today, and did not have long to wait for his answer.

Without warning, he saw Francella shoved Bichette out of the way. "This is going too slowly for me," she snapped. "Give me a tray of surgical tools!" She held her hand out, but the machinery did not respond.

"If you will just return to your seat, we can proceed," Bichette said. "You must have faith in my abilities. I know this patient well, and the Doge has entrusted him to my care."

"Like hell! Lorenzo has placed him in my care, not yours. You work for me, you dolt, and you will do as I say." The fingers of her extended hand twitched, as if giving hand signals to the servomachines, telling them to do her bidding.

"I have authorization from the Doge to perform complete medical examinations," the doctor insisted. "You must let me proceed."

She arched her shaved eyebrows in displeasure. "How dare you act as if I am interfering?"

Narrowing his eyes, he said, "That is not my intent. I'm sure we can work this out."

"I'm your boss, you fool. I own this facility, and Lorenzo put me in charge of the investigation. Don't you understand that?"

"But the Doge sent me a telebeam message yesterday afternoon, telling me how important my work with Noah is. He thought I might be on the verge of a momentous medical breakthrough, and that. . . ."

"He should not have communicated with you directly! I have an agreement with Lorenzo that all decisions concerning the fate of this"—she nudged Noah roughly in the side—"are up to me."

"With all due respect, Ms. Watanabe, you don't know what you're saying. You're too close to the situation, since it involves your brother, and you need to take a step back. Granted, you *own* this medical facility, but you don't know how to run every aspect of it. Prince Saito understood that, and he delegated important tasks." He glanced at Noah. "This is an important task."

"You think I don't know that? You say my judgment is impaired because *I'm* too close to the situation? What about you? I think you like my brother, and you're going easy on him, showing favoritism toward him."

"You could not be more wrong," Bichette insisted.

In a rage, Francella smashed a hand against a case and broke the plax. Reaching through the jagged opening, she brought out a sharp, gleaming knife.

Noah braced himself, but tried to show no fear.

She waved the instrument wildly in the air. Bichette backed out of her way, and she swished the blade close to Noah's face. In response, the captive did not close his eyes or flinch, and stared at her emotionlessly. He felt a spinning sensation, and a hum of energy all around him. Where was it coming from? Noah couldn't tell.

"This is not the way!" Bichette said.

Francella hurled the weapon in another direction, and it skidded and clattered across the floor. "Get me some results," she snapped, "or, by God, I'll do it myself!"

As she stormed out of the laboratory, Noah breathed a sigh of relief, but only a little one. Somehow he had an odd, unsettling sensation that his apparent immortality might be penetrated by that insane woman.

Chapter Twenty

Some disguises run deeper than any form of perception.

—Noah Watanabe

At the Inn of the White Sun, cleverly constructed inside the orbital ring over a jewel-like planet, only a few machines remained after Jimu and Thinker took sentient units to join the opposing forces of Doge Lorenzo del Velli and Noah Watanabe.

The orbiting way station was not as exciting as it had been in past years. However, since it lay beyond the war zone, podships still came and went, though with a different mix of races, and far fewer Humans or Mutatis. The sentient machines often said they missed those two races, for their abundance of exotic personalities, capable of interesting and unpredictable behavior.

Down on the glassy surface of the planet Ignem, the machines were still constructing their army, robots building robots, but they no longer had the same enthusiasm for the project, no longer had the same altruistic goal that had originally been instilled in them by Thinker. Previously, their cerebral leader had motivated them through reminders that they had been abandoned by their Human creators, discarded on junk heaps. He convinced the robots to build a machine army to serve Humans, with the goal of proving to them that the robots had worth after all, that they still had dignity. It was revenge in a sense, but with a loving touch, a desire to excel despite tremendous obstacles, despite being overlooked and tossed away. It was also ironic, considering how poorly they had been treated by Humans.

Now, far across the galaxy the machines serving the Doge and Watanabe were proving themselves, showing their value by performing work once limited to Human beings. On each side, Thinker and Jimu were adding to their numbers as they had previously on Ignem, building more and more sentient fighting machines.

Word of their successes got around the galaxy, even this far from the Canopan battle zone, and despite the podship problem. Travelers who had heard nehrcom news reports on fringe worlds brought bits and pieces of information back to the Inn of the White Sun. The two opposing machine leaders on Canopa were developing stellar reputations, or "interstellar" reputations, as one of the travelers quipped. . . .

According to the reports, the two machine forces had clashed in brief skirmishes when Watanabe's Guardians made guerrilla attacks against their enemies. To Ipsy, one of the left-behind units still at the Inn of the White Sun, it seemed unfortunate that robots had to fight their own kind, or that Human creators had to fight robots, either, for that matter. Ipsy was extremely proud of his machine brethren, but felt deep sadness as well.

A small robot, Ipsy had reconstructed himself with advanced computer circuitry. His real love was for combat, and if podship travel was ever restored to the Human-ruled worlds he wanted to join Jimu's forces, since he had always admired the ferocious fighting methods that robot had espoused.

The feisty Ipsy frequently picked fights with much larger opponents, so that he could test his personal combat skills. He won a few of the frays, but lost many more by wide margins, and was frequently forced to repair himself.

★ ★ ★ ★ ★

From Canopa, the Doge broadcasted orders to every planet in his Alliance, requiring all inhabitants—without exception—to submit to medical testing and thereafter to wear a micro-ID embedded in their earlobes, certifying that they were Human. Previously there had been testing, but it had been sporadic, with too many opportunities for shapeshifters to elude discovery. This time the Doge had his military and police leaders set up stringent systems to ensure that there would be no opportunities for anyone to escape the nets of detection.

On Lorenzo's newly christened capital world, a surprisingly small number of Mutatis were rounded up in this manner and thrown in his dreaded prisons—and it was the same elsewhere. But there were many suspects. It was reminiscent of the Salem witch hunts of the seventeenth century on Earth, as people constantly turned in their neighbors and personal enemies as suspects.

All across the merchant prince empire, anti-Mutati hysteria ran rampant, with widespread fear that shapeshifters could be hiding inside the bodies of anyone, impersonating people.

Chapter Twenty-One

Even in a corner with predators at your throat, there is always a way out, if you can only discover it.

—Mutati Saying

On the shapeshifter homeworld of Paradij, the Zultan spun inside his clearglax gyrodome, high atop his magnificent, glittering Citadel. During this procedure, his mind was like an advanced computer with all data in it available to him instantaneously. In addition, he had altered his body, and now looked like a cross between a saber-toothed wyoo boar and a Gwert, one of the intelligent alien races employed in scientific positions by the Mutatis.

At the moment, he was considering a very big problem, and needed all the inspiration he could muster.

With podship space travel cut off—the only practical means of transport across the galaxy—Mutati outriders had not been able to continue their Demolio attacks against Human-controlled worlds. Conventional spacecraft, such as Mutati solar sailers and the hydion-powered vacuum rockets used by Humans, were far too slow to be effective, except for intra-sector voyages. The Humans had learned this lesson the hard way when they sent an attack fleet against the Mutatis by conventional means, and it took more than eleven years to arrive, by which time the military technology was obsolete and easily defeated.

Nonetheless, there might still be a way for the Zultan to continue his Demolio torpedo attacks, busting enemy planets apart. Years ago, a Mutati scientist cut a piece of material off a podship—a thick slab of the soft, interior skin. He did it at a pod station while the ship was loading, and caused the sentient creature to react violently. It contracted, crushing the scientist and the Parvii pilot before they could send an emergency signal, but the piece of flesh was thrown clear and recovered by another Mutati.

After that, laboratory experiments were conducted on the tissue, and detailed analyses were made of the cellular structure. In the last couple of years, after many wrong turns, Mutati scientists had been able to clone the complex tissue, and had grown several podships . . . an unprecedented event.

However, while the lab-bred creatures appeared to possess many of the same attributes as authentic Aopoddae, they did not have all of them, and fell short in significant particulars. The scientists suspected this might have something to do with the power of the sentient creatures to control their own appearances, and—except for the influence exerted over them by Parviis—their own actions.

What the Mutatis possessed now were generic pods that did not display any individuality or variety. They all looked virtually the same, including their interiors and amenities, which often differed in authentic, natural podships. The clones had primitive access hatches and rough, archaic interiors, more like the insides of caves than the interiors of spacecraft capable of faster-than-light speeds. Not that any of the natural podships were luxurious; far from it; they did, however, offer some basic amenities that were lacking in the clones—such as benches, tables, and stowage areas for luggage.

So far, the Mutatis had met with no success testing the lab-pods. Several attempts to guide them and ride in them as passengers had been disastrous, resulting in crashes that killed everyone aboard, or in vessels that drifted aimlessly and had to be rescued by chase ships.

In addition, using rocket boosters, the laboratory-bred pods had been shot into space. From instinct, perhaps, the pods always accelerated beyond what the Mutatis wanted and reached such high speeds that they left their boosters behind and disappeared into space. Out of twenty-four such attempts, none of the lab-pods had arrived at the intended destinations on Mutati fringe worlds. They had a serious guidance problem, and all efforts to steer them precisely had met with failure. The artificial podships were like wild rockets shot by children in backyards. . . .

Emerging from the gyrodome, the Zultan was disappointed. Inside, God-on-High had appeared before him in a vision, telling him the guidance problem could never be solved. He'd experienced visions before, and had no idea that many of them were psychic influences from the Adurian gyrodome, altering his decision-making processes. He also didn't know that his research scientists were similarly influenced by minigyros they used, keeping them from ever figuring out how to control the lab-pods. The clandestine HibAdu Coalition didn't want any more important merchant prince planets destroyed, because they were slated to be prizes of war for the secretly allied Hibbils and Adurians.

Unaware of the layered plots enfolding him, Abal Meshdi went to the lab-pod development facility, and commanded them to make a ship ready to carry an outrider in a schooner, fitted with the torpedo doomsday weapon.

"The ship will be guided by God-on-High," the intensely devout Mutati leader announced. "If our Demolio is meant to hit the target, it will."

Chapter Twenty-Two

All things in life have a mathematical property to them: Everything you perceive by any of your senses, and everything that occurs to you in the apparent privacy of your own mind. No one can escape the numbers, not even in death.

—Master Noah Watanabe

From an observation ledge, Giovanni Nehr watched a machine manufacturing and repair facility inside one of the largest caverns in the underground hideout. He knew that Thinker had perfected some of these methods on the planet Ignem, but mostly the machines had engaged in repair operations on discarded robots there. Gio had served there himself, dressed in the very armor he wore now. Thinker was beside him now, a dull-gray metal box that only moments before had clattered shut . . . one of the cerebral robot's many turtle-like retreats into his inner self.

Directly in front of the shuttered robot a mist in the shape of a Human being formed in the air. But it was so faint as to be indiscernible to the eyes of any sentient race. Certainly Gio had no chance of seeing it at all. But the entity that drove the image saw him and Thinker, and absorbed information about them. The mist drew closer to Thinker, and swirled around him, like a spirit from another realm. . . .

On such a distant world as Ignem, it had been difficult for Gio to obtain the raw materials needed for new robots, particularly those rare elements required for the internal workings of sentient machines—elements that were closely guarded by industrial and political forces. Still, Thinker had found a niche by locating discarded robots around the galaxy that contained those elements, machines that he transported by podship and put back into service.

At Ignem, the sentient robots had been able to manufacture some new items, especially a popular computer chip that they sold around the galaxy. This brought in a nice stream of revenue, but had not had much of an impact on the overall market for new sentient machine components, which were dominated by the Hibbils on their Cluster Worlds.

Now, in the subterranean tunnels and caverns of the Guardians, the machines were doing something more advanced. With access to more raw materials and exotic components on the wealthy, mineral-rich planet of Canopa, they were actually manufacturing new sentient machines, in their entirety. This didn't have the efficiency of a Hibbil facility, but it was working well enough, and Thinker was innovating many of the manufacturing and assembly methods himself. He even had a prototype all-in-one machine that was designed to process raw materials through a hopper, convert them internally, and spit out a wide variety of finished components and products, somewhat in the manner of a hibbamatic. But the prototype wasn't working very well yet.

Thinker did have a real hibbamatic machine that Subi Danvar had obtained, also designed as an all-in-one production device by the Hibbils. But the Hibbil unit had not worked properly from the beginning, and would not hold any of the adjustments that the robot technicians tried to make to it. Thinker had learned afterward that it was a cheap model of the device, with inferior components and design shortcuts. While the merchant princes had superior versions of the machine, and had used them to produce defensive weapons on pod stations, the Guardians had not yet been able to obtain one of those, and had moral reasons for not wanting to do so. The high-quality hibbamatics were being used for planetary security, and despite the differences the Guardians had with the Doge and Francella, neither Thinker nor Subi wanted to compromise planetary defenses. At least the enemies on Canopa, though despicable, were not Mutatis.

So, the hidden Guardians had been making do with what they had, and it wasn't that much. Still, the flawed Hibbil unit had given Thinker some ideas on how to produce his own, and he was making the attempt.

Glancing over at Thinker's dull-gray metal box, Gio wondered why the robot leader often folded himself shut, something he refused to explain. To Gio it didn't make sense and seemed almost eccentric . . . a Human quality. A machine shouldn't need to focus its concentration in such a manner; it should be able to set its programs and block everything out electronically. . . .

The unseen mist swirled around Thinker, as if trying to merge with the robot. The ghostly form flickered and glowed around the gray box, like an aura for Thinker, but still Gio could not see it. Unconsciously, though, Gio's gaze followed its motion, as if he sensed something there. Then he looked back at Thinker.

Gio assumed the robot leader was just peculiar, and with peculiar people there was often no particular explanation. They just did things their own way, for their own unexplained reasons. Thinker and some of the other sentient machines seemed to have a number of Humanlike characteristics, albeit artificial ones. The machines were interesting personalities, Gio admitted, not the mundane sorts he might have expected.

They were surprisingly quiet down here on the floor of the cavern, Gio thought, all those robots moving back and forth, building their own little brothers. They were not nearly as noisy as a Digger machine boring through rock and dirt.

Finally, Thinker unfolded with a small commotion of metal. Turning his flat face toward Gio, he said, "My analysis of new, substantiated data points to the location of Master Noah. The information is sparse, but it is the best we've received so far."

Gio nodded. Earlier in the day, he had brought Thinker a new reconnaissance report, highlighting all the false leads the government had been disseminating on Noah in their efforts to conceal his whereabouts. But now the Guardians had real, proven data about a government effort to conceal a high-value prisoner.

For several moments, the robot did not say anything more. He just stood there, gazing down at the manufacturing floor with his metal-lidded eyes, drinking up details of the operations, processing and reprocessing the information in his data banks. . . .

After considering the problem at length, wondering how best to locate the missing leader of the Guardians, Giovanni Nehr had helped to obtain and assemble the data in the new reconnaissance report, and had influenced its findings. Considering his own input now, he felt rather proud of himself. He'd never seen the robot leader take so long to respond.

During all the time that Noah had been missing, Thinker had been pessimistic about finding him, saying that the possibilities were too large and there were not enough Guardians to complete an adequate search. But when Gio provided the latest report to Thinker, there had been a shift. The orange lights around the robot's face had blinked quickly; the mechanical voice had been more measured.

"I must contemplate that for a reasoned response," Thinker

had said, just before folding himself closed.

Now the orange lights around the perimeter of his face plate began to glow. Finally, he said, "I am prepared to answer now." The lights stopped blinking. With his gray metal eyes open wide, Thinker stared at Gio. Something glinted deep inside one of the intelligent eyes. "As a sentient robot, it is my primary goal in life to serve Humans, who were our original creators, and as such are almost godlike beings to us. At the Inn of the White Sun and the planet Ignem, I was consumed by one overriding desire, to build as many robots as I could and put them in the service of humanity. At that time, with all of my resources focused on that one goal, the full complement of my operating programs were at my disposal."

"For the life of me, I don't understand what you're getting at. What about the new recon report?"

"With all appropriate respect, Gio, you do not think like a machine, so your confusion is understandable. Consider the context of my remarks and realize, please, that I have now placed myself and my followers in service to humankind. I have attained my most important mission in life. I am here, doing what I want to do. The moment I began to work for Noah, my internal programming made certain automatic modifications. My personal initiative was shunted aside, since it might cause me to be overly aggressive. Robots must, by definition, be subservient and passive in the presence of Human masters such as yourself."

"I am Human, but I do not order you around. On the contrary, I am under your command."

"Only for training. Eventually, you will be my superior, since Humans always rise above machines. That is one of the basic laws of Human-machine interaction. You are superior creatures, and naturally exceed our capabilities. Now that we are in service to your race, we must be extra careful about what we do. I have sensed your previous displeasure about my inability to locate Noah. Other Humans, such as Subi Danvar, have been openly argumentative with me."

"That's all very interesting, but now I'd like you to give me your new probability calculations."

"Very well. Let me recheck them. For that, I don't even need to fold closed." He made a whirring noise, and presently began to spew out the names of the prisons on Canopa and other places where Noah might be, along with percentage probabilities of where he might be at any moment.

Listening carefully, Gio said, "There is a one-point-seven-one-percent chance that he is inside the Max One prison, and that's the highest odds?"

"There are many possibilities, even, as I said, a chance that he might not be at one of the government facilities I have listed. There is, in fact, a twenty-seven-point-three-two-percent chance that he is being held by a private party or a private company, which is a much higher overall percentage than the Max One odds. But when all of the private locations and all of the government facilities are considered, there is a greater probability that he is in Max One than anywhere else."

The robot paused, and blinked his metal-lidded eyes. "Are you following me?"

"I think so." Gio chewed on the inside of his lower lip. He was anxious to go out and find Noah.

"Keep in mind as well that these possibilities change from moment to moment and hour to hour, as I absorb new data from a variety of sources."

"OK, but tell me this. What are the odds that Noah is still alive?"

Thinker's mechanical eyes looked sad. "That is not something I wish to discuss. Will you excuse me from answering?"

Surprised at the emotional display, though it was undoubtedly programmed, Gio said, "Of course. I'll focus on Max One for the moment." He hurried off to tell Subi what he had learned.

Behind him, the mist lingered around Thinker, and then disappeared into the ether.

Chapter Twenty-Three

There are many forms of confinement, both seen and unseen.
It is often the unseen ones that are the most debilitating.

—Princess Meghina of Siriki

At the CorpOne medical laboratory, it had been another long day of tests on Noah, of unanswered questions and lines of scientific inquiry that seemed to lead nowhere. It was late afternoon, and Dr. Bichette stepped out of the room for a break, with his assistants. They left Noah where he was, secured to the examination table by electronic straps.

For some time now, Noah had felt a spinning sensation and a hum of energy all around him whenever he was under the electronic restraints. Where was it coming from? Noah had not been able to tell. Struggling to comprehend, his mind had vaulted away, and for a few minutes he had seen his friends Subi and Thinker, before the linkage broke.

Now the spinning sensation and energy hum became more intense, and he realized that he was generating it himself. His ankles and wrists felt increasingly hot. He struggled with the restraints, thinking something might be shorting out in the electronic system. The invisible straps were burning his skin.

Then, surprisingly, he pulled one wrist free, followed by the other. With only moderate effort, he also pulled his ankles loose and jumped off the table. Looking around, he decided to run up the stairs past the empty spectator seats. Reaching a door at the top, he opened it and found a corridor.

He ran with a burst of athletic speed. It was the first time he'd really been able to stretch his legs since being taken prisoner by the Red Berets, and he took full advantage of it. The corridor led to a bank of ascensores. At this early hour no one was around, and he felt strong despite not having slept much. He only needed to sleep for around six hours a night now, and this was continuing to drop, as it had been since Eshaz administered the Timeweb healing treatment on him.

Noah touched a pressure pad to order one of the high-speed lift mechanisms, and instantly he sensed that he had made a mistake. The pad felt odd, with a slick surface. A moment passed, and then he realized it had either read his identity or had decided that he was not an authorized user. Looking around, he didn't see any surveillance cameras, but they might be there anyway.

By the time alarm klaxons and bells sounded, Noah was running the other direction down the corridor, past the upper door to the operating theater.

He heard Dr. Bichette's voice on the loudspeaker system, shouting orders to the security staff. Just behind Noah a heavy metalloy door closed with an ominous thump, blocking the corridor. Ahead he saw another one coming down, and he rolled through only a fraction of a second before it slammed down. They were blocking sections off. Another door dropped ahead, and he found himself trapped in a small area, with no doors or windows.

Half a dozen security men escorted Noah roughly back to the

operating table, where Dr. Bichette and his assistants awaited them.

"He got out of the electronic straps," one of the security officers said. "Look at the burn marks on the table. How'd he do that?"

"I see you are going to require extraordinary measures," the doctor said in an irritated voice. "Get back on the table, please." Looking at the security staff, he told them to remain close by.

"I have a little genetic test to perform," Bichette announced as Noah lay down on the table. "For your own sake, let's hope it goes well and we discover what we need."

"The secret of my restorative powers," Noah murmured bitterly.

"Precisely. Tell your genes to talk to me. Incidentally, don't expect any favors from me, either. I didn't appreciate being kidnapped by your criminal gang of so-called Guardians, or the poor attitude you have displayed this morning."

Seeing no point or benefit in answering, Noah said nothing. He felt the numbing effects of drugs, and for a time he fought them. Then, setting aside the discomforts of the medical procedure, Noah drifted into a timetrance journey in his mind, venturing out into the space-time continuum, the vast celestial web.

Inside the alternate realm, he saw a blur of faces, and then one came into sharp focus. His Tulyan friend Eshaz gazed at him with pale gray eyes, inviting him to a place that was much safer. Noah merged into the form, like a man diving into warm water, and the countenance disappeared.

Abruptly he found himself thinking with the brain of Eshaz, remembering back to an ancient era when Tulyans had a mandate to care for the entire galaxy, and held dominion over podships. Those were halcyon days, the best of all time, and for the cosmic traveler it was an awe-inspiring experience.

That evening when Noah Watanabe awoke in his room, with the drugs wearing off, he still retained something of the Tulyan experience, as a comforting memory. Around him, he saw the orange glow of the containment field, and he recalled a guard who had experienced trouble with the field control of the system. At the time, Noah had assumed it was a simple electronic malfunction. Now he began to wonder if the energy field of his own body had contributed to it.

Reaching out, he touched the barrier with his fingertips. It looked solid, felt solid. On the other side, a guard watched him closely, his hand on the handle of a holstered gun at his hip.

Despite the new information pointing to Noah's whereabouts, Subi Danvar felt they needed more information before sending an armed rescue mission. So he decided to send Gio on yet another reconnaissance mission. It was not the first time Gio had been sent out, but on the prior occasions he had gone with other Guardians and robots.

This time, Subi was sending him alone. "You must leave and return carefully," the adjutant said at the appointed time, "taking great care not to allow anyone to follow you."

"I know how to be check for tracking devices and take other precautions," Gio assured him, before slipping out into the night.

As the armored man slipped through the darkness, his thoughts wandered. He liked Noah well enough, but mostly he wanted to ingratiate himself to his superiors. In his most private, illuminating thoughts, Gio admitted to himself that he was probably the most accomplished apple polisher in the entire galaxy, always working angles to worm his way into the affections of his superiors. His own advancement was paramount in his mind.

On the reconnaissance mission, Gio took along an electronic

device provided by Thinker. From the river bank opposite the stony, monolithic prison, he concealed himself behind bushes and scanned the outside of the jail. The walls were too thick to be penetrated, but he had a stroke of luck. Passing the infrared light over a wall, he saw a prisoner looking out the window of an illuminated cell, toward the water.

Unmistakably, it was Anton Glavine, the young friend of Noah Watanabe . . . and perhaps more than that. According to rumors in Guardian ranks, Glavine was actually Noah's nephew, but that opened up intriguing questions. It meant Francella must be Glavine's mother, and conjecture had been flying about who might be the father, even Lorenzo del Velli himself. In any event, Glavine's presence was a good sign. He and Noah were probably kept in the same facility, for ease in interrogating them.

Gio kept scanning, but did not learn anything more from that section of wall. Presently, Anton moved away from the window.

Now the scanner penetrated the water of the river, and looking just below the nearest visible wall of the prison, Gio was able to pick up startling details of the underwater portion of the wall.

He made out the outline of what appeared to be an underwater door, and at first he wondered why it was there. Then he realized it had probably been designed as a secret escape route—though not for prisoners. This structure had once been the castle of a nobleman, so it might have been his secret way out if he ever came under attack. There might even be an airlock on the other side of the door.

In ensuing weeks, Subi Danvar and Giovanni Nehr developed an ambitious and ingenious assault plan to get into the prison, not knowing that Noah had already been moved. . . .

Chapter Twenty-Four

I have often thought that the wild Aopoddae are too beautiful to be captured. Once, long ago, it was not necessary. We worked in harmony with them, and they came willingly.

—A Tulyan Storyteller

At the pod station over the Tulyan Starcloud, First Elder Kre'n stood with the rest of the robed Elders, awaiting the arrival of a most unusual podship, one that was guided by a rebellious Parvii. Eshaz was scheduled to return this morning on that vessel, and had sent word to the Council—by telepathic transmission through Timeweb—that he had a matter of utmost urgency to discuss with them.

Nearby, the Human teenagers Acey and Dux sat at a bench on the docking platform, with a guard posted to keep them in line. Since their unauthorized use of emergency escape capsules a few days ago, the pair had been monitored closely. The Elders were dismayed that the young men would behave so rudely and with such utter disregard for decorum, diverting equipment that might have been needed in a real emergency. Under the circumstances, the boys were not really welcome at the starcloud, but they were Eshaz's responsibility as his invited guests, and the Elders wanted to show him the proper respect.

The dignified Elders conversed in low tones, wishing Eshaz had never taken the boys under his wing when he had so many critically important duties that needed attention. But they knew Eshaz had done it out of a sense of honor, since they were Noah Watanabe's Guardians and he felt responsible for their welfare. Even in times of crisis, a Tulyan could not ignore honor.

"This is a most unfortunate situation," Kre'n said.

"But that is to be expected when timeseers are involved," noted the tallest of the Elders, Dabiggio, "especially this one who has worked with Humans so closely." Dabiggio, thus far the only member of the Council to become ill from what was being called the "web sickness," looked better to Kre'n than he had previously, with less redness, and healing skin lesions. The treatments were taking hold. But there were constant breakouts among the populace that needed to be dealt with on a priority basis. Fortunately, the long-lived Tulyans were a tough breed, and had strong adaptive genetics.

"He does tend toward eccentricity," the First Elder said.

"An understatement if I've ever heard one," Dabiggio said with a cough. He was not one of Eshaz's supporters on the Council.

As a podship pulled into one of the docking stations, arriving without the customary hieroglyphic destination sign on its side, Acey and Dux rose to their feet. They'd never seen one come in like this, and the boys approached it, intrigued. The big reptilian guard followed them closely, but made no effort to stop them.

A hatch opened in the mottled gray-and-black skin of the sentient craft, and a familiar alien stepped through the airlock onto the platform, a biped with a large head, scaly skin and slitted eyes. He was accompanied by Tesh, whom the teenagers had seen earlier with Noah Watanabe. She was one of the Guardians, and had seemed to be a member of Noah's inner circle, along with Eshaz.

"Good to see you boys," Eshaz said. "Excuse me for a moment." He hurried by.

Showing no surprise, Tesh nodded to the perplexed young men.

Dux didn't know what to say. Why were those two together? And what sort of a podship was this, with no other passengers? He'd never heard of chartered podships. The boys inched closer to the others, positioning themselves to listen in.

After greeting the elegant, robed Elders and introducing them to the attractive brunette woman, Eshaz asked to speak privately with the Council about a matter of "utmost importance." The group of Tulyans moved off to one side.

As Eshaz spoke with them, out of earshot of the teenagers, Dux noticed that the Elders looked even more troubled than before, especially a tall male whom he had never seen smile. They stared disapprovingly at Tesh, then at Acey and Dux.

Presently, the Council members conferred among themselves, huddling together and speaking in low, urgent tones. Unknown to the boys, Eshaz had made a most unusual proposal to his superiors. It was something he wanted Tesh to help them with, but he had not yet mentioned it to her, not wanting to do so until he had the necessary approval.

While the Council deliberated over his astounding proposal, Eshaz glanced over at Dux and Acey, and nodded to them stiffly. From staying in touch with the starcloud by Timeweb-enhanced telepathy, he knew the boys had been restless in his absence, and had caused a considerable amount of commotion. The Elders should be glad to get rid of them.

And Tesh, too, even though they had barely met her. Eshaz knew that his superiors had even more antipathetic feelings toward Tesh, since he had told them of her true identity as a Parvii, a member of the race that had been mortal enemies of the Tulyans since time immemorial. This revelation had especially disturbed Dabiggio, but Eshaz had neutralized him somewhat and had garnered the support of the majority of the Council by convincing them that Tesh was an outcast from her people, and that she possessed special talents that could be beneficial to the entire Tulyan race, and to the future of the crumbling galaxy.

By touching hands with all of the Council—the ancient truthing touch process that opened the gateways of the mind—Eshaz had convinced them of the utter truthfulness of what he was telling them. Now, as he looked on, Dabiggio went to Tesh and performed this lie-detection process on her by touching her face without telling her what he was doing. She knew anyway, since it had long been one of the pieces of information that the two races knew about each other. For Parviis, it was one of the inexplicable processes that Tulyans could do, just as the Parvii system of personal magnification was known to Tulyans, but not anything about *how* it worked. . . .

As the tall Elder completed the test and returned to his peers, Eshaz knew that Dabiggio and some of the Elders had other concerns. With his Council minority of supporters nodding in agreement, Dabiggio had debated it with Eshaz at some length. Eshaz had taken the position with him that all Parviis could not possibly be bad, and that one Parvii had never proven to be a threat, since they were only dangerous in swarms. . . .

"Even so," Dabiggio had said in a harsh tone, "they are a hive mentality, with a morphic field that compels them to behave in certain ways. We have never understood how far their telepathic fields range, so for all we know this Tesh could still be under the direct control of the Eye of the Swarm."

His slitted eyes burning with intensity, Eshaz had countered, "You're looking at an exception with her. In each race there are individuals who go beyond the range of any type of control." He grinned, and added, "Many of my people consider me something of a maverick, since I go about things in a different way."

First Elder Kre'n and most of the others laughed.

In sharp and dark contrast, Dabiggio kept a stern face, like a mask glued tightly onto the skin. "Add this episode to your maverick ways," he said. "But you must realize that there are reasons for the precautions of our people and for the traditions we have followed for millions of years. You can't just go out and bring an enemy into our midst."

"She is not an enemy, and these are not ordinary times. Tesh Kori is, like myself and Master Noah Watanabe, a member of the Guardians."

"It seems your loyalties are split, then."

"Not at all. The Guardians and Tulyans have similar goals, both wishing to preserve and enhance the integrity of the galaxy. As you well know, Dabiggio, I have remained loyal to the traditions of our race."

"But Tesh Kori has not remained true to the traditions and goals of her own people! She is a traitor to her own kind, and you want us to trust her?"

"So in your eyes, she can't do anything to gain your acceptance? I personally witnessed the animosity and vitriol in her dispute with Woldn, and I have performed the truthing touch on her."

"We have never questioned your integrity," Dabiggio said, in a softer tone. But he had spent much of his two-million year lifetime being surly, and his voice became harsh again. "I must say, though, that your judgment is another matter entirely. I'm thinking of the time you connected that Human to the web, to heal him."

"We've already been over the matter of Noah Watanabe,"

First Elder Kre'n said, "and it has no bearing on the discussion at hand. There is no pattern of bad judgments on Eshaz's part, only a pattern of independent thinking. Perhaps we need more of his kind in order to rise above the galactic crisis. Perhaps we need to think out of the box, as Humans like to say. All information indicates that Noah Watanabe is in fact an extraordinary person, better even than many of our own people."

Scowling, Dabiggio had muttered something, but kept it under his breath.

Daring to make another, broader point, Eshaz had said, "I think we should take steps to end the age-old animosity between Tulyans and Parviis."

"A heretical statement if I have ever heard one," Dabiggio said.

"What good has the Tulyan–Parvii conflict done for the galaxy?" Eshaz asked. "Each race has important talents that could help heal the galaxy, if we could only find a way to work together."

"Careful, Dabiggio," one of the other Elders said, "or Eshaz here will have your job. He's making sense."

But Eshaz had not shown—or felt—any satisfaction when he saw the reaction of extreme displeasure on Dabiggio's face. This one could be a dangerous foe, one he should not galvanize into action. "With all respect that you deserve for your own integrity and service to our people," Eshaz said to Dabiggio, "I am only suggesting that we explore new options. We can't keep doing things the way we have for so long. We are at the eleventh hour in the galactic crisis and the clock is ticking."

"You are one for extending olive branches, aren't you?" Dabiggio had said with a wry smile. "Both to me and to the Parviis."

Eshaz had returned the smile, with a deferential bow. . . .

★ ★ ★ ★ ★

Now he saw the Elders approaching him, with First Elder Kre'n ahead of the others. Eshaz held his breath.

"All right," First Elder Kre'n said, with a careful smile. "You have our permission to proceed."

"Fabulous, fabulous," Eshaz said. He bowed, and excused himself from them.

Strutting over to the boys, he patted them on the backs with tender care, then guided them over to Tesh. "If you will come with me," he said to her, "I have a most interesting proposal for you."

The Tulyan did not provide specifics until the four of them were alone in Dux's suite at the orbital Visitor's Center, awaiting the delivery of supper. They all sat on large chairs at a diamondplax table, furnishings designed to accommodate the enormous bodies of Tulyans, who were the largest of the galactic races. Tesh, Acey, and Dux sat on high pillows.

Leaning forward at the table, still dwarfing his companions, Eshaz looked at Tesh and said in a conspiratorial tone, "This is something I really didn't want to say within the telepathic field of Woldn back at the Parvii Fold, and not even inside a podship, where your leader's field presumably extends."

"No comment," she said.

Dux and Acey exchanged perplexed glances.

Eshaz took a deep, excited breath. "I am about to tell you something that Woldn would not like."

He paused as Tulyan waiters brought in large plates of food, the aromatic vegetarian fare that this race favored. In their entire history, they had apparently never eaten meat, seafood, or anything that had once been alive—other than the special plants that they grew for their leaves and other foliage, and trimmed without ever killing the plants. According to one of the main dining room waitresses, the Tulyans even had religious ceremonies and rituals involving the plants. It was a very serious, very spiritual matter to them.

Dux rather liked the dishes he'd been served here before, though Acey ate them only grudgingly, because he had no choice. As the waiters removed the lid from Dux's plate, he inhaled the rich odor of a golden stew. He thought it might be something they called *watilly,* which had what the waitress had called "a rainbow of flavors." Sampling it with a spoon, he wasn't so sure. This tasted slightly different, with a cilantro aftertaste. Maybe it was still *watilly,* but seasoned in a different fashion.

When the waiters were gone, Eshaz said, "I intend to hunt and capture wild podships, the way my people did in the early years of the galaxy."

Looking alarmed, Tesh protested, asserting that her people—and especially Woldn—would never permit it, and even if Eshaz was successful he would soon be swarmed and the pods would be taken away. This was the way it had always been when Tulyans obtained podships.

"I don't want any part of it," Tesh said.

"We seem to be missing some details here," Dux said.

"Wild podships?" Acey said, ignoring his cousin's comment. "How *fantastic!* We can go, too?"

"I've got to keep you boys out of trouble, don't I?" Eshaz wiped stew off his own chin, and grinned. "Of course, we will require transportation for such a grand adventure. That's where our friend Tesh comes in."

While the wide-eyed boys listened, Eshaz provided them with general information about Parviis and Tulyans, and their age-old battle for control of podships. He told them Tesh was not really Human, that she was a Parvii in disguise, and that she had piloted the podship that brought her and Eshaz here to the starcloud. Then he looked at Tesh and asked, "Do you want to add anything to that?"

She shook her head, and her emerald eyes flashed. "Perhaps later."

Reaching across the table, Eshaz touched her hand. Despite the magnification system he knew she had, Eshaz was able to connect with her cellular structure and read her thoughts, her innermost wishes and dreams. Earlier, he had done this to the Parviis who were clustered around him at the Palace of Woldn, probing the neuron highways of their brains, picking up some of their innermost wishes and dreams. He knew that Tesh had disagreed with Woldn before, and so had others. Now she was one of the most outspoken ones, inciting the displeasure of the leader. He had seen that firsthand, and now he learned more about her reasons, her independent way of looking at things, her strong sense of personal integrity and morality. Woldn had murdered passengers on podships, and she hated him for it. The terrible act had made her ashamed to be a Parvii.

She looked at him oddly, knowing that he was intruding on her thoughts, but letting him do it.

"Well, are you a Parvii first or a citizen of the galaxy?" Eshaz demanded, taking a new tack. "Can't you think of a situation where the health of the galaxy comes before the interests of your people? Noah's Guardians have performed recovery operations on only a handful of planets—not nearly enough. All of us need to do more." He paused. "Noah wants us to do more."

Now Eshaz found that her thoughts became troubled and murky, with flashes of near-decision that changed quickly and flitted off in other directions, some of which involved her personal feelings of attraction for Noah. In only a few moments, she explored too many ancillary considerations for him to follow. He didn't like to connect with mental impulses that shot in several directions like that, since it invariably gave him terrible headaches.

With a gentle smile, he withdrew his hand.

While Tesh considered his proposal, Eshaz said that Noah should expand his ecological recovery operations, to encompass more planets. In order to accomplish that, a fleet of Guardian-operated podships would be necessary, and Noah—if he ever escaped from imprisonment—could eventually merge operations with the entire race of Tulyans, the original caretakers of the galaxy.

"We Tulyans are working on methods of concealing podships from Parviis, and we think it might be possible to maintain control of every wild pod we capture." Pausing, he added, "Actually, it's something I've been wanting to discuss with Noah, but circumstances were never right—emergencies kept intruding."

"How do your people capture wild Aopoddae?" Tesh asked. "It is something I have always wondered about."

"I have already revealed a Tulyan confidence to you about our plans," Eshaz said. "Just as Woldn is not pleased with you, the Tulyan Council thinks I may be a bit too much on the eccentric side. Still, they have given me permission to go on a special mission—if you consent, of course. We know that you have sealed the sectoid chamber, preventing intrusion. On wild podship hunts, we always stop at a certain planet first in the Tarbu Gap, and I will need to pilot us there, since you cannot know the location."

"We are not enemies anymore," she said. "That much I will accept, but it must be reciprocal."

"Ah yes, to a degree. You concealed the location of the Parvii Fold from my truthing touch, hiding the galactic coordinates of your sacred place. Your people were the same to my touch; they told me nothing."

"And you Tulyans have your own sacred secrets as well." She

shook her head. "It's too bad you and I can't fully trust one another."

He smiled in a serene, perhaps ancient way. "Tell me where the Parvii Fold is, then, and I will tell you where the Tarbu Gap is. A quid pro quo."

"Just like that? But what if I give you the wrong information?"

"Then I will do the same for you. Don't forget. I have been traveling this galaxy for almost a million years, and I will know the truth . . . or the lie . . . of the coordinates you give me."

"It is at the far end of Nebula 9907," she said.

He narrowed his eyes suspiciously. "I have been to that region many times, and saw no galactic fold."

"There is an asteroid funnel that is veiled by a Parvii swarm that guards it constantly, a swarm that has changed its appearance to make it look like there is no opening at all."

"One of your nasty Parvii tricks," Eshaz said. He nodded his head. "Yes, that location rings true."

"And you Tulyans have no tricks of your own?" she said, with a smile. "Now it's your turn."

"Very well. The Tarbu Gap is in the Isuki Star System."

"Where?"

He grinned, revealing large reptilian teeth. "In the five hundred seventy-seventh quadrant, past the Tlewa Roid Belt."

She thought for a moment. "I'm drawing a blank."

"It is a region of burned-out stars, and of dwarf stars, both white and brown. It is one of the Aopoddae breeding grounds."

"I don't know how we missed it."

Eshaz shrugged. "It's a big galaxy. If you are ready, I shall give you coordinates to take us there."

"Have you used Tulyan mindlink to veil the region in some manner?"

"I have told you enough," he said curtly.

"Be nice to me or I'll inform Woldn, and he will have the swarms cut you off from that area. He will end your podship hunts forever."

"But your true allegiance is not to Woldn, is it?" Eshaz said. "It is to the well-being of this galaxy. I see it in your eyes, and . . . I felt it . . . in your touch."

Tesh did not look surprised. She looked down at her hand, where Eshaz had made physical contact with her, and smiled.

"Will you take us to Tarbu Gap?" Acey asked her.

"Just let anyone try and stop me," Tesh said.

The four of them reached across the table, and clasped hands.

Chapter Twenty-Five

From any point in time or space, the possibilities are endless.

—Noah Watanabe

While Giovanni Nehr was considering a plan to rescue Noah, he remembered seeing the underwater door of the Max One prison. The stone structure had once been a nobleman's castle, so he thought that was probably a secret escape route, with an airlock on the other side. But there might not be an airlock on the other side, or it might not be functional anymore.

To deal with that unknown, Gio now envisioned a scuba-commando team of Humans and fighting machines, attaching a mobile airlock to a wall underwater. They could then find a way to open the door and go through.

Finding Thinker in one of the robot construction chambers, Gio outlined his plan to him.

Blinking his metal-lidded eyes, Thinker said, "Your concept of a mobile airlock is intriguing, but it has never been done before. Granted, the underwater door on the prison may not have an airlock of its own, so your idea has some merit. But it presents difficulties, not the least of which is the method of sealing such a device against a wet surface, especially with the rock that the prison is made of. It's Canopan sangran, a material that cannot be climbed with adhesive shoes, since malleable foreign substances do not stick to it. In my data banks, I have information about the difficulties they had in formulating mortars."

"But they came up with a mortar, obviously."

"Yes, and I know the formula. But it requires materials that are not readily available to us on Canopa."

"There must be a way," Gio said.

"If we had the right materials, yes, but the lack of podship travel. . . ." Thinker hesitated. "Ah," he said.

"What did you come up with?"

"Come with me," Thinker said. He led Gio down a long tunnel into a side cavern. At a barracks building, he asked to see one of the new recruits, a young woman named Kindsah. "Tell her to bring her friend, too," he added.

After a few minutes, she came over. A stocky woman in her early twenties with curly black hair, she smiled readily. Gio had never met her before, but had seen her with an unusual little alien—one she had with her now, visible from the top of an open carrying bag in her hand.

Thinker explained the problem to her, and he said, "I've seen you demonstrating Lumey's flexibility, and the way he can change shape and stick to surfaces with the most powerful adhesive quality I've ever seen. Could he stretch himself thin and do what we need, forming a gasket?"

Reaching into the bag, Kindsah brought out the dark-brown amorphous creature that Noah Watanabe had originally rescued from an industrially polluted planet. "To save Noah, this fellow would do anything. Of course, he could do that." She touched the creature soothingly as she murmured to it, and in a few seconds it became long and thin.

"See if he can stick to this," Thinker said. He brought a large gray chunk of sangran out of a bucket of water, and extended it.

Like a snake, Lumey darted forward and adhered himself to the wet stone, so that no one could pull it free. Then, holding him by the tail, Kindsah swung Lumey and the heavy stone over her head like a lasso. Only when she stopped and spoke soothingly to the creature, telling it to let go, did it do so.

Next, Kindsah caused the creature to spread all over the floor of the cavern like the thinnest of crepes on the surface, face-up.

"This is going to work," Thinker said. He knelt down and touched Lumey gently with the metal tip of a probe, then looked at Gio. "Now let's solve the other problems presented by your plan."

Giovanni Nehr had not anticipated such a woeful possibility, but as he developed the rescue plan with Thinker and Subi Danvar, he feared that he may have painted himself into a corner. Too late, a range of unwelcome possibilities occurred to him. The bottom line: If his plan did not result in Noah's safe return, he could very well be demoted to a mere fighter again, no more significant than the dead-brain robots who followed Thinker. Or worse, Gio envisioned the end of his career path in the Guardians.

But he had to proceed anyway. He had no alternative. So he recommended the key details of a dangerous, risky plan. At every opportunity, he tried to spread the potential blame as widely as possible, even to the young female recruit who cared for Lumey. With such an uncertain result, he preferred to cushion his own fall. But everyone kept complimenting him on the boldness and cleverness of his ideas, and looking to him to spearhead the effort.

It soon became apparent to Gio that the blame—or credit—would all go to him.

In the plan, he set the time and means of infiltrating Max One prison, in a daring attempt to liberate the beloved founder of the Guardians. The penal facility had been constructed on a manmade canal to resemble its notorious, blood-stained predecessor on Timian One, the Gaol of Brimrock.

Finally, Gio and his team were ready to go, not knowing that Noah wasn't even there anymore. . . .

Chapter Twenty-Six

"The noble-born princes call themselves aristocracy and cavort about in fine trimmings, but they are empty shells, for they have earned nothing and only came into their wealth through the deaths of their ancestors. But each chain of inheritance actually began with someone *earning* the wealth. Hence, it is beyond comprehension how the noble-born princes can consider themselves superior to those of us who have amassed great assets through ingenuity and hard work. Alas, this has been a dynamic of history, the eternal clash of old and new money."

—Prince Saito Watanabe,
public address on "The Nouveau Riche"

Seated in a front-row seat of the operating theater, Francella Watanabe leaned forward in anticipation. Having been unavoidably detained by a meeting, she had come in late. It was late morning now, and every window shade in the facility had been drawn so that bright yellow sunlight only came in through slits.

Dr. Bichette, standing over Noah at the central table, was injecting him with something. Four burly security guards stood nearby, ready to spring into action if her brother tried to escape again. Electronic straps no longer held him, and guards reported that he had shown interest in the electronic containment field of his cell, apparently trying to think of ways to disable it, too. But this was a different, far more powerful system, and thus far it seemed capable of holding Noah. No one was taking any chances, though. Additional guards had been assigned to him around the clock.

Francella glared down at the doctor, who had also been a source of irritation. Bichette had displayed a maddening degree of independence to her, but she couldn't get rid of him. Like her father before her, Prince Saito, she relied on Bichette's expertise, and to his credit, the man did not seem to like Noah much himself. In a heated discussion the day before, Bichette had assured Francella that their goals were "not dissimilar," and that he would take care of the situation in his own way, but to their mutual satisfaction.

The pledge had been somewhat less than she would have preferred, but Francella wanted to maintain her own composure in this situation, and was trying to pull herself back emotionally from the experiments being performed on her brother. That was much easier said than done, she realized.

Besides, she had other important matters on her mind. Shortly before coming in today, she had conducted a virtual-reality nehrcom session with noble-born princes on other planets. Blocked from meeting them in person by the podship crisis, this was their only viable means of getting together. At her insistence security had been tight, and because of the high status of the participants, all of them had been able to obtain private rooms at the various nehrcom transmitting stations.

The video quality of the meeting had been fuzzy, nowhere near as good as the clarity of the audio. Jacopo Nehr, inventor of the cross-space transmission system, had never been happy with the video feature, even on direct hookups such as this that did not go through relay stations. Apparently he considered it something of a professional embarrassment, so often he acted as if the feature didn't exist at all. All Francella could do was to make the best use of the technology, such as it was. She liked to watch the body language of people with whom she was conversing, as that often told her more than their words. It told her something about their sincerity and loyalty, of paramount importance to her because of the nature of their meetings.

For years Doge Lorenzo del Velli had favored men who excelled in business, and he had been appointing them to important governmental positions . . . at the expense of the noble-born princes. Her late father and Jacopo Nehr were among the most conspicuous examples of commoners honored at the expense of nobles, as both had been appointed "Princes of the Realm." But there were many others at various levels of government, undermining the entire infrastructure of the Merchant Prince Alliance. In a sense it was ironic that she—not of noble birth herself—should find herself aligned with those who were, but it was how she felt about the matter nonetheless. The old traditions were important, and should not be discarded easily. Men like her own brother, if permitted to excel and advance, were part of the problem.

At the VR nehrcom session the noble-born princes had clamored for her attention, asking her to be more active in their cause. She assured them that she was doing everything she could, but for security reasons she could not reveal all of the details. That was true to an extent, because she was helping their cause by destroying her own brother. But she had to admit to herself that she had something else in mind that was far more important than anything she would ever reveal to them.

Through her own sources, she had learned that some of the princes felt uneasy working with a woman (and a commoner by birth), but because of her political power and influence, she was their best hope to overthrow Lorenzo and replace him with their own man. The new leader had to be a man; she had no delusions about that, or ulterior motives of her own. She wouldn't want the job anyway, since it would only invite competitors to plot against her, especially in view of her gender. Francella felt more comfortable as a power behind the scenes. She could be a puppeteer, and make the next doge dance on the end of her strings.

She had concluded the VR meeting as quickly as possible while assuring her allies of her devotion to them, and her ongoing, behind-the-scenes efforts to undermine Doge Lorenzo's authority and eventually overthrow him. It was all a political cesspool as far as she was concerned, but she didn't particularly want to take more severe action, such as assassination. After all, she and Lorenzo had been bedmates for years now, and she didn't want to completely do away with him. She just wanted him out of office.

Now, in the laboratory, she focused on her most pressing interest. The square-jawed Dr. Bichette, in a white medical smock, was flanked by a pair of female technicians, similarly attired. The trio wore belts containing a variety of medical instruments and even stunners, should the patient become unruly and somehow break free of the electronic restraints that were holding him down.

At the moment, they seemed to be sedating Noah.

Her brother's purported immortality condition had not yet been verified, and there were certain things she needed to know. At the thought, she felt a slight trembling. In her discussion with Bichette she had emphasized their importance. He'd said he understood, and would perform the research properly, to fully exploit the information they obtained.

In previous laboratory sessions, Bichette had taken blood and tissue samples from Noah, and had performed a variety of experiments on him. Today, the doctor looked back at Francella and said, "I'm glad you are here. You will want to see this. The patient's ability to regenerate body parts seems to be linked with his reported 'immortality' condition, and if so, it is important to understand how it all works." Without further comment, he turned to his work, watching as the technicians took vital signs, including checking the dilation of the pupils. Unconscious, Noah heaved deep breaths, with his chest rising and falling perceptibly. Bichette opened one of Noah's hands and then swung the arm and hand onto a metal side table.

At a nod from one of the technicians, Dr. Bichette called for a C76 surgical scalpel, holding his hand out as the servo machinery in the room whirred to life, and a mechanical arm reached down to him from the ceiling.

Grabbing the scalpel, he made a quick motion with it, cutting off her brother's right forefinger. Noah jerked, but did not awaken. His breathing became less regular, and more agitated. Tossing the finger on a tray, the doctor moved to the bottom end of the table. This time he called for a surgical saw, and cut off the big toe on Noah's left foot, the same foot that had regenerated after being amputated earlier.

Again Noah jerked, and this time his eyes fluttered open before he drifted off once more, probably experiencing a nightmare. Francella felt no sympathy for him, never had. If he ever injured himself when they were children, she always enjoyed it, and now she felt a comfortable, pleasant sensation, a wash of memories from those times.

While Francella watched, fascinated, one of the attendants recorded everything with a holocam. In less than a minute, the finger and toe regrew, forming red appendages that changed in hue moment by moment, returning to the natural, light pigmentation of Noah's skin.

The technicians wrapped up Noah's severed finger and toe, and marked them for laboratory analysis. Dr. Bichette tossed the scalpel on a table, and looked thoughtfully at Noah. Francella wondered if his thoughts paralleled her own. Surely, he must have considered the possibilities. As for her, convinced that her brother really had eternal life, she was anxious to obtain it for herself, too.

Francella left her seat, and moved to the doctor's side. He glanced in her direction.

"I've been thinking about injecting his blood into my own bloodstream," she said.

Overhearing this, one of the laboratory technicians looked alarmed.

"I would not recommend that," Bichette said. "There are many analyses to complete before anything like that can be considered. Even then we would not want to try it on a Human being first." He shook his head. "There are many steps to follow."

Francella did not like the sound of that. She detested delays, had in mind the things she wanted to do. With the gift of eternal life, she could accomplish so much. The problem of her brother would remain, since he would also have the gift, so she would always—literally—have to keep him under control. For all eternity, she would be the master and he the slave.

Unless she found a way to obliterate Noah and all of his bodily tissue. But without cellular material, how would he regenerate? By magic? She experienced a mounting rage, and didn't know how long she could keep it in under control. Her trembling increased, and a shudder coursed her spine.

Leaning over Noah as he slept fitfully, she whispered in his ear: "I've always hated you. You were Daddy's favorite, his chosen successor, and the two of you acted like I didn't exist at all. I got nothing but the leavings, whatever you didn't want."

She felt an urge to slap him hard, but resisted because of the witnesses. Grimacing, she husked, "The tables have turned now, and I'm in control."

Chapter Twenty-Seven

> Any prison, no matter how ironclad it might appear to be, has multiple weak points. Security is only an illusion, and often only works *because* of the illusion.
>
> —Noah Watanabe, *Ruminations*

Shortly after midnight, three men, a woman, and six robots, all in black, slid down a muddy embankment and slipped into the water. The river, murky and slow-moving, chilled Gio at first despite his body suit, but he warmed as he swam across underwater, using his tankless breathing mechanism and making hardly any noise. The others followed him almost soundlessly. He felt a rush of exhilaration. With luck his commando team would rescue Noah Watanabe, and maybe even Anton Glavine. But Glavine was of secondary importance. The commandos' priority was clear, and everything had to go smoothly.

Gio wished he had a floor plan of the prison, but such information was highly classified. He had tried obtaining the layout, but at Thinker's suggestion he had made a blanket inquiry, concealing their intent by making it for all government-operated buildings on Canopa. No inquiries had resulted in anything useful, not even when bribes were offered.

The Humans under Gio's command wore night-vision goggles, but the six robots didn't require such gear, since their visual sensors adjusted automatically, absorbing the narrowest rays of light.

In actuality the commando squad had an additional member, since one of the ten squad members—Kindsah—carried Lumey in a backpack. Reaching the base of the rock prison wall, the young female Guardian removed the alien from her pack, and massaged Lumey gently. Looking at the amorphous creature in the red darkness, Gio imagined that Lumey might be feeling his own excitement and anticipation, since Noah had rescued him from an industrial slag heap.

For a moment, Gio almost had a change of heart. It was a strange sensation, as if he was about to take an unfamiliar path. Since first encountering Noah, he'd held some affection and respect for him, but with Gio such feelings had distinct limitations, not coming anywhere near the abiding, narcissistic love he felt for himself. For as long as he could remember, Gio had been a survivor, wary of outsiders, not trusting anyone, not even his family. His attitude sharpened even more after his brother became famous and got so much adulation.

In the red darkness, three of the swimming robots held the mobile airlock, with the flat side toward Kindsah. She petted the alien in her hands, and Gio saw it stretch as thin as a rope and attach itself to the perimeter of the airlock's flat side, forming a living gasket. Through some inexplicable means, the creature seemed to understand its role.

With Gio in the lead, the commando team submerged, and secured the airlock around the underwater doorway of the prison, with Lumey playing his part perfectly, and even leaving an opening in the center that matched the size of the door itself. Opening a hatch on the airlock, Gio swam inside first, followed by two of his team members, one of whom was a robot with security disabling capability.

They waited while pumps drained the chamber of water. Then they worked on the heavy metal prison door, using a fast-acting acid that ate the metal away. In a matter of moments the old door broke away, opening into darkness.

"Searching for alarm components," the robot reported. It discharged a flying unit that went ahead, through the hole. Designed by Thinker, it would neutralize any motion detectors, noise sensors, or other alarm features while making prison authorities think the system was still in operation.

In the red light of his goggles Gio made out a large, empty chamber beyond. A minute later the flying probe returned to its host robot, blinking a green light.

"Our remote camera isn't working," the robot reported. "I can't get any images of what's ahead. The probe found an alarm and decommissioned it, though."

"Let's go!" Gio said, after considering for only a moment. He led the way through. As they reached the rock interior floor of the prison, a clearplax door on the airlock closed behind them. He saw a door open on the other side of the airlock, letting water into the chamber, along with three more members of the commando team who swam inside, including Kindsah. The process repeated, and in a few moments the entire squad stood inside the prison.

With Gio in the lead, they ran from corridor to corridor and cell to cell, always keeping close to a wall, slinking around corners, moving stealthily through dim illumination. This entire level was unoccupied, though a room containing racks, garrotes, electrocution machines, injection tables, and a variety of other diabolical devices showed signs of recent activity, with scraps of food and leftover cups scattered about on the floor and tables.

Behind Gio, the robots moved with impressive silence. He didn't know how they accomplished it. Leading them up to the next level, he waited to confirm that the entire alarm system had been disabled, then hurried along the corridor. As he rounded a corner he saw a guard just ahead, and froze in his tracks. One of the robots fired a stun pellet, dropping the guard with a soft thud.

Most of the cells were unoccupied, but not all of them. As the commandos ran by, some of the prisoners asked what they were doing. Others called out for help, but Gio ignored all of them. He couldn't rescue everyone, couldn't afford to direct any energy in the wrong direction, slowing the thrust of his force.

Anton Glavine, whom Gio had seen standing at a window earlier, was nowhere to be seen. The commandos checked floor after floor, not finding Noah, either. But it was an immense facility.

On the limited number of levels they reached, they fired stun pellets, knocking guards into unconsciousness. The commando team's security robot got its remote camera working, and in a blur of speed, the flying probe searched every remaining section of the prison. There were many more guards on other levels, but no sign of Noah or Anton.

Just as the flying probe searched the last area, Gio glanced at his wristchron, and saw that he only had a couple of more minutes before they had to leave. Gio's imagination ran wild. Maybe Noah and Anton were being interrogated in a hidden room, or even tortured. The Doge's prisons were notorious hell-holes.

Hearing voices just ahead, around a corner, he stopped. Holding up his hand, the rest of his team paused with him, and listened. The alarm robot sent the flying probe ahead. Studying a small screen on the robot, Gio saw the camera flicker as it sent a fuzzy signal.

On the image he saw Anton Glavine, seated at a chair with uniformed Red Berets around, interrogating him. No sign of Noah Watanabe anywhere, but on this level and on the route to reach it there were more guards than his small force could overcome. To Gio it looked too risky to attempt a rescue of Anton.

"You have such a convenient memory," one of the interrogators said, a burly man with a black beard. "Somehow you can't recall anything about where Guardian headquarters is, but you admit being there? How is that?"

"I don't know," Anton said, "but I'm telling you the truth." He smiled grimly. "Maybe it's stress-induced, and you should let up on me."

"I wish they'd let us use more efficient methods on this one," the man said, "and on Watanabe. I'd get the information out of both of them."

"So, he hasn't told you, either?" Anton asked.

"Obviously, or we wouldn't be pressing you. At least he doesn't have a cock-and-bull story like yours, and he admits knowing. He keeps talking about honor and duty. Makes me want to puke."

The interrogators paused as a woman in a hooded cloak emerged from a side door, carrying a tray of food. As she set the tray on a table, Glavine was ushered over and seated. He glanced at the woman, then began to eat quickly. The Red Berets stood to one side, talking and not paying attention to the pair.

With a quick motion the woman whispered something to Glavine, then hurried away. He looked surprised at whatever she had to say. Just before she departed through a doorway her hood fell open for a moment, revealing blond hair and a heart-shaped face. She slipped away, unnoticed by the guards.

She was the most stunningly beautiful creature Gio had ever seen. He played the holo-image back on the robot's screen, then froze the frame. And recognized her. She was, unmistakably, Princess Meghina of Siriki! But what was the famous courtesan and companion of the Doge doing here, serving food to a prisoner and trying to conceal her identity?

An odd feeling came over Gio, a mixture of questions and the sense that all he was seeing, while fascinating, would not result in finding Noah. Anton might be a good secondary target to rescue—in view of the rumors about him—but he seemed to have an important benefactor, a noblewoman. Were they lovers? Was Lorenzo really his father? One thing seemed clear: Any attempt to get him now would certainly result in a firefight, and he'd be on the losing end. If Anton had been alone in an isolated cell, it might have been different. But this was much more complicated. Anton was the focus of too much attention.

Noah didn't seem to be here, but wherever they were keeping him they would undoubtedly move him to a more secure place after an assault on Max One. Better to retreat and regroup.

Gio gave the necessary comsignal, then led his team back the way they had come. In a matter of minutes, he and the others were outside and in the water again, with the exception of one robot, who sealed himself in the airlock and pumped water out of it. Afterward he would reseal the underwater door to the prison, using a mortar patch he had brought along. It would not look the same as the original door, but in the murky darkness of the prison should go unnoticed for a time.

As Gio emerged from the water and crawled up the riverbank on the other side, he felt dismal. He had developed an excellent rescue plan for the facility, but it seemed likely that Noah had been moved. Maybe he wasn't even alive.

For Giovanni Nehr's career path, a very bad scenario had come to pass.

Chapter Twenty-Eight

When making important leadership decisions, take care to avoid certain emotions such as anger or envy, since they can be dangerous to your mission. But don't avoid emotions entirely. Always follow your gut instincts.

—Noah Watanabe

Thinker had developed a veiling energy field to protect the subterranean headquarters, a system that was superior to the original infrared scrambling system he had set up. Now he felt even more confident that Noah's enemies would not locate their headquarters inside rock-lined underground burrows. Most of the hidden facility lay deep beneath hills near Noah's former ecological demonstration compound, but some of the newer chambers were close to the edge of his old property.

With the improved technology, the robot was not concerned about security. They could burrow directly beneath the old administration buildings if they wanted to, and would not be detected.

Learning of this, Subi liked the irony, and at first he thought it might be an unexpected action that Noah had taken himself—a slap in the face of his enemies. But Subi's better judgment told him to maintain caution. . . .

He had trouble making some decisions. With Noah missing—incarcerated or worse—Subi felt out of balance. For the months of the Master's absence he'd been trying to keep the Guardians going, and he had done reasonably well in recruitment, bringing in hundreds of young men and women, along with the new machines that Thinker was building. Subi had helped obtain materials for the robots, and had given the robot leader specifications for the mechanical fighters and support workers that he needed.

On the surface, seen through the eyes of the Guardian membership, the organization seemed to be doing well. They were not only growing in number; they were making successful, destructive raids against the Doge's Red Berets and Francella's CorpOne assets. But to Subi, those successes only masked the deep pain he felt inside, the terrible, gnawing fear that he would never see Noah again.

Is he dead?

On one level, it seemed impossible to him; Noah Watanabe was the strongest person he had ever met, and even had an odd restorative power that Subi had observed himself, the ability to regenerate an amputated left foot. Cellular regeneration. Amazing. But Subi still assumed Noah was mortal, a container of cells that would eventually decay and die.

The loyal adjutant didn't want to think that way, and tried to remain optimistic. He would follow Noah off a cliff if ordered to do so, would do anything for the great man. With loving attention to detail, Subi was keeping the Guardians going for Noah, caretaking them until his friend and mentor returned. But what if that never happened? What if the worst had occurred?

He could not share such terrible thoughts with anyone for fear of destroying the organization, could only live with his terrible fears each day, constantly trying to put them out of his mind.

In Noah's absence, Subi had to make do in any number of ways. The adjutant missed being able to consult with his boss on tough decisions, or having Noah ask him for his advice. He missed their walks together on the Ecological Demonstration Project, and hearing the renowned man identify every plant they passed. He missed conducting classes together on EcoStation. Now, with all of that gone, Subi had to motivate young minds in new ways. He still conducted classes, still taught ecology, but it was not the same. Holo-images of plants, shown to students in underground caverns, were not the same as the real thing.

It was all second-rate, except for Noah's own writings on galactic ecology, which Subi prepared for classroom education and distributed to the students.

On the operating table at the CorpOne medical laboratory, Noah sensed evil forces at work against him, and felt their debilitating effects on him. He heard his loathsome sister's taunting voice, but could not focus on her words. Drugs were keeping him submerged.

His tortured mind struggled and groped, searching for escape, and he did manage to achieve a timetrance, but it was not the serenity he longed for, not a haven to restore his energies and his desire to fight on. He felt dismal.

Like an injured predator, he attempted to gain control over a podship that was docked in a pod station, wanting to take the vessel out on the podways. But as his mental tendrils reached out and touched the podship, it jerked away from him, and fled into space.

Yet Noah kept reaching out, and this time he took a different direction. . . .

Just before Noah's capture, he had asked Thinker to download a backup copy of his brain into one of the robot's data banks. The Guardian leader had been thinking about his own mortality, and wanted to make sure his teachings were directly available to his followers, in case something happened to him.

For some time afterward the cerebral robot contemplated the best means of preserving and presenting the information in Noah's mind. Finally he came up with something beyond what either of them originally contemplated. He created a three-dimensional color likeness of Noah on a large square screen, visible by opening a panel on the front of the robot's torso. It looked and behaved like the original person, and even interacted with anyone speaking to the screen. For further realism the image had freckles on its face, as well as tiny scars and blemishes on the 3-D body, all precisely correct from every side.

Anxious to show off his new creation, Thinker went to Subi Danvar's underground office, and entered unannounced.

The adjutant stood at a work table, thumbing through a pile of paper documents. Hearing the metallic sounds as the robot entered, he turned. "I'll just be a minute," Subi said, going back to his work.

As Thinker waited, he slid open the new video panel on his chest, and the image of Noah Watanabe flashed on.

"Hurry it up, hurry it up," the simulacrum said in a voice that very nearly matched the original.

"Eh?" Startled, Subi dropped the papers, scattering them on the floor.

"You heard me," the Noah said. "Now come over here where I can get a better look at you."

Timidly, Subi approached the screen, where the face of Noah Watanabe stared at him in displeasure.

"What is this?" Subi said, looking up at Thinker's metal face, just above the screen.

Thinker did not reply, but the video image did. "I'm not in the habit of being ignored by a subordinate. Speak to me, Subi, not to the robot."

Perplexed, Subi backed up, staring all the while at the screen. "Thinker, tell me what's going on here."

The robot formed a stiff smile. "When Master Noah was with us, I used my organic interface connection to download the contents of his brain. All perfectly harmless, I just made a copy, with no harm to the original. I did it at his request, to leave a backup copy of him behind. A dated copy, of course, only containing memories and experiences that were in place on the date of the interaction."

Just then a swirling mist formed around the screen, unseen by anyone. They did, however, see the image of Noah flicker.

"I think it has a short circuit," Subi said. "You'd better shut it off."

"Absurd," Thinker said. "I have instant access to every one of my circuits, and they are all operating perfectly."

"Then why is Noah's face flickering?"

"My circuits report no malfunction."

"You must be wrong, my friend." Subi saw the image of Noah partially concealed by a gray film, as if a fog had gotten inside the screen. "Robots can make mistakes too, once in a while."

"I'm no ordinary robot." Thinker whirred, and then looked down at the screen on his own chest. "Mmmm. Peculiar. Perhaps I should fold shut and contemplate this." For some reason, though, he delayed.

The foggy gray film inside the screen looked peculiar to Subi, and gave him an unsettled feeling. It swirled around, and then seemed to dart into the image of Noah and vanish entirely. Simultaneously, the eyes and face of Master Noah looked more alive, more alert, and still Thinker did not fold himself shut. . . .

"You're looking rather stressed," Noah said to Subi. "Perhaps we can have one of our old talks again, and I could give you some advice that will be of assistance?"

"I doubt that," Subi said. He tapped the robot on the head, and said, "Thinker, this . . . *thing* . . . uses computer programming to carry on conversations?"

Hesitation. Then: "*Bio*computer programming. It acts like the original, reacts like Noah really would to any given situation."

"So, *it* could still lead us?"

"Well," Thinker said, "I have already discussed this possibility with the programmed likeness, and it doesn't think that would be practical."

"Kindly do not refer to me as a thing or an it," the image said.

"A most peculiar sensation," Thinker said. "The spoken words are not emanating from my operating circuits."

"That's because I really *am* Noah. Not in the customary sense, since my corporal form is somewhere else. Even so, I have come here, and I'm with you now at this very moment. Now listen carefully, and I'll tell you where they're keeping me."

"Most unusual," Thinker said.

"Good one," Subi said. "Nice trick, Thinker."

"Not a trick," the robot said. "Something is going wrong . . . going wrong." With the repeated words, Thinker's voice merged with Noah's, and came from the screen.

Subi reached out, and touched the face on the screen.

But the voice from the screen grew weak, and said, "I can't hold the connection any longer. . . ." In a few seconds the voice faded out entirely, and the strange animation of the image went away with it, leaving it less lifelike and more in the nature of a video recording, as it had been originally.

Chapter Twenty-Nine

It is said that the Supreme Being had a first thought, a second, and a third. So it was in the beginning, and shall be again.

—A legend of Lost Earth

To Noah, it had all been like a strange dream, but he knew it had really happened. And, though he repeatedly tried to make the connection again with his image in Thinker's torso, he found it impossible to accomplish. On other occasions he had traveled along the strands of the web to go wherever he wanted, but other times—such as now—it seemed to block him. The harder he tried to return to his friends, the more impossible it seemed to be.

In his heart, he suspected that he needed to back off on the attempts. Then perhaps, the cosmic pathway would open for him again like the embrace of a lover.

As a robot, Thinker struggled to explain the strange event, but Subi offered an explanation right away. He theorized that there had been a computer malfunction that made Noah's simulation seem to come alive.

"I have no record of a malfunction," Thinker said.

"Therefore, you have a malfunction on top of a malfunction."

"Perhaps, but my probability programs point in an entirely

different direction, to the cosmic structure they call Timeweb. I have only sketchy information on it, what has been reported to me about certain unusual properties of communication and travel. As you know, Master Noah made me the official historian of the Guardians, and the trustee of his life story. At that time, despite numerous experiences in Timeweb, he did not understand how the network functioned. Maybe he has a deeper comprehension now that he has gone from us, but we can't contact him to find out. I suspect that no *living* organism will ever gain all information about something so vast and complex."

"Are you implying that you could gain a full understanding of it?"

The heavy lidded eyes blinked. "Of course. I have a much larger capacity for data storage than any Human."

"But is Timeweb all about information and data sorting? Noah told me it has certain spiritual qualities that he didn't think could be grasped in any purely logical way."

The machine whirred, but only for a moment. Then: "That could be the case. To be most effective, I must remain open to all possibilities, however implausible they may seem at first."

"Maybe there's hope for you after all," Subi said with a gentle smile.

"The best answer I have now," Thinker said, "is that an aberration in the cosmic structure transported Noah's mental image all the way here. Think of a radio or audiovisual signal skipping through the atmosphere of a planet, or through the galaxy. The signal comes and goes, depending upon surrounding conditions."

"Do your programs say if it can happen again?"

"Not enough information. . . ."

Over the course of several days, Thinker checked the simulacrum circuitry and pronounced it fit. He, Subi, and other

Guardians interacted with the Noah-image several times, and each time it was a straightforward matter, with the image operating as the robot intended. The electronic simulation provided them with its advice and instructions based upon AI-enhanced probabilities that were calculated from Noah's actual past experiences.

The Guardians even asked the simulation about the strange, brief moments when it had seemed to be something more. "Oh, you only imagined that," the Noah said, after a moment's hesitation. "It never happened. Your perceptions are not real."

Grudgingly, Subi accepted this.

As time passed, he and his followers obtained advice from the computer-generated Noah about how best to make guerrilla raids against industrial polluters, and they were successful in destroying an immense gaserol plant operated by a business associate of Doge Lorenzo. With the help of Noah's alter ego, the Guardians pursued the most serious damagers of the environment, no longer limiting themselves to the forces of Lorenzo and Francella. This made the Guardians more unpredictable, and harder to defend against. . . .

In heavy armor that disguised him as a machine, covering his entire body instead of only part of it, Giovanni Nehr was sent on a new outside mission. Even after Gio's failure at Max One, the Noah simulation had recommended no punishment for him, and the placement of no obstacles in his career path.

Thus, Gio found himself on still another reconnaissance assignment. This time he was supposed to infiltrate Jimu and the fighting machines that were in the service of the Doge. With considerable finesse he accomplished this, obtaining a position with a robotic yard crew working at the Doge's cliffside villa. There, Gio confirmed earlier intelligence reports that Jimu had his robots reproducing at a very high rate. One day, Gio saw more than a thousand of them performing efficient, deadly fighting formations in a practice session near the villa.

After a week of spying Gio returned to Guardian headquarters, and reported to Subi Danvar and Thinker, who stood just outside the Brew Room. "We don't want to oppose those machines in direct battle," Gio said. "They're too numerous, too skilled."

"I projected as much," Thinker said, after listening to more details. "They have access to far more raw materials than we do, can build at a much higher rate."

Again, Subi consulted with the likeness of Noah Watanabe, who flashed on at the center of the robot's chest. "Subi, you don't really need me," Noah said. He stared intently from the screen.

"How can you say that?" Subi protested. "The Guardians are nothing without you."

Noah's likeness scowled. Then it seemed to move away, and paced around a simulated chamber.

"Master Noah, come back here," Subi pleaded.

Noah did so, and returned to the foreground of the screen. With a kindly expression, he said, "Thinker has been updating me with reports of your activities and decisions. My loyal adjutant, you are the wisest of leaders. Your decisions are sound."

"Not as sound as they could be. I've done my best, but. . . ."

Interrupting, the simulacrum said, "The best hope of the Guardians is not to consult with an electronic version of me, but to follow your leadership instincts. You've been right to continue your guerrilla raids, while building your own forces, Human and machine. I especially like your idea of calling the robots 'ecomachines.' I never thought of that."

"But I never said anything about that," Subi said. "How did you . . . ?" He paused, and looked up at the metal face of Thinker. "You downloaded *my* brain, too?"

The metal face smiled, and the metal-lidded eyes blinked in acknowledgment. "While you slept."

Angrily, Subi said, "You had no right. I didn't give you permission to do that!"

"Earlier, I avoided doing that to Noah without his permission. This time, however, I. . . ."

"Well, what?"

"I ran probability programs and arrived at the answer that you would appreciate joining Noah's simulacrum in my internal world."

"Well I don't, and I don't want you to ever do that again to anybody. Do you understand?"

"Yes, sir, but I was only trying to be helpful."

"Don't forget what I told you."

"I never forget anything. I'm a machine, with perfect recollection."

Subi shook his head. "You still have a lot to learn."

"As you can see," the Noah copy said, interrupting them from the screen, "I know you very well, Subi. Thinker's screen of me is clever, but you should not rely on me any longer, my friend. It can only weaken you."

A tear ran down Subi's cheek. "My decision is this, Noah. I will continue to speak with you from time to time . . . as a friend. You thought I only saw you as a boss?"

"No, and I never saw you as only an adjutant, either." The simulacrum's eyes looked sad, even capable of crying. Then he turned and walked away, into the darkness of a simulated tunnel.

Chapter Thirty

Each world is different from every other one, and Tarbu is the most unique of all.

—From a Tulyan Story

In the vast galaxy, some life forms had existed for eternity, while others had evolved over the eons, so that only remnants of their ancient pasts remained . . . the faint genetic dustings of history. So it was with planets, and entire galactic sectors surrounding them.

Tarbu was a world run by Tulyans in much the same manner as it had been millions of years ago. As mortal enemies of Tulyans, the Parviis knew it existed but had never been able to determine its location. It was the Tulyan equivalent of the Parvii Fold, mysterious and hidden, filled with the arcane ways of its inhabitants. Both regions, as if designed by God for such purposes, had been cut off from other star systems by cosmic conditions—the Parvii Fold by its pocketed, far-out-of-the way location, and Tarbu by electrical disturbances that prevented Parvii brains from detecting it—or the existence of the Wild Pod Zone beyond, in a region of dim, dwarf stars.

According to Tulyan legend, the Sublime Creator established Tarbu and the protected region on the other side of it as a sanctuary for podships and for the Tulyans who were supposed to be their pilots. It came to be known as the Tarbu Gap. In this belief system, the Sublime Creator constructed the relationship between Tulyans and the spacefaring Aopoddae in the first place, but Parviis subsequently altered it in horrific ways, for their own selfish purposes.

Eshaz led his companions off the podship that had just traveled across space, then strode through an airlock to the station platform, talking to them constantly, giving them a preview of the remarkable wonders all of them were about to share.

Fascinated, Dux hung on every word. To the teenager, this pod station orbiting Tarbu looked like any other, with its mottled gray-and-black surfaces, along with the organic texture of its construction, not dissimilar from podships themselves. He had heard it said that both podships and pod stations were living variations of an ancient race that had been created in unexplained ways, and which continued to behave mysteriously, like an immense, galactic-scale organism. When considered in that manner, it sounded frightening to some people, but Dux had never felt that way himself. Each time he rode in a podship or stepped onto a pod station, he felt more at peace than anywhere else, and infinitely calm. It was like some people felt in the presence of water, as if the liquid was a link to the past when Humans swam the seas of Lost Earth, before evolving to walk on land and become what they were today.

"Eshaz mentioned something to you in passing," Tesh said, "the Parvii Fold. He and I have an arrangement of trust, or I would not permit him to speak in this manner, and he would never have brought me here. To his race, the Tarbu Gap is as sacred as the Parvii Fold is to mine."

"Don't forget the Tulyan Starcloud," Eshaz said. "We have more than one sacred region."

She nodded. "And perhaps there are others as well, on both sides."

This elicited no apparent reaction from the big Tulyan, as he led them across the platform of the pod station.

Staring at Tesh, Dux furrowed his brow. "Eshaz said you aren't really Human. What did he mean by that?"

"I am like you and not like you at the same moment," the pretty brunette said, as they all paused at an empty shuttle bay. She touched one of Dux's shoulders. "I am a Parvii, one of the major galactic races, even though most races do not even know we exist."

"You certainly look Human," Acey said, "so what's the difference?" He always liked to know how things worked, and studied her attractive form with new interest.

Dux noticed Eshaz standing off to one side, watching them with a somewhat amused expression.

"Your race—*humanus ordinaire*—is an offshoot of mine," she said. "We are genetically linked, but so vastly different now that the similarities are more superficial than significant." She paused. "We may look alike at the moment, but watch this." Touching her own wrist, she seemed to disappear in a faint mist. Then Dux heard her, a tiny voice down on the deck.

"Don't step on me!" she shouted, looking up at them and waving her arms.

Kneeling, Dux and Acey stared at the tiny Human shape, like a Lilliputian in the Land of Gulliver.

"I wonder what other surprises Tesh and Eshaz have for us," Acey said.

"We have hardly begun!" Eshaz boomed, towering over them.

The boys tumbled backward, when Tesh suddenly shot up and became full-size again. As Acey and Dux regained their footing and stood with her again she said, "Eshaz and I have come to an understanding of epic proportions. Historically, Tulyans and Parviis are mortal enemies, like Humans and Mutatis, but we have agreed to work together for the greater good, for all of the races and sectors of the galaxy."

"Noah Watanabe is the binding force," Eshaz said. "All of us are eco-warriors serving his cause, his interpretation of galactic ecology. Agreed?" Through slitted gray eyes he peered down at Acey and Dux.

"Agreed!" the boys exclaimed.

"We knew we could count on you," Tesh said. "Or at least, that's what Eshaz told me. You see, he read your minds."

"How did you do that?" Acey asked.

"Leave me *some* secrets," Eshaz said good-naturedly. Then, looking at Tesh, he said, "Speaking of that, I will readily admit that certain thoughts of yours are . . . how shall I put it? They are veiled, but not completely. I speak of personal feelings you have for Noah Watanabe, beyond anything professional in your capacity as a Guardian."

Dux saw her redden in apparent embarrassment.

"The way you look at him, for example," Eshaz added, "and the particular tone of your voice in his presence. I find it interesting."

"What do you know about it?" she said, indignantly. "You're not even Human."

"And *you* are? As far as I know, Humans don't do the magic act we just witnessed."

Composing herself, she smiled. "I'm closer to Human than you, my friend. In any event, you do not even have a mate. What is your experience in personal relationships, anyway? For that matter, how do Tulyan people *reproduce?* I know you have males and females, since First Elder Kre'n is female, or so we are led to believe. Do you mate in the customary manner?"

Now Eshaz smiled, as he was finding his own amusement in the interplay. "You have touched upon one of the matters we do not discuss with outside races."

"It is similar for me," Tesh said, "but it is not a racial matter at all. I do not discuss affairs of my heart with anyone. They are too personal."

"But you must discuss them with someone," Eshaz said. "With the person you have such feelings toward."

"That goes without saying," she said. Her green eyes twinkled. "My feelings for Noah are personal. So are my feelings for you."

Eshaz laughed, a deep rumble. "A Tulyan and a Parvii," he said. "The most interesting proposition I've ever received. And I have lived for a very long time, indeed."

Tesh pushed him good-naturedly, but he was so large and heavy that he didn't move. Her voice rose. "I didn't *proposition* you, you big oaf!"

"I will be more cautious of you in the future," he said, with a wide reptilian grin. "In all matters, you are dangerous."

In a short while a shuttle arrived, to transport them down to Tarbu. For some reason, Dux had been unable to see the planet at all when they arrived at the orbital pod station. There had been no mists or clouds, though, nothing to obscure his vision. Now, as they plunged down in the shuttle, the planet seemed to take shape before them, emerging from space like something appearing out of nothingness, as if had popped out of a void, from an entirely different dimension. As they dropped down into the atmosphere, the light was an eerie brownish gray, with no visible sun or cloud cover. Just an oddly illuminated sky.

Dux and Acey stood silently at a window of the shuttle, not saying anything, only able to absorb with their eyes and their souls.

As they set down on the landing pad of the shuttleport, Eshaz said, "We call Tarbu the 'porcupine planet,' since most of its surface is covered with thorny vines, even beneath the snow at higher elevations, and underwater. The stuff is incredibly tough, but grows so slowly that we've been able to trim it for surface travel and habitation."

The Tulyan put on a custom-fitting protective suit made of thick green material, and said, "You three will have to remain here, since we don't have suits for . . . aliens. I need to go off the beaten path a bit and find a special variety of vine."

"Have you forgotten?" Tesh said, "I can shut off my magnification system and ride in one of your pockets."

"Very well."

She reduced herself, and climbed onto one of Eshaz's thick hands, which he extended down to her. Carefully, he selected a side pocket for her, with a flap that she could open and close.

Then, looking sternly at the boys, Eshaz said, "Can I trust you two to stay out of trouble for a few hours? I don't want you causing mischief here, like you did at the starcloud."

"We won't let you down," Acey promised.

"But you know that, don't you?" Dux added. "After all, you read our minds, and know our hearts."

"That I do, laddies," he said. And he turned and left with his tiny Parvii passenger. They made a most unlikely pair.

The planet was covered with thorny underbrush, but Tesh soon learned that the inhabitants had cut ingenious labyrinthine passageways on the surface, and had built multi-level structures inside the growths. Eshaz's protective suit was necessary, he explained, because many of the thorns contained drugs, toxins, and a variety of other potentially harmful substances, and should not be touched indiscriminately.

"There are a variety of thorn bushes here," he said, "containing different things, and it takes an expert to identify them."

"Sounds like a thorny problem," she quipped, from his pocket.

"That it is," he said humorlessly.

Eshaz took a narrow passageway to the top of a knoll, where he emerged into a broad clearing. There he pointed out several prickly thorn bushes around them, in a variety of colors. "Our vinemasters cultivate these with great care," he said. "They are ancient growths, going back to the beginning days of our race."

Just then, a pair of Tulyans emerged from the undergrowth. They were much smaller than Eshaz, and at first Tesh thought they might be a sub-race.

"Greetings, Eshaz," one of them said, in a high-pitched voice.

"And to you, my young friends," Eshaz said.

"You desire cuttings today?" the other asked in a similar tone.

"These are vinemasters," Eshaz said, looking down at his pocket passenger.

The Tulyan pair looked at her closely, and one of them asked, "Is that a . . . Parvii? *Here?*"

"It is," Eshaz said, calmly.

"And the Overseer approves of this?" the other asked. The voices of the vinemasters bordered on hysteria.

"I am here by direction of the Council of Elders," Eshaz replied, calmly. "Shall I wait while you go and consult the Overseer?"

"That will not be necessary," a voice said. Another Tulyan appeared, this one as large as Eshaz, with a creased, bronze face and deep-set, slitted eyes. He looked very, very old. "I have been in contact with the Council, and they told me to expect our distinguished visitor."

"Tesh, meet Pluj, the eminent Overseer of Tarbu."

Peeking out of the pocket, she waved to him.

As the Tulyans talked, Tesh felt out of place, and had a lot of questions to ask, but she didn't feel the time was appropriate. She remained unclear about the ages of the "young" vinemasters, since she had heard that a Tulyan lived for millions of years, and was, in effect, immortal. It appeared that they had some type of breeding system anyway, and that these were the

Tulyan equivalent of children. She suspected that this could still make them tens of thousands, or even hundreds of thousands, of years old.

Eshaz and the Overseer, followed by the vinemasters, walked up and down rows of thorn growths, selecting the vines that Eshaz needed—for a use that was not discussed among them, and which had not yet been disclosed to Tesh.

On the way back to the shuttleport, with Eshaz carrying five large wooden cases that were strapped together, she asked him how old the vinemasters were.

"Oh, much older than you might think."

"But are they children?"

"Not in the sense that you mean, or they would never be entrusted with such important responsibilities. The way we breed and age is quite different from any other race. One day, I will explain it to you, perhaps."

"We'll trade stories," she said, in her tiny voice.

"Yes, we'll do that, perhaps around a campfire."

She laughed. . . .

Later that day, Eshaz and Tesh returned to the shuttleport with the burnished wood cases, containing the special thorn vines and other supplies (including foodstuffs) that had been provided for them by the vinemasters.

When this was completed, Eshaz provided new galactic coordinates to Tesh, and pointed into a region of space where few stars were visible. "That way," he said.

With a nod, she hurried forward to the navigation room, one of her own secrets. Eshaz smiled as he watched her shrink and disappear into a corridor.

One day, he mused as the podship took off, *our races might not keep such secrets from each other.*

Chapter Thirty-One

Nothing works by itself. Everything in this galaxy, from micro to macro, is linked to something else.

—Master Noah Watanabe

Even when podships crisscrossed the galaxy, the Zultan Abal Meshdi had not enjoyed traveling beyond the worlds of the Mutati Kingdom. Such journeys had invariably proved a disappointment to him, showing him planets and peoples that were far inferior to his own, far less than his glorious homeworld of Paradij and the jewel-like Citadel from which he ruled the multi-planet shapeshifter empire.

For him, Paradij was the center of the entire universe, but once this had been a barren, unappealing world. The Mutatis, after being driven to planets like this by Human aggression, had completely terraformed it, with massive hydraulic engineering and planting projects that transformed gray into green and blue. In their centuries-long task, generations of shapeshifters had been guided by God-on-High. This beautiful place was proof of what they could accomplish with determination and holy guidance.

As Meshdi strolled through his ornamental gardens one morning, he marveled at the towering fountains on each side of the stone path, water spouts that had been engineered to change color and shape by the hour, so that they looked new to him all the time. They were reflections of Mutatis themselves, who could metamorphose their own appearances at will, thus preventing boredom and constantly opening creative possibilities.

He considered the beauty around him a reward for his good deeds in a prior life. Certainly, no mortal being could ask for more.

Truly, I am blessed.

From this cosmic jewel, the Zultan ruled the Mutati Kingdom. He sighed. If not for constant Human aggression, this would be more than enough for him. But they forced him to lash out, to draw a line in space that he would not permit them to cross.

The Zultan adored technology, especially the personal gyrodome in his suite and the various types of minigyros, devices provided to him so generously by his Adurian allies. Each day he used the large unit to purify his thoughts, giving him the clarity he needed to lead his people. And whenever he went out, he liked to wear one of the portable minigyros on his head, not only to maintain his own thinking processes, but as an example for his people. In increasing numbers, they were using the devices as well.

The loyal Adurians, while adept at technological innovation, were nonetheless not as skilled in robotics as Hibbils, who were allied with his enemies, the merchant princes. The Humans also had their nehrcom cross-space communication system, which enabled them to remain in contact with one another instantaneously, across vast distances. Surprisingly, that had been the invention of a Human, Jacopo Nehr.

But in a blessing from God-on-High, the inventor's discontented brother, Giovanni Nehr, had come to Paradij to reveal the secret of the technology. The naïve Human had turned it over to Meshdi to get even with his brother and to ingratiate himself with the Mutatis, thinking he would be rewarded with a proverbial king's ransom. Instead, Meshdi, after accepting the information, had placed the traitorous man in prison. Somehow he had escaped, but no matter. Now the Mutatis had the technology, or at least a large part of it. They were able to communicate across space with their own system, although the reception was fuzzy and sometimes went offline. His scientists were working on the problem now, along with other important military matters.

In particular, the Mutati scientists had successfully cloned podships, and were now hard at work on the next step, solving the very difficult guidance problem. But it had occurred to Meshdi that the guidance of podships might not be technological at all. He still had technicians working on it, but in the meantime he was relying on God-on-High to guide the sentient pods to their destinations. For a Mutati, that was always the best course of action.

Recently he had ordered the launch of a lab-pod against Siriki, a key enemy world chosen because of its proximity. With much publicity, a brave Mutati had been selected to pilot a schooner that would be carried aboard that pod, a schooner that was being fitted at that very moment with a planet-busting torpedo. The holy Demolio, his doomsday weapon that had been so successful in destroying four enemy planets, prior to the cutoff of podship travel.

Frenzied preparations were underway on Paradij, and soon all would be in readiness.

For some reason, the Adurians had expressed concern about continued attacks against enemy targets. He couldn't understand why, as they weren't providing him with good reasons, only requests that he delay for a "better opportunity," whatever that meant. The fools would not deter him, even if they were allies. War was war, after all.

Technology alone cannot win this war, Abal Meshdi thought.

God-on-High must guide our bombs.

Upon returning to the heavily fortified keep of the Citadel, an aide handed him a nehrcom transmission, written in ornate script by one of the royal scribes. The communication was from an operative on Canopa who had been able to sneak into one of the Doge's nehrcom facilities.

The Zultan was pleased to learn of Human-against-Human warfare on Canopa, with Noah Watanabe's Guardians fighting against the forces of the Doge and Watanabe's own sister. With the blessing of God, they would all annihilate themselves, thus reducing the number of targets that the Mutatis needed to strike. . . .

On far-away Canopa—now the capital world of the Merchant Prince Alliance—Doge Lorenzo amused himself by torturing a Mutati prisoner while General Jacopo Nehr looked on. They were in a deep dungeon of Max Two, which had become the largest prison on the planet, as a result of recent additions. One day the Doge might change the names around, but it was low on his priority list.

As a result of his recent emphasis on identifying Humans through medical examinations and then labeling them with implants, many disguised Mutati infiltrators had been uncovered. The Doge's police operations had been going well.

This particular Mutati was what Lorenzo called "a screamer." The creature started crying and howling on the way here and continued in a frenzy of emotion when the pain amplification machines were used. So much energy this one had, and how it hated being caught! It increased Lorenzo's pleasure.

Two guards used sharp pikes to keep the Mutati from escaping, prodding it each time it tried to veer one way or the other. All the while, dancing around the victim, Lorenzo used a large pair of clippers to cut off flaps and folds of fat from the creature's body, causing it to writhe in pain and attempt to create shapes that could not be cut so easily.

Cackling gleefully, Lorenzo saw it as a game. Snip, snip, snip! He danced around the creature, looking for new places to cut, moving in quickly and then retreating. Piles of flesh lay all around, saturated in purple Mutati blood.

"I think that's enough," Nehr said. "Unless you want to kill this one. Keep in mind, we can still get information out of it, using other methods."

"Oh, you spoil my fun," Lorenzo said as he tossed the clippers aside. "You're just like. . . ."

He paused when he noticed the blond Princess Meghina in the doorway, watching. She glared at him, her eyes dark and angry.

"I'm disappointed in you," she said. "You know how I feel about this." Meghina could hardly contain her fury.

"What do you think dungeons are for?" Lorenzo asked. "To sing lullabies to our prisoners?" She watched as he wiped blood off his hands with a cloth.

"There are galactic conventions against this sort of thing," she said.

"There are also galactic conventions against blowing up enemy planets. Or there should be. We lost four worlds to these bastards, and billions of people! Surely, you can't begrudge me a little revenge."

"They did a horrible thing, but I don't like what the war is doing to you," she said. "This is not good for you."

"I'm sorry," he said, looking suddenly like a child who had just been scolded.

Behind him, Meghina saw the pitiful Mutati rolling over its own severed bloody parts, incorporating them back into its shapeshifting body. Despite its suffering, the Mutati focused on her for an instant with its bright black eyes, before she broke gazes with it.

Had the creature recognized her true form? She had taken a calculated risk coming down here, because some Mutatis—albeit only a small percentage—had the ability to recognize another of their kind no matter the disguise, by detecting aural and electrical signatures that were unique to the individual. She faced another risk as well, the new requirement that everyone get a medical examination and an implanted device certifying that they were Human. Because of her high status as a noble lady, she and others had not been required to undergo the process. But that could change.

Nonetheless, she stood her ground. "I would like you to discontinue this barbaric practice," she said, following Lorenzo as he left the chamber.

The beautiful Princess Meghina, while born a Mutati, had remained in Human form for so long that she could not change back. She hated Mutatis herself, but could not condone the sort of treatment she had seen today, for any reason. Not knowing his courtesan wife's dirty secret, Lorenzo was devoted to her and valued her advice, and her opinion of him. It was only out of noble custom—Meghina understood this—that he had trysts with numerous other Human (and even alien) women. She did the same herself with men, in her own fashion.

Deep in conversation, the royal couple traveled a short distance by groundjet, to the Doge's cliffside villa. By the time they reached his bedroom suite and she was nibbling at his ear, he finally acceded to her request. She had more than his apology now; she had his promise that he would not torture any more Mutati prisoners.

But Lorenzo had his own mind about such matters. He had learned to tell important people what they wanted to hear, without really altering his behavior. From now on, whenever he had an urge to torture a shapeshifter, he would still do so, but would take care to conceal the act from her. In this time of war, with all the stresses of leadership, he needed to maintain his diversions.

Chapter Thirty-Two

> It is curious that two of the oldest races in the galaxy—the Parviis and the Tulyans—both rely upon paranormal methods to gain control over sentient podships. But in this context, what is "normal," and what is not?
>
> —Tulyan Wisdom

As their podship approached the Hibbil Sector, Eshaz spoke like a tour director to the boys sitting beside him. Dux and Acey alternately chattered excitedly and listened to him.

"Wild podships migrate here at this time of year," Eshaz said, "for breeding. They're like herds of whales on Lost Earth, but cover vast distances of space. We Tulyans understand the ancient patterns of the deep-space pods, and chart them. I expect we'll see some action soon."

The podship bumped gently against the exterior bumper of a pod station, and Eshaz said, "Just a brief stop for a permit. Then we'll go on to the Wild Pod Zone. It's still a good distance away, with very dim, collapsed suns. Not like this." He pointed up, at a rather ordinary-looking yellow sun.

Tesh guided the sentient craft to a dock inside the station, where furry little Hibbil workers secured the vessel with lines.

Moments later the hatch opened, and a dozen Hibbil policemen marched aboard, dressed in black-and-gold uniforms. The men's bearlike faces twitched irritably, and their dark eyes glanced around, as if they were looking for contraband. Their gazes focused first on the Tulyan, then on the burnished wood cases that lay on the floor, still strapped together.

"Doing a little podship hunting?" the lead policeman asked. His nametag read, YOTLA.

"Seen any wild ones lately?" Eshaz asked, stepping toward the officers.

"Not for some time," Yotla said with a grin, "but it's a big zone out there and they're probably hiding somewhere. I'll take your permit fee now."

With a nod, Eshaz passed him a golden cylinder. "Our fee and application are inside."

Dux saw that the cylinder contained precious jewels. With a furry hand the Hibbil officer activated a button on the side, and a complex series of blank holo-pages popped into the air. "You haven't filled out the forms," he growled.

"My answers are the same as the last time I was here," Eshaz said, with a yawn, "so I included enough extra payment for you to complete the documentation for me." He glanced at Dux and grinned, "Saves a lot of time."

With a grunt the officer resealed the cylinder, and departed with his companions.

The podship got underway, and proceeded slowly away from the orbital station, then accelerated, but not to web speed. An hour passed, and they reached a region of space that was dotted with half a dozen white dwarf suns, and two that were brown, and even dimmer. Eshaz chattered about how they had once been bright orbs, filled with nuclear energy, but over billions and billions of years they had collapsed. "Most races think there is very little life out here," he said. "But we know better. It is a prime hunting region."

Eshaz pointed out a porthole at black-and-gold ships patrolling a sector that he called the entrance to the Wild Pod Zone, vessels with unusual, angular hull designs and bright search beams that illuminated space around them. One of the beams focused on them, causing Dux to squint.

"Hibbils wield considerable military power and are fiercely territorial," Eshaz said, "so we have found it most convenient to simply pay them off."

"Their ships look fast," Acey said.

"None faster, for intra-sector bursts," Eshaz said. "The Hibbils are a totalitarian society, run by a corrupt military junta. They claim jurisdiction over a broad region, far beyond the traditional boundaries of their Cluster Worlds." With a sneer, he added, "They pulled the planets out of orbit and linked them together mechanically. Hibbils fear a chaotic breakup of the galaxy, and think this will save their civilization from destruction."

"I'd like to go to their homeworlds sometime," Acey said. "I've heard they're tech masters."

"An interesting race, perhaps," Eshaz admitted, "but they are among the worst industrial polluters in the galaxy. They provide supposedly low-cost machines for the merchant princes and for the leaders of other races, but there are hidden costs—damage to the planets they raid for raw materials, and more depleted worlds than the Guardians can ever restore."

As Acey and Dux looked through portholes, the podship headed slowly out into the darkness of near-space, leaving the Hibbil ships behind.

Chapter Thirty-Three

There can be great beauty in change, even if propelled by violence.

—Mutati Saying

In his natural state he was the most dashingly handsome of Mutati men, with great folds of fat around his midsection, a perfectly symmetrical triple chin, and overlarge eyes on his tiny head. As he made his way through the crowd, in a golden outrider uniform decked with medals and ribbons, terramutati women swooned at his feet, and aeromutati females darted overhead, blowing him kisses as they flew by. Many Mutati men had applied for this glorious position, and Kishi Fapro had been chosen over all of them, not only for his good looks but for his enthusiastic willingness to die for the sacred cause of his people.

For weeks his holophoto had been shown everywhere on Paradij, and in grainy nehrcom video transmissions to other worlds throughout the realm, so that everyone envied him. Surely he would occupy a special place in heaven after his heroic sacrifice, even higher than his earlier counterparts who had given up their lives flying Demolio torpedoes into enemy planets. Fapro represented a new beginning, with the Mutatis working even closer with God-on-High than before, relying upon him to guide the holy bomb to its target. It was "a mating of religion and technology," the Zultan had said, displaying his proclivity for turning a phrase. After this success, the Mutatis would rain holy bombs on every merchant prince planet, and the long war would be won.

No one would ever see Kishi Fapro again, except in the holo-images that would live beyond the expiration of his flesh and in a variety of curios that were sold bearing his likeness. He would also live on in the endearing memories of everyone who watched him now as he marched steadily toward the gleaming black schooner, smiling and waving to the crowd, showing no fear whatsoever.

To enthusiastic cheers, he stepped inside the vessel and fired up the engines. In a matter of moments he lifted off, and streaked up to the orbiting pod station. As holocameras watched him all the way and projected the images to screens all over the Mutati Kingdom, the outrider guided his craft into the cargo hold of a laboratory-bred podship.

Excitement mounted as the podship taxied out of the pod station and moved into position a short distance away. Then, bearing the black schooner and its deadly bomb, the lab-pod accelerated into the sky. In a bright flash of green light seen on the surface of Paradij, the Mutati doomsday weapon left the atmosphere and disappeared into space, pointed toward the merchant prince world of Siriki. On the other end, there would be no arrival at a pod station. This time, the entire podship, with its precious cargo, would strike the planet directly, triggering the deadly explosions.

On a platform amidst the cheering onlookers, the Zultan Abal Meshdi uttered a prayer from the *Holy Writ.* He was convinced that God-on-High would guide the lab-pod to destroy their hated enemy—and that it would occur in a matter of seconds.

Following the prayer, he raised his arms and shouted to the

crowd, "Our doomsday weapon is on the way!"

A day passed. . . .

At a nehrcom station on Siriki, the Human operator received an odd signal. His instruments revealed that it was from the Mutati homeworld of Paradij, but he knew that was impossible, since the Mutatis had no nehrcom units.

The signal was first weak, then stronger. It repeated several times. The operator checked the source, and was astounded. Quickly, he relayed it to another operator on Canopa, a woman. She in turn went personally to the Office of the Doge on Canopa, where she handed a one-page report and a slender plax recording tube to the Royal Attaché, Pimyt.

"An odd transmission came in, sir, purportedly from the Mutatis on Paradij."

After scanning the report and listening to the signal, Pimyt looked up and said, "I'll take care of this from here. You are to mention it to no one."

"That is my sworn duty, sir," the operator responded, with a slight bow to the furry, much shorter Hibbil. "I brought it directly to you."

"You understand, of course, that this is a hoax? It could not possibly have come from Paradij, because the Mutatis have no nehrcom system."

"That is my understanding, sir."

"We're putting the Doge's best investigators on this, and they'd better not learn that you discussed it with anyone."

"You can count on my silence, sir."

"Tell the Siriki station to destroy all records of this. Then destroy yours, too. I want no copies of this to exist, not in your memory or anywhere else. It is a matter of utmost security to the Merchant Prince Alliance."

"I understand, sir. With your leave, I'll take care of it right away."

Pimyt waved a hand dismissively.

When he was alone in his office, the Royal Attaché muttered, "What is this? What is that fool Zultan up to now?" He stared at the report. "Sending a signal here?"

Pimyt's reasons for being upset ran through circuitous pathways. Secretly, he and his Hibbil people were allied with the Adurian race under the HibAdu Coalition, with the goal of bringing down both the Merchant Prince Alliance and the Mutati Kingdom. The conspirators, after infiltrating themselves into key positions such as his own, had not yet seen the right time to make their move. They were still laying groundwork, getting control of weapons and personnel, setting things up.

For a long time Hibbils and Adurians had been treated in a condescending manner by two races that considered themselves superior to them. His own Hibbil people, ostensibly an ally of the Humans, had actually been under the collective boot heel of the merchant princes during all that time: politically, economically, militarily, socially, and in every other imaginable way. It had been much the same story for the Adurians, except that it was the Mutati Kingdom keeping them down. Finally, unable to endure any more mistreatment, the Hibbils and Adurians had aligned themselves into what they called the HibAdu Coalition. In large measure this secret alliance was so that they could exact revenge against their tormentors, taking everything that was of value away from the merchant princes and the shapeshifters—their worlds, their profits, and more. In the coming war, the Coalition intended to wipe out ninety percent of the populations of the two offending races, and enslave what was left.

But the Mutati Zultan was a madman and a wild card. Pimyt's secret collaborator, the Adurian Ambassador VV Uncel, had been stuck on Paradij by the podship crisis, and must certainly have made attempts to influence the Mutati leader. Pimyt knew that the ambassador had convinced Mutatis to use gyrodomes and minigyros, devices that weakened their brains in subtle ways and made them easier to conquer. However, unable to stay in touch with Uncel during the most recent crisis, Pimyt didn't have updates. Neither of them could risk sending nehrcom transmissions back and forth between enemy planets, so Pimyt could only hope for the best.

This new signal episode troubled him a great deal. When added to an earlier event in which Jacopo Nehr detected Mutati nehrcom transmissions on his own mobile transceiver, apparently sent by mistake, it gave the attaché additional cause for concern. The cross-space transmission leak had occurred after the cessation of podship travel, so he had not been able to follow up on it. In the errant transmittal, he heard the whiny voice of an Adurian saying that Mutatis, with no access to podships, could no longer launch Demolio attacks against merchant prince planets. The sound quality had been fuzzy, with no video at all, and Nehr had come directly to Pimyt with the information—since the two of them had a private arrangement and the Hibbil would ruin Nehr if he didn't cooperate. The Adurian voice on the transmission had been, unmistakably, that of VV Uncel, though only Pimyt realized that.

The Royal Attaché paced nervously around his office. He had been fortunate with both of the Mutati transmissions, and had taken steps to keep a lid on them. But he couldn't contain the information forever, and soon it would get out that the Mutatis had their own system. If Nehr ever came clean and revealed Pimyt's knowledge of the internal workings of nehrcom units, merchant prince investigators might soon wonder if Pimyt had passed the information on to the Mutatis. Actually, the Mutatis had obtained it independently from Nehr's disloyal brother, but the connection was still there, and Pimyt could be compromised.

"Why did the Zultan send a signal to Siriki?" Pimyt said to himself, staring at the one-page report. He scratched his gray-and-black head, then dropped his jaw, as he recalled how the Mutatis had confirmed a number of Demolio strikes by sending nehrcom signals to the planet and seeing if it was still there.

Siriki? Did he try to destroy the planet? Has he found a way to launch the bombs again?

It seemed unlikely, but in this chaotic galaxy, he could not rule out the possibility. But what could he do to find out? He had only been able to send coded nehrcoms to his own operatives on other merchant prince worlds, containing military instructions, mostly involving infiltration and setting things up for future attacks by the HibAdu Coalition, making the attacks easier and more likely to succeed. But the conspirators could not act without podships, and neither could the Zultan of the Mutati Kingdom.

No one could.

On Paradij, there was much confusion and unease among the people.

A nehrcom transmission verification system revealed that their nehrcom signal was received on Siriki a day later. It did not bounce back as undeliverable, as anticipated. Thus the Demolio had never arrived.

Rumors spread more rapidly than a royal birth announcement. What could have possibly gone wrong?

The Zultan Abal Meshdi tightened up his nehrcom security. Then, paying little attention to the mutterings of the populace, he called for new volunteers, announcing in a planet-wide broadcast, "We need to send more outriders, again and again! Which of you will be our instruments of God?"

Paradijan Mutatis thronged to volunteer for their sacred duty.

Chapter Thirty-Four

> Each life is made up of large and small pieces. None of those pieces, not even the tiniest, is insignificant, for they all contribute to the whole, to the person you see standing before you in the mirror.
>
> —Jacopo Nehr

In a particularly foul mood, Francella marched down the corridor of her central medical laboratory. It was lunch hour, but she had no appetite for anything, except venting her anger. All morning long she had been at the site of one of her largest manufacturing facilities, now reduced to smoking rubble by a hit-and-run Guardian attack. Her brother, even though she was holding him prisoner and conducting medical experiments on him, was still the inspirational leader of those malcontents. Originally, he had styled them as "eco-terrorists," but in her eyes they no longer carried an environmental banner. They were simply terrorists.

Throwing open the double doors of the company cafeteria, she stomped in and found Dr. Bichette at a large round table, one of five in the room. The core of each table revolved slowly like a lazy susan, so that diners could select sealed packages of food, all kept steaming hot in gelplax containers. As she sat beside the doctor, he was pressing a button on the edge of the table to select an item. As he did so, the package slid down a short ramp onto his plate. In contact with the air, the gelplax melted away, revealing a stir-fry meal.

"We need to talk—now," she began.

She saw the immediate sag of his face and shoulders that she had noticed before, whenever she wanted something from him. Sometimes he didn't show enough respect to suit her, but he was still considered one of the best medical research directors in the Merchant Prince Alliance, and had assembled a team of brilliant specialists who were intensely loyal to him. If she ever fired Bichette, they would all go with him. In any event, with no access to personnel on other planets, he had assembled the best possible team on Canopa. So, even though he irritated her on a regular basis, she continued to put up with him.

"I've been thinking about your latest report on my brother, and my own daily observations. You and your researchers are painfully slow; I can't stand it. The two major lines of experimentation—cellular regeneration and immortality—have made woefully little progress."

"Actually we have made considerable progress, but it's too technical for you to understand. The details are in the report, the gene splicing, the cell structure analysis, the. . . ."

"Don't be condescending. I read it all, and it's gobbledygook. I don't think you're getting anywhere at all, but you don't have the guts to put that in your precious reports, do you?" She leaned toward him, but spoke louder. "Admit it! You're not getting anywhere!"

"You're mistaken. We're doing our best on a complex project."

"Let me see. Next you're going to tell me it could take years for results."

"Why, yes. If it's solvable at all, it might not be possible to accomplish it for decades. This is cutting-edge science."

"That's what I thought you'd say," she said, rising to her feet. "Finish your lunch."

She walked briskly out of the cafeteria. Glancing back, she

saw him picking at his food, deeply troubled. . . .

Five minutes later, Francella passed one of her own CorpOne guards and entered her brother's room. He was sitting up in bed, eating from food on a lap tray. With a sharp glare, he looked at her.

She closed the door, and locked it. Francella wanted the secret of immortality, and not because the Doge had ordered her to discover it, through her research team. She wanted it for *herself.* But there were too many uncertainties, and she might die before it was made available to her.

The recently healed fingers on her brother's hands were faintly pink, from Bichette's repeated cuts there. The latest report had said that continuous acts of cellular regeneration on the same appendages were causing the skin to heal more slowly. It seemed to mark a limit to the powers of Noah's body, but the experts were not sure how significant it was.

Francella felt a sudden rush of rage and cruelty. She hated him. Her fingers tightened around the handle of a weapon in her pocket, then released. Instead of using it, she took a conciliatory tone with him and said, "Why don't we make an effort to get along? All you have to do is tell me what you know about your condition."

His hazel eyes flashed angrily, and he cleared his tray with a sweep of one hand. Dishes clattered and broke on the floor. "You were responsible for that force of fake Guardians that attacked CorpOne headquarters, weren't you?"

"Of course not. Don't be preposterous."

"I think you're lying, and that you're responsible for our father dying. After all the destruction you've caused to this family, you want us to be pals now?"

"You're in no position to speak to me like that!"

"I'll answer none of your questions." He struggled to lift his legs from the bed, but they had been deadened by implanted injections of drugs, and he couldn't move them. The doctors had found another way to keep him immobile.

"Oh, dear brother, would you like to be released?"

"Yes, damn you!"

Impulsively, she brought the weapon out of her pocket and activated it—a silver-handled laserblade. She clicked it on, causing the tip of the barrel to glow ruby red.

"You seem to be having trouble with your legs," she said. With a burst of burning red light, she began to cut off his right leg, at the thigh.

The drugs in Noah's legs were not painkillers. He learned that the moment the hot light began to sear through his skin, then severed tendons and melted bones. His leg felt as if it was on fire.

He screamed at her and flailed, trying unsuccessfully to reach the weapon. Blood gushed from the open wound, but coagulated quickly. As his body began to restore itself he felt a shift in the pain signals that were being transmitted within his body, a coolness like foam applied to a fire. Such an odd sensation.

But it was only short-lived relief. Calmly and precisely, Francella severed his other leg, even as the first one was beginning to grow back. She must be deaf to his screams.

A mad, fascinated gleam filled her eyes. With shaking hands, she tossed his appendages in a medical waste bin.

"I'm no longer waiting for the 'experts' to perform their 'tests' on you, dear brother. I'm taking charge of your case." She cut across his middle body, only going halfway through and digging the hot light—at some lower setting—around on his interior organs. All intentional, he presumed, to maximize his suffering. Belly pain. Spurting blood. Noah didn't know if he could keep staunching the injuries.

Through his excruciating, almost otherworldly pain, Noah

heard the guard calling for his sister, and knocking on the door. "Is everything all right in there, Ms. Watanabe?"

"Yes, you idiot. Now go away!"

The man said something Noah couldn't understand, then grew quiet. He was probably going to get Bichette.

Noah howled in agony and cursed her.

With blood spraying all over her, Francella cut off the new legs before they completed their regeneration process, then hurriedly amputated both of his muscular arms.

"Let's see how immortal you really are!" Francella shouted. "If I destroy all of your body tissue, how will you regenerate? Will you get smaller and smaller, with less cellular material to use for repairs?"

"How dare you use me as a guinea pig? I'm your brother! We're fraternal twins!"

"You're like a lizard," Francella said, her eyes frenzied, "growing parts back. Is that what you've become, a slimy little lizard?"

Noah bellowed at her defiantly. "You bitch! I'm ashamed we're in the same family!"

She smiled, and he fell silent. The blood flowing from his wounds—where the arms and legs had been sliced away, and the stomach had been cut open—stopped, and skin began to grow back.

Then Francella hacked away at his head and the rest of his body, cutting and recutting the moment she saw anything growing back. Noah's consciousness ebbed, and he felt himself drifting out into the cosmos, on a stream of blood that stretched across the continuum of time and space. . . .

The research scientists knocked the door down, and tried to calm her, until she threatened them with the instrument. She was drenched in blood. They backed away.

While Bichette and his associates watched in dismay, Francella continued to hack her brother into smaller and smaller pieces. Finally, she paused, breathing hard. None of the parts were moving anymore. Nothing appeared to be growing back.

She fell to her knees, screaming and sobbing. Someone took the laserblade out of her hand.

Dismayed, she realized that she had acted out of anger and frustration, and she hoped she had not killed him, but only because he was needed for the ongoing experiments. Could Noah still regrow parts, and if so, in what form? Bizarre thoughts flashed through her brain. Would multiple copies of Noah develop, one around each of the severed pieces?

As she watched, Bichette and the others conferred, then piled the body parts together in a gory heap.

But Noah was—against all odds—still alive, extending mental and physical tendrils into the alternate dimension of Timeweb, probing, receiving mass and nutrients from the cosmic organism that supported his remarkable body. He felt the powerful presence as it filled and restored his bodily functions.

Yet in his unbearable, unrelenting pain, Noah would have preferred death, the long sleep that eluded him.

Far across the galaxy, Tesh and her companions on board the podship proceeded through one dwarf star system after another in the back regions of the Hibbil Sector. The Parvii, the Tulyan, and the two Humans on the vessel did not actually have daytime or evening, not by the standards of their lifetime experiences, and there were no bright suns in this region. But they did know when they were fatigued, and based upon that they reached what Eshaz called a "diurnal arrangement," under which the wristchron Acey wore became their ship's clock.

Under this arrangement they agreed upon a time to rest, in

preparation for the hunt that would begin the following "day". . . .

When the agreed-upon time for sleep arrived, Tesh left the sectoid chamber and sealed it, after giving the sentient vessel the command to float in space within a specified area. Now, with the lights low in the passenger compartment, she and the others lay in recumbent chairs, sleeping.

Suddenly Tesh sat up and cried out, "Noah! Oh my God!"

Around her she heard the soft snoring of the teenagers, and the rumbling, deep snorts of Eshaz. Apparently the three of them had not heard her, but she sensed that something was wrong: Noah Watanabe was in terrible danger, and she could do nothing to help.

In her inexplicable but certain grief she shouted his name, as if calling to him across the vastness of the galaxy. "Noah!"

Somehow, her traveling companions continued in their slumber. She could not understand why, or why she felt as she did. Tesh remembered Noah's freckled, handsome face, and his intelligent brown eyes.

And she wondered if she would ever see him again.

Chapter Thirty-Five

Each of us has a place of sweetness where we can go to soothe our troubled spirits. Sometimes it is a fellow Mutati or a physical location, but most often it is imaginary, and we are only able to escape there for fleeting moments.

—War therapy session notes, Dij

The Emir Hari'Adab had a different method of clearing his mind than that employed by his powerful father, the Zultan. Instead of connecting his brain to Adurian gyros, which had become something of a fad, Hari liked to glide around the star system on a solar sailer. Though he was a sizeable Mutati himself, he felt like a mote inside the craft, with its giant silvery wings glinting in the sun. It was so silent out here, and infinitely peaceful. Usually it made his troubles seem far away and inconsequential.

But not today.

He sailed along the ecliptic of the Dijian System, following the apparent path of their sun through the heavens. Only a few hours ago, he had been towed out here by a rocket plane, and then left to drift. But that was all for show, to avoid criticisms from sailing purists. Secretly, his solar sailer had backup rockets.

Technically, he knew he wasn't really solar sailing, at least not the way a true spacefaring aficionado would look at it. Periodically, his craft was aided by short, silent bursts of rocket power. In an officially sanctioned solar-sailer race, he would be disqualified for violating the rules, but for these private moments he liked the extra energy boosts, instead of having to wait and pick up speed gradually over the reaches of space, using the rapid-absorption solar panels on the craft.

I feel like my brain needs that, he thought. *A little extra oomph.*

At his command, the craft dipped and then soared under combined sail and rocket power, as he tried to improve how he felt. The unusual, custom-built craft had a variety of entertainment options. One of them, the on-board gravitonics system was off now, but if switched on could give him the sensation of being on an amusement park ride. He didn't want that right at the moment, didn't need a thrill. In fact, he realized now, he needed the complete opposite of that. He needed to slow down the sensations and mental processes that were causing him so much anxiety.

Hearing a surge as the rockets kicked on, he shut them off, too. And just drifted. Looking through the overhead and side windows, he marveled at the glittering beauty of the outstretched wings, how they seemed to be reaching for a breath of cosmic wind from God-on-High, the way he was looking for the same thing now, heavenly inspiration.

Hari believed in God, and was more devout than most Mutatis. But his personal beliefs fell far short of the religious fanaticism his father was spreading around the realm, causing increased hysteria in the people when they were most vulnerable, not helping them at all.

On numerous occasions he had voiced his opinions to his father, always doing so respectfully and in private. Lately, Hari had been protesting the aggressive Demolio program, and he had always opposed the war against the Merchant Prince Alliance, favoring peaceful resolution instead.

Repeatedly the Zultan had rebuffed him, suggesting to his son that he needed to "gyro" himself or other such nonsense.

Hari didn't think his father had ever been that intelligent. Oh, the elder Mutati was smart enough to keep from accidentally stepping off a ledge, but he didn't have the degree of mental sophistication that was needed to lead a great people. He was more like a next-door neighbor, entertaining to be around, but not a real leader.

The newest incarnation of the Demolio program was a step off a ledge of another sort, and the Zultan was dragging his people down with him. To Hari, the use of laboratory-cloned podships was a violation of nature, a sacrilege against God-On-High himself. Thus far the Emir had only told his father he opposed aggressive military tactics, without framing his discontent in religious terms. To do so would risk a huge emotional outburst from the Zultan, who considered himself the sole arbiter of all important religious and political issues.

The cutoff of podship travel had effectively confined Hari to the desolate Dijian star system, although he could take this sailer to the adjacent Paradij System if he so desired, a journey of a little over a month. For one reason or another he had avoided doing that. Most of all he didn't relish the thought of a big confrontation with his father, whom Hari blamed for causing natural podships to go into hiding.

Through it all, Hari had led the people of his solar system in a buildup of military defenses, causing them to rally around him. He considered himself patriotic, didn't want Dij or any other Mutati planet overrun by foul-smelling Humans. But his father was going too far. The frenzied Zultan Abal Meshdi had orchestrated the Mutati people, bringing them to a dangerous fever pitch.

The Zultan even forced Mutati children to sing military songs in school, and encouraged them to make gruesome drawings of dead Humans. Lost innocence. Another sacrilege.

While Hari was doing the best possible job under trying

circumstances, he felt a deep sadness in his heart, one that could not be remedied on this private sailing venture. With a scowl, he sent a telebeam message, ordering the rocket plane to come back and get him.

The following day, Hari'Adab and his girlfriend, Parais d'Olor, sat atop a rocky, barren cliff overlooking the sea, talking. It was a perch above their favorite stretch of private beach.

For this occasion Parais had metamorphosed into a very large butterfly with rainbow designs on her wings. Periodically, as she considered their important topic of conversation, she fluttered off the cliff and floated around on sea breezes, before landing beside him and tucking her wings.

Hari had never understood the long-standing enmity between his people and Humans, and wished that rational minds might prevail, heading off further bloodshed. But his father, always rabidly militaristic, had insanely destroyed four Human-ruled planets, and intended to wipe out all the rest of them as soon as he could get another delivery system perfected. It made no sense to the young Emir, and he felt himself shaking with rage and frustration.

Gazing into Parais' cerulean blue eyes, he imagined the children they might have one day, offspring that would be aeromutati like her, since female genes were dominant. So many shapeshifters . . . and Humans as well . . . had found mates in the time-honored ways of love, and just wanted to raise their families in security.

But such dreams were only illusions, waiting to be shattered by the next episode of war.

Chapter Thirty-Six

Victory is invariably achieved through a series of carefully calculated steps.

—Jimu of the Red Berets

In recent weeks Thinker had been looking at Giovanni Nehr with increasing disdain, and even some suspicion. The man's behavior seemed particularly odd after the debacle of his failed attempt to rescue Noah from Max One Prison. Cocky and outgoing before that, he had become introverted and secretive. He stopped going to the Brew Room for beers and barely interacted at all with the robots, even though he still wore the armor Thinker had given him back on Ignem.

Even more troublesome, with Subi Danvar's blessing Gio was spending an increasing amount of time away from the subterranean headquarters, supposedly because he needed to perform additional reconnaissance missions to find out where Noah really was. But Thinker had his doubts. Gio wasn't very good at reconnaissance—he had failed to discover in advance that Noah wasn't even at that particular prison.

Still, Subi said he still believed in him, and Thinker thought this might be because the adjutant wanted to give him a chance to redeem himself. Humans were like that, always trying to give one another second chances. In his data banks the robot leader had countless examples of such generous behavior, countering the aggressive, even criminal actions of other members of the Human race.

But Thinker wondered if Gio deserved a break like that, or it was a waste of time and resources. Of greater concern, was he actually going out on reconnaissance missions, or could he possibly be a spy? Was he providing updated information on Guardian forces to the enemy? It seemed entirely possible.

Without Gio's knowledge, Thinker had been observing and psychoanalyzing him, and had determined that he had a pattern of currying favor with superiors in order to gain his own promotions and other favors. Gio had behaved that way with Thinker when the robot commanded him, and had done the same with both Noah and Subi. This was another unfortunate aspect of Human behavior, their tendency toward sycophancy.

Thinker had serious doubts about whether Gio was serving the interests of Noah or the noble cause of the Guardians. His background as the brother of the top general in the Merchant Prince Alliance made him even more suspect. Supposedly the Nehr brothers had quarreled and no longer spoke to one another. But what if that was a lie, and Gio's unexpected appearance at the Inn of the White Sun—where he volunteered to join the machine army—had been a clever ploy?

These thoughts troubled the cerebral robot.

One afternoon Thinker was supervising the machine troops inside four large, connected caverns as they performed training exercises. He saw Subi Danvar enter the chamber and stand off to one side, where he watched the machines as they marched and simulated weapons fire, shooting silent beams of light at each other . . . the equivalent of blanks.

Thinker clanked over to Subi and began to voice his concerns about Giovanni Nehr, who was supposedly out on a recon mission at that moment, but might be doing other things instead.

The adjutant, after listening attentively, scowled. Then he said, "I don't see it that way. Gio's as dedicated as any of us."

"I'm not so sure. But there's one sure way to find out. With your permission, I could read his thoughts." Thinker brought a tentacle out of his body, and it hovered overhead. "My organic interface," he said.

"Put that damn thing away. I told you how I feel about downloading Human thoughts without permission. It's not ethical."

"I believe the issue here is survival, not ethics. All's fair in love and war?"

"I won't hear of it. You're violating Human rights. It's not the right thing to do, and Master Noah would never stand for it."

Thinker snaked the tentacle back into its compartment. "But what if I'm not wrong?"

"You *are* wrong. Believe me, I know a lot more about people than you do."

Just then, Gio strode into the chamber and looked around. He appeared to be quite agitated, and was perspiring heavily. Joining his two superiors, he loosened his body armor and said, "I found a huge training camp for the Red Beret machine division, in the Valley of the Princes. They've converted industrial buildings to manufacturing robots, and have more fighting machines than we ever imagined, at least thirty thousand of them, and growing fast."

"That many?" Subi asked.

"We can never keep up with their production rate," Gio said. "We have one advantage, though," he added. "They don't know where we are."

"Pray it stays that way," Thinker snapped, displaying an uncharacteristic machine emotion. With a sudden movement, he clanked away, to tend to his own, much smaller army.

★ ★ ★ ★ ★

On the jewel-like planet Ignem, beneath the orbital ring containing the Inn of the White Sun, the remnants of a machine army had been performing repetitious troop exercises. Since the departures of Thinker and Jimu, they no longer had effective leadership, and had grown stagnant. They were not increasing their numbers, and only performed minimal repairs on themselves to keep what they had going.

In particular they had lost the inspiration that had been provided by Thinker, the greatest computer brain among them.

For some time now, the increasing malaise had irritated the feisty little robot, Ipsy, to the point where he had been challenging more robots to fights than ever, selecting among the largest and most heavily armed of the bunch. They were only too happy to accommodate him, and he usually lost. But the dented little guy kept coming back at them, and did gain some degree of respect in the ranks for his unflagging courage. But the officers had still refused to listen to his pleas for a more effective army, and would not make any improvements. Finally, the officers had ordered Ipsy to stay away from Ignem, and banished him to the orbital Inn.

But even that had not slowed him down, as Ipsy turned his aggression toward reinvigorating the operations of the Inn of the White Sun. For months he had been traveling to alien worlds that were still accessible, where he'd been skillfully promoting the services of the facility. Possessing a font of new promotional ideas and a relentless, hard-working attitude, he was bringing in a good income for the machines, almost as high as it had been before the Human and Mutati empires were isolated from the rest of the galaxy.

Finally, with control over a mounting treasury, he sent word down to the officers on Ignem that he wanted to spend the funds on improving the army. In a return message, they declined his offer.

Ipsy seethed, but refused to give up.

Chapter Thirty-Seven

Life always rises from death . . . in infinite, and sometimes startling, forms.

—Tulyan Wisdom

It was unlike anything seen in a medical journal in the history of mankind, or in the annals of any other galactic race. Dr. Hurk Bichette, at first horrified and repulsed at what Francella did to her own brother, now stared in disbelief at the grisly scene before him . . . Noah's bleeding, severed body parts piled inside a clearplax-covered life-support unit.

Did something just move there? The doctor wasn't sure, and the gauges showed nothing at all, no sign of life. The system, particularly the mini-atmosphere of the large, coffin-sized enclosure housing the remains, was supposed to preserve any life that remained, but that probably didn't amount to anything at all. The trauma to the body had been so severe that no one, not even a person imbued with the powers Noah had displayed, could recover from it.

Alone in a small, heavily guarded chamber, Bichette walked slowly around the plax case containing the grisly remains of the body, chunks of flesh, bone, and brain matter. On the left, a fragment of skull with Noah's red hair on it, matted with blood. In the center an eyeball, severed and amazingly intact, staring into nowhere . . . no change there in the forty-two hours since the horrific incident.

Punching buttons on a panel, he brought up original holo-photos of the remains, and compared them with what he was looking at now. Everything was the same, except for the increasing decay, and the stench. Disappointment filled him.

From a medical standpoint, it was more a matter of observing and hooking up monitoring equipment than anything else; this wasn't the sort of patient who could be helped by any known medical treatment. Noah had to recover on his own, drawing resources from his secret, mysterious source.

Bichette rubbed his own eyes. They must be playing tricks on him. Even through the sealed plax, Bichette could still smell the putrid odors of blackened, decaying flesh, a smell that seemed to permeate everything. He didn't think he could ever put it out of his memory, or erase the recollection of what he had seen the madwoman do . . . his demented boss.

In the background, from another room of the medical complex, he heard Francella shouting at someone. The day before, the two of them had reached an understanding, that she would stay away from Noah from now on and not interfere in any way with procedures that needed to be done. She said she just wanted a vial of Noah's blood, which she took with her. The conversation seemed moot now. A mortician would be of more use here than a doctor.

No, wait. What is that?

Bichette stopped dead in his tracks, and watched in astonishment as the damaged brain matter writhed and gathered together, then stopped moving. Moments passed. Slowly, the brain matter began to combine with a mass of flesh, and then inched toward the intact, still motionless eyeball.

A wave of fear passed through Bichette. He started to yell for his assistants, but changed his mind. The doctor felt a personal connection to this case, almost an ownership over it.

I'm witnessing medical history.

How could the body possibly be regenerating, after such severe trauma? With cellular material destroyed and gone, what was he using for nutrients, for energy? Flesh and bones should not be able to grow out of nothing. Medical science was not magical. And yet, this was happening anyway, defying the most basic laws of science and creation.

The mass of brain and flesh had now encircled the eyeball, touching it, cradling it like a precious child. Abruptly the eyeball moved, and looked directly at Bichette.

The doctor stood frozen in his tracks.

Moment by moment, the flesh and bone gathered and metamorphosed, while a holocamera recorded everything.

Some would call the creature before him an abomination, and Bichette knew he had to keep information about it from going public. That would only invite unwelcome inquiries, and perhaps even worse—an attack on the facility by the Guardians. Already they had made a commando assault on Max One, where Noah used to be kept.

By the end of the morning, the entire head had regenerated, and it lay face up with facial features that clarified minute by minute, bringing out the scarred, one-eyed countenance of Noah Watanabe. The top of his skull had patches of reddish hair that were gradually filling in. The missing eye began to emerge from the skull and take shape. Through the changes, the face grimaced, as if in continuing pain, and no sounds came forth. Wounds healed, but at the bottom of the head, where the brain stem remained visible, the ragged tissue did not cauterize, and remained open and moist with blood.

As all of this occurred, the life-support system collected information and transmitted it to the gauges. The vital signs were weak, but improving. This *creature*—and that was all

Bichette could call it at the moment—did not have any body, but it still had an erratic pulse.

Hours passed. All of the remaining cellular material began to gather at the base of the skull where the brain stem had remained exposed, and gradually covered it over. By the end of the afternoon, the head had become the seed of a new body, which grew from the neck down, filling in the upper body and then the rest . . . the arms, hands, legs, feet. In all respects, it appeared to match Noah's previous form, with scars that continued to heal and fade.

At last, in the middle of the night the process stopped, and the instruments showed that Noah—as if exhausted from the effort—was slipping into a fitful slumber. He kept drifting off, but every few moments he would suddenly twitch and reawaken. The eyes looked blankly at Bichette.

All through the process, as Noah's features solidified and the scars disappeared, his face had been a mask of pain. The suffering had been troubling to the doctor, but he had been afraid to administer medications out of fear that they might interfere with the arcane regeneration processes occurring in the body. But now, looking at the intact, regenerated person, he took the chance. Opening a panel in the life-support case, he injected a powerful mix of opiates into Noah, then closed the case.

According to the instruments, Noah slipped into more comfortable sleep, going deeper and deeper through the stages, but occasionally coming back to REM state, dreaming.

Afraid something might go wrong, Bichette remained at his side, and checked the monitoring mechanisms on the plax case, including the alarm system. Finally, assured that he could do no more for the moment, the doctor fell asleep himself, on a gurney. . . .

During the entire restoration process Noah had been linked to

Timeweb in its alternate dimension, a cosmic intravenous line feeding nutrients into his body, from one realm to another. During the restoration process, he'd been thinking of venture deeper into the cosmic realm, but had been too fatigued for any attempt. He felt pain in every muscle, bone, and joint of his body.

He had also thought of Tesh, recalling in particular the intelligent beauty of her face and the confident way she comported herself. Noah wondered how she was doing, and hoped all was well with her.

Then he became aware of the medications kicking in, dulling his senses. At first Noah was angered at the intrusion, feeling his abilities slow and his mind reel back in. As moments passed, however, he welcomed the drugs and the relief they gave him from all of his troubles.

Very little occurred in the CorpOne medical laboratories without the knowledge of Francella Watanabe. Either she received reports on the various activities, or she could see them firsthand, through holocams inside the principal laboratory rooms.

From her office in the complex, she had watched the entire process in three-dimensional holo-images that floated in the air. It had been almost as good as being in the room with her brother and Bichette, and had the advantage of keeping her at a distance, preventing her from interfering with the unknown forces that were bringing Noah back to life.

Too often she had stormed around the building, yelling at people, venting her frustrations, even slashing the face of a scientist as he cowered in her presence and tried to fend off the surgical knife she swung at him. The man had been lucky to escape her full rage. In fact, she'd had to use all of her willpower to avoid going into the chamber where all of the real action was occurring.

While slashing at the scientist and chasing him down the corridor, she had demanded answers from him. "What will happen if I inject Noah's blood into my own body? I'm his fraternal twin. What bearing will that have?"

"I don't know," he had whimpered. "I just don't know."

"Get out of my sight, then!"

The wounded man had disappeared around a corner, presumably to find a doctor himself. The fool was lucky she didn't kill him.

Now at the end of a long day, Francella did not feel any weariness at all. Curiously, while she loathed her brother and wanted only the worst for him, she felt exhilaration at his Lazarus trick, since it confirmed to her that his blood had supernatural powers. She could use it to gain eternal life for herself. Doctors and medical-research scientists knew nothing of immortality; she shouldn't even have asked them about it. They only knew how to treat injuries and illnesses, and how to analyze diseases.

Nothing like this.

In fact, this sort of thing, if widespread, did not bode well for the medical profession at all. With death vanquished, people would not need doctors. But those professions did not need to worry, since she would not permit the secret to get out. Even if he could not be killed, her brother could still be kept in captivity and used for whatever purposes she desired. She envisioned Noah continually providing her with blood and other cellular materials, a lab animal kept alive to be milked of its nutrients.

The excited woman smiled to herself. In the low light of her office, she stared at the vial of blood that sat on her desk, at the rich, wine-colored elixir inside the small plax container. She touched the surface of the plax, and knew she had the secret of perpetual life at her fingertips.

Connecting the vial to a dermex medical instrument, she pressed it against her left arm, injecting the contents into her own bloodstream.

As the fluid raced into her veins, Francella felt supremely confident. It was said that twins had special, even paranormal connections, and she had convinced herself that this was true. The demented woman thought she was giving herself eternal life, but in reality something quite unanticipated would occur. . . .

Chapter Thirty-Eight

> I think about my sister often. Sometimes I imagine that I already know her better than I know myself.
>
> —Noah Watanabe

Like a fetus to an umbilical cord, Noah had remained linked to Timeweb during the intense ordeal of his physical restoration, as he returned to life, defying all odds. He had, in a very real sense, gone through a remarkable process of rebirth, on a scale beyond that of any other creature who had ever walked the worlds of the universe, or moved from star system to star system.

The drugs administered to Noah had caused his mind to release its tensions, which should have enabled him to drift into peaceful, restful slumber. But the act of letting go had resulted in an unexpected consequence. Through a veil of consciousness, he saw his sister in her private office, removing a dermex unit from her arm. With a satisfied smile on her face, she leaned back on her chair and closed her eyes.

Noah felt himself forming into a mist as he had done before. Looking down, he saw that it had again taken the shape of his physical form. It floated around the room, even touching Francella briefly when he passed close. The moment the mist came into contact with her, she opened her eyes and sat straight up.

Since he was her twin, Noah sensed how deeply troubled she was, and he knew that virtually all of the hatred she could muster—a considerable amount, indeed—was focused on him, even though she did not know he was there with her. He realized as well that there was nothing he could do about it. She would always feel that way, to the last breath she took. Her wide-open eyes reflected the internal sea of her madness.

He saw her shiver and shudder. She grabbed a coat, hurried to the door, and rushed out into the corridor.

Noah followed, a mist in her wake that clung to her like a shadow.

"You sense I'm here, don't you?" he shouted.

Nervously, she looked behind her, and almost tripped as she picked up her pace and left the building. He heard the noises she was making, but didn't know if she could hear him. Just another oddity added to the long list he was accumulating in his mind.

A limocar took her home, and Noah stayed with her all the way, riding invisibly on the seat beside her. She kept twitching, looking around, talking to herself and scrunching in a corner, trying to assure herself that she was not crazy, that she just needed some rest. "I've been working too hard," she said.

He was enjoying this, making her nervous, lingering where she couldn't do anything about it.

Once, just before they got out of the limocar at her palatial home, she passed her hand through the air where Noah sat in his misty form, but her expression was perplexed and she said nothing about him, didn't use his name.

The vehicle was coming to a stop, still rolling slowly, when she leapt out, ran inside the main entrance of her home and locked the door behind her. Francella then instructed her personal servants to lock all doors and windows, and to draw the shades in every room.

As the attendants scurried about their business, Noah stuck to her, trying to scuff against the skin of her arms and face whenever he could, which had the effect of further agitating her. She went straight to bed, fully clothed, and pulled the covers over her head.

Noah took that as a barrier. Even in this circumstance, where he was functioning outside of his corporal form, he didn't want any hint of incest. Instead, he would wait for her to awaken, and would resume the torment.

He realized as he did these things that he had stooped low (though nowhere near to her level), and he felt shame, but only a modicum of it. His rage gave him righteousness, and more than anything he wanted to see her dead.

Now he felt full shame. This was not like him, not at all. As he watched her sleep—the lump under the covers—he felt his resolve weakening. At the same time his connection to the ethereal realm seemed to slip. The images in her bedroom grew more faint. He heard Francella snoring, and felt himself floating involuntarily back to the locked room in the laboratory where they kept him. . . .

When Francella awoke the following morning, troubling thoughts of the incident still clung to her like raindrops from a storm. But she reminded herself that she had been fatigued when the strange energy seemed to chase her out of the office, and she ascribed it to her own imagination.

She hoped it was that, wanted to think it was, and that it had nothing to do with the blood she had injected.

Chapter Thirty-Nine

> There are many forms of children.
> They do not always need a physical form in order to breathe.
>
> —Saying of the Sirikan Hill People

For weeks, Princess Meghina had been making clandestine visits to a man, always in the middle of the night. Wearing a dark, hooded cloak, she moved silently down a rock-walled corridor, clinging to pockets of darkness.

As a renowned courtesan, this was not particularly unusual behavior on her part. She liked to be discreet. Her customary appointments, however, were with princes and other refined noblemen, from the best families in the galaxy. The man she was seeing now had noble blood, but only on his paternal side. He didn't live in a magnificent palace or a castle on a hill. The object of her affection was a prisoner in the Doge's prison, but not a lowly detainee. This one had status.

She had paid off the right guards with Sirikan gemstones, and thus far her secret remained intact. Since first laying eyes on Anton Glavine at the pod station where he was arrested, Meghina had felt an instant attraction. It was always like that with the men in her life, an immediate connection that soon became physical.

But to test herself, she always liked to go through a selection process with her potential paramours. Anton was far more handsome than most of them, but that had little to do with it, as far as she was concerned. Of utmost importance, each of her lovers needed to occupy a special and unique niche in the galaxy; they must not be cut from cookie-cutter molds.

Her dear Prince Saito Watanabe had qualified with flying colors. The self-made tycoon, born into relative obscurity, had raised himself by his own hard labors and force of personality. As for the Doge Lorenzo del Velli, he had his own individuality, particularly his forward-thinking way of elevating commoners to nobility based upon their accomplishments in life. He had done exactly that with Saito, with Jacopo Nehr, and with others. It took courage for him to take those actions, bucking thousands of years of noble tradition. The hardships that her prospective lover, Anton Glavine, was going through now would ultimately build his character. She liked that in a man.

As Princess Meghina hurried down the corridor, she reminded herself that she also had an important humanitarian purpose in mind. It was obvious to her that the mysterious young man had not been treated in a manner befitting his station. He was, after all, the son of Doge Lorenzo, and could even become the ruler of the Merchant Prince Alliance one day, given the right political winds. But she didn't care about the politics.

It struck her with some excitement that she had never done anything quite like this before, grooming a relationship to this extent, and she laughed a bit at herself. Perhaps she was going a bit "rock happy," losing some of her senses from being confined to one planet, albeit a large and wealthy one. For much of her life she had flitted between glittering worlds, and her restriction to this one made her feel dismal much of the time.

This nocturnal adventure lifted her spirits; each day that she had an appointment she looked forward to it, even though the two of them had only held hands so far. She hadn't pushed for more, not even a kiss. She hadn't told him of her attraction for him, though she could tell that he knew it anyway. Thus far she had only confided that she was interested in his well-being, and would tell him no more. To her credit, she pulled it all off with an air of mystery.

At first the young man had seemed confused by her attentions, and then grateful. In return for her payoffs to the guards, she had obtained better treatment for him. So far he had been spared intensive interrogations or torture, but one of the guards told her he didn't know if he could promise that for much longer.

Though she had given him no name, Anton had recognized her, and had told her so. Once when he started to utter her name, she'd pressed a hand against his mouth. "Shhh," she had said. "We don't want the wrong people to find out I'm helping you."

Some of the guards had recognized her, despite her efforts to remain cloaked and to conceal her features as much as possible. In delivering her payments to the guards, Meghina's intermediary had commanded them to look away whenever "the lady" came to visit. Most of the guards had done so, but she had seen a couple of them peeking, trying to get a glimpse of her. One of them might have seen her full face a couple of weeks ago, when her hood slipped off as she was leaving.

Tonight, as she moved stealthily down the corridor, she was surprised to see another female visitor, already with Anton in his cell, speaking to him in low tones. The princess recognized Francella Watanabe immediately, unmistakable with her high forehead and shaved eyebrows. She wore a long black coat.

Slipping into a darkened alcove only a few meters away from the orange bars of the cell's containment field, Meghina eavesdropped on the conversation.

"Are you well, my son?" Francella asked. She stood inside the cell, while he remained seated on the lower bed of his bunk.

Looking away from her, he said, "I've told you before. I have no feelings for you, so we have nothing to discuss. Why do you keep coming back?"

"Because I neglected you for too long. I beg you to forgive me, my son. Am I not worthy of your slightest sympathy?"

"You are only worthy of my contempt."

"At least you have *some* feelings for me," she said, with an emotional edge to her voice. She looked down, then said, "I could help you more, if you'd give me a chance. Already I have prevented them from torturing you."

Anton didn't respond, but it occurred to Meghina that he had at least two female protectors now. Undoubtedly the guards were playing both of the women to maximize their payoffs, saying to each that they didn't know how much longer they could continue to protect the prisoner.

Moments later, Francella used a transmitter to release the containment field, stepped out, and then reactivated it. Without another word she swept down the corridor, while Princess Meghina remained in the shadows. In his cell, Anton threw something metal that clanked on the rock floor.

Stepping out of the alcove, Meghina said, "You're popular tonight."

He looked at her, his face filled with tragedy. "I'm sorry, but this isn't a good time. Can you come back another day? I appreciate what you're doing for me, but I just don't. . . ." He seemed at a loss for words.

"You don't need to explain," she said, softly. "I understand."

As Meghina left the prison the same way she had entered, she felt no sympathy for Francella; the selfish woman gave up her maternal rights when she abandoned him as a baby. Of that she was certain.

But the Sirikan princess was not sure what to make of Francella Watanabe's involvement now . . . this adversary she loathed so much, who competed with her for the affections of Meghina's own husband, Doge Lorenzo. Admittedly, the courtesan and the Doge had reached an understanding between them, an open marriage. But she wished he had better taste in some of the other women he saw.

It arrived, like so much information, as an unconfirmed rumor, a horrific story of butchery committed against Noah by his own sister. A new Guardian recruit, a young woman, came to Subi and Thinker with the dreadful tale.

"Everyone's talking about it," she said. "I don't know who said it first, or where it came from."

"His own sister, eh?" Subi said, seething.

"That's what they saying."

Subi sent out investigators to scour Rainbow City and the Valley of the Princes, seeking hard information. Finally it arrived, late that night. One of the investigators had spoken with a medical researcher who claimed to have actually seen the carnage.

Under cover of darkness, Subi led a commando squad himself. In a frenzy, the Guardians stormed CorpOne's headquarters complex, the inverted pyramid and surrounding buildings. Quickly, they took control of the complex and killed or captured all of the guards.

Feeling a rush of adrenaline, Subi then ordered his squad to aim incendiary rockets at the headquarters building. He hesitated before giving the order to fire. This was the most famous of Prince Saito Watanabe's buildings, and the most architecturally interesting. The late prince had been Noah's father, and as such he deserved respect. Especially since Noah came to feel that the two of them might have been close, if not for the vindictive interference of his own sister.

Francella.

But rage suffused Subi as he envisioned her face, and her terrible acts, not only against Noah but against her own father. Over a megaphone, he shouted: “Everyone in the building, you have five minutes to get out.”

Some of the offices had lights on, while most were dark. He saw movement up on one of the top three floors that had been leased to Doge Lorenzo.

Within minutes, a dozen people rushed out of the building on the ground level, and were taken into custody. No one important; just mid-level office staffers and janitorial workers.

Subi made a chopping motion with his right arm, a gesture he selected intentionally, as a visual reminder of Francella’s terrible crime against Noah.

A volley of incendiary rockets struck the building’s top levels exactly where Thinker had told him to hit, causing the entire structure to collapse and burn. It burned like a torch, lighting up the Valley of the Princes.

Chapter Forty

> "There are new experiences, and then again there are *new* experiences! This blows the top off my skull!"
>
> —Acey Zelk, comment to Dux Hannah

Early in the morning, according to the artificial diurnal time established by the hunters, their mottled gray-and-black podship proceeded slowly through the Hibbil Sector, taking a roundabout, seemingly wayward course. In this manner they hoped to avoid alerting their prey. . . .

Inside the low light of the passenger compartment, Eshaz opened the large shipping cases and brought out a protective suit like the one he had worn on Tarbu. After putting it on, he removed the contents of the other cases, and arranged various items on the deck and on top of a bulkhead table.

These included thorn vines in varying colors, all carefully wrapped in broad leaf packages. Each parcel was marked in a Tulyan dialect that Dux could not read, labels that Eshaz said identified the toxins and drugs in the vines, along with the sizes of the clippings. Other cases held vials of liquid and powder, small bowls, fire cylinders, herbs, music spheres, pigment rings, a big alloy cauldron, and an intricately folded, gilded harness that was decorated with mythological animals. Cheerily, Eshaz described some of the items as he brought them out.

In complete fascination, the boys watched as he mixed liquids, powders, and herbs in the bowls, took scrapings from the thorn vines, and combined everything in the cauldron, which he heated by inserting the fire cylinders into receptacles around the bottom of the thick alloy casting.

"I'll let this cook for a while," he said.

"Sort of a witch's brew?" Acey asked.

"Your terminology limits comprehension," Eshaz retorted. "A common Human frailty. When roaming the galaxy, you must avoid thinking in preconceived terms."

Acey nodded, but he looked puzzled.

Dux took a deep breath, and tried to keep his own mind open.

Presently Eshaz murmured incantations and tossed the music spheres overhead, which played monastic-sounding chants and polyphonics and then floated down into the boiling cauldron, melted into the liquid, and were silenced.

"It's time," Eshaz said, looking around.

"What?" Acey said.

"Tesh is coming to a stop."

Running to a porthole, Dux and Acey looked out into a region of space that was oddly illuminated by a pale bluish-gray light that had no discernible source. Acey went to another porthole. "I don't see any wild podships," he said.

"Nonetheless, we are in the right place."

Now, using long spoons, Eshaz dipped solution out of the cauldron and poured it into silver vials, which he sealed with sharp-pointed tops and placed into a bag. Then, removing the protective suit and his other clothing, he smeared iridescent pigment rings on his body, changing the scaly bronze surfaces of his skin to a network of intricate, colorful designs.

His slitted eyes were glazed over now, and he seemed to take no notice of Dux or Acey. Invoking new incantations, he handled the thorn vines without protective clothing, and wrapped a selection of them around his waist, then used straps to secure the bag of vials to his chest. He placed a bright red vine on his head, wearing it like a crown, and murmured what Dux imagined might be a Tulyan blessing.

As the boys watched, spellbound, Eshaz grabbed the gilded harness, which was still folded. Opening a hatch, he leapt out into the eerily illuminated vacuum of space, and quickly closed the door behind him. Through the mysterious workings of the podship, there was no explosive decompression that might have been caused by the inrushing vacuum of space. Instinctively, the boys held their breaths, then began breathing a few moments later, uneasily at first but with more comfort as the cabin oxygen level replenished quickly.

"Look!" Acey said, pointing upward.

A filmy window began to form on the top of the passenger compartment, and the teenagers saw Eshaz harnessed to the top of the podship, leaning forward.

The Tulyan felt the craft accelerate along a course that he had specified for Tesh. Squinting to peer ahead, he made out a herd of podships there, moving in their typical vee-formation away from him. As he neared them at a higher rate of speed, he saw that they were one of the largest wild-pod herds he had ever seen, with at least seventy individuals.

"Ubuqqo, atra mii," he murmured in his ancient tongue. "Thanks be to the Sublime Creator."

In the time-honored way of his people, Eshaz held two silver vials—one in each hand, pointed toward the podship formation. At his mental command, the vials shot out of his hands, faster than any projectile weapon. Grabbing more vials from the bag, he released one after another, and all hit their targets, sedating the podships one by one from the rear of the formation—though they continued to fly with their visual sensors looking forward, and did not send warnings to the leader.

Gradually the entire formation slowed down—with the exception of the alpha pod—and came to a dead stop in space.

Inside the passenger cabin beneath Eshaz, the teenage boys pressed their faces against portholes, staring out. Limited by his Human sensations, Dux had not felt the accelerations, decelerations, or turns of the podship in which he rode. Now, as if experiencing a dream, he saw a herd of podships come into his view. Most of them appeared to be drifting.

Their own podship, still under the guidance of Tesh, floated slowly past the sedated creatures. . . .

When he was just behind the lead podship, which remained unaware of the flurry of silent activity behind it, Eshaz reached deep into his mind, and focused all of his energy. He must be especially precise now, capturing the alpha pod and taking full control of it. It could not be sedated like the others or permitted to escape, or it would react by reviving them and leading all of them to commit suicide.

At the last possible moment, just as the alpha pod seemed to sense something, Eshaz made a floating, zero-g leap onto the creature's back, connected his harness, and dug thorn vines into its sides.

The podship was a big one, with ragged scars on its sides, perhaps marking prior attempts to capture it. The creature squealed out, an ancient protest that Eshaz heard despite the vacuum, and he held on.

Like a wild stallion of Lost Earth, the creature bucked, spun, whirled, and tried to throw off its rider. With expert precision, Eshaz brought out more vines and dug the sharp thorns into the creature's hide, injecting toxins. Finally the podship settled down.

On top of the pod, Eshaz lay flat, facing downward. Spreading his hands out, he felt the creature tremble, as it sensed what was about to occur. The Tulyan felt himself dropping slowly, like sinking into a thick bog. He merged into the flesh, and into the creature's primitive brain.

The podship altered appearance. Eshaz's face and eyes formed on the front, on a scale equal to the much larger size of the creature, and its skin became scaly, a gray-bronze hue that combined the two races. Immersed in every cell of the Aopoddae, Eshaz changed the direction of the vessel, causing it to veer off to the right. The other wild pods followed.

Exhilarated, Eshaz accelerated onto a podway, with the entire formation following, and Tesh's pod just behind them.

From the sectoid chamber, Tesh heard Acey and Dux hooting with excitement inside the passenger compartment. Then, as the podships reached open space, beyond the protection of the Wild Pod Zone, she saw a small contingent of Parvii scouts on one side, keeping pace with them. Her emotions warred with one another.

Eshaz, leading the pack of sentient spaceships, must have seen them, too, because he urged the alpha pod—with its hybrid, reptilian face—to greater speed. The unpiloted podships accelerated, keeping up.

But the Lilliputian scouts kept pace, too.

Tesh knew they were communicating with others within telepathic range, summoning a full swarm . . . enough to take control of the wild podships. She and Eshaz had discussed this possibility, and knew they wouldn't have much time to escape. In one sense she felt like a traitor to her race, but she knew her actions were absolutely necessary.

Chapter Forty-One

There are countless ways to die, but only those specified in the sacred texts guarantee your entrance into heaven.

—*The Holy Writ* of the Mutatis

On the Mutati capital world of Paradij, the Zultan Abal Meshdi lounged on oversized pillows in his palace harem, watching as his personal menagerie of shapeshifters danced for him. Fifteen of the most beautiful Mutati women of the three subspecies—terramutati, aeromutati, and hydromutati—danced on the floor, in the air, and inside a large tank of water. They moved in perfect synchronization, kinetic kilos of undulating flesh, the most graceful he had ever seen. But this evening he did not feel any desire for them. He had too much on his mind, had worked too hard for too long. At last everything was coming together: all of the important pieces were moving into position.

He had never witnessed such a malevolent, misanthropic frenzy all across the planet, and it pleased him immensely. In each city, town, and hamlet, every citizen was contributing mightily to the war effort against humankind, marshaling resources, channeling energy, performing all of the small and large tasks required for the ultimate, grand victory of the Mutati Kingdom.

As the inspirational leader, the Zultan knew he had been the catalyst for this new thrust, but lately the whole thing was taking on a life and energy of its own. Bioengineering laboratories were creating an abundance of lab-pods, while factories were churning out simulated merchant schooners with built-in Demolio torpedoes, and training facilities were preparing the outriders. Buildings everywhere carried giant electronic murals of the Zultan, along with holos of the most popular outrider volunteers, those Mutati men and women who would pilot the planet-busting bombs to their destinations.

Rumors abounded that the Zultan himself would ride one of the deadly Demolios to glory, and he allowed the stories to persist. They did no harm, and actually served to inspire the people even more, by showing that he was willing to give his all for the cause. Privately, he had no intention of getting to heaven that way. His own deeds spoke for themselves; he had already paid for his ticket.

I'll come up with some good excuse, he thought, as he watched the bulky beauties perform a shapeshifting dance, contorting their abundant mounds of flesh in provocative ways. *Some delaying tactic to keep others boarding the lab-pods ahead of me.*

His thoughts shifted as he watched a lithesome hydromutati slide through the water. He could never marry that subspecies or conceive children with a non-terramutati, but the *Holy Writ* did permit certain dalliances. . . .

Though Noah's body looked substantially restored, with all of its exterior parts and appendages, scars remained that were slow to heal, along with faint, pink discolorations on his freckled skin. His internal organs ached, especially his kidneys and lungs. Signals reaching his brain told him the organs were healed and functioning well, but they remained traumatized, like separate, sentient life forms huddling inside his body. The pain had been excruciating. Any other Human would have died under such a violent onslaught, but Noah, with his enhanced life functions, lived through more agony than any other person had ever endured in the entire history of his race. The trauma had gone on and on, without relief—with the exception of intermittent, unpredictable mental excursions that diverted his attentions elsewhere, but for only brief moments. During the worst of it he would have welcomed death, but the Grim Reaper had not awaited him with open arms.

In his continuing suffering, with his paranormal linkage to Timeweb, Noah was in the process of discovering something new and disturbing, over which he had no control. . . .

Subi Danvar jumped back from the screen on Thinker's chest, as if he had just seen a ghost. He had been talking with the simulated Noah about the wonderful times they used to have at the Environmental Demonstration Project, and on board the orbital EcoStation.

Suddenly the image of Noah shifted, and a three-dimensional likeness of him seemed to float out of the screen into the underground cavern. At first, Subi thought it was a holo-image, but it didn't have the same quality of illumination, and he saw no projector. The image floated around the chamber, then landed on its feet a short distance from Subi. It looked diaphanous, like a living mist in Human form.

"Do you see that?" Subi asked Thinker.

"See what?"

"There!"

"The cavern wall, you mean? What?"

"Not the wall! Noah! Don't you see him?"

"Noah is not there. I'm afraid you're having an illusion, perhaps initiated by my data screen. I'd better switch it off." He did so, and closed a panel over the screen.

With trepidation, Subi walked over to the image. Timidly, he extended his hand toward it.

"Don't try to touch me!" Noah said.

Subi recoiled. Looking back at Thinker he asked, "Did you hear that?"

"Hear what? Poor man, you need to get some rest."

Stubbornly, Subi reached toward the image, and put his hand through it. As he did so, the apparition faded entirely.

"I told you not to touch me!" Noah yelled, as if from afar. "It's more than the dimensional stretch can tolerate!" He disappeared entirely, and took his voice with him.

Chapter Forty-Two

Though Lorenzo keeps his business affairs private, it is known that he holds a number of corporate directorships around the galaxy, a network of interactions that form the economic basis of his power.

—*Pillars of the Merchant Princes,* a holodocumentary

The destruction of the CorpOne headquarters building had forced Lorenzo to relocate his offices and royal residence to the orbiter that had formerly been Noah Watanabe's prized EcoStation. While the Doge hated to retreat, he had been pleased that he still had this facility solidly under his control, and that the pesky Guardians could not possibly get to him there. The space station, now fully armored and fitted with the most advanced security systems, also had a formidable squadron of government patrol ships constantly on alert.

Deep in thought, the Doge walked through the module containing his new offices, where a construction crew worked at an efficient but inadequate pace. He would order Pimyt to speed them up. Office work still needed to be done, so his staff had been operating out of makeshift quarters nearby.

Proceeding down a long corridor into another module, he entered one of Noah's former classrooms and waved at Princess Meghina, who was discussing the ongoing work with a contractor. With her good taste and love of exotic projects, she was helping immensely, and Lorenzo had put her in charge of this section.

Originally Lorenzo had been about to make drastic changes to this area, tearing out not only the classrooms but also the connected mini-forest area that Noah's people had cultivated. It had all looked absurd to him, and he'd wanted to move gambling equipment in for a glitzy new casino. Meghina concurred with the casino idea, but talked him out of changing this particular module, telling him that plants created oxygen, valuable on a space station. She pointed out what a holovideo told her—that the forest ecosystem was a self-sufficient, scaled-down version of life on Canopa, with small birds and other creatures filling ecological niches. She then suggested that they turn the classrooms into an attractive casino dining hall, with the miniature forest surrounding it, separated by the invisible electronic barrier that was already in place. All excellent ideas, he had to admit. The gambling equipment would have to go elsewhere.

Almost oblivious to anyone in the corridors of the orbital station, Lorenzo stalked ahead. Subordinates fell silent as he neared them, and they scurried out of his way. Behind him, four Red Beret guards kept pace, watching out for his safety. He had other things on his mind.

With the Mutati war forced into the background, Lorenzo del Velli still faced tremendous difficulties. In particular, he was concerned about reports of discontent against him among the princes on various planets. His political problems were complex and worrisome, exacerbated by the continuing guerrilla attacks by Guardian forces against government and corporate installations on Canopa. There had even been copycat incidents on other planets, reportedly done by sympathetic groups that were not formally aligned with the Guardians. With no access to nehrcom stations, the Guardians could not possibly be coordinating the attacks, but they were occurring nonetheless, and weakening him.

The underpinnings of opposition against Lorenzo ran deep. For some time, the noble-born princes had been critical of him for stubbornly appointing commoners such as Saito Watanabe and Jacopo Nehr to important government positions. The noble-born princes, descended from aristocratic lineages that went back for thousands of years, were not happy about this at all, but Lorenzo had brought most of them over to his side anyway, by pointing out the necessity of rewarding exceptional skills. None of the nobles could deny the sterling business accomplishments of either Saito or Jacopo. And, while Saito was dead now and his operations were more low-key under his daughter Francella, Jacopo Nehr was still in the limelight, having been promoted the year before to Supreme General of all Merchant Prince Armed Forces.

Rounding a corner forcefully, Lorenzo almost bowled over a little man carrying a briefcase, going the other way. One of the office functionaries. A paper shuffler. The office worker apologized profusely, bowed, and hurried on his way.

The Doge headed for a room at the end of the corridor—his communications center—which he saw through an open doorway. Lights blinked in there and small robots whirred back and forth, performing functions that were even lower than those of the typical office worker.

Lorenzo knew which noble-born princes were closest to him, because they were the ones most vocal in their support. Of course, some of that could be a ruse, and he was alert to that. He remained most concerned and troubled, however, by the ones who were remaining silent and detached from him. Having alerted his own government agents by nehrcom on the various Alliance planets, he had the princes under constant surveillance, thus far without turning up any specific evidence against any of them. It was most perplexing to him, and frustrating. The disloyal princes seemed to have taken a page from the Guardian playbook, lying low and making their own form of guerrilla attacks against him.

As he entered the communications center, Pimyt greeted him. The little Hibbil carried an electronic notebook under one arm. "We are ready to broadcast," Pimyt said. "Here are the prompter notes."

"I don't need notes," Lorenzo snapped, shoving the furry little man aside. "I know what to say."

He went to a console, and a technician in a black singlesuit turned on the machine, bathing the Doge in soft white light. Later in the day he would broadcast through nehrcom relay to the people of every planet in the Merchant Prince Alliance, his version of the ages-old fireside chat. It was a recent suggestion from Pimyt, and Lorenzo had taken a liking to the idea, as a way of keeping him in the minds of the people. With the cessation of podship travel and the mutterings of noble-born princes against him, Lorenzo's task in this regard was proving to be increasingly difficult.

But first he had a more limited broadcast, just for the Canopan people. To show his concern for their security, Lorenzo had been making regular public proclamations on the purported progress his forces were making in rooting out Noah's forces, the cowards who made guerrilla style attacks against corporate and government facilities where many of the citizens worked.

While Pimyt stood by nervously, holding the electronic notepad, Lorenzo began to talk extemporaneously. In a blatant lie, he told the people to pay no attention to the increasing number of destroyed buildings and other assets on Canopa, that Guardian losses were very high and they didn't have the resources to go on much longer.

Bolstering the spin he was putting on events, he accompanied his speech with holo-images of Noah in captivity, to prove that the Doge was in control of the situation. In reality they were older pictures of the rebel leader, before Francella hacked him to pieces. The current images of Noah, though his body had regenerated, made him look like a torture victim, with pinkish scars and other wounds that were not healing as rapidly as in the past, when he experienced less grievous injuries.

As Lorenzo completed the address, he stepped away from the white light. The technician transmitted recorded messages, boilerplate material that accompanied every one of the Doge's pronouncements.

Lorenzo walked away, ignoring Pimyt for the moment, who scuttled along behind him babbling the usual sycophantic nonsense. The merchant prince leader's new orbital office headquarters would offer him additional security, but he wanted to spend more time down on Canopa as soon as possible, and this made him grumpy whenever he focused on it.

By rights, his offices and his residence should be down there, not up here. His empire seemed to be shrinking around him. Once, he ruled hundreds of wealthy planets of the Merchant Prince Alliance from the glittering capital world of Timian One. Now, with the capital destroyed and Canopa increasingly dangerous for him, he had retreated to a very small place, and only maintained tenuous control over the remaining planets.

He still ventured down to the surface of Canopa on occasion, but only accompanied by a cadre of Red Berets, led by a trusted colonel who had been in his service for almost a decade. These men were the fiercest of Human and machine fighters, trained in the most advanced weaponry and sworn to protect their Doge at all costs.

Ever the optimist, Lorenzo always had interesting operations underway. For some time before the destruction of his Canopan offices, he had been expanding this space station by bringing in new armored modules and floating them into orbit, intending to turn the facility into a gambling resort called The Pleasure Palace. Word of this got out, as he wanted. But it had the unintended result of causing some of the discontented princes to criticize him for it. Still, he thought he could turn the tables on them.

Even with the forced relocation of his offices, he would proceed with the casino plans, and would demonstrate to the Alliance that he could not be intimidated by criticism. Besides, the facility would make a lot of money for him, enabling him to fulfill his love of gambling in a dramatic, very public way. Admittedly the whole enterprise was a risk, but the raw creative excitement energized him, and he felt confident that it would succeed in a big way.

Chapter Forty-Three

A thought can be the most beautiful thing in all
of existence . . .
Or the most malignant.
—Fragment from the teachings of Lost Earth

Even though Francella's CorpOne headquarters building no longer existed, Doge Lorenzo was still obligated to make ten years of exorbitant lease payments to her. The same held true for the opulent cliffside villa that he had vacated. Both properties were part of the same ironclad contract, drawn up by her attentive lawyers. The merchant prince leader had hardly bothered to look before signing, bless his foolish heart. Francella so loved to manipulate him.

Now as she supervised the movement of her furnishings back into the villa, Francella glanced in a mirror that two men had just hung in the parlor. Moving close to the glax she looked at her forehead above the shaved eyebrows, and at the skin beneath her eyes. She thought her face was smoother than before, that faint lines had vanished, and she looked younger than her thirty-eight years.

Excitement infused her. The injection of Noah's blood was beginning to take effect! She felt exuberant.

With a new quickness in her step, Francella took a break and wandered along the loggia, past the open-air gallery of imperial statues. Across the Valley of the Princes, she saw Rainbow City clinging to the sheer walls of an iridescent cliff, with midday sunlight glinting off the jewel-like buildings.

At the end of the loggia, she entered a large room that had once been piled high with her father's most special treasures, and which now stood empty. She remembered going there as a child and admiring the priceless jewels and artworks, which the tycoon had collected during a lifetime of travels around the galaxy. Thinking back as she strolled around the empty room, she noted scratches on the marble floor and the walls that needed to be repaired.

But just for a moment, as if she were a small girl again, she plopped herself on the floor in one corner, on the exact spot where she used to sit. The plush handmade carpet was gone now and the floor was very hard, but she felt calmer with each passing moment.

Francella was about to get up when she noticed something on the wall. A display case had been there for years, and now, just above floor level she saw a vertical line on the wall, perhaps a third of a centimeter in height. Dropping to her knees, she examined it.

When she touched the wall it sprang outward, revealing a compartment beyond.

Her heart raced. Could a treasure be inside? She thought she had placed all of the valuables in safekeeping before the Doge moved in, but what if her father had hidden something here, perhaps the most precious of his possessions?

Reaching inside, she thought at first that the hiding place was empty. Then her fingers tightened around a small, hard object, the shape of a coin. Bringing it out into the light, she saw that it was not that at all, but was instead an old-style computer disk, the retro-though-dependable type her father had preferred to use.

She might have held this very one in her hand, years ago. Once, as a four-year-old, she'd seen a pile of them on a table and had placed them in a pocket of her dress, thinking they were coins and she could buy candy with them. Finding the disks in her pocket, a maid had scolded her and put them back without ever telling her father.

Francella sighed. In many ways she missed the innocence of her childhood, before the desolate realities of life began to embitter her. In her own way, she had always loved her family, and even Noah, despite the enmity they held for one another. She had also loved their father, the old prince, dearly, but had found it necessary to get rid of him and blame the death on her brother. Under different circumstances, if she had only been treated as an equal with Noah—without all the favoritism that Prince Saito showed toward him—things might have been entirely different.

I am not a monster, she thought. *I only do what I have to do.*

But she would not let sadness intrude on her fine mood. This computer disk could be something valuable. Francella took it into her study, where a technician was setting her equipment up.

"Can you read what's on this disk?" she asked.

He whistled. "That's an oldie. Should be able to, though. I've got a converter in my bag." He set up the converter, then made several equipment adjustments and tossed the disk into a hopper. Seconds later a copy—one of the modern data shards embedded in a clearplax ball—rattled out into a tray, along with the old disk. He handed both of them to her.

In privacy, Francella activated a palm-sized computer, and watched the holo screen appear in front of her eyes. The writing on the screen had been encrypted, but she ran through the codes her father used and saw the words shift into Galeng. This was Prince Saito's electronic journal. Feeling a rush of excitement she scrolled and found references to herself and to Noah, with the old man wishing the two of them would stop quarreling.

Then she caught her breath.

"The love of my life is Princess Meghina," he wrote. "But she is secretly a Mutati who cannot shapeshift back. She is more Human than anyone I know, more filled with love and loyalty and compassion and a passion for life. I love her dearly, and can never turn her in. This is a secret I shall carry to my grave."

But the harlot is Lorenzo's wife, Francella thought. *He must know, too.*

Reading on, she discovered otherwise. "I am the only Human who knows this explosive secret. So skillful is her deception that the Doge has no idea of her true identity. Nor can he ever know. I am confident that history will sort this matter out for the best, but to protect Meghina during her lifetime I have taken steps to prevent release of the information for many years, until long after the participants in this little drama are gone."

Ecstatic, Francella saw an opportunity to accomplish two important goals at once.

Formulating her plan more that afternoon, she began to think about how best to spread rumors—through channels to protect her own identity—about Princess Meghina's scandalous secret. Along with that bombshell, she would add a twist of her own, the assertion that Doge Lorenzo had known about it all along.

When released—it would take a little time to get everything set up—the story and all of its related suspicions would spread like fire on dry grass. Had the Royal Consort avoided medical examinations, or had her records been falsified? Who was covering up for her, the Doge Lorenzo himself?

Yes, the puzzle pieces would fit together nicely, enabling Francella to get rid of that loathsome woman once and for all. And eliminate the Doge at the same time, thus advancing the cause of her allies, the noble-born princes who wanted to bring Lorenzo down and replace him with a leader sympathetic to their cause.

My son Anton would fill the bill nicely, she thought as she dispatched three messengers from her study.

But Francella knew this was just wishful thinking. Anton hated her so much that he would hardly speak to her. And she knew very little about his politics . . . except his affinity for her despicable brother, and his refusal to reveal the location of Guardian headquarters. Such a disingenuous story Anton was telling, that he'd been experiencing memory gaps.

She sighed with resignation, knowing that she could not force all of the puzzle pieces into place. At least she had recognized an opportunity and was about to jump on it. Not a bad day's work, after all.

Chapter Forty-Four

We all gamble anyway, with every breath we take. Why not make it fun?

—Plaque signed by Lorenzo del Velli,
entrance to The Pleasure Palace

With money from investors and his own sources, Lorenzo completed construction work on The Pleasure Palace in a matter of weeks, along with his connected offices and living quarters. The high class casino-resort had luxury apartments for wealthy customers, which he offered at reasonable rates in order to entice them to the gambling tables. Even in these uncertain times, gamblers flocked there, primarily the nobility and business leaders of Canopa, but also a number of wealthy travelers who had been stranded on the planet when podship travel ceased.

Each night Lorenzo played the perfect celebrity host for his well-dressed guests, and was often seen in the company of his elegant and mysterious courtesan-wife, the Princess Meghina. Liras poured in, so much wealth that he quickly had to enlarge a high-security vault wing on the orbiter.

The space station became a most unusual royal residence for the Doge, an orbital wonderland where he could indulge his taste for high living and make a great deal of money in the bargain. To an extent he was pleased with the new setup, but military and political concerns continued to occupy much of his time. Every day before going to the casino, he met with his attaché Pimyt. In particular, they prepared important nehrcom transmissions to every planet in the Merchant Prince Alliance, making certain the defensive positions remained in place on every pod station, and that military forces were as strong and alert as possible.

All orders of this type went from Lorenzo to Pimyt, who in turn was supposed to either transmit them himself at the nehrcom station on Canopa or convey them to General Jacopo Nehr.

As before, the devious Hibbil underhandedly modified some of the messages, causing merchant prince military installations to move or actually *reduce* strength . . . adjustments that were accomplished subtly and almost imperceptibly, a little at a time.

His inside knowledge of the location of Human military forces and their strength was a huge espionage coup for the Hibbils and their secret Adurian allies.

As far as Lorenzo knew, his orders were being taken care of properly, but he couldn't stop worrying. There were still no podships connecting the planets of his Merchant Prince Alliance—or those of the enemy Mutati Kingdom. It was as if the Human and Mutati worlds had been separated from the galaxy and discarded, like rotten apples from a barrel.

Chapter Forty-Five

> Tell me what you actually see in me, and not what my detractors *tell* you to see.
>
> —Princess Meghina, private note to Doge Lorenzo

Lorenzo didn't like the way Pimyt looked when he entered the royal bathing room, as if he didn't care enough, or as if it was a matter that was completely out of his hands. How could the little Hibbil act so detached when Lorenzo's world was crashing around him? Wasn't it bad enough that he'd had to relocate to the orbiter? And now this? The rumor had hit Lorenzo like a Mutati torpedo, burrowing in and detonating inside his brain.

"It's a monstrous lie!" the Doge thundered. Rising naked from an immense bathing pool, he grabbed a robe from one of the two female attendants who had been washing him.

"Undoubtedly you are right," Pimyt said. "But we must act quickly to dispel the story before it gains too much traction. Already it is inflaming the populace, causing them to ask questions. They want your response."

"The people are demanding that I address them? How absurd. I speak to them whenever I wish, if it pleases me." He glared at the attendants, and they hurried away.

"I understand that, of course." The Hibbil's red eyes seemed to brighten, like embers that had been fanned. "Is that your response, then, My Doge?"

"Don't be an idiot! Obviously, this is an unusual situation, requiring emergency action. Prepare my shuttle immediately, and my escort of Red Berets."

The little alien bowed, but maintained his irritatingly detached demeanor. "It will be done."

A short while later the shuttle landed, and the Doge's elite special police whisked him into a gleaming black groundjet for the ride to Rainbow City, perched on a cliff top. Lorenzo fumed all the way.

When the groundjet finally came to a stop in front of a large building with white pillars, he didn't wait for attendants to let him out of the vehicle. While his security forces scrambled to keep up, he marched into the ornate lobby and across it to the high-speed ascensore for the ride to the top floor, the fifty-seventh. He told the guards and Pimyt to remain in the lobby.

Princess Meghina called these her "royal apartments," but in reality she had converted an upscale apartment building into a palace. As the Doge stepped out of the ascensore, he hardly noticed the expensive statuary and artwork in the entrance hall, most of which he had paid for himself.

"I've been expecting you," Meghina said, bowing to him as he marched toward her. Barefooted, she looked tired and bleary-eyed, as if she had been crying. Her long blond hair hung haphazardly about her shoulders, and her saffron daygown was wrinkled.

"Is it true?" he shouted, standing right in front of her and staring up into her face. Even without shoes, she was slightly taller than he was. He hardly needed to ask the question. He saw the answer in her expression. A mask of sadness.

"All I can say is it's not what you think. Yes, I was born a Mutati, but I always hated my own people. I always wanted to be Human. I am *not* a spy!"

Stunned, he could not think of anything to say.

"In my youth I studied Humans and longed to be one of them," she said tearfully. "My Mutati peers criticized me for that, but I stood up to them, and took a huge risk by intentionally remaining in Human form so long that I could not change back."

"And our daughters?"

"I falsified my pregnancies, all seven of them . . . even had the genetic records altered. The girls are not related to either of us."

Raising a hand to strike her, he hesitated. "I could kill you for this!" he thundered.

"I almost wish you would," she said. "I have done you wrong. But please believe me, I did not intend to hurt you."

"Oh, you didn't intend to hurt me! Well, that makes it all right then, doesn't it?" He lowered his hand. "You are to remain here under house arrest," he commanded, "until I decide what to do with you."

"Yes, of course." Her voice became very small.

As he left, Lorenzo didn't care about any of her excuses. He was only concerned about damage control because of the immense political harm that had just been done to him.

On the lobby floor, he pushed past his guards. Not seeing Pimyt at first, he knocked the smaller Hibbil down, then stepped on his arm and continued on his way.

Sirens blaring and horns honking, the merchant prince leader and his military escort sped through the streets of Rainbow City. Presently his black groundjet stopped at the security gate of the CorpOne medical complex, and then proceeded toward the large central building.

Having already bypassed security, a small squadron of Guardians—men and robots—stood on a rooftop inside the complex.

Other Guardians were in position a short distance outside, waiting for the moment to rush in.

Moments before, Thinker had folded himself shut, saying he had to consider something important. Now Subi and the others waited beside him, looking nervously in all directions. In a bold daylight raid, they had been preparing to move against the central medical laboratory on the other side of the street, where Francella Watanabe had recently been observed by Giovanni Nehr. They had also brought a new weapon with them, for just this purpose.

But at the eleventh hour Thinker had something more to work out.

Just then, Subi saw a black groundjet and other vehicles pull up at the main entrance to the big laboratory building. Somebody important. He wondered if it could be the Doge Lorenzo himself. Nervously, Subi glanced at Thinker.

Still no movement from the robot. . . .

Back in their underground headquarters the day before, after Thinker and Subi had studied Gio's reconnaissance report, the robot had thought it might be possible to capture Francella and destroy the medical facility.

"She would be a valuable hostage," Thinker had said as they stood in Subi's unadorned office. "So I came up with a little gadget to help out."

On his torso screen, the robot had then shown Subi schematics of what he called an "isolation weapon," which would destroy buildings while providing protective cocoons for people, so that no Human casualties resulted from their attacks. "I came up with it after our strike against the CorpOne headquarters building, when we had to wait for the structure to be evacuated."

"That was a major building collapse," Subi had said. "You mean people could actually survive that?"

"Absolutely. This new weapon would scatter protective cocoons moments ahead of the destructive explosives, thus protecting everyone."

"But wouldn't rescue parties have to still dig people out of the rubble?"

"No. The cocoons have mechanisms that will cause them to rise above the explosion, and then float down without harm on the nearest spots away from the rubble."

"You're sure this will work?"

"Fully tested. Everyone will be perfectly safe. . . . We can use it to go after Noah's sister," Thinker had said.

"And if Noah is inside, and still alive. . . ."

"He will be absolutely safe. I have worked this out with great precision, and the weapons are already constructed. I must inform you, however, that your concerns about his welfare are probably too late. He is very likely dead, wherever he is."

"I know," Subi had said. Rage had infused him with a desire to capture Francella, and he added, "OK. We go tomorrow. Let's start getting ready. This won't just be about getting even with her. It will be about weakening our enemies, cutting off the head of the monster."

"Mmmm. Francella cut Noah, so we cut her out of her own protective cocoon, separating her from the forces that surround her. . . ."

On the rooftop Thinker suddenly opened and said, "I just corrected an inspection malfunction. The isolation weapon's design was thoroughly tested, but there is a manufacturing defect in this particular unit that needs to be corrected. Otherwise, we will kill everyone in the building."

"What?"

"We must return to headquarters and fix it."

Just then, one of the Guardians nudged Subi. Looking to his

left, the adjutant saw two men on top of an adjacent building, stepping out of a stairwell onto the roof. "They saw us," the Guardian said.

Subi and his companions ran. In less than a minute, leaping down stairs, the squadron reached the alley where they had left two commandeered CorpOne vans. Thinker showed remarkable agility in keeping up. As they tumbled aboard the vehicles, shots rang out, and Subi saw uniformed CorpOne security officers running toward them.

The vans accelerated and barreled down the alley in the opposite direction. A blast hit the back of the second van, tearing into the torso of Thinker, who had bravely placed his metal body there in order to protect the other passengers. Subi narrowly missed being hit.

"Thinker!" Subi shouted, as the vans barreled through the entrance gate, then turned onto a main arterial and accelerated. Behind them, other Guardian forces—looking like ordinary Canopans and robots—moved into various positions to block pursuit.

Inside a robot-assembly area of Guardian headquarters, robotic workers worked feverishly to reactivate Thinker's central processing box, an armored core that contained the AI-brain and its micro-control systems.

In a matter of hours Thinker was rebuilt, and soon he was better than ever, with none of the scratches or dents he'd had previously. The first time he folded open, a crowd of Guardians stood watching, including Subi and Gio.

With a broad smile on his flat metal face, Thinker said, "Did anyone miss me?"

He tinkered with the screen on his own chest, causing an image of Noah Watanabe to appear, as before. Everyone clapped and cheered, and gathered around to welcome the robot back.

Then, under Thinker's direction, he had robots make dents and scratches on his rebuilt body, roughly matching those he'd had before. "I don't want to look like a green lieutenant," he said.

Chapter Forty-Six

Ironically, the crisis in Francella Watanabe's soul and her morals made her more Human. While her body was degenerating toward its inevitable end, she finally became something that had always eluded her before.

—Secret notes of Dr. Hurk Bichette

As days passed, Francella became convinced that the injection of her brother's blood really was changing her for the better. Moment by moment, she felt more invigorated and thought she looked younger. After a while, she came to realize that she should not examine herself in the mirror so frequently, since it made it hard to notice the changes. Still, she persuaded herself that a metamorphosis was occurring.

Believing that her brother harbored the secret of eternal life, Francella had taken a big risk in seeking it for herself. But she'd thought through the options beforehand, and determined that she stood to gain more than she might lose. On the plus side, she could attain eternal life, while if something went wrong she would lose only the remaining decades of her short, mortal existence. But the crazed path of reasoning that led her to attack Noah and inject his blood into her own body had not prepared her for the stark reality.

One morning she finally looked at herself very closely in the mirror, and jumped back in surprise and horror. Then she inched closer. Unmistakably, a cobweb of fine lines covered her forehead and cheeks, with dark blue circles under her eyes. She was changing, but not in the way she had anticipated.

Behind her, a mist formed, and took the shape of a person. But she didn't notice, and after a few moments the ghostlike form faded.

As Noah drifted back into his corporal form in his locked sleeping room at the medical laboratory, he realized more than ever that he did not understand how to use his powers in Timeweb. He wasn't even certain if he could call them "powers" anymore. Once, when he'd been able to control podships, that might have been an apt description. But so much had happened to him since then, so many complexities within complexities. Podships had every reason to fear and distrust him, due to his part in recommending that Doge Lorenzo install sensor-guns on merchant prince pod stations to prevent Mutati attacks, weapons that were used to destroy several podships. That difficult decision on his part accounted in large part for the aversion of the sentient spacecraft to him, and perhaps for his difficulties in negotiating other aspects of the immense cosmic web.

He also suspected that the grievous physical injuries inflicted on him by his demented sister might have a bearing on his current difficulties, causing some sort of irreparable brain damage that led to him drifting in and out of Timeweb, with little or no control on his part. Those physical traumas might have interrupted his development in the ethereal realm.

It was most peculiar, the way he had visited his Guardian followers in this manner, and Francella as well. They were like two ends of his emotional spectrum, from abiding love to intense hatred. The Guardians were his vision for the galaxy, representing the hopes and dreams he had for mankind as the Human race fanned out into the stars. He wanted Humans to behave responsibly in ecological matters, reversing the age-old trend toward rampant consumerism and the galactic-scale dumping of garbage.

He had recovered physically, but what toll had it taken on who he was, and *what* he was? He remembered Tesh Kori thinking for a time that he was a monster who needed to be destroyed, after she saw the first episode when his amputated foot regrew, and numerous subsequent episodes when his body accomplished the impossible.

As Noah lay in his locked room, a shudder of fear ran down his spine. His access to Timeweb was not necessarily a blessing, not if he couldn't understand it fully. There had been glimmerings of possibilities revealed to him, amazing things he had seen and experienced. An immense, galactic-scale environment called Timeweb, far beyond anything he had envisioned when he coined the phrase "galactic ecology." Eshaz had healed him by connecting him to the cosmic filigree, and there had been astounding mental excursions, far beyond anything the Human mind could possibly imagine. So far beyond, in fact, that they had to be true. He had no doubt that these things had really happened to him, and that he had been given a view of something that only the gods should know about.

One thing seemed very clear to him, and he could do nothing about it. His feelings of frustration and inadequacy were made worse by his own uncertainty, making him like a rudderless ship in a paranormal void. He had seen and experienced too much . . . and not nearly enough.

The cruel unfairness shocked and disappointed Francella. How could her brother, with all the privileges and advantages he'd always had over her, get the better of her yet another time? It seemed to be the work of a dark power. She was like a progeria victim, aging at an accelerated rate. A leaden heaviness set in over her and she slumped to the floor, weeping and wailing.

Servants came to her, but she shouted them away. In her suffering, she didn't want them around.

Later that day she had to go to CorpOne's new temporary headquarters for a meeting, inside a hastily constructed complex of modular buildings. Under high security, a new office structure was under construction nearby, and as she made her way down an interior corridor she heard the drone and clank of machinery.

Dr. Hurk Bichette approached her, carrying a sheaf of documents. He flipped through them as he walked. Seeing her, he paused and said, "Ms. Watanabe. Are you feeling well?"

"Get out of my way," she said, pushing past him.

But he scurried to keep up with her. "You look pale," he said, "and tired. Have you been getting enough sleep?"

Francella felt a deep fatigue. None of the stimulants she had taken were helping, and she hadn't bothered with makeup. "I have an important meeting," she said, referring to an earnings report she was going to receive from her top executives. "And after that, I'm going up to the orbiter to see the Doge."

With a worried expression, the doctor looked at her closely and said, "I want to conduct comprehensive medical tests on you. See me first thing when you get back, all right?"

"Yes, yes," she said, and hurried into the conference room. Darkness seemed to be descending around her, but she vowed to keep going until she dropped.

Chapter Forty-Seven

Among the galactic races, we've always been the preeminent survivors, able to overcome any obstacle and defeat any challenge. This time, however, facing galactic chaos and determined foes, we must be more resourceful and brutal than ever.

—Woldn, the Eye of the Swarm

Before the Parvii scouts had been able to summon their multitudes, Eshaz had accelerated onto a podway, with the Aopoddae herd behind him. Knowing he had only seconds to make good his escape, he pressed the pods to greater and greater speeds, faster than he had ever gone through space in his long lifetime. They did not resist him. By controlling the alpha pod, he gained absolute authority over all of them.

Taking a web shortcut that Tulyans used in bygone days, Eshaz—having merged his face and form into the flesh of the creature—had led the herd of wild podships directly to the Tulyan Starcloud. With Tesh and the unpiloted pods right behind him, he'd slipped into the protection of the starcloud.

Now, with Tulyans rushing to take control of the other sentient vessels that he had brought in, Parvii swarms were gathering in space, but kept at a distance by the protective mindlink of the Tulyans, a powerful energy shield that repelled them.

In the past the Parviis had been able to break through, but

this time the Tulyans were much stronger and sent their enemies spinning away in rage and confusion. . . .

Inside the inverted Council Chamber a short while later, Eshaz stood with Tesh, facing all twenty Elders. The tribunal of Tulyan leaders sat solemnly at their long bench, as they asked probing questions. Two of the younger Elders on the Council had reddish patches on their skin from what was being called "web disease," linked to the deterioration of Timeweb, and they looked tired. The tallest Elder, Dabiggio, had previously suffered from this malaise himself, but now he looked much healthier, with most of his skin lesions having healed. Even so, Eshaz knew that this was a matter of utmost concern for the Tulyan people. There were increasing numbers of breakouts of the sickness throughout the starcloud, and—though Tulyans seemed able to overcome the debility—it drained their collective energy, diverting them from the important tasks they needed to perform for the welfare of the galaxy.

First Elder Kre'n had called this emergency session to deal with the situation of the Parvii swarms. Over the millennia the enemy multitudes had come and gone, and they had been able to find holes in the mindlink to compromise it . . . until now. The telepathic shield seemed to be a complete wall to them, without weak points.

But the Elders were not assuming anything, and they would not let their guard down. So far their ancient enemies were being kept at bay, but in the flux state of the galactic ecological crisis and the ongoing hostilities among the races, the Council had vowed not to take any chances.

As the worried Tulyans met, the swarms kept coming into their galactic sector, in larger numbers than anyone could recall, even the most aged of the Elders.

Leaning forward and scowling, Dabiggio led the interrogation of Eshaz and Tesh. The towering Elder made pronouncements more often than he asked questions, but Eshaz had come to expect this sort of behavior when dealing with the cantankerous old Tulyan. He seemed to have a deep and permanent scowl etched into his face.

"You're in contact with the swarms, aren't you?" Dabiggio said, his gaze lasering at Tesh. "If we kill you, will they scatter back into space?"

"I reject my people, since I do not agree with their aims. Unlike Tulyans, the Parviis are a selfish race, concerned only with their own welfare and their own power. As for your questions, if the morphic field still extends to me, I no longer feel it. When Woldn declared me an outcast, I think he totally cut me loose. If you were to kill me, I don't think the swarms would even know it."

"Shall we test your theory?" Dabiggio asked, his voice like a razor.

"She did not lead the swarms here," Eshaz said, interjecting, "since Parviis have known for millions of years where we are. She did us no harm, and actually benefited us with the capture of more than seventy podships."

"Seventy?" Dabiggio scoffed. "Why, in the old days we used to capture ten times that many on a hunt!"

"But it's one of the biggest herds I've seen. Over the last nine hundred thousand years, this ranks as a significant capture, much more than the three or four we typically bring back at a time."

"They are probably Trojan horses," Dabiggio grumbled, "filled with Parvii swarms hiding inside, ready to pounce at the most opportune moment."

As Eshaz and Dabiggio debated, Tesh became small and flew up onto First Elder Kre'n's shoulder. "Touch me and know the truth of my words and my actions."

With one finger, Kre'n touched the face of the tiny creature, and then smiled gently.

"What about you, then?" Tesh asked as she made a slight buzzing noise and flew in her wingless way over to Dabiggio, where she landed on the counter in front of him. "Test me yourself," she offered. "I put my life in your hands."

"Your life is *already* in my hands," the big Tulyan said. He just stared at her, without even touching her skin against his.

Showing no fear, she landed on the end of his large snout, so that the unpleasant old Tulyan could not avoid cellular contact. For several moments he just looked at her cross-eyed, in such a comical manner that it made Eshaz smile. Several of the Elders tittered. Finally, Dabiggio waved a hand near her, and she flew back to Eshaz, where she landed on his open palm.

Dabiggio sat back in his chair, looking very displeased. But he said nothing more, and let others ask their questions. Every Tulyan knew that Dabiggio had long been angry over not being selected by his peers as First Elder. His resentment had gone on for hundreds of thousands of years, as he continued to find himself unable to secure the top job. Even so, he had enough political clout to remain on the Council, as the leader of the minority faction.

Now he seemed disinterested as the other Elders completed their questioning of Tesh and Eshaz, and dismissed them. Eshaz had long felt sorry for the unhappy Elder, the way he was always so miserable. Of late, though, that sympathy had turned into his own irritation.

CHAPTER FORTY-EIGHT

In this universe, it is undeniable that there are secrets within secrets, layered infinitely into Timeweb. As but one example, Jacopo Nehr may not have really discovered the secret of nehrcom transmissions; perhaps he only thought he did. Web-dependent nehrcoms, and web transmissions by other races, may only be the tip of the iceberg, or keys to the outermost layer of a puzzle box. There are intriguing legends that nano-creatures inhabit the web, living inside its strands. Are they yet another, undiscovered, galactic race, and are they responsible for instantaneous, cross-space transmissions?

—From a Tulyan study of cosmic mysteries

On board the space station orbiting Canopa, Jacopo Nehr sat in his office, awaiting an appointment with the Doge's attaché. From this utilitarian work space, provided for him by the government, the Supreme General gazed glumly out on the twinkling nighttime lights of Canopa's cities, visible through broken cloud formations.

He heard voices out in the corridor as people walked by. His office, like many of the rooms on the orbiter, had inadequate soundproofing, allowing noisy intrusions that irritated him and distracted him from his important work. In another linked module, the former classrooms constructed by Noah Watanabe and his Guardians had been converted into an exotic dining hall with a miniature forest around it. What a waste of space. But because of the insulating quality of the forest and the module itself, Nehr wished his office was in there instead, so that he could enjoy some peace and quiet.

The orbiter was like an immense child's toy, a maze of modules and tunnels that had been lifted into orbit and connected, some by the Guardians and many more by the Doge after he took over. Now it featured The Pleasure Palace Casino, a Grand Ballroom, an Audience Chamber, and royal apartments, along with other features . . . and more construction was ongoing.

In the public furor over her secret identity, Princess Meghina remained secluded in one of Doge Lorenzo's apartments, under his protection. After admitting in a brief broadcasted statement that she was in fact a Mutati (a damage control strategy recommended by the Doge's aides), she no longer appeared in public because of the outrage that would cause. People were evenly divided. A surprising number accepted her claim that she was more Human than Mutati, while others were deeply suspicious of her and critical of her royal protector.

Since retreating to the orbiter, Doge Lorenzo had become nervous and agitated, making him difficult to be around. Even though his new casino was generating tremendous profits, he kept worrying about more things that might go wrong, and had fallen into the habit of adding to the list of unfavorable possibilities each day and trying to take immediate actions to thwart them. Jacopo Nehr worried about his long-time friend, and felt tremendous loyalty toward him for the favors he had done for him.

Many of the modules contained thousands of the Doge's Red Beret troops, his personal contingent of the Merchant Prince Armed Forces. An elite group of Human and machine fighters, they were absolutely devoted to his protection, and remained close to him wherever he went.

One of the largest modules contained the Royal Court of the Doge, now only a shadow of its former grandeur on Timian One. Despite the proximity of the opulent casino in adjacent modules, it had become an exceedingly sober court, without the gaiety and fanfare of its predecessor, which seemed part of a bygone, halcyon era. Now the vast majority of members (and the patrons of the casino as well) were Human noblemen and ladies from Canopa, no longer such a melting pot with colorful characters from other planets. The only exceptions were a handful of aliens who happened to be on Canopa when podship travel was cut off.

Just then the door slid open and Pimyt marched in, carrying a valise under his arm. The Royal Attaché, with a haughty expression, slapped half a dozen communiqués on the desk, written on the Doge's parchment stationery. Tired of being a flunky for this furry little master of extortion, Jacopo wanted to refuse further cooperation. But as he looked at the irritatingly smug expression on the Hibbil's face, Jacopo knew that he had no choice, that he must keep transmitting the messages to other planets . . . or Pimyt would carry out his threat to reveal Jacopo's most precious trade secrets and ruin him. It was so difficult to deal with business matters, and so unfair, when he had other important duties to handle as the highest military commander.

"You will take care of these for me," Pimyt said.

The troubled general thumbed through the papers without focusing on them, wishing he could be anywhere else, far from there.

With podship travel cut off, Jacopo's financial situation had become precarious. His factories on the Hibbil Cluster Worlds could still export robots and other machine products, but not to the Merchant Prince Alliance . . . nor to the Mutati Kingdom, though Jacopo never dealt with the vile shapeshifters anyway. Interplanetary financial relationships, and the entire galactic monetary system, were far different now. Keeping him afloat, a number of banks had accepted his promissory notes sent by nehrcom, and he had leveraged himself in order to build new manufacturing facilities on Canopa. Other banks had given him deadlines, saying they would foreclose on properties that were within the reach of their agents, and orders would be sent out by nehrcom.

How ironic it would be, Jacopo thought, if his assets were seized because of orders sent via his own cross-space transceivers. For business reasons he had established his own nehrcom transmitting stations on Hibbil worlds, all under the strict built-in security system he had established for all installations, a system that would destroy the stations if anyone ever tried to tamper with their inner workings. He knew Pimyt had not learned how nehrcoms worked from any one of those facilities; it was an absolute impossibility. But something else had gone wrong, and the meddlesome little fur ball had learned the details anyway.

He focused on Pimyt's latest communiqués. One was to the Human-ruled planet of Renfa, ordering the disbanding of a squadron of attack spacecraft. In recent months Jacopo had been the conduit for other military and business messages from the attaché, and the general had assumed that Pimyt and his Hibbil friends were engaged in war profiteering, controlling contracts for the construction of new military bases and for the manufacturing of war materials, making exorbitant profits in the bargain. He assumed they might even be stealing weapons and selling them to neutral parties—not imagining that they would sell to anyone remotely associated with the Mutatis.

"You will take care of these for me," Pimyt repeated. "Do it tomorrow."

Jacopo nodded, then spun his chair and gazed out into the starry night sky. He heard the door slide open behind him, and the Hibbil muttering as he left.

Just then Jacopo heard the voice of his own daughter, Nirella, who entered the office. "What's wrong?" she asked.

He went to greet the stocky, middle-aged woman. "Nothing, nothing. Just the usual." He had to keep the shameful secret to himself, that he was being blackmailed.

"I wish you wouldn't work so late," she said. "I worry about you."

"Don't," he said, mustering a reassuring tone. He ushered her to the door. "I don't have that much more to do tonight."

"All right, Daddy," she said. Giving him a peck on the cheek, she departed, leaving him to his troubled thoughts. Staring off into space, he felt dismal, with very few connections to anything that made him happy. His daughter was one of the few remaining links to his earlier celebrated life.

In her early forties and unmarried, Nirella admired her father and worked closely with him. Few people knew that she co-discovered the nehrcom transceiver with him almost twenty years earlier. The two of them had been on a business trip to one of the Inner Planets, setting up distributors for Jacopo's precious-stone export business, one of his enterprises at the time. In that operation he had specialized in selling exotic, priceless gems. Following a long day of fruitless negotiations with the Wygeros who controlled that sector, Jacopo and Nirella had been going over their business plan in their spacetel suite. Suddenly they had stopped, as static and loud voices filled the air.

Close examination of the suite had revealed that they were, in fact, alone. But crawling around on the floor, Jacopo found the source of the noise, a tiny piece of translucent green stone that had lodged in the sole of one of his shoes. As he pulled the fragment free and held it up to the light, the fuzzy, staticky sounds had still come from it. Nirella had started to say something, but had fallen silent. Wisely, it turned out.

Both of them had recognized the green rock fragment as a substance their miners had only recently discovered on a remote planet . . . a deep-shaft emerald brought up by a drilling machine from more than fifty kilometers beneath the surface. Preliminary reports—made at their Canopa laboratory just before they departed for the Inner Planets—indicated it was harder than any known substance in the galaxy, with a crystalline, piezoelectric atomic structure. The voices they had been hearing in the spacetel room were those of their own company gemologists in the corporate laboratory far across space, talking about how rare the green stones were. The gemologists were speculating on what the market value of the newly discovered stones might be, and revealed a skimming operation they had been conducting, stealing precious gems from the corporation.

Kneeling beside her father, Nirella had exchanged startled glances with him, and neither of them had spoken while the static and voices continued. There were several things going on at once. Dishonest employees in sensitive positions were pilfering company assets, and somehow their duplicity was being communicated across more than a hundred light years of distance. Based upon outside events referred to in the distant conversations, it seemed to be *instantaneous* communication, too.

Simultaneously, Jacopo and his daughter had realized the immensity of what was occurring.

Without any doubt, instantaneous cross-space communication would be one of the most astounding, valuable discoveries in the history of the galaxy. But looking at his daughter, Jacopo realized that he was not alone in the knowledge. As he considered the immensity of this secret, the twenty-four-year-old woman unsheathed a stiletto from her waist and handed it to him. "Slit my throat quickly if you must," she said. "Do it the way I taught you."

Having developed potent fighting skills from an early age and honed them over the years, Nirella had been a reserve Red Beret captain at the time. She was his bodyguard as well as his business associate. He trusted her implicitly, but both of them knew that a secret of such magnitude was mind-boggling. Refusing to accept the weapon from her, he looked deep into her almond-shaped eyes, trying to see her soul, the part of her that would remain faithful through all temptations . . . or would betray him. Such a secret went beyond family blood. *Way beyond it.*

And he had told her to put the knife away. . . .

Citing a "personal emergency," Jacopo had subsequently canceled all further negotiations with the Wygeros and had caught the first outbound podship, accompanied by his daughter. Transferring twice en route, they reached Canopa in short order, and strode into the laboratory, surprising the gemologists. Nirella did her job well, cutting their throats without spilling any blood on the interesting new stones.

In ensuing weeks, Jacopo and his daughter performed their own experiments in secrecy, with each of them on a different planet, transmitting back and forth. In this manner, the optimum cuts and configurations of the emeralds were developed for perfect sound quality. Subsequently, Jacopo's miners found the special emeralds deep beneath the surface of other planets around the galaxy, and after testing them he took steps to provide security over all of the resources.

But even with all of the research they conducted, Jacopo and his daughter never figured out *how* the gems transmitted across such vast distances . . . only that they did. Ever since then, Jacopo had paid Nirella more than she had ever imagined it possible to earn. She became his equal partner in the enterprise, even though he took all of the credit for it in public, and strutted about like a great inventor.

She never seemed to mind, and for that, he loved her even more.

Chapter Forty-Nine

If you consider any question and its apparent answer, you will come to realize that you still have a lot more to think about. Profundity is only a function of the power of the mind.

—The Tulyan Conundrum

The Tulyan Starcloud was a planetary system at the edge of the galaxy, surrounded by weak suns. Concealed from them by mists during their previous stay in the orbiting Visitor's Center, Dux and Acey had only imagined what was down there, based on descriptions provided by the staff of the spacetel. But those words had been grossly inadequate for the wonders they beheld now as they returned from deep space, not coming close to what they were meant to describe.

The beauty made Dux gasp and stare in speechless wonder. It was an otherworldly place that no one could tell him and his cousin about; they had to see and experience it for themselves.

While Tulyan handlers took control of the podship herd, Eshaz said he would take the boys and Tesh on a tour around the starcloud. Tesh had refused to give up control of her podship, and had instead sealed the sectoid chamber in the way of her people and left the pod tethered to other vessels, floating in secure space, protected by the powerful energy shield of the strongest Tulyan mindlink ever conceived. Eshaz explained to his guests that Parviis had previously penetrated their security system, but that would not happen again. Every Tulyan on the starcloud was focused on this important assignment, and had created the most dense and unbreakable telepathic field in their history. It should be more than enough, Eshaz promised.

Following Eshaz onto a wingless, pencil-shaped vessel, Dux noticed a circle design etched into the hull, which the Tulyan said was the sacred sigil of his people. After seating his guests in the cabin, Eshaz activated the computerized pilot system, and the small ship took off. It made hardly any noise as it flew. Presently, they were flying between the three planets in the unusual solar system.

The legendary starcloud was unlike any place Dux and Acey had seen before, in all the travels they had made around the galaxy, on their vagabond adventures. The Tulyan lands over which they flew were pristine, a fairy tale realm of lovely meadows, sapphire-blue lakes, tall forests, and craggy, snow-clad mountains.

"Each night the skies are filled with comets and meteor showers," Eshaz said, "a truly remarkable ethereal display. Some of the heavenly travelers can be seen in the daytime as well, moving and flashing across the milky white backdrop of the starcloud."

"Sounds eerily beautiful," Dux said.

"It has that quality," the big Tulyan agreed. "We have a defensive system called the Tulyan mindlink, and it is said that some of our most powerful Elders actually hitch telepathic rides on comets and meteors, and ride them into space."

"Wow," Acey said. "Wish I could do that."

"You're probably not smart enough, cousin," Dux said. "And neither am I."

"Nor I," Eshaz said. "This universe is full of wondrous things you can never do, no matter how long your life is." He looked sadly at the boys, as if thinking of something he didn't want to say to them.

While the pencil-shaped vessel flew on, going in and out of the mists, Eshaz said his people did not live in cities. Rather, the four million inhabitants were widely separated in small settlements on the three gravitationally linked planets of the system. Tulyans lived quite simply, and one of the few examples of advanced technology they had was the starcloud transportation system they were using now.

"Thc sigil of your people, the circle design on the hull of this ship," Dux said. "What does it mean?"

"Everything in life goes in a circle," the Tulyan responded, "from life to death, from happiness to sadness, from beauty to chaos. We are all eternal beings, and yet we are not. Riddles and circles mirroring each other, truths and deeper truths, layers and layers of reality, all returning to a cosmic speck of singularity, a starting and ending point. That is what existence is all about, as my people have determined, with all of their collected wisdom."

Pausing, Eshaz added, "We Tulyans are a very ancient race, perhaps the first in the entire galaxy. We go far back, through the mists and veils of time."

Presently he brought the pencil ship down in a field of red and yellow flowers on the largest world of Tuly. Disembarking, he led them along a path to a knoll where he lived, a black, glassy structure overlooking an alpine lake that was surrounded by gnarled little trees.

"This is the finest spot in the entire universe," he announced, as he swung open a heavy door and went inside. "I am very fortunate, indeed."

The walls of his home, both inside and out, were of a deep black obsidian-like material. When sunlight glinted on it the hard surface became translucent and revealed glittering points of light deep in the surface. For Dux, it was like peering into the universe itself.

After dinner that evening they went outside, where fiery comets and meteors swept through the mists of the starcloud, seeming to put on a show just for them.

Far across the galaxy, Noah remained imprisoned at the Corp-One medical facility on Canopa. He had made numerous efforts to escape from the facility, and when the physical attempts had failed, he had resorted to mental excursions, using his powers in Timeweb. But those powers were nowhere near what they had once been, back in the days when he had been able to make mental leaps across space and pilot podships by remote telepathy . . . in the days before he advised Doge Lorenzo to set up sensor-guns at pod stations around the galaxy, to prevent deadly Mutati military ventures. The shapeshifters had been using a terrible weapon they transported in schooners aboard podships. Entire merchant prince planets had been blown to oblivion, scattered into space dust. Drastic measures had been required, and Noah had been at the center of the effort.

As a result, several podships had been destroyed by sensor-guns. Circumstantial evidence suggested to him that the sentient spaceships had detected his culpability in the matter, and had taken steps to block his access to the cosmic web. Such efforts (if they occurred) had not been entirely successful, since Noah had still been able to burst out into the cosmos, for paranormal journeys. But his efforts had been erratic, unpredictable, and very frustrating.

Now, after exhausting himself for hours in such efforts, he lay on a cot in his locked room, and found that he was caught in yet another locked room, a nightmare of the mind. In the dream he was trapped in a deep hole, with a huge Digger machine towering over him, piling dirt on top of him. Tesh Kori was at the controls of the machine, laughing fiendishly as she buried him.

Noah screamed, but to no avail as she piled more dirt on. Somehow, even with the scooping activity he could still see her, and still retained a glimmer of life. He howled at her in protest, "How can you do this to me? Don't you know I love you?"

The roar of machinery drowned out his words, and then he heard only the ominous sound of dirt being piled on top of him. Darkness flooded him. He was completely buried. Moments of horror passed, in which he wished he could die, but somehow he did not. Then he sensed something opening up beneath him. The planetary crust cracked, and he tumbled into a deep, stygian void, a frozen vault of time.

He remembered hearing legends of another galaxy beneath his own, and as he tumbled into the unknown he felt chilled to the very depths of his soul. Various races called it the "undergalaxy," the place of eternal damnation.

Struggling with every last ounce of strength that he possessed, Noah flailed his arms and slammed into something. He woke up, and in the low light he saw that he was back in the CorpOne room again. His left arm throbbed where he had struck a side table, knocking it over.

Was this better than the nightmare his mind had displayed? Both scenarios were dismal, and offered him no respite. Not even death.

Chapter Fifty

"Every time you make a decision you are taking a gamble. In fact, the apparent act of not making a decision is really a decision per se, and is thus inherently a gamble. Since there is no way to escape risk, the only course is to embrace it."

—Remarks of Lorenzo del Velli,
Grand Opening of The Pleasure Palace

"Even from captivity, he has made a fool of you," Francella said. She sat with Lorenzo in the dining hall of the space station, surrounded by the miniature forest of dwarf oak and bluebark canopa pines that her brother had planted. "His Guardians attack us at will, then go into hiding. They're causing a lot of damage, ruining industrial facilities and other key assets."

"A classic guerrilla war," Lorenzo observed. "Not easy for a military power to fight. It can go on for years."

Leaning close to a cup of iced mocaba juice, the Doge inhaled, causing a narrow stream of brown liquid to rise from the cup through a narrow, invisible energy tube. A decadent manner of drinking, requiring hardly any effort, but he seemed to find it amusing.

"If you would stop playing with your gadgets," she huffed, "we might make progress in this little war." With a sneer, Francella lifted her own cup of mocaba and drank it in the conventional fashion after deactivating the energy tube. She tasted the sharp, cold flavor.

Something caught her eye in the woods, a movement that seemed unusual. Not birds or the small forest creatures that had been transplanted to the orbital enclave. A faint mist drifting in the air? She rubbed her eyes. When she looked in that direction again, nothing appeared to be out of the ordinary.

"I do not *play* at war," he said, a hurt and angry expression on his face.

"But it goes on for too long. If you dedicated more effort to rooting out the evil, it would end. Why do you go easy on your enemies?" Beyond the Doge, she saw small, speedy birds flitting from branch to branch, kept separate from the dining hall by an invisible electronic barrier.

"You are mistaken. I want nothing more than to end this nuisance, this swatting of gnats. But your brother's forces—led by his adjutant—are a crafty lot, and have their own robotic forces."

Pausing, Lorenzo looked at her closely, an inquisitive expression on his face. "You do not look well, my dear."

That morning, she'd had makeup applied artfully by a personal servant, but obviously it was not enough to conceal the ravages of her ailment. Rage seeped into every cell and atom of her body. Somehow her brother had lured her into his spider web, and caused her to take the blood that would kill her. A deadly trick, and he had the immortal gift of being able to regrow his body, a gift that had undoubtedly been denied to her.

Thoughts of revenge filled her. If she could not kill him, she wanted to destroy everything he had built in his lifetime, all of his plans, his hopes, and his dreams, turning them into a nightmarish charnel pile. Everything would die that he had worked for, and he would be left a broken shell, never able to escape his eternal confinement.

"I want the Guardians annihilated," she demanded. "They killed my father and destroyed CorpOne headquarters."

"It will be done," the merchant prince leader promised.

"Immediately!"

"Of course. Now I want you to see a doctor."

"All right," she said. But she did not see what good it would do. . . .

In ensuing weeks the Red Berets, and especially Jimu's machine forces, stepped up their activities. All over Canopa, people were arrested and brutally interrogated. It was something Jimu did well.

Having been banished to the Inn of the White Sun by the machine officers on Ignem, the feisty little robot Ipsy pressed on. Despite the large amount of money he had garnered from his clever business operations, the officers had been paying little attention to him, and had rejected his offers of financial assistance to build a bigger army. He could not understand why, as military robots, they cared nothing for increasing the power and might of their forces. Without Thinker to guide them, they were only stupid machines, with no direction or sense of purpose. They just marched around down on the surface of the planet and engaged in foolish skirmishes.

Yet, through hard work and an aggressive marketing strategy, Ipsy impressed the civilian leadership of the Inn. As a consequence, they promoted him to the directorship of the Inn of the White Sun. Very quickly, the little machine grew increasingly officious and ordered much larger civilian robots around in a gruff tone, demanding excellence from them. Under his management, the Inn was becoming more popular than ever, even though few Human or Mutati travelers journeyed there anymore, because of the limitations on space travel.

Chapter Fifty-One

Consider sight. No matter what you gaze upon, there is always something beyond, something unseen. Consider the other senses as well, and every thought, and you will see it is true for them as well.

—Noah Watanabe

Now that Francella Watanabe knew she was dying, her surroundings took on an entirely different cast . . . more harsh and glaring, with hardly any noticeable loveliness or color. She could not imagine ever enjoying anything again, the beauty of music, the taste of fine wine, or laughter among friends.

She felt that way about the soft dawn pastels that flooded across the sky now, which provided her with little enjoyment at all, certainly not enough to divert her from her bleak emotions. Essentially numb to her surroundings, Francella tried to walk up a walkway toward CorpOne's largest medical laboratory building, but her steps were arthritic and painful. Every joint and muscle in her body ached. Even at this early hour, Dr. Bichette had better be there, as she had demanded. She had telebeamed him in the middle of the night with her orders, but he had sounded remote and peculiar, not his usual cooperative, obedient self.

All the pleasures of life seemed to have been taken from her prematurely, and it did not seem fair to her. Francella was not dead yet, and by rights such things should not be taken from her until the very last moment of her existence, and her last gasp of breath, which should have been many years from now.

On a deep level, she knew that she had been dying ever since she took her first lungful of air, more than thirty-eight years ago. Every mortal in the galaxy was given a death sentence at birth. The only question was when they would succumb to the frailties of the flesh, and under what circumstances. It was all so uneven, and so cruelly unpredictable within a predictable framework, the distinct limitations of the bodily container.

She wanted to lash out at everything and everyone, to be even harder on people than she had been before, but somehow that seemed purposeless to her at the moment, and might even increase her unhappiness. Perhaps if she had been a more pleasant person, it occurred to her now, the Supreme Being might have blessed her with a less demanding, far happier life. But the difficulties she had experienced since her childhood had made her the way she was today, had molded the hard edges of her personality. She had only reacted to challenging situations, the primary of which had been the curse of having a brother like Noah. From the beginning, their father had favored her fraternal twin over her, giving him a charmed life while cruelly shunting her aside. As a result she had been forced to assert herself and develop a strong personality, one that could not be trampled upon.

Nonetheless, deep in her soul she had a sensitive side. And with death staring her in the face, she was terrified.

Francella limped into the laboratory's coffee shop, where she had told Bichette to meet her. To her relief the doctor was there, accepting a large cup of mocaba from a machine. In a slow, sleepy voice, he said, "This is already my second cup, but it doesn't seem to be doing much good."

"Huh." She stared at him, didn't get anything for herself. He drank nervously, and seemed to be avoiding eye contact with her, as if afraid to anger her by focusing on the obvious—that she appeared to have aged ten years in only a few weeks. She hadn't bothered to wear makeup today, and knew the effect must be startling to him. The muscles in her legs ached from the walk.

Finally, he glanced at her and asked, "Are you ready?"

"That's why I'm here." Her voice creaked and she felt tired, overburdened with her problems.

"Of course."

They walked side by side down the corridor, saying nothing, encountering no one at this hour except for one of the maintenance men, wearing coveralls and a tool belt. The man looked at her oddly as she hobbled along painfully, and she stared him down.

The examination went much as she had anticipated, a numbing blur of probing instruments and medical jargon coming from Bichette's mouth. Essentially, she was taking this man into her confidence in revealing her physical debility to him. But she had no one else to turn to on this important health matter, no one else to give her advice. Though she had never admitted as much to him, she considered Bichette something akin to a friend. For years he had served her father and CorpOne well, as more than a mere doctor or the director of CorpOne's Medical Research Division. But friendships were not something Francella had cultivated in her life. There had been no time. Other matters had been more pressing, more immediate, and she'd had to put certain things on the shelf of someday.

Now she felt the loss, and very much alone.

After checking her blood, cellular activity, and vital signs, and comparing them with earlier readings, Dr. Bichette gave her the bad news, which was not unexpected: "You are the same blood type as your brother, but for some reason the injection of his blood is causing you to age prematurely, like a progerian. Your cells are breaking down too quickly."

"Is there an antidote?" she asked, weakly.

"None that I know of. It would be nice if we could reverse the procedure you did, removing your brother's blood and all of its effects from your body, but I know of no way to accomplish that."

"You would like to lecture me for my impulsiveness," she said with a menacing glare, "but *don't.*"

He nodded.

"Come with me," she ordered. Limping, she led the way to Noah's quarters, which were an entire section of the laboratory. By the time they got there, lab technicians were arriving, beginning to check equipment and charts, laying out the tests and procedures they would conduct on him today.

Francella saw her brother sitting in a comfortable chair, calmly reading a holobook that floated in front of his eyes. He looked fully recovered now, even completely unscarred, and this infuriated her.

Feeling increasingly frustrated, she wanted to do him serious harm, in any way she could. Across a speaker system, she spoke to him, in a voice cracking with emotion. "You tricked me, didn't you? I did exactly what you expected, taking your blood, and you knew what would happen to me. I'm dying. Does that make you happy?"

He shoved the holo book to one side (where it continued to float in the air) and then stared at her, his face emotionless. "Listen to me carefully," he said. "You have everything to do with your problems, and I have nothing to do with them. Just because you have always resented me, and you have always distrusted me, does not make your feelings rational. I have never done anything to you."

"You always got the best from Daddy, and I got the dregs."

"You're blaming me for *his* actions?"

"I blame you for taking what he gave you when we were growing up, and enjoying it, without once thinking of me."

The remark struck home. She saw him flinch, and think about it.

On a rack by him, she saw some of Noah's severed body parts in cryogen tubes, awaiting further tests. She had cut all that skin and bone off him, but had been unable to finish him off. Like a lizard with a bottomless reservoir of regenerative matter, he kept growing everything back.

Turning to Dr. Bichette, who stood at her side, she ordered him to take a vial of blood from her and inject it in Noah. A bit of revenge. As she gave the command, she made sure the speaker system remained on, and watched her brother for a reaction. But he went back to reading his holobook, looking entirely relaxed.

She tried to control her anger.

Shaking his head, the doctor said, "Noah is a medical miracle, unlike any case ever recorded. You should not interfere with his cellular functions."

"I already did, when I cut him up. This is just a different procedure."

He looked alarmed. "You are not qualified to make medical decisions."

"In case you haven't been paying attention, Doctor, my family corporation owns this medical laboratory and everything that's in it, including you . . . and Noah."

She had used the term "family corporation," and this gave her pause. It was owned by a family of *one* now . . . Francella herself.

Summoning a medical technician, Francella repeated the command to her, to make the blood transfer. The aide looked at Dr. Bichette. Reluctantly, he nodded. They all went inside the room with Noah, where the aide took three vials of blood from Francella.

Her brother showed no reaction whatsoever when a technician made the first dermex injection in his forearm. Within seconds, his arm turned dark red, then black. Noah looked totally unconcerned. In five minutes, the arm fell away, a gory mass on the floor. He hardly looked at it. On his body, the limb began to regrow.

In fascination, the doctor and his staff watched, along with Francella.

"The rest of his body is rejecting the injection," Bichette said, "keeping the poison away."

"Poison?" Francella snapped.

He leaned close to her and whispered, "No offense intended, but your blood is tainted. You know that."

Struggling to retain her composure, Francella ordered additional injections on different parts of Noah's body. In a flurry, trying to please her, the staff did as she wished.

But each time it was exactly the same. Portions of her brother's flesh changed color and fell away, but soon began to regrow, replacing lost mass mysteriously.

"Sorcery," Francella said.

"You cannot harm him," Bichette said at last. He watched her warily, maintaining his distance from her.

"I can keep him locked up for the rest of his life."

"You mean for the rest of *our* lives. He is likely to outlive his jailers." The doctor looked at her oddly, in a way that Francella did not like, as if measuring the remainder of her lifespan.

While Francella considered the situation, it occurred to her what a curious pair of twins she and her brother were, with her aging rapidly and him reconstituting himself at an incredible pace, growing new cells even as hers were decaying.

"Your life may be shorter than mine, Doctor," Francella said in a menacing, creaking tone, "if you don't find a cure for me."

Chapter Fifty-Two

> Beginnings and endings: we pay so much attention to them, and yet, we do not really see. It is said that even gods must begin someplace, and end as well. But such reference points are not the sharp demarcations we think they are; they only seem to occur when we *notice* them. Before that, and afterward, there is a continuous flow of one thing leading to another, and back around again. It is the flow of time and space and wonder. It is the flow of joy and sadness.
>
> —Noah Watanabe, *Drifting in the Ether* (unpublished notes)

As his name suggested, Thinker had spent much of his life in contemplation, and was not known as a robot of action.

There had been exceptions, such as the times he had led his robot troops in practice battle maneuvers on Ignem, but that had not been his forte. Rather, he had a proven knack for gathering information and organizing it in his ever-expanding data banks. For some time now, he had been searching unsuccessfully for facts about the whereabouts of Noah Watanabe, but most of it had been rumors. In the robot's own data banks, he had the earlier download of the contents of Noah's brain, but that was of little help in determining where others were hiding him.

He also kept running through details of the strange experience in which Noah had seemed to come to life in the simulation that Thinker carried with him in his robot torso. Most peculiar, and most unexplainable, except he kept coming back to the probability that said it had something to do with the cosmic infrastructure that spanned space and time.

Thinker's information on that paranormal realm was sketchy at best, but it seemed clear that Noah Watanabe had a connection with it—or *thought* he did—that enabled him to enter and leave it on both a physical and ethereal basis. The robot had a difficult time comprehending anything that was not entirely tangible, but supposedly Master Noah could project his mind out into the far galaxy. Unfortunately, the Guardian leader might only be imagining that, from a unique form of Human insanity. One thing was certain. The whole concept of Timeweb was most peculiar, indeed.

Concerning Master Noah's location, the robot had other sources of information. The day before, he received a reported sighting of Noah as a passenger under restraint in a blue-and-silver security vehicle, the colors of CorpOne. He had already added this to all of the other information on the Guardian leader in his robotic data banks. This, when added to the earlier information, enabled Thinker to run a decent probability program. He had done this once before on Noah, before the two of them ever met. At the time, Thinker had been searching the galaxy to find him and the Guardians, so that the cerebral robot and his followers could join the group of eco-warriors. Now the search area was much smaller—Canopa and nearby planets—but the situation was far more urgent. Master Noah was in danger.

The new probability program pinpointed Noah. He had to be in the CorpOne medical laboratory complex.

Now he opened up Noah's simulation, causing his image to appear on the robot's torso screen.

Glancing down at the screen, though he could "see" the image without doing so, Thinker said, "Greetings, Master Noah. You will be pleased to learn that we know where you are now, and that we have set in motion a plan for your rescue."

"A *good* plan, I hope," the simulation said.

"Even better. An excellent one. We embark tonight."

"I am pleased to hear that."

"One thing, though, Master Noah. I have burned through my circuitry trying to understand the unusual properties of the realm you call Timeweb."

"Au contraire, my metal friend. *I* did not make up that name. It is already long-established."

"Of course. I was only using what you Humans call a figure of speech. It has occurred to me that I should perhaps make a further effort to comprehend Timeweb before we make the rescue attempt. After all, you seem to have both physical and mental properties that are extraordinary, and the more data we have the better. I am running through more programs as we speak."

"And you expect me to give you something new? But you know I can only reveal what I knew when you used the organic interface to download the contents of my mind."

"Logically, that is so. But there was a recent episode when you—the simulation—seemed to come to life. Subi and I saw a strange mist dart into your image and disappear. At that very moment, your eyes and face seemed to become more animated. I have confirmed that this occurred, Master Noah, but there is no explanation for it . . . and you spoke words that were not in my operating circuits."

"Am I speaking such words now?"

"No. I know what you are going to say a fraction of a second ahead of time."

"So, it is as if you are talking to yourself?"

"That statement has no relevance in a mind of my caliber

and complexity. Many times, one portion of my circuitry will 'talk' with another portion—or portions—of it. There is no Human correlation that you would be likely to understand."

"With the exception of insanity. From your probes, I see that you have investigated that with respect to my mind."

"As I should. Just one of the possibilities that I must explore."

"And your conclusion?"

"I do not have enough information about Timeweb to offer a conclusion, but all indications are that the ethereal realm does in fact exist. It could be true that the realm exists but you are still—pardon me for saying so—mentally unbalanced. Sanity is not an exact science with Human beings. It is more a matter of coping and balance. All of you seem to have aberrations."

"No argument about that."

I will leave your simulation operable for a while, but you do not look animated, as you were before."

"Are you going to leave me on during the rescue, too? That would be odd, me rescuing myself."

"My analysis tells me to shut off your programming before we leave, to keep things less confusing. We don't want a circumstance where you think you must take charge of the operation. No, Master Noah, in this instance I must override you."

"For my own good."

"Exactly."

"See you soon, then. Good luck."

"And good luck to you, Master."

That evening, Thinker and a small band of robotic commandos waited in the darkness outside the largest laboratory building. Transmitting an electronic signal, Thinker read the security code, disabled it and hurried through, ahead of the others.

Scanning forward, the robots disabled the motion and sound

detectors and all pressure pads in the corridor, then surged onward, making surprisingly little noise for mechanical men. Thinker had designed this squad for stealth, and had fitted everyone with sound-softening mechanisms for their moving parts. Two Human guards were struck with stun darts, and slumped at their posts as the robots hurried past them.

Through the glax wall of a room, Thinker saw the Guardian leader lying on a bed, in low light. As if sensing something, Noah opened his eyes, even though the commandos made virtually no noise.

The robots had no way of knowing it, but Noah had been lying awake in his cell with his eyes closed, feeling trapped and dismal. Moments before the arrival of the commandos, he had been engaged in a mental struggle, and had succeeded in entering the paranormal realm of Timeweb. But as he vaulted into the heavens and tried to connect with podships, they had scattered away from him yet again, fleeing into space. Wherever he went, however he tried, it was the same. The podships avoided him like a dread disease.

At one time Noah's sojourns into the cosmic domain had been welcome respites for him, an exhilarating means of refreshing his mind. He had piloted podships by remote control, but he couldn't do that anymore. Not even close. The glorious experiences were gone, lingering only in his memory.

Then, sensing something, Noah opened his eyes just as the commandos burst into his room.

Another form of escape had become available to him.

Accompanied by the robots, Noah hurried into the corridor, in bare feet and pajamas. "Let's go!" he said.

The squad ran down the corridor with him in their midst, forming a protective metal cocoon around him.

Just before exiting the building, Thinker placed an incendiary bomb, and set the timer.

Francella's villa overlooking the Valley of the Princes had several interesting features, one of which she had discovered only recently. Accessed through a hidden doorway, she'd found a large sealed chamber cut into the cliffside beneath the villa, a sparse room with a hundred comfortable chairs fronting a podium and a transceiver box hanging from the ceiling. Documents left in the room said it was a nehrcom relay station her father had set up for corporate reasons, to keep critical business operations secret, and he had paid the Nehrs handsomely for it. The facility came with Jacopo Nehr's impregnable, built-in security system.

To her delight she'd discovered that the equipment was still operational, so she had arranged for a virtual conference that was about to begin. At her invitation half a dozen noblemen sat in chairs fronting the podium, wearing elegant surcoats and leggings.

Switching on the system from the podium, Francella saw holo projections fill the rest of the room, additional chairs with noblemen from all over the galaxy either in them, or taking their seats. In addition to these projected nobles were the ones from Canopa who actually sat in front of her.

As the meeting progressed, Francella noted that the video clarity was even worse than usual, as it flickered on and off. The audio quality—always crystal clear before—was poor as well, with bursts of static and brief, irritating periods of dead silence. All of the attendees were noble-born princes, some of whom were openly critical of Lorenzo the Magnificent's governmental policies.

Over the nehrcom transmission the dignitaries voiced several complaints about this. Then a plump man in their midst, Prince

Giancarlo Paggatini, said from his projected image, "Some nobles believe in you, Francella, while others are only here on fact-finding missions, to see what you're all about. I'm one of the latter."

"Please believe me," she said. "I want to see a reversion to old ways, before the Doge began appointing princes without regard to their ancestry. He has forsaken the tried and true ways, abandoning the traditions that have always formed the cornerstones of our civilization."

"But you are a commoner yourself," Paggatini said. "Your father was one of Lorenzo's appointees, and you've always been . . . close . . . to the Doge. Why should we believe you?"

"Because I no longer believe in Lorenzo. He must have known that Princess Meghina was a Mutati and concealed it, the liar. It's a scandal! He denies knowing, but how can anyone trust him after this? And after what he's done to all of you, denying you your birthrights."

The conference participants conversed back and forth across the galactic link, discussing all the reasons they despised Doge Lorenzo. In loud, angry voices they complained that he was awarding appointments that belonged to princes, and hiding a Mutati. In addition, he was focusing too much of his efforts on his luxurious orbital casino, The Pleasure Palace, while neglecting important matters in the Merchant Prince Alliance.

"It's more like the Plunder Palace," a tall prince with a monocle quipped, eliciting the laughter of his companions. "He's profiting at our expense." This was Santino Aggi, a notorious drinker who slurred his words now, as he often did.

"It's his fault the nehrcom isn't working right, too," another nobleman said.

As the conference nehrcom continued far into the night, Francella and the princes discussed options for dealing with Doge Lorenzo. Ultimately the conversation turned to getting rid of him, one way or another.

"There is one more thing to discuss," Francella said, having waited for just the right moment to bring it up. "Some of you have heard about what happened at the pod station, when I shot Noah and he healed, right in front of our eyes. Just before that, a young man shouted at me to stop. He called me 'Mother.' We had him arrested, and he is still locked up."

"Anton Glavine," Giancarlo Paggatini said.

"That's right. He really is my son, and Lorenzo is his father. The implications are clear. We have the next Doge, the one who is entitled to the position by his bloodline."

"The princes are not obligated to choose a Doge's son," Paggatini said, his cheeks reddening. "If Lorenzo abdicates . . . or dies . . . we can elect someone else."

"But we're here to uphold tradition, aren't we?" she said. "And primogeniture is one of the oldest traditions in the Alliance, the eldest son taking over the duties of his father. Anton deserves the chance. Anton *del Velli.*"

"We need to think about this," Paggatini said.

"What about Anton's political views?" another asked. "Who will he appoint to high offices?"

"I can keep him in line," Francella said.

"He'll appoint nobles to high office instead of commoners?"

"He will," she said, assuming that Anton—as the son of nobility himself—would be inclined to agree with her views on this issue. All she'd heard about him indicated that he was a decent person and she thought he'd eventually forgive her. No matter the unkind words he'd spoke to her; she had seen something more gentle in his eyes, perhaps a longing for his mother. And she had to admit to herself, she'd been feeling an increasing maternal instinct toward him herself. This made her want him to do well.

As they discussed Anton, and Francella continued to expound

his real and purported virtues, a number of the noblemen began to warm to the idea of him as Doge. This pleased Francella immensely. Just as she had hoped, they were beginning to rally around Anton del Velli as a figurehead. She had financial reasons for her political plans, as she expected to receive a generous share of her son's tax collections . . . money she needed badly.

Though Francella Watanabe had concealed it with deft manipulation of financial records, CorpOne—the late Prince Saito's pride and joy—was near bankruptcy. While her father was still alive, she had drained the assets of his company, transferring a large amount of money off-planet and converting it to hard assets in her own name—assets that were rightfully hers, but which were subsequently lost in the destruction of Timian One. To make matters worse, the unrelenting Guardian attacks on her Canopan operations were cutting so deeply into profits that she could not make the payments on huge operational loans that she'd had to take out.

The following morning Francella received the bad news about Noah's escape from her medical facility, and the destruction of the main building. Already, Noah was sending telebeam broadcasts around Canopa, trying to rally more people to his cause.

Furious, Francella confronted Dr. Hurk Bichette in front of the smoking ruins. He shook with fear for his life. "I assure you that we can still find a cure for you," he said.

"And how do you intend to support your research, when my brother's dismembered body parts, along with blood and tissue samples, were destroyed in the fire?"

"We have you," he said, "and the secret lies somewhere in your blood, in your cellular degeneration."

"The *secret,*" she said, in a dejected tone. "Noah's body regenerated from a mass of cellular material, after I cut him into a thousand pieces. I ask you this in your precious research: How does he do it? Sorcery?"

"We'll find out."

"Noah and I are twins," she said, her voice suddenly determined. "If he can do it, I should be able to, too."

Dr. Bichette did not reply. He stared glumly into the embers of the medical building.

Chapter Fifty-Three

I asked the Master if we should do something more to ensure the silence of Anton Glavine, and he paled at the suggestion. Then he reddened with anger, and said to me: "My nephew would never reveal the location of our hidden headquarters, not even under torture. I have looked into the heart of the man, and he is pure and loyal. He is as dedicated to our cause as any of my followers."

—Security Log, entry of Subi Danvar

Standing in front of the screen on Thinker's chest, Noah looked at the 3-D color likeness of him that the robot had fashioned He and the machine leader stood inside one of the robot-assembly chambers at the Guardians' underground headquarters. It was late morning, but sunlight did not penetrate to this level. Nonetheless, Noah felt upbeat, with renewed vigor.

"So you've been running the show in my absence, eh?" Noah said to the electronic simulacrum. "Why couldn't you . . . or should I say, *didn't* you . . . do more to locate me?"

"I do not know what you mean," the image said, lifting its chin haughtily.

"Is it possible you didn't want to find me, so that you could take over my leadership position?"

"I did no such thing! You of all people should know that is not in my character. I am motivated only by honor and duty!"

Looking on, Subi Danvar laughed out loud, and even Thinker

vibrated a little, his programmed equivalent of amusement.

"Everyone has a dark side," Noah said thoughtfully. "Perhaps it took a computer simulation to find mine." He scratched his head. "I wonder."

"Why don't we discuss something that makes sense?" the facsimile asked in an indignant tone. "Why don't you ask me where Tesh is? You've been thinking about her, haven't you?"

"Well, where is she, then?"

"Tesh is with Eshaz and those two teenage cousins, Acey and Dux. According to the last report, they are at the Tulyan Starcloud. I know this because Eshaz sends information to one of the handful of Tulyan Guardians in our employ, a female named Zigzia, and she passes it on to us. In your absence, we learned that they call her a 'webtalker,' and she utilizes some ancient means of communication, presumably involving the galactic infrastructure. Zigzia is one of the younger Tulyans, only three hundred thousand years old. Why, just yesterday she—"

"Enough!" Noah said. "I don't babble like that. There is a defect in your programming."

"The copy is just nervous in your presence," Thinker interjected. "He only wants to please you."

"The information about Zigzia is correct," Subi said. "As a security measure, I pressed the Tulyan Council and got the information—but only on a sketchy basis, without details."

"Interesting," Noah said. Then, staring at the screen, he added, "Maybe this really is my dark side, with all of my latent defects revealed."

"The dark side is always associated with the flesh," the facsimile said, raising his voice. "And as you can see, I have none."

"An intriguing argument," Noah agreed. "However, I think

it's time for Thinker to update you with another download from me."

"Perhaps it should be two-way," said the face on the screen. "I know things you don't."

"No thanks," Noah said. "I'll have Thinker analyze your data and give me a report." And to the robot he said, "Shall we, my friend?"

"As you wish, Master." Thinker closed the panel on his chest, and brought out the organic interface tentacle, with its glistening array of needles.

Doge Lorenzo del Velli was making a lot of money from his orbital gambling resort and casino. Earlier that morning his architects had modified plans for an enlargement of the facility, and the redline schematics appeared on a screen built into the top of his desk. A set of computer keys and touch pads enabled him to make notes on the screen, which were transmitted to his staff for immediate action. Looking up, he watched through his office window as two modules were floated into position by spacetugs and locked in place.

Urgent demands from Francella Watanabe sat on his desk, asking for even more Red Beret action against her brother's Guardians, who continued to make attacks on her Canopan operations. He shook his head. She had been especially foolish to allow Noah's escape and lose a large medical laboratory. He wished he had not given her full control over the prisoner, but she had been quite insistent . . . and it had been her brother, after all. Now the rebellion could only escalate, with its titular head back in charge.

Barking a command into a speaker, Lorenzo delegated Francella's requests to his Royal Attaché. The Hibbil would take care of them in his usual efficient fashion, leaving the Doge to attend to more interesting matters. Looking back at the desktop screen, he made some additional notations on the schematics, where he thought more gambling machines could be fitted in. Already his casino was immense, but demand was high and he didn't want to miss any opportunity to maximize profits.

His architectural instructions were heeded. But on the other matter his Hibbil attaché sent only lackluster instructions to Canopan military and police commanders, telling them to "look into" Francella's request.

Where the Adurians were widely known for their biotech laboratories, the Hibbils were known for providing efficient manufacturing facilities, and especially for the low-cost machines they produced in large quantities on their worlds. In his own office next to that of the Doge, Pimyt envisioned a Hibbil torture machine that he intended to hook up to Jacopo, Francella, and even Lorenzo. If only there weren't so many delays and unexpected problems.

Working undercover (Hibbils on Human worlds and Adurians on Mutati worlds), the conspirators had been planning to overthrow them and take over. Years ago, in an initial effort to destabilize the Mutati leadership, the Hibbils' Adurian "allies" had cleverly insinuated gyroscopic "decision-making" devices on the shapeshifters, causing them to pursue foolish military actions against the Humans . . . actions that focused their political and military energies in the wrong direction, away from the true threat . . . and were destined to fail.

In order to give the Mutatis a false sense of accomplishment, the Hibbil-Adurian cabal had caused decisions to be made that resulted in the destruction of Mars, Earth, and Plevin Four. The later obliteration of Timian One, however, was not supposed to have occurred . . . and was an expensive mistake, since the Hibbils were supposed to take that wealthy planet as a war prize. This caused considerable friction between the conspirators.

Under great pressure, the Adurians assured the Hibbils that they would take care of the problem through minor adjustments to the Zultan Abal Meshdi's gyrodome and to the portable gyros used by the populace—accomplished through undetectable electronic signals. The Adurians were insistent that it would not happen again, and in recompense they offered to transfer certain Mutati assets from the Adurian side of the ledger to the Hibbil side, after the Human and Mutati governments were overrun by combined Hibbil and Adurian military forces.

Then podship travel had been cut off mysteriously, and Pimyt had gone through a period in which he had been out of contact with his conspirators on distant worlds, since he had not wanted to risk sending nehrcom messages from the Merchant Prince Alliance to transceivers that should not even exist in other star systems. Eventually he had been able to set up a relay system in which he sent coded messages to other MPA planets, and they were in turn relayed to HibAdus on other planets. The arrangements had been complex—requiring much more than the customary bribes, promises, and threats—but he had accomplished it, so that intermittent messages could be sent back and forth.

When the communication links resumed, Pimyt learned that the Mutatis had discovered how to clone podships in the laboratory, and that the crazed, hate-filled Zultan had been using the lab-pods to send Demolios against Human targets. Gyro manipulation had not altered his thoughts, since his loathing for Humans was too deeply entrenched. Fortunately, the lab-pods had serious navigation malfunctions, and there'd been no strikes. Just a lot of effort and fanfare. But just by sheer luck, Abal Meshdi might eventually hit a valuable target, or his scientists might solve the technological glitches.

After conferring with the Hibbils, the Coalition had been able to use gyro manipulations to force Mutati scientists to make complex adjustments to all artificial pods being produced, so that their guidance systems could never work. Thus Meshdi's psychological need to attack Human targets was fulfilled, but it would never amount to anything; he could not cause any significant damage.

With the infiltration of Mutati lab-pod facilities, the Coalition accomplished something more. They learned how the cloning process worked for lab-pods, so that they could begin to make their own lab-pods on Hibbil and Adurian worlds. In conjunction with that, they had the Hibbils design navigation systems that actually worked, guiding the vessels across the vast distances of space. The Hibbils had also been able to fit customized fixtures into selected vessels, so that they were more useful as warships, or so that some of them were more comfortable than others.

But through it all, even with these successes the Coalition remained troubled as to why podship travel had been cut off to and from all Human and Mutati worlds. No one had any idea how that could have happened . . . and, if not for this unfortunate circumstance, the secret plan of the Coalition would certainly have been completed by now. They had their lab-pods, but it was taking time to grow the new fleet.

Pimyt was a key player in the Hibbil side of the arrangement, which bore some similarities with the Adurian program. Humans were by far the largest consumers of Hibbil machines, and many of those units—even the ones manufactured by Jacopo Nehr's factories on the Cluster Worlds and shipped out prior to the podship crisis—contained (without Jacopo's knowledge) certain subtleties that would in time turn them against Humans. Pimyt smiled at the thought. Even the sensor-guns that had been connected on short notice to pod stations throughout the Merchant Prince Alliance were not for the benefit of Humans.

They were to protect the planets for the conquerors.

Chapter Fifty-Four

Ultimately everything is happenstance, isn't it? You can take steps to accomplish a particular goal, and you think you are improving the odds of success, even ensuring the result you want. But it is not really so. There is always something out there that you cannot possibly anticipate, a monster waiting to crush your hopes and dreams.

—Anonymous, from Lost Earth

On the pod station orbiting the Mutati homeworld of Paradij, the Zultan Abal Meshdi led a prayer service, attended by a throng of his people, who stood in silence on the sealed walkways of the station.

He, like everyone present for this traditional religious holiday, wore a simple white gown, and they all had minigyro mechanisms on their foreheads. It was nighttime, and in the low natural light cast by the pod station the gyros threw eerie VR-light on the faces of the participants. His voice came across speakers to the assemblage, many of whom could only see him on projection cameras.

Every square centimeter of the pod station was packed with fleshy Mutatis, and some of those who could not fly overhead used their shapeshifting abilities to make themselves more comfortable, turning into a variety of creatures that could climb walls and windows, or hang from ceilings. Today was the Feast of Paradij, honoring the occasion centuries ago when nomadic

Mutatis first settled on the most sacred of all planets.

As was his right, the Zultan had selected this holy day for yet another Demolio launch against the enemy—hoping that a spill-over of blessings from God-on-High during the celebration would aid the war effort.

The previous launch against the merchant prince planet of Siriki, and recent attempts against other enemy worlds, had been unsuccessful thus far, even when they tried slightly different trajectories against the same targets, like gunners trying to find the range. Their laboratory-bred podships, while they looked like the real thing and reached tremendous speeds in space, continued to have perplexing guidance problems that sent them veering wildly off course.

For today's attempt, a system of deep-space relay telescopes had been pointed toward distant Canopa, where a massive explosion was expected. By the law of averages something had to eventually hit its intended target, if only by accident. Or so his scientists claimed. But the Zultan wasn't so sure about that. The galaxy was a very large place.

He completed the prayer and blessing, then lifted his arms and gave the command everyone had been awaiting.

Silently, the laboratory-bred podship took off and disappeared into space, with its deadly Demolio torpedo inside.

At an improvised nehrcom station on Dij, the Zultan's son, Hari'Adab, and Parais d'Olor listened to a report on the latest launch. The Mutatis had not yet perfected their cross-space transmission system, and static interfered with the sound quality, along with something that caused the signals to surge and fade.

The pair stood silently with their hands clasped in front of them, the position of Mutati prayer.

Minutes passed with excruciating slowness. Hari heard chatter over the line as a commentator provided calculations on how long it should take for the lab-pod to arrive at Canopa and blow it to oblivion. Lab-pods didn't need to go anywhere near the pod stations where the Merchant Prince Alliance had set up sensor-guns. Theoretically a cloned podship could emerge on the opposite side of Canopa and then blow the planet into space dust.

Finally enough time elapsed, and there was no report of an explosion. Hari and Parais heaved sighs of relief. Their prayers had been answered.

Chapter Fifty-Five

All things come to an end. There are no exceptions.

—Tulyan Saying

It was like having front-row seats for the most spectacular show in the cosmos. As if they were living creatures, small comets and meteors swooped so close to Eshaz's home that he imagined jumping aboard one of them and flying it straight to heaven. He never tired of the spectacular galactic displays, not even after seeing them for hundreds of thousands of years.

His three guests sat with him in large rocking chairs on the porch, oohing and aahing like spectators at a fireworks display. Even the Parvii woman seemed impressed, and she had undoubtedly seen a great deal in her travels around the galaxy. Hours ago, they had all received great news, a report that Noah Watanabe had been rescued from a CorpOne medical laboratory. Already Eshaz had obtained permission from the Council to send a congratulatory message to him at the next regularly scheduled transmission time over Timeweb—a message that would be received on the other end by Zigzia, a Tulyan working for Noah's Guardians. This evening's galactic show was the frosting on an excellent day.

Truly, I have been blessed to live here, Eshaz thought, savoring the beauty of the night. But he worried over how much longer such natural delights would last, galactic wonders that were probably unrivaled in the entire universe. So far the sacred starcloud had not shown any signs of the deterioration affecting other star systems as the Timeweb infrastructure unraveled, that living organism linking all galactic life forms.

"There are so many excellent stories I could tell you," Eshaz said in the low light, "for I am very old by your standards, and rich with experience." He rocked in his creaking chair. "Eons ago, my people were masters of the entire galaxy, and could journey to the farthest stars in the blink of an eye. We controlled podships then, before Parviis swarmed in and pirated them away."

He glanced at the shadowy, magnified profile of Tesh, who had chosen to remain too small for the Tulyan rocker, and added, "Our enemies were always an irritant, and eventually became much more than that. It was the beginning of the end, and prevented us from performing our large-scale caretaking work. For too long we have tried to patch things together, but it has not been nearly enough."

She looked over at him, with the saddest expression on her face. The remorse of one Parvii meant little to Eshaz. It was not nearly enough, but he still enjoyed her companionship, and had done important work with her. They had captured podships together, an unprecedented collaboration in the history of the galaxy.

The big Tulyan stopped rocking and said, "Even with their domination, Parviis don't have all of our powers. I am a time-seer, one of the Tulyans who is sometimes able to peer short distances into the future."

"In order to obtain travel privileges for his people," Tesh interjected, "Eshaz's services . . . and the services of other Tulyans like him . . . are made available to the Parviis. Woldn, and all the Eyes of the Swarm who preceded him, have always worried about the future."

"Your people have a guilty conscience," Eshaz said.

"Perhaps that is true, though I suppose all of us feel the guilt of our ancestors."

In a faltering voice, Eshaz said, "I was ordered to timesee for Woldn, but something blocked me . . . chaos in the galaxy, I think. But I sense something important anyway, that Noah Watanabe holds the keys to the future."

"In what way?" Dux asked.

"I wish I knew. He might not even understand how to use them himself." The ancient reptilian shuddered as a cold breeze emerged from the mists, and the sky went dark.

Chapter Fifty-Six

Eternal life does not equate to eternal happiness. In point of fact, the opposite is far more likely.

—Noah Watanabe

Francella stood on the largest loggia of her palatial cliffside home. Gripping the railing, she looked dejectedly out on the moonlit Valley of the Princes, focusing on her own destroyed buildings down there . . . the headquarters and the main lab that had been sabotaged by the pesky Guardians. Then her gaze drifted down to the cliff face beneath the railing, and the welcome relief that could be only a few moments away for her.

For Francella Watanabe, her entire life had been a waking nightmare in which she had striven to be noticed, but in which her rightful position in the family and in society had been denied. As far as she was concerned, most of the blame for that went to her twin brother, but it also irritated her that their father had permitted it all to happen in the first place. A self-made industrialist, Saito had been opposed to the indolence and inherited wealth of noble-born princes. He professed to honor hard work and ingenuity, so logically he should have honored and rewarded her efforts. But it had never been that way. She'd been forced to work twice as hard as Noah to gain any measure of respect with their father, and ultimately she received only the grudging, secondary attention given to a mere daughter.

That lack of respect for her as a person and as a woman carried over even now, despite the fact that she owned and controlled the immense assets of CorpOne. She saw it on the faces of officers of the company and in members of the Doge's Royal Court, in their subtle looks and tones of voice. On the surface they appeared to give her deference and jumped to comply with her wishes, but she always sensed an undercurrent. She was not the great Prince Saito Watanabe. Nor was she Noah Watanabe, who—despite having been declared a criminal—was still widely admired among the people.

She felt the moisture of her own teardrops on her hands as she continued to grip the railing. It would not be difficult for her to climb over and tumble into oblivion.

To Francella, the atmosphere of hard work in which she had grown up was a fraud and a farce, a purported ethical base that never really existed. Any semblance of ethics she'd seen had been tainted with exclusionary clauses that left her out of the inner circles of merchant prince society. As a woman and a Human being, she resented that.

Feeling betrayed by her family, it was easy for her to abandon them. She had arranged for the death of her father, and had neatly blamed it on her brother. Likewise, she had been spreading rumors against Doge Lorenzo, and had allied herself with his political enemies, the noble-born princes. It had been easy for her to turn against people who did not respect her. Now she would champion the cause of the noble-born aristocrats, and in the process would advance the position of her own son Anton, and of herself. After all, he was of noble blood from the loins of Doge Lorenzo, and she could not be expected to ignore that.

Through it all she had become a political chameleon, doing whatever it took to survive in a male-dominated society filled with intrigues and double dealings. She thought her own schemes had been well laid out, and they did give her some measure of influence over difficult situations.

But something eluded her. From birth, she had been allotted the normal Human lifetime. That was limited enough, yet now, through a terrible misfortune and injustice, even that was being taken away from her. Each time she looked in the mirror or saw others react with aversion to her appearance, she felt the erosion. The end was drawing near. . . .

Unable to sleep that night, she had been pacing the corridors of her villa in a robe, desperate to come up with a solution. Earlier in the evening she had taken a couple of spinneros, pills that were manufactured by her company as antidepressants. They were not working on her, perhaps because they were lousy drugs, or because she was too far down to bring herself back.

She envisioned herself summoning the necessary courage and jumping off the cliff. But would that really be courage? Wouldn't it be more brave to fight harder than ever for life?

Her despair shifted quickly to anger, and she turned away from the railing. She had never been a quitter or a loser. Her enemies would have to drag her kicking and screaming from this life, from everything she deserved. As long as she still had breath, she would fight.

Dressing hurriedly, she summoned her chauffeur and ordered him to notify Dr. Bichette that she intended to call on him within the hour. She wanted a firsthand status report on her condition, and what he was doing to combat it. No matter that it was the middle of the night. If she could not sleep, neither should Bichette.

At the last minute, Francella slipped a puissant handgun into the pocket of her jacket. If she didn't like what he had to say, she would administer her own form of discipline, and—assuming she let him live—she would put a black mark in his personnel file. Actually, a bloody mark sounded better to her. It was her right as his employer, after all.

At the front entrance, the chauffeur handed her an envelope. "The doctor sent this over right after I contacted him."

After slipping into the back seat of the limousine, she opened the envelope, while the vehicle hummed along the maglev track. Reading the note, she said to the driver, "Take me to Lab Two instead of his home. He's waiting there."

Her pulse raced. The message read, "I have good news." What did he mean?

Arriving at the laboratory, she found that the doctor, fully aware of his precarious position, had been working around the clock. He looked pale and gaunt, and had not shaven in some time. A vein throbbed at his temple, as it did whenever he became agitated. "I'm glad you're here," he said in his deep voice, grasping her hand and shaking it. "Your timing is elegant."

Dr. Bichette reported interesting developments in the research. From duplicate medical records that were kept in a separate location and not destroyed in the lab fire, he and his staff had compared Noah's previous DNA structure with what it was now, and had spotted significant differences, particularly involving how genes transferred during cellular division. In a normal person, a small number of cells had age-related chromosomal defects that were held in check when the person was young, but expanded their domain as the person grew older.

"But in the case of Noah Watanabe," the excited doctor said, "these defective cells no longer exist. His basic DNA structure has been completely revamped, making him better than new."

Francella found these comments fascinating, but she was impatient to hear more. "What does this mean for me?" she demanded.

Looking increasingly nervous, the doctor continued. "When you injected yourself with Noah's blood, it gave me an idea. I began to wonder if his DNA might be used as a blueprint to make a new product, an elixir of eternal life."

"The Fountain of Youth," Francella said.

"It seems entirely possible. Computer projections indicate that an injection of elixir could make some people live for a very long time."

He started to go into more detail when she interrupted. "Begin production at once."

His eyes widened. "But more studies are required first, tests on animals and willing Human subjects."

"I do not have the luxury of time. You are to immediately suspend all other medical operations and focus our resources on the elixir."

Chapter Fifty-Seven

> Certain robots have no sense of honor programmed into them, or they have overridden it, and will destroy anything that stands in their way.
>
> —Thinker, entry in his data banks

Upon learning of Noah's escape from the CorpOne facility, Jacopo Nehr summoned his top officers to the orbital space station. In his office there, the Supreme General of the Merchant Prince Armed Forces said, "I understand robots broke the prisoner out of the medical lab. Is that true?"

Colonel Umar Javit, commander of the Red Berets, stepped forward. A big man with broad shoulders, he said, "It is, sir."

"But how could robots sneak in and do that? Aren't they clanky and noisy?"

"There are ways to muffle sound, a fact I learned by asking robots under my own command the same questions."

"I've heard about your robots," Nehr said, thoughtfully. "They're doing a good job for you, aren't they?"

"Better than most men, sir. They've been self-replicating, too, building more of their kind quickly. I had twenty machine volunteers in the beginning, and now they number in the tens of thousands."

"Impressive. Put them to work on this Noah situation. Add them to the Human Red Berets that are already looking for him. Find Noah and his hideout and destroy them."

"Shall I take prisoners, sir?"

"Only enough to obtain intelligence information." He grimaced. "Doge Lorenzo and Francella are anxious for results."

"We are to kill the rest of the Guardians, then? I mean, the Humans?"

"Right. Their robots can be reprogrammed, after we get important data from them."

"And what are we to do about Noah Watanabe? From what I hear, he can't be killed. There are even doubts about whether he is really Human or not. I mean, he's not like Princess Meghina, really a Mutati. The shapeshifters are as mortal as we are."

Nehr nodded. "He's in his own category, isn't he? Capture him, kill him if you can with overwhelming firepower. Whatever it takes to stop his operations."

Underground, his location veiled by the security system that Subi and Thinker had improvised, Noah stood with Zigzia, a female Tulyan who was around his own height, but who probably weighed three times as much as he did. She wore a green-and-brown Guardian uniform. For her race, Zigzia was on the small side, even for a female. Noah had dealt with enough Tulyans to be able to distinguish one from another by facial features, and he thought this one had an interesting look to her, with intelligence in her dark, slitted eyes.

"Please repeat my message back," Noah said.

"To make certain I have it right, you mean?" She looked a bit perturbed, and a crinkle formed along her bronze, scaly snout. "I have a perfect memory, just as Eshaz does."

"Of course. I don't wish to be insulting. As I understand it, virtually all Tulyans have such a memory. But there *are* a small percentage of exceptions."

"With all due respect, Master, you think I might fall into the latter category?"

He shook his head. "I'm sure you don't. I am told by my people that you have precise recall, and that you have transmitted numerous messages between us and your Council of Elders on the Tulyan Starcloud. It's just that this is the first time I have dealt with you personally, and I have a certain way of doing things."

"I accept your apology," she said.

"My. . . ." Noah smiled. "Yes, you could call it that."

With a twinkle in her eyes, the bulky alien repeated his message back to him in its entirety, even including the vocal inflections and pauses in his original, when he uttered it moments ago. Word for word, she got it exactly right, and he nodded with satisfaction.

"Very good," he said. "Most impressive. OK, go ahead and send it."

She grinned, revealing large teeth. "The regularly appointed time is this afternoon."

"Yes. As specified by your Council. One of these days I shall ask you to show me in detail how the system works. Something to do with the web, as I understand it."

Disapproval registered on her face. "That is correct, but the Council has not authorized me to say more."

"To an outsider, you mean?"

"No, Master Noah. You are as close to being Tulyan as any Human I have ever met. Among my people, you are held in great esteem. But only the Elders can decide what is revealed to you."

"I understand."

She bowed, and left to perform her various tasks.

In his soon-to-be transmitted message, Noah asked about Eshaz and Tesh, wondering how they were doing and what they were doing. On the surface it appeared to be entirely business-like, focused on their operations as Guardians, and Noah's request that they return as soon as possible. Noah also had an interest in regaining jurisdiction over the podship that Tesh had with her, even if he was never able to pilot one of the sentient vessels himself again. With the ship at his disposal, many things were possible.

In several voyages across space, each taking only a few moments, he could move his entire force of Guardians to another planet. But what would he accomplish if he did that? He didn't want to mount an army to attack the merchant princes. Instead, he wanted to work with them against the Mutatis and the Parviis, who were so problematic in different ways. The podship—presumably operated by Tesh—would enable him to personally move around the galaxy quickly if he needed to do so, and it might also be a bargaining chip in dealing with young Anton, who was the odds-on favorite to be the next doge. Noah harbored hopes that his past close relationship with his nephew might be beneficial to the cause of humankind. He just needed to figure out the best way of reaching out to him.

Noah wanted Eshaz, Tesh, and the podship back for professional reasons, to be sure, but behind the official communication he concealed his strong desire to see Tesh. He missed her. On a very personal level, it was a situation that he wanted to figure out how to handle, how to reach out to her. But in this galaxy, with all of the problems he faced, other matters were more pressing. . . .

On the other end of the transmission, Eshaz was forced by the Council of Elders to answer vaguely, without details of what they were doing. They saw through Noah's words, to his true feelings. Eshaz defended Noah, saying that the man would never let personal feelings get in the way of important work. But Eshaz had to agree with his superiors. In his own experience, he had seen something extra between the two Humans.

Under tight control by the Elders, Eshaz's transmitted response to Noah read simply, "Congratulations on your rescue from imprisonment. We trust that you are doing well, and look forward to working closely with you again."

When Jimu received his command to find and destroy Noah and his headquarters, it tied in with something the robot had been planning to do anyway. Recently, there had been reports of undercover Guardian machines operating around Canopa, eluding capture. He would concentrate on finding them, and ferreting out their secrets.

Moving quickly, Jimu ordered a roundup of every sentient machine that showed its metal face on Canopa. Household, factory, and office bots were brought in for questioning, along with every other type of mechanical device that had the capacity to think. Interface probes would be used, and even disassembly, if necessary. Whatever it took to find out where each machine had been, and what it was programmed to do. . . .

A week later, Jimu heard about some unusual robots that had turned up, and one in particular. As excited as a robot could be with his programmed emotions, he hurried to a government warehouse on the outskirts of Rainbow City. There he found a contingent of his Red Beret machines surrounding an armored Human and a dented bot that had folded itself shut. He recognized them immediately, from information in his own data banks. Both were famous in machine lore.

Without a doubt, they were Giovanni Nehr and Thinker.

"The robot won't open," one of Jimu's sergeants said, "and we're worried about damaging his programming if we try to force the issue. He's really sealed himself up."

Striding up to the prisoners, Jimu said, "Hello, Thinker. Remember me, old friend?"

To his surprise, Thinker opened without delay. Having erased part of his internal programming, the portion that revealed the location of Noah's subterranean headquarters, Thinker had set all of this up intentionally, wanting to be captured. He had his own plan in mind, with two important goals . . . one involving Jimu and the other involving Gio.

Back at the Guardian hideout, the cerebral robot had left a full backup copy of himself, and instructions that if he didn't return within three hours, this copy would be inserted into a new body, and the one he occupied now (including its internal programming) would be automatically deactivated. With respect to Gio, whom he did not yet entirely trust, this was an important test, sanctioned by Noah Watanabe himself.

Using his advanced programming, Thinker had taken preparations to send an electronic signal that would wipe out Gio's memory of the headquarters location if he even started to utter the wrong words, or if any attempt was made to separate the two of them. Additional memory-wiping signals, though designed for robots, would be sent to all sentient machines within hearing range, if necessary. The robot had made adjustments to his own programming to set it up. Normally Thinker could not harm Humans or meddle with their minds, but he was able to tweak that by placing Noah's safety, and the security of the entire Guardian organization, above all other concerns.

"You're on the wrong side, old friend," Thinker said to Jimu. Around the perimeter of Thinker's face plate, orange lights blinked on. They began to pulse slowly and hypnotically, with the light receding and returning like the tide, dimming and brightening, dimming and brightening.

"But we both work for Humans," Jimu said. "How can that possibly be wrong?"

Abruptly, an interface probe shot out of Thinker's torso and locked into a port on Jimu's body, which now bore the cardinal-red markings of the Doge's elite force. It took only seconds to transfer the data to the wayward robot, after which Thinker withdrew the probe.

"Now do you understand?" Thinker asked.

"All Humans are not worthy of our loyalty and devotion," Jimu intoned. "But Master Noah is."

"Welcome to the Guardians," Thinker said. He clasped metal hands with Jimu.

Jimu, instilled with sudden fervor, now issued new commands to the robot force in the warehouse. "We will not fight our own kind, especially not the revered Thinker. We all owe him a duty, for what he began in the White Sun Solar System where your brethren were first renovated, after having been discarded as worthless by the merchant princes."

"Giovanni Nehr knows the way," Thinker said.

Moments later, the motley group filed out of the warehouse, with Jimu ostensibly at the head of a Red Beret squadron. But an armored Human right behind him provided directions.

In ensuing weeks, Thinker and Jimu worked together from Noah's headquarters to decimate the robotic ranks of the Red Berets. During what looked like typical patrols or troop exercises, a number of the Doge's machines began to slip away and go over to Noah's side—a trickle at first that would gradually increase.

Chapter Fifty-Eight

The concept of voting is like a pebble in a pond, enlarging outward from personal decision points concerning small matters to larger and larger matters.

—Anonymous, perhaps from a politician of Lost Earth

Despite his vices and extreme avarice, Doge Lorenzo had attempted to coordinate an effective military defense system on all planets in the Merchant Prince Alliance. As a matter of routine, he left most of the details to the professionals such as General Jacopo Nehr, but the Doge had his own ideas and concerns about such important matters. Sometimes he went into Nehr's office on the orbiter and discussed military issues with him, but usually Lorenzo passed his orders through his attaché, Pimyt, who in turn relayed them down to the nehrcom transmitting station on the surface of Canopa for dissemination to other planets.

Lorenzo had also continued to reward scientific and business achievements by appointing commoners to princely positions. But he had failed to keep abreast of changing political tides, and failed to see the strength of the opposition to him until it surfaced in a big way. Now his political opponents—while concealing their identities—were lobbying for a vote of no-confidence in the Hall of Princes, and had garnered enough support to make it happen.

Today was the day of the vote.

Accompanied by his guards, the self-proclaimed Lorenzo the Magnificent took a shuttle down to the surface, and then a groundcar to the government complex in Rainbow City. At one time these buildings had been devoted to Canopan affairs, but now they served a larger purpose because of the destruction of Timian One and the merchant prince capital there.

His car crossed the city's central square and stopped at the largest building, a domed structure that was now the Hall of Princes. The vote would be taken inside during a nehrcom conference session.

As he took his seat on the central stage, he wondered how many princes were aligned against him, and which of those who claimed to support him were actually working against him behind his back. He sighed. His grandfather had told him to be wary of political alliances, since they could blow away like leaves in the wind. Lorenzo realized now with a sinking sensation that he had forgotten that admonition, and had let his guard down while his enemies massed against him. He felt tears of sadness and rage welling up inside, and fought them back.

Many of his questions would be answered soon, when the princes placed their anonymous votes. For years he had been able to avoid even having a vote of confidence, since he had so many supporters who opposed it. But now, with the increasing opposition, the vote would be taken. He did not expect to lose, but the mere fact of the vote troubled him.

A handful of Canopan princes filed into the chamber and took their seats, along with a number of princes who had been visiting when podship travel was cut off. Gradually the other seats filled with holo-images, projections from other worlds. The transmitted images were so realistic that Lorenzo had to look closely to see the difference: they had a slight, almost imperceptible lack of sharpness. He nodded to some of his friends and long-time allies, including Anese Eng of Siriki and Nebba Kann of Salducia. They nodded back, most of them from far across the galaxy.

With a worried scowl, Lorenzo folded his arms across his chest and waited. He cast his own vote with a control panel on the arm of his chair, and saw the princes doing the same out in the chamber. They had an hour to complete the process, and many of the dignitaries whispered and murmured among themselves, making last-minute decisions and deals.

He didn't like the facial expressions he saw on many in the chamber, including noblemen he had long considered his friends and allies. Stony countenances that seemed to look completely through him, as if he wasn't even there. Could the vote possibly go against him? He wished he could say something here on his own behalf, but by long tradition that was impossible. All of the politicking had been done before this, with secret deals and payoffs. But it might not be enough.

Nervously, Lorenzo summoned an aide. "I'm not feeling well," he said. "Perhaps I should go to an anteroom."

The aide, a small but powerfully built black man, spoke in a confidential tone. Dib Venkins had always been outspoken, but his advice was consistently good. "Couldn't that be seen as a sign of weakness, Sire?"

"It would look worse if I fall over."

Nodding, Venkins helped him to his feet and escorted him through a side doorway, while the whispering and murmuring increased. Maybe this would garner him some sympathy votes, the Doge thought. Pimyt hurried to lend assistance.

In the anteroom, Lorenzo refused to sit, eat, or drink. "Leave me," he said to the aide.

After the black man left, Lorenzo told Pimyt why he'd had to leave, then said, "How can they even call for this vote, after all I've done for the MPA? I've put money in the pockets of everyone in that chamber, and this is how I'm rewarded?"

"All ballots are not in yet," Pimyt said. "I have people making last-minute deals, pressing for the support of anyone who's on the fence. It is difficult to do, however, since so many princes are keeping their cards close to the vest. As you know, Francella has her people doing their best on our behalf, too. I just spoke with her this morning."

He nodded. "You're doing the best you possibly can, and I appreciate it."

Lorenzo heard a rap at the anteroom door, and Pimyt let Francella in. She wore a long white dress, with a pale blue sash and a gold broach bearing her initials on her lapel. He saw the unmistakable aging on her face (despite the attempts to cover it with makeup), and a slight stoop to her posture. He felt a deep concern for her welfare. It was good of her to come when she was not feeling well.

"May I come in?" she asked, looking over the top of the much shorter Hibbil and smiling at Lorenzo.

Feeling the need for emotional support, Lorenzo nodded. He rested his hand on a copy of the *Scienscroll* that lay open on a stand, and this gave him some comfort, as if a higher power was watching over him.

Hurrying to his side, Francella placed a hand on his shoulder. "We're doing everything we can," she said, "but it doesn't look good."

In disbelief, he looked at her. "I'm going to lose?"

"The revelation about Princess Meghina is too large to overcome, it seems."

"I didn't know she was a Mutati!"

"I believe you, but it has the appearance of concealment on your part, and some people are willing to believe the worst about you. There is this, too. Word has it that my brother spread the story about Meghina and your involvement."

"Noah did that?"

"It's in his nature, and he's out now, back with the Guardians."

"But how did he find out about Meghina?"

With a shrug, Francella said, "Who knows? But Noah hates you for helping me."

"I could kill him for this!"

"I already tried that."

"Just the same, there are still things we can do. If we get our hands on him again, we can seal him in plax and bury him, or drop him in the deepest part of the ocean."

"My brother's cells do have some value, so it would be better to seal him up somewhere and stab needles into him to extract blood whenever we need it."

"A cure for you," Lorenzo said.

"Precisely."

A wave of sadness overwhelmed the Doge, and words caught in his throat.

"It's Noah's fault that this vote of confidence is going to go against you," Francella said. "I hoped for a different result, but the polls are clear." She looked downcast.

"Maybe you're mistaken," Lorenzo said, staring at the *Scienscroll* that still rested under one hand. "I could still pull off a miracle."

She did not reply.

With a sudden movement, Lorenzo dropped to his knees in front of the *Scienscroll* stand. He could not hold his emotions back, and tears streamed down his face.

On either side of him, Francella and Pimyt knelt, too, and the three of them prayed silently together for several long minutes.

"I don't understand how this happened," Lorenzo finally said, opening his eyes and looking at his most trusted associates. "I just don't see how this could have possibly happened. Don't the princes know what I've done for them?"

"Maybe there will be a miracle after all," Pimyt suggested.

But Lorenzo heard otherwise in his tone, and saw hopelessness in his face. He was only going through the motions.

Looking at his long-time lover on the other side, Lorenzo thought she looked dismal, and seemed to age moment by moment. The Doge sensed powerful forces aligned against him, attacking even those closest to him.

"If it does not go well," Francella said, "we must salvage what we can. Our best hope may lie with our son, Anton."

"As the next Doge, you mean?"

She nodded. "I have made inquiries through intermediaries. Anton could garner considerable support."

"Because he's a del Velli, but does not have my baggage."

With a tight smile, she said, "And you could still exert a powerful influence over him behind the scenes."

"I don't know him well enough to say that."

"But I do, and he'll do as we say."

"We must consider the ramifications of this," Pimyt said, obviously agitated. "It would be a big step, with obvious risks."

"If it goes badly for you out in the hall," she said to Lorenzo, "we must move quickly and present Anton to them before anyone can mount an opposition candidate."

Pimyt did not say anything, and to Lorenzo his attaché seemed unable to keep up with the fast pace of events. At least Francella had considered the possibilities.

Reluctantly, the Doge nodded. "Let's go back in," he said. Trying to summon his courage, he rose shakily to his feet.

When he walked back into the large chamber with Pimyt, it was eerily silent. All eyes were turned on Lorenzo.

He saw the tally on a screen that hung from the high ceiling:

For Doge Lorenzo del Velli: 578
Against Doge Lorenzo del Velli: 955

Angrily, he tried to control his shaking. He had lost the vote of confidence. It wasn't even close.

Just then, Francella Watanabe strode into the chamber and marched down the central aisle toward him, accompanied by their son, Anton Glavine.

The real and the projected princes rose to their feet and the chamber erupted in applause. To Lorenzo's surprise, he heard a clamor arise in favor of his bastard son.

"Doge Anton!" they chanted. "Doge Anton!"

Francella and Anton mounted the stage and stood in front of him. "This is our miracle," she said to Lorenzo. "I've made all the necessary arrangements, made the payments and promises. The princes will haggle back and forth a bit, but only for the sake of appearances. The vote for Anton will only be a formality."

The Doge sat down. His Human enemies were more subtle and devious than the Mutatis, and had succeeded in pulling out the Doge's underpinnings of support so suddenly that he was shocked. The situation with Anton was intriguing, but Lorenzo couldn't accept him too easily, or that would garner opposition to the new Doge.

So, feigning more rage and discontent than he really felt, Lorenzo jumped to his feet. "You haven't heard the last of me!" he shouted, as he stormed out of the hall.

Even though the princes wanted Lorenzo's resignation, they could not force it, not even after the vote of no confidence. A number of legal procedures still had to be followed to remove him from office, and that could take years, as it had in the past with other merchant prince leaders. Lorenzo knew something of merchant prince law, and had the best lawyers to represent his interests.

In private, he told her what he had decided to do, and finally she said, "Yes. I see the wisdom in your words."

The princes and their representatives held meetings far into the night, while Lorenzo conferred with Pimyt and a staff of attorneys. During a meal break on the stage, with tables set up for those who were on Canopa, Francella went over to Lorenzo and said, "I told them you are too stubborn to resign, my dear, but you must be cautious. The noble-born princes are not in a patient mood, and we are at war against the Mutatis and against the Guardians. They are talking about using wartime provisions against you, and. . . ."

"Don't try to snow me," Lorenzo said, raising his voice so that others could see him seeming to argue with her. "My people know the laws better than you do. I can take steps to remain in power for a long time."

"Some of your opponents are saying that you could be overthrown violently," Francella said. She glanced back at Anton, who sat at her table but thus far had remained silent.

"Supreme General Jacopo Nehr is totally loyal to me," Lorenzo countered. "He can bring most of the armed forces to my support on a moment's notice." Pausing, the Doge smiled and added, "Nonetheless, for the good of the Alliance, I have decided to take a different course of action. Tell them I will abdicate, but only under certain conditions."

"And those conditions are?" Francella asked. She sounded irritated, but Lorenzo assumed it was only for show.

"Watch me," he said.

Calling in old favors, Lorenzo and his staff made a flurry of last-minute political arrangements. Despite his bluster, he knew his political opponents could attack him militarily, and the armor on the orbiter wouldn't stand against a full-scale assault. Still, that would be an unprecedented, egregious act, and might very well lead to civil war all across the Alliance.

Making the best of a bad situation, Lorenzo slipped cleverly out of the noose his opponents had prepared for him. He agreed to abdicate immediately, and accepted exile to his space station, where he would operate The Pleasure Palace Casino, guarded by a contingent of Red Berets. Under the arrangement, he would be permitted to keep his corporate directorships, and would receive the title of Doge Emeritus, along with a generous annual pension.

He also had the new, secret understanding with Francella, which might prove to be more lucrative than the gambling casino. Immediately after the agreement with Lorenzo was signed, the princes conducted a private vote, and Anton del Velli was elected Doge.

Chapter Fifty-Nine

Everyone wants to be seen and noticed. It is an aspect of the Human condition. It is also an aspect that we constantly attempt to select and frame the pictures in which we appear.

—Master Noah Watanabe

Anton Glavine, a former maintenance man and later a prisoner, never imagined that he would one day become the highest-ranking official in the Merchant Prince Alliance, the Doge of all humankind. The suddenness of his ascension stunned him. After a midnight vote he felt as if he had been plucked from darkness and lifted into the light, with limitless possibilities for his life. Great riches had been opened for him as the heir to the House of del Velli and the Doge's share of taxes he would receive, even if they only came from Canopa and the rest was on paper, due to the cessation of podship travel.

In the beginning Anton had to follow a tight course, at least until he gained enough power and influence in his own right to speak out and say what he felt. His concerns ran deep. Principal among them was his enigmatic mother, about whom he had mixed feelings. Anton tried to view her sympathetically for the woman's mental illness, which seemed obvious. He appreciated the belated attention she had given him, her overtures to make up for the time they had lost between them, more than twenty years. Anton tried to feel love for her, but that was not easy, and he didn't know if he ever could.

She might have done terrible things to the person he admired most in the entire galaxy, his Uncle Noah Watanabe. Anton had heard stories about Francella performing violent laboratory experiments on her own brother and how he had survived through some miracle and then escaped. If she really did that to him, Anton could never forgive her. He would even see that she was prosecuted, but thus far they were only stories, without evidence.

Francella was claiming that the descriptions were exaggerated, and that she had really conducted controlled experiments, with full medical technology and personnel available for life saving purposes. According to her claim, supported by Dr. Bichette, Noah gave permission to have his body cut into pieces, knowing that they would grow back, and he issued a challenge, asserting he could not be killed. Anton had seen him do that on the pod station, when Noah told his estranged sister to go ahead and shoot, since that could not harm him. He claimed immortality, and evidence suggested that this actually was the case.

Though Anton did not fully understand why, he knew that his mother had always hated Noah and had unfairly blamed him for the attack on CorpOne headquarters that killed old Prince Saito Watanabe. She might even have been responsible for that aggression herself, but Anton did not have any evidence pointing in that direction. Only the suspicions of her brother and other people. Anton wanted to believe the best about his mother. What a shame it would be to find her after all this time and then discover that she had no redeeming qualities at all.

He also found it troublesome that Francella seemed to be a master at pointing fingers, including the recent incident with Noah, the earlier attack on CorpOne, and the way she had recently cast suspicions about Doge Lorenzo, asserting that he knew all along that Princess Meghina was not Human, and had concealed the facts. That tactic was one of the key reasons for his fall from power. As far as Anton was concerned, it had not been entirely above board, but perhaps that was the way of merchant prince politics, just another day in the arena of political combat. Soon, he would learn more about how the game was played. For now, he was a child thrown into the ocean and told to swim.

Trumpets blared, and on all sides noblemen and ladies bowed their heads to Anton as he walked down the central aisle of the Hall of Princes, with his mother just behind him. Anton wore a glittering gold-brocade cloak and uniform, draped in jewels and medallions, while his regal-looking mother was adorned in a long white gown and golden headdress. Outside, the central square fronting the government buildings thronged with people, celebrating the inauguration of the new Doge, the leading prince of the realm.

On one level of awareness, Anton felt tremendous pride, and a certainty that this lofty position was his birthright as the son of Lorenzo. But he also felt a great deal of responsibility, and a fear that he might not be up to the task. He vowed privately to do his best, and to assert himself as soon as he could, getting out from under the skirts of the woman behind him and prosecuting her if he found evidence that she had committed any crimes. Anton knew he had to be his own man. He would grow into the job, beginning with humility and diplomacy and gradually changing, revealing his own personality and goals. It was a difficult time to ascend to this position, with the ongoing hostilities and the strange cessation of podship travel. He doubted if any ruler before him had ever faced such monumental obstacles.

He noticed General Jacopo Nehr and his daughter Nirella standing by the aisle. The woman glanced at Anton and smiled.

She looked to be around twice his age and was rather stocky—but he found her attractive and reportedly she was still able to bear children. Her father had been lobbying through the political channels of the merchant princes, offering her in marriage to the new Doge. Anton still had feelings for Tesh, and he didn't want to think about matrimony just yet. Nirella seemed pleasant enough the few times they had met, but he needed to get to know her better before making a commitment—no matter the obvious political and economic benefits of joining two influential merchant prince houses.

Anton continued down the aisle, then took a deep breath and climbed the steps of the central stage, where a white-robed Merchant Priest awaited him, holding a bound copy of the *Scienscroll.*

Having rehearsed this event, Anton strode up to him and stopped, while Lorenzo and Francella stood stiffly on one side. Due to the limitations on space travel that prevented merchant prince nobles and their entourages from journeying great distances, common citizens were permitted to sit in the great hall on this occasion, beside those noblemen and ladies who lived on Canopa. Around the realm, other noblemen and ladies, as well as billions of citizens, watched the proceedings via nehrcom links.

The priest told the assemblage in the hall to stand. Then he sprinkled holy water on Anton and read words from the *Scienscroll:*

> "For ours is a realm fashioned and favored by the
> Supreme Being;
> Truly, our blessings and glories are many!
> Hear this now, in every princely land:
> A new ruler rises like the sun, to shine brightly
> on us all!"

At a nod from the priest, Lorenzo stepped forward and handed his son a sapphire signet ring, on a tiny pillow. Then he stepped back.

Anton shivered with delight as the priest reached out and placed the ring on the third finger of the young man's right hand. Every merchant prince wore such a ring, and they had collectively given this as a gift to him. In recent days, he had been wearing it, getting used to it. The ring was his bond to the other princes, signifying that he was allegiant to them, one of their peers. Now, by virtue of the inaugural ceremony and the blessing of the priest on the ring, Anton had risen to first among his noble peers, simultaneously subject to them and their ruler.

Trumpets blared again, while the crowd cheered and stamped its feet in a traditional welcoming gesture. On one of the most unexpected occasions in all of Human history, Anton Glavine, the bastard son of Lorenzo the Magnificent, was inaugurated Doge Anton del Velli of the Merchant Prince Alliance.

The following day, he would move into the palatial cliffside villa vacated by his father, and still owned by his mother. Suddenly Anton's life had accelerated, and he hoped he could keep up.

After the grand ball that evening, Francella sat alone in her dressing room, reflecting on the big day. It had pleased her to see her son and Nirella Nehr dancing together, and engaged in animated conversation. She would be happy to see the two houses merge through marriage, giving Francella access to one of the great fortunes in the galaxy.

The day had gone extremely well, and she felt considerable pride—but not for her son, though that might come one day, if he showed the sense of duty she hoped he had. For the moment, she felt extremely proud of herself, for rising above adversity and achieving what seemed impossible. She had not only toppled a sitting doge without him knowing of her involvement, but she had installed her own son in his place. Truly remarkable.

And, while she had been unable to stop the agreement under which Doge Lorenzo saved himself from disaster, at least she had made the best of the situation. Her son's new position would bring great revenues into the family in the form of skimmed taxes, and she intended to receive a considerable share of them. In addition, she envisioned a sizable financial reward when her company began producing and selling the new elixir based upon Noah's DNA. She would use it herself, and would sell it to selected clients on Canopa for more than a king's ransom.

A name for the product occurred to her, and she made a note of it in a recording device built into one of her lockets. She would call it the "Elixir of Life."

Chapter Sixty

> All galactic races share the need to learn. It is part of the genetic coding for survival, a process that instills life and vitality into the collective organism. When learning stops, the cells eventually become necrotic, and death looms.
>
> —Finding of CorpOne medical research study

A month passed that seemed like much longer to Anton Glavine. In his new position and responsibilities, he had many concerns.

For one, the mustachioed young Doge wondered what had happened to thousands of Red Beret robots, which seemed to have vanished. He suspected that his uncle and his Guardian machines had something to do with it, since it was now known that clever programming and inventory adjustments had been made to conceal the disappearances. The remainder of the Red Beret robotic force was under lock and key now, with the machines decommissioned and guarded.

Anton wondered about the fate of Noah, too, who continued to elude discovery and for some reason had reduced the number of guerrilla attacks, around the same time that the robots disappeared. General Nehr suspected that the Guardians were preparing for a new, much larger attack against Red Beret and CorpOne facilities, and that a machine army would form an integral part of their new plans.

But where were the Guardians? His mind ached from trying

to figure it out. Once, Anton had known the location of their hidden headquarters, for he had been a trusted member of Noah's inner circle. Then, mysteriously, the information had vanished . . . or had gone into hiding, like Noah himself.

One of his interrogators at Max One had referred to it as a "convenient memory," and perhaps it was that, or a selective memory. Or maybe it was, as Noah suggested, stress-induced. In any event, Anton had not been lying. He really could not remember.

Anton recalled his early life with Noah, and being on the orbital EcoStation with the great ecological teacher and his Guardians, but there were significant gaps after that. The Doge saw faces in his memory, such as those of Subi Danvar, Tesh Kori, Giovanni Nehr, and the robot Thinker, and meetings with Guardians, but he could not recollect the backgrounds, could not tell where the meetings took place, or many of the details that were discussed. Anton also remembered the dramatic events at the pod station, where Noah confronted Doge Lorenzo and Francella Watanabe. Both Noah and Anton had been taken into custody that day, and imprisoned at Max One.

An odd thought intruded, that the gaps in data suggested he might actually be a robot, or a bionic man, and someone had tampered with his internal programming. But that was preposterous. He knew he truly was Human, and that he was the biological son of Doge Lorenzo and Francella Watanabe. Medical tests had proven it.

But why can't I remember more about Noah? he wondered.

Oddly, he had so many concise memories of other things about Noah. It occurred to him that maybe he was protecting his uncle from harm by enemies, and had somehow blocked the memories in his own mind.

Perhaps I don't want to know, because if I did, I would have to go after him and harm, or even kill, him. This man who has done so much for me, and whom I have always admired more than any other.

The harder Anton tried to remember, or to figure out what was preventing him from doing so, the farther away the memories seemed to go. It was almost as if some higher power was interfering with his thought processes, preventing him from revealing secrets that were hidden and layered deep in his psyche.

A higher power that was protecting Noah Watanabe.

The youthful Doge worked hard each day, studying holohistories and other electronic documents to learn as much as he could about the merchant princes and the most important commercial and industrial worlds. Much of his training regimen was provided by his mother, but he went beyond anything she put in front of him, and he opened up his own channels of inquiry through his staff and the local government library. Nirella Nehr was a big help as well. In her position as half owner of her father's corporate empire and its nehrcom transmission system, she obtained information from all over the galaxy and shared it with him. They were spending a lot of time together, and rumors were circulating that a royal wedding would soon take place.

While undergoing an intense, on-the-job learning process, Anton was anxious to put his own new policies into force. He had a lot of ideas, including reaching a cease-fire with Noah. But his own position was complex. First he needed to be more sure of himself and of how his mother would react to such a step. Anton had been probing her on this issue, talking about political necessities that might point to the necessity of a cease-fire, and how a cessation of internal hostilities could benefit the entire Human cause. Thus far she remained unconvinced, but gradually her arguments were becoming less vociferous, less emotional.

As Anton accumulated information, it amazed him how much he had not known previously, especially about history and politics, and how many important activities were going on without the public having any knowledge of them. Instilled with fresh enthusiasm for the new things he was learning, he looked forward to getting up each morning and going about his activities. He was so excited about his new life, in fact, that he began sleeping a couple of hours less each night than before. In part this was because he was so tired at the end of each day that he slept more soundly. Essentially, he had two speeds now: like a hyperactive child, he went full tilt all day, and then fell sound asleep. In some respects he felt like a child, too, discovering new things with each waking moment.

While Anton got to know Nirella, it surprised him what a close bond they were forming, despite the difference in their ages. They clicked together, but she didn't press him for marriage, and claimed it was her father doing that, and Anton's mother. "I hear that's the best way to ruin a great friendship," Nirella said once.

He liked her sense of humor, and the way her blue eyes danced when she laughed. As time passed he thought less and less about how much older she was, and began to think of both of them as around thirty . . . the approximate mid-point between their ages. One evening as they shared a late meal, Anton surprised himself by proposing to her and sliding a glittering engagement ring across the small private table.

"Are you sure?" she asked, holding the large diamonix ring up to a candle to see it better.

"Is that a yes or a no?" Nervously, Anton polished off a glass of redicio wine, then refilled it.

"You are the Doge," she said. "If you want to marry me, I cannot say no."

"Don't be silly. I give you permission to turn me down."

"To be honest, I would marry you even if you weren't the Doge, and I think you would do the same if I weren't filthy rich."

He smiled. "You're right. I wish we'd met earlier."

"If we had, I'd be a child molester."

"I mean two or three years ago. I feel like I'm missing out on life when you're not around."

"What a sweet thing to say." She extended her left hand. He slipped the diamonix ring over her wedding finger, and then leaned across the table to kiss her.

Far across the galaxy at the Inn of the White Sun, the sentient machines had grown tired of Ipsy's officious, dictatorial methods. The feisty little robot's opponents formed a resistance movement that gained momentum quickly.

Before Ipsy could take counter-actions, he found himself exiled and tossed aboard a podship bound for the Hibbil Cluster Worlds. The other machines did this as a cruel joke, thinking that the Hibbils (who preferred their own regimented machines) would deactivate the patched-together Ipsy and dump him on a trash heap.

The royal wedding, held a scant week after the proposal, was by no means typical. At Nirella's suggestion, they made it an electronic event, broadcasting it all over the Merchant Prince Alliance by nehrcom. Even on Canopa, the couple invited only a few guests to the small theoscientific chapel where they exchanged vows, choosing instead to transmit the proceedings.

Francella, not a typical mother herself, did not complain, and neither did Jacopo or his shy and unassuming wife, Lady Amila Nehr. The parents seemed so pleased at the union that they didn't care how the formalities were accomplished. Lorenzo had no say in the matter at all, though he was invited and did attend. Keeping his feelings to himself, he sat quietly at the rear of the chapel with his Hibbil attaché Pimyt, while Francella and members of the Nehr family sat in the front.

The chapel, constructed almost entirely of prismatic glax, sat in a park in the Valley of the Princes. It had been the late Prince Saito's favorite place to go for serenity and contemplation, and seemed to Anton like the perfect spot for him to begin his exciting new life with Nirella. The altar contained a life-sized sculpture of the Madonna cradling models of technological devices, including a silvery vacuum rocket and a white, bubble-shaped nehrcom transmitting station.

When the participants began the ceremony, the weather had been cloudy, and through the prismatic roof of the structure Anton saw that the sky was a dismal gray. Then, just as they were about to exchange rings, the sun peeked around the cloud cover and shone a narrow beam of light on their hands, making the rings sparkle and gleam.

"I'd say that's a good sign," Nirella said as they kissed.

He laughed, and heard soft chuckles from the small audience.

To conclude the ceremony, the white-robed priest passed each of them a chalice of holy water, which Anton and Nirella sprinkled on one another.

Just then, Anton jerked in surprise when he saw two men enter the chapel and take seats at the rear, on the other side of the aisle from his father and the Hibbil. The late arrivals were Noah Watanabe and the bride's adventurous paternal uncle, Giovanni Nehr. What were they doing here, and how had they gotten past security?

"Look!" Anton said, pointing.

"A little wedding present for you, darling," Nirella said with a gentle smile. "You've been talking about the need for a cease-fire with Noah, so I thought we might have a little family reunion on our wedding day."

Anton exchanged nods and smiles with his Uncle Noah, across the chapel.

"I checked with your mother before inviting him, and told her what I had in mind. She was resistant at first, then agreed, especially when she realized that my father, as the MPA military commander, was arranging a cease-fire at the highest level, just for us."

"My mother didn't try to stop it?"

"No. Maybe she's changing."

"One can only hope."

"The public isn't being told that Noah is here, and no images of him are being broadcast from the chapel."

Anton nodded. "This is great, because I don't want to fight with Noah anyway. I'd been hoping something could be worked out, so that we could devote our full attention to our real enemy, the Mutati Kingdom. Podship travel could resume at any moment, and the war with it."

"I forbid you to talk shop on our wedding day," she said. "Now, go to him."

Beaming with delight, Anton made his way toward Noah, and they met halfway. As he passed his mother, the young Doge heard her muttering in displeasure, but she did not seem inclined to make a scene. Anton wondered if his wife had made a demand, and had gotten her way against her new mother-in-law. He hoped the two women would get along. It would be difficult if they did not.

"Congratulations, Nephew," Noah said, giving the young Doge a robust handshake. "Pardon me for being so familiar, but I still remember when you wore short pants."

"I'm glad you could make it," Anton said. "And you, too, Gio. It's great to see both of you."

"We're hearing good things about you," Noah said.

"And I'm hearing very little about you," came the Doge's rejoinder. "We have a great deal to discuss, but my wife says I can't talk shop on our wedding day."

"We can't stay long today," Noah said, "but perhaps we might get together another time." He looked up at a nehrcom unit mounted in the ceiling. "Your public awaits you."

The two men clasped hands again, and then the visitors hurried away.

CHAPTER SIXTY-ONE

The variations of God are infinite.

—Noah Watanabe, *Commentary on Sentience*

"I shouldn't have gone," Lorenzo said. "The tension was so thick in that chapel, you could cut it with a knife." He and his Hibbil attaché stood in a new casino module, watching robots move heavy gambling machines into place.

"To the contrary, My Lord," Pimyt said, rubbing his own furry chin. "It is always valuable to attend such events, for the purpose of gathering information."

"Perhaps, but I felt like jumping out of my seat and strangling Noah."

"Francella wanted a chance at him, too, and that's what made it so interesting. To her credit, she—and you, Your Magnificence—rose above petty grievances, and showed up for the sake of your son."

Arching his gray eyebrows, Lorenzo said, "My grievances against Noah are hardly *petty.* He and his Guardians undermined my leadership, and then he leaked the story about Meghina being a Mutati."

"You have evidence of that, Sire?"

"A gut feeling. Instinct."

"Mmmm. Interesting. Nevertheless, on a galactic scale, when you view the big picture, the immense societal tides that are flowing as we speak, all such interactions really are *petty*."

"I don't have to keep you around, you know," Lorenzo said. "You've always been rather haughty, and now that I've been deposed you have become openly impertinent."

"I only speak frankly, My Lord, which is what you need at the moment." The furry little Hibbil bowed. "I have always considered you a friend, and only want what is best for you."

With a hard stare, Lorenzo nodded and lowered his voice. "I suppose you're right. Very well, but do not speak to me in that manner when we are in the presence of others. We'll keep it our little secret, eh?"

The dark red eyes lit up. "Oh yes. I love secrets." Rubbing his furry chin, Pimyt said, "I wonder if Francella will keep her bargain with you, if she will truly allow you to influence the new Doge. We haven't heard much from her since the vote and the inauguration."

"She's been busy. Don't worry, Pimyt. Francella and I have a long relationship, and she'll come through for me, as she promised."

"I hope you're right."

They walked around a robot work crew, then exited the module and strolled down a glax-walled corridor, which offered stunning views of the armored space station modules, profiled against Canopa far below. It was mid-afternoon.

Ducking into an office that had formerly been occupied by General Jacopo Nehr, they closed the door and sat in comfortable side chairs. Pimyt had to hop up on a cushion and arrange pillows behind himself for back support. His uncovered feet dangled over the floor. The new Doge Anton had decided to keep General Nehr on as commander of the Merchant Prince Armed Forces, a decision that undoubtedly had a great deal to do with the fact that Nehr was his father-in-law.

"It will be interesting to see how much of an ally the general remains to us," Lorenzo said. "When he left, he expressed gratitude for the appointments I gave him, and he promised to always look out for my welfare. But things have changed, and we'll have to see how it all turns out."

"Now you're the worrier," Pimyt said, with a tight smile. "Jacopo will keep his word. I know this for a fact."

"And how can you be so sure?"

"That is my business, Sire, to keep such details in line. I have always been good at them, don't you agree?"

"Without question." The Doge Emeritus narrowed his eyes. "You almost sound like you have something on him."

A tight smile behind the salt-and-pepper beard. "I have something on everyone, Sire. Except you, of course."

"I wonder. Now let's talk about how to further our interests, and I'm not just talking about financial matters. Politics is in my blood, and always will be."

"I know that. Well, there is some dissatisfaction among corporate princes about the inauguration of Anton, who was brought to power by his mother and the noble-born, anti-corporate princes. A number of dissatisfied, self-made princes have contacted me, offering to form an alliance with you. They have not forgotten how you always rewarded performance instead of bloodlines."

"Good," Lorenzo said, nodding. "Form the alliances, and we'll build from them. But do not say anything against Doge Anton or Francella. We don't want our comments coming back to bite us."

"You are a master of diplomacy, My Lord."

Since escaping from the medical laboratory, Noah had been playing catch-up, learning about the guerrilla operations that had been undertaken by Subi and Thinker, and the assimilation of thousands of new robots that had formerly been Red Berets.

One morning he stood in a large underground chamber, getting an update from Giovanni Nehr, who wore his customary armor, making him look like a machine-man hybrid. Gio had been assigned to work closely with the new robots. The two of them watched as Jimu inspected hundreds of fighter bots, who stood in formation. While they had been extensively checked and reconditioned, some still had cardinal red markings on their metal bodies, which Noah mentioned.

"I'll make sure they're all cleaned off," Gio said.

"Hmm," Noah said, nodding, "but I'm more concerned about what's inside the robots, their programming. An enemy could implant latent operating instructions that are designed to activate at a certain time, or under certain circumstances."

"That would be a nasty trick."

"And devastating."

"Thinker already thought of that, and these robots have passed his rigid tests. He's checking others now by interfacing with them, and even tearing them down completely."

"Is he tearing all of them down, or only on a random basis?"

"The latter, Master Noah. Thinker ran probability programs, and he assures us that the likelihood of such problems is infinitesimal."

"I want all of them torn down anyway. It's better to be slow and safe."

"I'll tell him."

"Hear me well. I want the probability reduced to *less* than infinitesimal. All of the new robots are to be disarmed and placed under guard until they are fully cleared."

Gio saluted, and went to inform Jimu of the increased security measures.

That evening, as he had done on a number of occasions since returning to the Guardians, Noah attempted to reenter the cosmic web. In darkness he lay in bed, letting his mind float freely. He felt a slight tugging at his consciousness, and this gave him hope. Was he going back in?

But the sensation dissipated, and afterward he lay awake, wondering what was going wrong. Had he lost his previous powers entirely? And did that suggest he would lose his immortality as well? Most of all, it troubled him that he had not been able to remotely control podships for some time now. The last occasion that he had done it efficiently, without being rejected by the creatures, had been before he recommended drastic measures to the former Doge Lorenzo del Velli, measures that resulted in setting up the deadly pod-killer sensor-guns. Did the creatures know, somehow, that Noah had been responsible?

He had many more questions than answers.

Lorenzo knew he was licking his wounds, but he hadn't done so poorly in the exchange of his merchant prince leadership role for the life he led now. He was still one of the five wealthiest men in the galaxy, and remained widely respected. Under the new agreement, he had his own powerful paramilitary forces, Red Berets that had been assigned to protect him for the rest of his life. His space station—with a population now of more than twenty thousand persons—was well-armored, and surrounded by defensive gunships that were always on patrol.

As days passed, the Doge Emeritus formalized his new alliances, and had one brief meeting with Francella Watanabe. She told him, just as he had anticipated, that she had been busy with all of the arrangements involving the new Doge, and she and Lorenzo had to go through what she called a "cooling off period" before the former Doge could get more involved in Anton's affairs. Biting his tongue and not complaining, Lorenzo accepted her assurances. He was coming to accept the new arrangements, and understood that important political relationships did not always move forward quickly.

Even in his present position, Lorenzo had to be alert against Noah and his Guardians. Their guerrilla attacks and other disruptions had long been a thorn in his side, preventing him from dealing with other pressing problems. He was certain that Noah still wanted to get even with him for taking over the ecology compound, the orbital space station, and planetary recovery operations around the galaxy. All of that, when added to the likelihood that Noah had leaked the story about Meghina being a Mutati, made Lorenzo and Noah natural enemies.

"I'm going to get him before he gets me," Lorenzo said to Pimyt, during an afternoon meeting, held just before the opening of a new casino expansion module. Behind the stocky, gray-haired man a holo floated, an overview of intelligence reports that had come in on the guerrilla activities of Noah's Guardians. A timeline with it showed that they had stepped up their attacks against corporate installations on Canopa, though there seemed to be a slight reduction in attacks against government facilities.

"Good strategy," the Hibbil replied. "We know one thing. With podships cut off, he could not have gone far."

Now, with assurance from Francella that she would keep Doge Anton in line, Lorenzo instituted a renewed all-out effort to locate Noah's secret headquarters and annihilate him.

Chapter Sixty-Two

There are certain big events that mark historical turning points. It is invariably possible to look back on them years later and recognize them. For the most momentous events, however, you know them the instant you see or participate in them, the moment they are set into motion.

—Jodic Am'Uss, Official Historian of the Tulyan race

There were particular things that Eshaz could not reveal to the teenage Humans or to the Parvii woman. The full power of Tulyan mindlink was but one of many examples. He didn't know how he could put that phenomenon into words anyway, because he didn't fully comprehend how it worked . . . only that it did.

To discourage military aggression by outsiders, the Tulyans had leaked information that they had a powerful mindlink defensive system, and that certain Elders could actually hitch telepathic rides on comets and meteors, taking them on fantastic trips through space. These were true statements, but mindlink was much more than that. It had dimensions that had not been known to the Tulyans in ancient times when they were defeated by the Parviis, but which had been developed and perfected over the past century and a half. In galactic time, that was not very long ago at all.

It was not known by outsiders that the spectacular nighttime displays of comets and meteors in the starcloud were actually the result of the collective telepathic powers of the Tulyan people, under the guidance of powerful Elders. It was also not known that the Tulyans, considered a pacifist people, could now harness the energy of these cosmic bodies and turn them into weapons.

Previously the Parviis had broken through weak spots in mindlink, and had entered with their swarms, taking control of podships that were being hidden by the Tulyans. For weeks now, Parvii swarms had been gathering outside the starcloud, increasing their strength and trying to find the opportunity to break through again. This time they wanted to take over the seventy podships that Eshaz had brought back, along with the vessel that was under Tesh's control. But, with the tenuous, perilous condition of the galaxy, and the need for Tulyan caretakers to spread out in greater numbers, the Tulyans could not permit that to happen. They needed *more* podships, not fewer of them. They needed to end the cycle of Tulyan capture and Parvii attack.

The Council of Elders vowed that this time there would be no mindlink lapse, no opening for the relentless enemy to exploit. And for the first time in the history of their race, the Tulyans were going to do something unexpected, going on the offensive with their own telepathic weapon.

At the appointed time, in full daylight, Eshaz left his three alien companions at his home, and climbed alone to a high point of rock that overlooked his property, telling them only that he wanted time for contemplation. Reaching the pinnacle, he closed his eyes and focused all of his mental energies in the manner that the Elders had instructed him to do. In doing this, he, like other Tulyans involved in the effort, were energy boosters for the Elders, who were themselves performing more complex defensive and guidance functions.

They called it a telekinetic weapon.

In the universe of his mind, Eshaz saw the misty starcloud and its three planets, looking as if they were floating in a bath of milk. He felt the energy level rising, and then saw fiery comets and meteors approaching from space as if drawn to a magnet, along with glowing asteroids. At the last moment the celestial visitors veered off and headed for the largest swarm of Parviis, terrifying the tiny creatures and scattering them into space.

Eshaz felt a supreme relaxation of tension, and opened his eyes.

Like an island oasis in the troubled galaxy, the Tulyan Starcloud floated serenely and peacefully in the ethereal mists, as if nothing unusual had occurred at all, just as it had looked since ancient times.

It was the way the galaxy should be, unchanging and constant . . . eternal. But beneath the surface, beyond what Eshaz could see, he knew that the fabric of existence was shredding.

The Parviis, who had been thwarted in their desire to penetrate the mindlink energy shield, were now dispersed into the frozen void and sent spinning off in confusion, with their morphic field disrupted. As a result they lost contact with Woldn, who had been in their midst and had been controlling their movements.

Their connection to the Eye of the Swarm interrupted, billions of the tiny creatures flew off in all directions. Furious, Woldn dispatched squads to locate them. But when only a small portion of his people returned, it became clear to him that the others had perished, and that his power base had been eroded.

He hoped it was only temporary.

With the Parviis in disarray, the Tulyan Council of Elders sent out more than seventy hunting teams aboard as many podships, to the Hibbil Sector and to galactic sectors far and wide, where the wild podships migrated at this time of year.

Eshaz, having earlier merged with an alpha pod in order to capture an entire herd, piloted the same vessel now. He was the Aopoddae ship and it was him. The spacefaring vessel bore his reptilian face on the front of its hull, and its skin had taken on a scaly, gray-bronze hue.

Inside the passenger compartment stood six Tulyan hunters, anxiously awaiting the opportunity to go to work, to practice the ancient methods of capturing the mysterious, sentient creatures. Acey and Dux were on board with them, but Tesh—at Dabiggio's insistence—remained back at the Starcloud Visitor's Center. There had been something of a tug of war between her and the Council through intermediaries, and Tesh had held firm that if she was not permitted to join the hunt she was not going to release control of her podship to anyone. So, it remained sealed and motionless, floating in its docking bay at the starcloud. Through regular truth-touching to verify her motives and allegiances she was declared pure, and by majority vote the Council judged that she had at least earned the respect she was demanding.

But, like all Parviis, she had other information deep in her mind, and knew things that the mortal enemies of her people could never draw out of her. Not unless she told them. . . .

"Eshaz wants you boys to enjoy yourselves," said one of the Tulyan hunters in the alpha pod. A squat reptile with an angular grin, he went by the name Viadu. "Old Eshaz says you're experienced hunters."

"I wouldn't go quite that far," Dux said. "We were just observers the last time out."

"Well you're part of the team now, though you can't go outside and wrangle."

"Maybe we can," Dux said. He glanced over at Acey, who

was removing articles from a pack he brought along.

"What do you have there?" Viadu asked.

"Just something I put together with spare parts, while I was banging around in the Visitor's Center. It kept me busy."

Dux knew what it was. As he and the Tulyans watched, Acey brought out a helmet with a plax face plate, and a green protective suit modeled after the larger Tulyan models, to keep from being drugged or poisoned by thorns. He put the gear on.

Looking at him, the Tulyans laughed.

"Hey," Acey said, "I'm pretty handy with things, and I really can breathe inside this thing. I tested it. Made one for my cousin, too, but he's not as brave as I am."

"Not as *foolhardy,* you mean," Dux said.

"So, you want to go upstairs, eh?" Viadu said, to Acey.

The young man nodded vigorously, inside his outfit. His voice came through a built-in speaker, sounding thin: "This suit is perfectly sealed, and has oxygen for me to breathe. It's also thermally protected, since we Humans weren't born with much insulation."

"All right, but there are certain things you can't do, since the pods only respond to telepathy."

"I just want a front row seat up there," Acey said.

"All right, but if you get in the way, I'm sending you back down here."

"Agreed," the teenager said.

The Tulyans unpacked shipping cases and got into their own protective suits, after which they brought out thorn vines wrapped in broad leaf packages, and other items they would need. One of the Tulyans mixed liquids, powders, herbs, and thorn scrapings in small bowls, then tossed everything into a cauldron and heated it with fire cylinders in the alloy casting. Dux and Acey had seen Eshaz do this before, but they found it no less fascinating now.

Viadu murmured incantations and tossed spheres overhead, which played serene music and then floated down into the cauldron and melted into the boiling liquid. Working fast, the Tulyans filled silver vials with the liquid, then removed their protective suits and smeared pigment rings on their bodies, creating the network of intricate, iridescent designs that they had previously seen Eshaz create.

The Tulyans, slipping into a collective trance, murmured incantations and handled the multicolored thorn vines without protection, wrapping them around their waists and making red crowns for their heads. Bravely, Acey stepped forward, and Viadu wrapped a vine around his protected torso, along with a red-vine crown on his helmet.

Dux began to feel afraid for his cousin, but didn't say anything. They had already discussed this at length, and Acey would not be deterred. Being more circumspect, Dux thought it was too reckless, but he had tested the oxygen and thermal systems in the two helmets and suits himself, and had assured himself that it all worked. As far as Dux could tell, Acey had done his usual excellent job in putting the gear together.

A few minutes later the podship slowed, and Dux heard the Tulyans saying wild podships had been sighted. Moving quickly, Viadu opened a hatch and leaped outside, pulling Acey with him. The hatch closed quickly behind them. Through a filmy window that formed on the ceiling, Dux saw them standing on top of the sentient spaceship, leaning forward. From listening to the Tulyans, Dux had learned something that reassured him somewhat about Acey's safety. They said that all podships had protective fields around them, enabling pilots to ride outside, even at high speeds.

Eshaz guided the craft toward the rear of a formation of wild podships, and Dux saw Viadu use thought-commands to fire sedative vials at the creatures, causing them to slow, one by one. The alpha pod, sensing pursuers, turned around to confront them. Eshaz steered straight at him, and Viadu leaped onto the back of the creature, connected the harness, and dug thorn vines into its sides. Soon he merged into the flesh of the podship, and his face appeared on the prow.

Next the other five Tulyans in the hunting party went onto the top of Eshaz's vessel, one at a time, and in short order they captured five more podships and metamorphosed them into amalgam creatures with Tulyan pilots, while additional hunting teams came in and helped mop up the herd. From a porthole in the passenger compartment Dux watched in astonishment as Tulyans and podships seemed to create another race of hybrid spaceships.

Utilizing methods more mystical than technological, the Tulyans first fought Parvii swarms with comets and meteors and then wrangled more than three hundred additional wild podships, which they returned in short order to the security of the starcloud.

It was a historic day, and a reminder of legendary glories.

Chapter Sixty-Three

It is said that wisdom comes with age. I have lived for almost a million standard years, but I still have a great deal to learn.

—Ruminations of Eshaz

For the past month, Francella Watanabe had locked herself on the lower floors of her villa, refusing to see anyone. In all that time, she had not been to the laboratory complex or to her new CorpOne offices, and had not responded to requests from Lorenzo for appointments. While Lorenzo had relocated his office and residence to the orbital space station, he still had an unexpired lease for the top-floor suite of her villa, though he had not been seen there in some time.

Each day Francella sent telebeam messages to Dr. Bichette, asking for progress reports on the new elixir research program. He and his staff of brow-beaten, under-pressure scientists worked around the clock, with the desperate feeling that they were not just trying to save Francella's life, but their own as well. To enforce her orders, Francella had sent CorpOne security troops to ring the laboratory complex, and was not letting anyone out. Food was sent in, and the sleeping arrangements were improvised. Bichette sent constant, increasingly nervous responses to his menacing boss.

Failure was not an option.

The reason for Francella's isolation at the villa was obvious to anyone. The last time Bichette saw her she had been aging rapidly, at a pace that must have terrified her. He had been frightened himself, just seeing the way her face changed, day by day. Now it must look much worse, so shocking that no amount of makeup could conceal it.

One afternoon the doctor's medical assistant, Reez Carthur, sat at a desk preparing a response to Francella, informing her of the latest research results. As with the prior communiqués, the information was accurate, but he put the lab results in layman's terms, so that Francella could understand. Carthur spoke into a microphone, which transcribed his words and typed them into the telebeam transmitter.

Just then, Dr. Bichette burst into her tiny, windowless office. "Don't send it," he said. "I have an important update."

With great excitement, he dictated a message, telling Francella that at last he and his dedicated staff had been able to synthesize an elixir using Noah's blood, but there were distinct limitations. He told her they had taken a genetic blueprint from the plasma, but it was so complex that it defied any form of written or electronic documentation. Curiously, though, they had still been able to get the DNA of the plasma to transmit manufacturing instructions through a computer network, to produce an elixir. Computer projections indicated that the elixir could extend the lifetimes of Human beings.

He paused, and thought to himself. *Could extend.* The computer projections indicated something more as well, a bit of information he was not revealing to her yet. The elixir would only work on a small number of people, what he called a "micro percentage" of the population. It seemed best to omit that tidbit for now, and hope for the best. He had tried to get a probability of success percentage from the computer, but so far he had been unable to obtain it. The only answer had been, repeatedly: "Data incomplete."

Another detail troubled him, and thus far he kept this to himself, too. In the elixir manufacturing process, tiny amounts of Noah's original blood plasma would be used up, so production could not go on forever . . . unless they could take him captive again, or otherwise gain access to him. So many problems, but indications were that the plasma they had on hand would be enough to produce millions of capsules. . . .

Francella did not respond by telebeam. Instead, she showed up in person hours later, looking haggard and demanding a dose of the miracle drug. Only thirty-eight, she looked twice that age.

"We're not in production yet," Bichette said.

"I'm not made of patience," she said, something he already knew from personal experience.

"As I understand it, you don't want us to scientifically test the elixir before you take it? We only have computer projections at this point."

"You understand me perfectly."

Bichette heaved a sigh of resignation. Apparently she had not noticed the distinction he had made in his telebeam message to her, that the elixir *could* extend the lifetimes of Human beings. She wanted it to work so much that she was willing to take the optimistic view, and overlook any downside. Afraid to argue with her or point out pitfalls, he had no choice except to do as she demanded.

Under Francella's withering eye, Dr. Bichette and his staff rushed to set up a small-scale manufacturing facility in one of the laboratory rooms. In less than twenty-four hours they began producing capsules of blood-red elixir.

"This is not to be swallowed," Dr. Bichette said, having taken a capsule directly from a machine hopper and handed it to her. "Instead, it is to be squeezed between the fingers and injected into the skin by tiny needles."

With shaking hands, Francella squeezed the capsule. She closed her eyes, then opened them and looked angry. "I don't feel anything yet."

"We don't know how long it's supposed to take. We tried to get that information out of the computer, but got no answer. Besides, I suspect it's different for every person."

The used capsule in Francella's hand had become flat and gray. She tossed it aside. "Give me more," she said.

"Listen to me, please. Wait for a few days to see if you start feeling better. We'll check you and monitor your progress."

"Do as I say."

Stepping close to her, Bichette placed a reassuring hand on her shoulder. "Please listen to me on this. I care about you, and I don't want you to overdose."

"You'd better be right about this," she said, then whirled and left.

Chapter Sixty-Four

> For our race, web caretaking is the most ancient of tasks, the one for which we were born. Alas, alas, alas. So much in our heritage remains unfulfilled.
>
> —Lament of the Tulyans

For Tesh, it had been a stunning sight that had captured her full attention and a wide range of emotions, seeing hundreds of podships arrive at the Tulyan Starcloud, all bearing the faces of Tulyans on their prows, reminiscent of the figureheads on sailing ships in the old days of Lost Earth. For this epic event, she had been standing on a sealed observation deck of the orbital Visitor's Center, along with many excited Tulyans and a handful of dignitaries of other races.

As a Parvii, she knew she should not have felt that it was a wonderful moment, but she had been unable to escape the sensation of delight, and a chill had run down her spine. . . .

Now two days had passed, and as she stood alone on the same observation deck, she had not changed her impressions or her sentiments. It seemed to her that her own people had been in the wrong for much of the galaxy's history and she had been an unwitting part of it, a contributor in her own limited way. Long ago, Parvii swarms used powerful telepathic weapons to steal the fleets of podships away from their original custodians, the Tulyans, and then took actions to round up every last sentient spaceship that the Tulyans happened to get their hands on. For Tesh, born into the situation only seven centuries ago, she had not been provided with a context about this that would have enabled her to understand the immensity of the historical act.

She wondered if she had been brainwashed.

In orbital space, she watched a Tulyan face appear on one of the tethered ships. It was not Eshaz. The ship moved around to the other side of the formation, and disappeared from view.

Suspecting that Parvii belief systems had been imposed on her in subtle and deceptive ways, Tesh wondered how far the historical fraud might have gone. Did the Eye of the Swarm and others close to him know the true nature of the situation, or was he a pawn himself, having been fed false information that had become part of Parvii lore? Her people had no written history, only the oral traditions passed on from generation to generation, so she had no place to go and look anything up, no documentation. At least not through her own race. That was unfortunate. She wondered as well what documents or other forms of proof the Tulyans had, and if they might be tricking her now in some way.

But her heart told her otherwise, an innate sensibility that she always carried with her. Was the truth right in front of her eyes? From her private vantage point, she saw almost four hundred captured podships moored in nearby space, the bounty of two hunts, including the one she went on with Eshaz and the teenage Humans. The Council of Elders had decided to tether them at the center of the starcloud for maximum security, a strong point where the mindlink energies of the race were maximized.

Increasingly it seemed to Tesh that the decay of Timeweb might in large degree be the fault of her own race, for removing the Tulyan web caretakers from their jobs and only allowing a few of them to go about their work, not nearly enough for such a massive job. Considering this, with doubts seeping into her consciousness, she began to feel great shame. Not for doing anything wrong herself, since she must have been a dupe like so many others, but for the very fact that she was a Parvii. Such thoughts! Did she carry within her cells, within her DNA, the dark remnants of her genetic past, the shameful detritus of those in her race who had been directly and consciously to blame?

Yes. The truth stared her in the face.

But she knew that she needed to set these worries aside at this critical juncture in history, and begin anew with a fresh awareness and fresh eyes, doing her very best to right the wrongs of the past. As a result of those wrongs, the entire galaxy was out of balance, and crumbling away. She had to reveal certain information to the Tulyans, and saw no alternative. . . .

As she watched, two other ships took on Tulyan faces, and moved to other moorages. Even though she had seen the extraordinary piloting process several times now, Tesh didn't know if she could ever get used to it. The Tulyan method of piloting podships was so different from that of the Parviis. In a sense it seemed more personal to her, merging as they did with the sentient spacecraft. She wondered how the Aopoddae felt about it.

Prior to meeting Eshaz and sharing time with him, Tesh had considered his people her enemy. After all, they were a race that wanted to take away what Parviis had, control over the enigmatic podships that traversed the galaxy at tachyon speeds. She had seen Tulyans over the centuries, whenever they came around the Parvii Fold to perform timeseeing duties and other tasks, and whenever they rode as passengers in ships she piloted . . . but now she was beginning to perceive them as a tragically lost people, making a desperate, last-ditch attempt to regain their power and perceived purpose.

They are no longer my enemy, she thought as tears formed in her eyes.

With remarkable clarity she was beginning to see the error of Parvii ways, of aggressive actions that might have led to the extinction of any other galactic race except the Tulyans. Ironically, they were tough and resilient and were actually fighting to survive, unexpected qualities in a race that had professed pacifism for so long.

All her life Tesh had known that Tulyans were nearly immortal, since they were immune to disease and other forms of cellular degeneration, though it was known that they could be injured or even killed in accidents. Now she was beginning to understand that their twin curses of longevity and pacifism had forced them to watch as the galaxy and its Timeweb infrastructure disintegrated in front of their eyes. It must have been a terrible penalty for them to pay, a constant reminder of their supreme failures and of their once-glorious past.

At long last, their pacifism was over, and so, perhaps, was their longevity. The increasing physical discomforts the Tulyans were experiencing suggested that a process of bodily disorder and deterioration might be beginning in their race. Additionally she had heard that hundreds of Tulyans had disappeared, while working on their limited assignments around the galaxy. Though Tesh was not inside their skins, she felt as if she was beginning to get inside their heads, suffering with them, thinking more like them than a Parvii.

Nevertheless, it troubled her that her own people had scattered outside the Tulyan Starcloud and flown off in disorder. To her knowledge, nothing like that had ever happened before. Tesh knew full well what Woldn would do next, but she could not permit that to happen. . . .

That morning at the Tulyan Starcloud, Tesh approached Eshaz, in the lounge of the Visitor's Center. She slid into a seat opposite him at a table, after raising the chair to conform to her body size, which even in its magnified state was still considerably smaller than Tulyans. Since this was a diplomatic facility, the furnishings were designed to accommodate a variety of racial types and sizes. The two of them ordered cocaxy drinks in frosty, frozen glasses. It was as if Eshaz had waited for her to arrive before getting anything for himself, even though they had made no arrangements to meet.

"We received a message from Master Noah," the Tulyan said. "He asked about you."

"So?" She tried to still the quickened beating of her heart. "How is that of interest to me?"

Reaching into a body pouch in his side, he brought out a piece of folded parchment and placed it in front of her. "A transcript of Noah's message," he said. "A touch on your skin could tell me how it is of interest to you."

Tesh took a sip of the tart, aromatic drink and scanned the document, which had been printed in the widely understood language of Galeng. Noah's words were few, and she finished them quickly. "It's just an official communication; nothing personal here at all."

"That depends upon how you look at it. Right after mentioning your name, he asks that you and your traveling companions return as soon as possible."

"Don't be silly. I'm looking at his words now, and they refer to all of us, not just me."

"On the contrary, there is a certain emphasis, a *weightiness* to what he is saying. Our diplomatic people have examined it carefully, and there is no doubt. He is asking about your welfare, and wants to see you."

"Well, maybe you're right." Tesh smiled stiffly. "After all, I am not without certain charms. But I must discuss something else with you, something of far greater consequence than the fates of two people in a huge, crumbling galaxy."

Eshaz nodded solemnly. "Proceed."

The Parvii woman had something very important to say, one of the secrets of her race. She struggled to express herself, having practiced how she might say this, but faltered under the enormous gravity of all the warnings she and her ancestors had received against revealing such information. Finally she paused, unable to get the words out the way she wanted.

Reaching across the table, Eshaz made contact with the crackling energy field that was Tesh's second skin, touching her projection-enlarged left hand. In performing this truthing touch, he absorbed her thoughts as Tulyans could do with another galactic race . . . but she knew he still didn't obtain the information she had to reveal to him. She sighed deeply, trying to calm herself.

Presently Tesh told him without speaking, *My people are very aggressive, with angry tempers. You Tulyans may have won a battle with your newfound telepathic powers, your mindlink. But you have stirred up a huge hornet's nest, and the Parvii potential is much greater than yours. We have rapid breeding methods, and the capacity to use the most devastating psychic weapons in the galaxy, with the concentrated focal power of millions of Parviis at a time. In ancient times, my people employed these devices against Tulyans and other races, destroying entire fleets and planets.*

She paused, letting the information sink in. He didn't transmit any thought response, or say anything, as if he knew she still had more to say.

Continuing her internal monologue, she told him, *The ancient knowledge is still available, held in sacred reserve by our war priests. As you know, I am an outcast, no longer in contact with Woldn's morphic field, but I still sense that something big is brewing. I know my people well, and what the legends say we will do in a time of dire need. At this very moment they have sought sanctuary in the Parvii Fold, where breedmasters and war priests are working together for a retaliatory strike.*

Now Eshaz pulled back. His gray, slitted eyes flashed with alarm. "This is very disturbing."

She spoke, too. "A great deal is at stake. I want you to accompany me on a diplomatic mission to the Parvii Fold, before my people can regenerate and mount a counterattack. We must convince Woldn that war between our races is suicidal, and. . . ."

"And that we need to work together to preserve and repair the galactic infrastructure of Timeweb," he said, interrupting. "Tulyans and Parviis must use the entire podship fleet cooperatively for the most massive project in history. Thousands of ships to transport repair teams all over the galaxy, to as many trouble spots as possible. For the sake of harmony, Parviis can pilot the ships, while Tulyans such as yourself can perform the web repairs."

"You and I are beginning to understand each other," she said with a slight smile. "Let's hope it bodes well for the others we must convince."

"You would return to the Parvii Fold?" Eshaz whispered to her. "But you are an outcast, forbidden from returning to your people."

"I must risk everything, as all of us must. The stakes are too high for any concerns about personal safety. Yes, I would do that, and much more."

Finally, Eshaz sat back, and stared across the table at her.

She pushed the cocaxy drink away.

"I will seek the advice of the Council," he said.

Eshaz requested an emergency meeting with the Elders, and they assented. He told them Tesh's story, and her astounding proposal. A short while later they summoned her before them, and listened attentively to the details. She told them she wanted Eshaz to accompany her to the Parvii Fold, perhaps with a diplomatic team of Tulyans. Then she clasped her hands in front of herself, awaiting their decision.

"You say you want Parvii pilots to transport podships around the galaxy, containing teams of Tulyan repair teams," First Elder Kre'n said, after a brief conference with the other Elders. The Tulyan leader paused, as if expecting a response.

"That's right," Tesh said, filling in the quiet that had fallen across the great chamber.

"Tulyans and Parviis can never work together in a meaningful way," Kre'n declared. "We agree that web repairs are needed, but for that we don't need Parviis at all. We can pilot podships *and* do the infrastructure repairs. Your request is denied."

"But you are in grave danger!"

"So are we all." Kre'n waved an arm dismissively. "You have our permission to leave the starcloud on your 'diplomatic mission,' but *alone*. It will serve no purpose for any Tulyans to accompany you, as it could inflame the passions of Woldn in an unproductive way."

"Not even Eshaz? Woldn knows him."

Eshaz grabbed her by the arm, squeezing it. "Don't argue with the Elders."

She pulled away. "I'm not. I'm just. . . ."

"Their decisions are carefully thought out," Eshaz said, "and based on reasons you could never understand." He glanced up at their unsmiling faces, then back at her. "The Elders will not reconsider."

He escorted her forcefully out of the chamber.

"Your people can never defend against a Parvii telepathic onslaught," she said, in the corridor outside. "You have no concept of the terrible destructive force that war priests can generate. They have a focal weapon, drawing upon the primal energies of the universe."

His eyes widened. "I have heard stories of such a thing, legends. But we have a highly advanced form of mindlink now, which we didn't have in the old days. We will not fall so easily."

"But why risk a battle with the Parviis? No matter how it goes, it will be a waste of valuable time and resources."

"Go quickly," Eshaz said, as they reached the smooth plax deck outside. "I will remain here with my people in our small moment of triumph and renewal, working with the few hundred wild podships we have, practicing with them on the podways that are protected by the starcloud."

"Your moment of triumph will not last long." She narrowed her eyes. "Is that all you're going to say to me? Just go, and good luck to you? Don't you understand the immensity of this?"

"The Council has spoken. We must do as they command."

"You've argued with them before."

"I've tried to *persuade* them of certain things. But after working with them for so long, I know when it is utterly hopeless, and when it is certain to raise their ire. I must say, they don't trust you, don't really believe you. The truthing touch did not reveal any of this additional information, so they're assuming it's an insidious Parvii trick, and they wonder what else you might have hidden. They would rather spend their time and energy on shoring up the defenses here."

"I'm very worried about this. Woldn is going to strike back, using ancient weapons."

"With the stakes so high, we won't be routed easily."

"I hope you're right," Tesh said. "But won't you come with me?"

"No."

"Why not?"

"For reasons you can never understand. Now go! You're wasting time."

While packing her things and readying for departure, Tesh heard a rap at her door. Touching a remote pad to open it, she greeted Acey and Dux.

"Eshaz told us about your diplomatic mission," Dux said. "Let us go with you."

She frowned. "For the sake of adventure, or to really help?" she asked.

"I don't think I can give you a good answer to that," Dux admitted. "If I say what you want to hear, you'll think I'm lying."

"That's about the only thing you could have said to please me," she said, with a grin that flashed white teeth.

"We won't get in the way," Acey promised. "We just want to go with you as your friends."

"Be careful," she said. "You might say something that doesn't sound sincere."

Acey looked crestfallen, and Tesh added quickly, "I would like both of you to come along as my friends. I appreciate your devotion, and I've come to believe that all the races must work together. Woldn will not be pleased to see you, but such contacts must begin someplace."

"So we are emissaries?" Dux asked.

"Isn't every member of every race, whenever they come into contact with another galactic species." Looking both boys over, Tesh added, "You couldn't possibly be spies."

"Do you include the Mutatis in your vision of races working together?" Dux asked.

"Well, perhaps there are exceptions," she said, with a small smile. "You must be on your very best behavior, though, and the trip will be dangerous. There are tremendous perils on the way to the Parvii Fold, and as I told you I am an outcast, forbidden to mix with my people ever again."

Dux, who could wax philosophical at times, responded, "Safety is never more than an illusion anyway, no matter where . . . or who . . . you are."

"I travel light," she said, in a cheery voice. "How about you guys?"

"We're ready!" Acey said. . . .

Eshaz secured the necessary departure permission from the Council for the last-minute inclusion of the teenage boys. The Elders were only too happy to let the Parvii woman go, along with the Humans.

"Even assuming the best about her, she is on a fool's mission," Dabiggio said.

"So it seems," Kre'n said, wrinkling her bronze-scaled face in worry. "But what if we're wrong?"

"Not even worth considering," the big Tulyan responded.

In the tension of the Council Chamber, Eshaz wisely remained silent, then bowed and left.

After delivering the clearance to Tesh, Eshaz caught a shuttle home. On the way, he saw her podship slide away from its docking bay and head into space. The sentient craft accelerated, and vanished in a flash of green light.

Chapter Sixty-Five

> It is a deadly, ancient clash of inbred racial purposes, those of the Tulyans and those of the Parviis. And at the middle of their conflict is yet another race, the Aopoddae, the most enigmatic of all . . . and perhaps the most important.
>
> —Noah Watanabe, *Reflections on my Life,* Guardian Publications

On board the podship, Tesh left the teenagers in the passenger compartment, then entered the sectoid chamber by herself. The boys understood in general terms that she was piloting the ship, and had asked her for details, but she avoided telling them very much. They were her friends, but she had not felt comfortable discussing certain subjects with them yet, things that she had been taught from an early age were important Parvii secrets.

Already, she had gone farther than any Parvii was permitted. If Woldn learned what she told the Tulyans, she could be put to death, but the galactic stakes were so high that she had to take the chance. Secrets. She was beginning to think it was a dirty word, and a tool with which she and others like her had been controlled for so long.

Tesh was violating another prohibition now, in taking the boys to the Parvii Fold. Oh, she had excuses worked out in her mind for Woldn, that the Human teenagers were Guardians as she was, and they were working with her to maintain the integrity of the galactic web. This was all true, but she would have to do a lot of smooth talking to convince the Eye of the Swarm. There was also the matter of the Tulyan she had befriended, an alien who had been facing similar challenges regarding his own racial secrets. To Tesh, and she suspected Eshaz felt this way as well, such secrets didn't matter anymore. The integrity of the entire galaxy was at stake, not territorial claims or racial power structures.

She was beginning to doubt many of the "sacred" teachings that had been passed on to her during her lifetime, and had been wondering how much of the information had been a clever web of deceit. Now she was taking two of her Human friends to the most clandestine of all Parvii gathering places, which could subject her to severe discipline from Woldn, but she was willing to face that possibility. She felt newly strong and defiant, and could not wait to tell him with determination and absolute certainty what needed to be done for the sake of the galaxy.

It took longer than Tesh had anticipated for her to cross space, since she ran into a stretch of bad podways on the far side of the Oxxi Asteroid Belt, and had to slow down. Only a few years ago, when she piloted other podships on these and other routes, she only rarely encountered this sort of problem. Eshaz had told her that entire galactic sectors had collapsed since then, from the continual entropic decay of Timeweb. This was of increasing concern to her, as it was to the dedicated Tulyan caretaker.

After almost two hours, the podship finally entered the treacherous Asteroid Funnel leading into the galactic fold of the Parviis. Inside the passenger compartment, Acey and Dux looked out portholes and saw grisly clusters of tiny Parvii bodies outside floating in the vacuum . . . along with the tumbling, luminous white stones of the funnel, stones that were slowed by the collective mass of the corpses. So was the podship, which had to carefully negotiate the funnel in order to elude the stones and thick groupings of bodies.

In the green glow of the sectoid chamber, Tesh was even more horrified than her two passengers, but she kept advancing toward her destination anyway, with tears streaming down her face. This was the most terrible Parvii tragedy she had ever seen, and in all likelihood the greatest in their entire history.

Finally the spacecraft emerged into the immense, pocketlike Parvii Fold, where even more chaos became apparent. There were clusters of bodies everywhere in sight, floating and bumping into one another, and more podships than she had ever seen before—thousands and thousands of sentient spacecraft overflowing the moorage basin. Some of the vessels were tethered together, but many were not and just floated aimlessly in the airless vacuum, as if even the life force of the sentient creatures themselves had gone out of commission.

Around the faintly glowing Palace of Woldn, Tesh saw a comparatively small swarm of Parviis—a few million of them flying to and fro lethargically, with nowhere near their usual hummingbird energy. As she tethered her ship, she saw that the grand palace was weakening, since the Parviis holding it together were losing strength and causing structural deficiencies and inconsistencies in the simulated gravity system. Many of them had a sickly, yellowish sheen to their bodies.

Leaving her personal magnification system off, Tesh entered the large palace by riding in on a shoulder of Dux Hannah, who walked beside Acey Zelk. Both of the boys wore their thick green protective suits and helmets, to enable them to breathe and to survive in the subzero environment. They were like giants entering the building, but the structure was on such a majestic scale that they still had plenty of headroom.

Inside a vaulted chamber on the second level, Woldn lay on a bed formed by his fellow Parviis and fabric, while a small number of his advisers sat or stood nearby. None of them were flying, and many looked gaunt as they walked about arthritically, with the natural color drained from their faces.

Like a Lilliputian speaking to giants, Tesh told her Human companions to find a place to sit off to one side, and they did as she wished, on the simulated marble floor.

Approaching the Eye of the Swarm, Tesh told him where she had been, and asked what had happened to him.

"You!" Woldn exclaimed, half rising out of his bed. Tall by Parvii standards, and wiry-thin, he wore a dark robe. "I forbid you to be here! And you bring Humans? What madness is this?"

"I have come nonetheless," she said, in a gentle voice. "For your sake, my honored leader, and for the sake of all galactic races. We come on a mission of utmost importance."

"What sort of drivel is this? Leave my sight, before I have you killed."

Four of his aides moved toward her, but stopped when Acey made a motion to intervene. The Eye of the Swarm was sending them telepathic commands.

"You always were outspoken, weren't you?" Woldn said, to Tesh. "Is there no escape from your meddling, even on my deathbed?" He sat up, arranging tiny pillows around him. "Once, I had high hopes for you, but you let me down. You let all of us down."

Tesh moved closer to him, and felt herself engage with his weakened morphic field. Though Parviis could transmit thoughts telepathically to one another, and could limit what information they passed to each other through this means, she instead opened her mind and did not attempt to conceal anything from him. Feeling the outflow of her thoughts, Tesh watched the expression on his narrow, creased face as he assimilated the data and perused it. She revealed her ideals to him, how she thought Humans, Tulyans, Parviis, and other galactic races needed to work together.

"You have experienced a great deal in your life," Woldn said, at last. "Important things."

"Yes," she said, softly.

"Your intentions are good. I see that. But I cannot agree with your reason for coming here. You ask too much. My people will never work on equal terms with Tulyans or Humans. For millennia, for as long as the memory expands and the stories are told, Parviis have been the dominant race of the three. That will not change under my leadership."

She said nothing, and hoped that he would cogitate further, analyzing the information she had provided from new angles. But he was sick and weak, and might not have the capability to do so.

In a diminished, cheerless voice, Woldn said that the new defensive weapons shot by the Tulyans—comets, meteors, and radioactive asteroids—had caused immense harm to the Parviis, disrupting the energy fields that connected them paranormally with their brethren, throwing the tiny people into disarray. The damage extended to some Parviis who had been piloting podships out in deep space, causing them to fall off course into uncharted regions. It also killed most of the breedmasters and war priests, preventing the symbiotic segments from organizing a retaliatory force to strike back at the Tulyans.

"It is terrible to see what has happened to my brethren," Tesh said. She nodded toward an uncovered window, where bodies floated in space.

Woldn nodded, then continued. He said he withdrew all of his people into the Parvii Fold, along with every podship still in their control . . . more than one hundred thousand of them. But in what had become known as "the Tulyan Incident," at least eighty percent of the Parvii people had died. It was the greatest catastrophe in their history.

She stood and listened sympathetically while Woldn lamented

at length, wondering how the tragedy could have possibly occurred when he and his followers had worked so hard, the way his people always had. Parviis had swarmed the perimeter of the Tulyan Starcloud many times before and had dealt with Tulyan defensive measures, always getting through eventually to recapture podships—but never in the past had Parviis been injured or killed by Tulyans. It used to be easy to blockade the Tulyans for punishment, driving them crazy by confining them to their impenetrable starcloud, but it was much different now.

"If I survive this," Woldn said, "I don't want to risk going back there for a long time." He swung out of bed and paced around slowly, in his robe.

"The Tulyans have developed a weapon we never expected," Tesh said, "but our troubles go beyond anything they did to us. Our plight is another symptom of the deterioration of Timeweb. We Parviis can no longer go our own selfish way as we have in the past. We must cooperate with other galactic races from now on . . . and especially with the Tulyans, whom we have always sought to dominate and humiliate."

"We have never charged for galactic transportation services," Woldn said indignantly, "and have provided them faithfully for millions of years."

"With the exception of charging Tulyans for their limited travel rights," she said, "by making them timesee for us."

"Well, yes," he admitted, folding his arms across his chest. "But that's so minor in the overall scheme of things that it's hardly worth mentioning."

Tesh knew that the historical currency of her people was not money or precious jewels; it was the thrill of mastering the magnificent podships . . . the supreme ecstasy of piloting them across vast distances, while keeping other galactic races from doing so. But Woldn's impassioned argument was making no headway with her at all. It didn't alter, in the least, what needed to be done.

In a firm voice she said to him, "Your morphic field is weakened and might never recover. Forgive me for saying so, but you might die. Have you appointed a replacement?"

He stopped pacing. His shoulders sagged. His entire body sagged. "My heir apparent is dead, along with three backups. The entire order of succession that I established." Gazing sadly at her, he said, "Once I considered you a candidate, with your strong will and intelligence. But you went too far in your defiance, and disappointed me."

Her eyes twinkled softly. "I never would have guessed how much you liked me."

"I have never *liked* you. I have only observed you carefully, and have discussed you at length with my top advisers."

"And now?" she said, grasping at possibilities. "Is there still a chance for me? You have seen the loyalty in my heart, the great vision I have for the galaxy."

He shook his head stubbornly. "Because of your rebelliousness I would never teach you the way of the morphic field, no matter the situation. But the secret will not die with me. I will heal, and so will my people." He looked away from her, as if uncertain of his words.

Going closer to him, Tesh said, "But if you die without a successor, there will be no Eye of the Swarm. With no one to take your place and establish a Timeweb-spanning morphic field, our people can no longer pilot the fleet of podships across the galaxy. I think you should make all of the podships available to the Tulyans immediately, so that they can accelerate their critical work. Do it with them: Parvii pilots to transport Tulyans, so that they can do the web caretaking tasks."

"*Their* critical work? What about *our* critical work? Without the podships, we would be nothing."

"I'm not suggesting that you turn the ships over to them. As I said, we can maintain Parvii pilots."

"It's a trick. I don't trust them."

"Then put a small swarm into each podship, enough telepathic power to defend it."

"No. We are weakened, we are ill."

"We need to get beyond this discussion," she said. "The Tulyans must maintain and repair the galaxy the way they used to, long before you or I were born."

"If we lose the podships," he said with a glare, "what is our purpose? We will go extinct."

"Our prospects are not good now. Besides, every race in the galaxy will go extinct if you don't cooperate."

He stood speechless for only a moment. "In time my people will heal," he insisted, "and everything will be back to normal again."

"There's nothing more I can say to you then," Tesh said, angrily.

"Everything will be back to normal again," he repeated, with a far-away look in his eyes, as if his mind had slipped out of gear.

Frustrated at her inability to sway him, Tesh departed with her two friends. Before getting the podship underway she stood in the passenger compartment and told them, "I can't tell you how disappointed I am at Woldn's selfishness. I hate to say it, but if all of my people die, maybe that would be the best thing that could happen."

"Maybe he'll change his mind," Acey said. His wide face was etched with concern.

"I don't think he ever will," she said.

"Why don't we go see Noah and consult with him?" Acey asked. "We know he escaped from his sister's laboratory, so he's probably back at Guardian headquarters now."

"Maybe you're right," Tesh said, brightening a little. "I'd like to see him, and with any luck it shouldn't take us long to get there."

"One thing though, Acey," Dux said. "We'd better steer clear of Giovanni Nehr, or we'll do something we'll regret."

"Guess you're right." Acey looked dark, then grinned disarmingly. "Hey, we should *thank* him. If he hadn't boxed us up and shipped us into space, we wouldn't have gone on the wild pod hunts, or ever seen the Parvii Fold."

"Just stay away from him," Dux said. "No threats, no nothing."

"All right." Acey thought for a moment, and asked Tesh, "What about the Doge's electronic surveillance system around Canopa? We can't just swagger back into the pod station and take a shuttle down to the planet."

"There is a way of taking the podship directly to Canopa," she said, "circumventing the pod station and the most advanced scanner nets. It's a tricky landing maneuver, but I can do it."

"Is it dangerous?" Acey asked.

"You bet." Then she squinted at him and added, "But that only makes it more appealing to you, doesn't it?"

Chapter Sixty-Six

We believe that the Aopoddae may have evolved from something quite different, and that they did not always look like the podships they are today. We have long known that they are shapeshifters, for they can adjust their cabins, cargo areas, and other on-board components. It has been assumed that they are not Mutatis, but if this assumption is incorrect, our enemies have plans we cannot possibly fathom.

—Doge Anton del Velli

After crossing space, Tesh took her podship down to the surface of the planet Canopa, avoiding the orbital pod station and landing in a wooded clearing near the concealed entrance to Guardian headquarters.

To accomplish this, she had taken a circuitous, multi-speed route that enabled her to pass undetected through the electronic surveillance net in Canopa's skies, using skills she had learned from one of the most talented of all Parvii pilots, Ado. Centuries ago, under his very special tutelage, she had been taught that there were instances of pod stations being damaged or destroyed, so that Aopoddae vessels occasionally had to take alternate landing measures. Ado had taught her how to elude electronic security and virtually anything else in her path, from tumbling rocks in the Asteroid Funnel to objects floating through the atmospheric envelopes of planets. . . .

A squadron of robots entered the clearing as she and the teenagers disembarked. Noting green-and-brown Guardian colors on the machines, Tesh sighed in relief.

"I'm Jimu," a small, patched-together robot announced in a formal voice. "I have identified each of you by your spectral characteristics. Please follow me."

The three visitors followed, though they knew the way.

Just inside the entrance to the subterranean headquarters, Noah greeted them stiffly.

"They landed a podship out there in the meadow," Jimu said. "My robots are putting an electronic net over it to prevent detection."

"We saw it all on a security screen," Noah said, shaking his head in disapproval.

"It was a bit tricky getting through the planet's security net," Tesh said, "but I can do it again to get out of here. The way I do it, they don't even know I'm getting through."

Noah motioned to Thinker, and told the boys to go with the cerebral machine. They walked away slowly, but lingered to eavesdrop.

Scowling at Tesh, Noah then said, "You were undetected by the planetary net, but we picked you up on our system?"

"Different systems, different results. I came in fully aware of both systems. Look, Noah, I could explain it to you in detail, but there are other matters we need to discuss first."

"We don't know if you consider us Guardians anymore," Acey said. "But we want to stay with Tesh wherever she goes."

"Just go with Thinker right now," Noah said in a firm voice. "I also have some things to discuss with Tesh." Frowning, he watched the flat-bodied robot walk away with Acey and Dux.

As the boys entered a burrow tunnel, Acey told Thinker excitedly how he and Dux went on two podship hunts, and rounded up almost four hundred sentient spaceships. The boys provided some of the most colorful details.

To Thinker, this was entirely new information, beyond anything in his data banks. He asked for more specifics, and found himself intrigued and astounded by what he heard.

Somberly, Noah turned to Tesh. "I'll decide the priorities here," he said, "and I don't like your daredevil flying. If you brought a podship in, that means the Mutatis might do the same, and use one of their doomsday weapons against Canopa . . . or against another Human-ruled planet."

"I don't think that could possibly. . . ."

Noah cut her off. "If the Mutatis learn what you have done, a new avenue of attack could be opened. If they can land without a pod station, it becomes a lot harder to prevent attacks."

"I am among the elite of all Parvii pilots, and hardly anyone can match my skills. Besides, all of the Mutatis that we saw in merchant schooners have been denied access to space travel . . . just as Humans have been cut off. The shapeshifters don't have their own podships, and neither do your people."

"You shouldn't have come without calling," Noah said. "You put all of us in danger."

A silence fell between them. Noah shot a hard stare at her, and when she gave him a hostile look in return, he wondered if she could see beyond his veneer to the attraction he felt for her. Now that Tesh was no longer with his nephew Anton, there was nothing to keep her and Noah away from each other. Nothing except for the tension that constantly existed between them. Now something sparkled in her eyes, like a little dance of light. A glint of attraction for him? But it only lasted for a moment, before her own veneer replaced it.

Noticing that she was beginning to shake slightly, Noah placed a hand on her shoulder and said, "I wish . . . I wish for so much, but there have always been complications surrounding us."

Her eyes flashed. "What are you trying to say?"

"That we should understand one another better, that we should. . . ." He looked away, and instantly regretted letting his guard down with her.

Upset, she pushed his hand away and said, "I'm a Guardian, and that's all." He had trouble reading her. Previously she had pursued him physically, but now he wondered if that had only been a ploy on her part, to manipulate him for her own purposes. Still, he couldn't help wondering what it would be like to make love to her, this woman of a different race. She certainly was attractive, especially when angry. Feeling a slight flush, he took a deep breath and struggled to suppress his emotions.

"We have certain feelings for each other," Noah said, choosing his words carefully. He felt awkward, though. "Or should I say, *toward* each other. In any event, the emotions are there, and we both know it. But whatever those feelings are, and wherever they could take us, I have always known that we need to set them aside. Whether it is affection or loathing, we cannot let them get in the way of our duties. Our priorities must lie elsewhere."

"Nothing else occurred to me," she huffed.

He said bitterly, "Then we agree on something after all."

"I have important information to tell you," she said. "I just came from the Parvii Fold, and. . . ."

This elevated Noah's anger, reminding him of the way she brought her podship in. "Yeah, you flew through the security net and imperiled us all. I told you how I feel about that. Listen, I have other things to do now, so we'll have to talk later." Before she could respond, he whirled and stalked off.

★ ★ ★ ★ ★

To Noah Watanabe, problems were piling on top of problems, big ones coming in so quickly that he was feeling overwhelmed by them. Tesh's unapproved podship landing would require some thought. For the time being, he notified his security force to put her and the boys on lockdown. They would not be allowed to leave the headquarters without his express permission.

The evening before, Noah had been trying to deal with another big challenge, his continuing inability to enter Timeweb or control podships. Again, he had failed to make the necessary mental leap, and he'd been left wondering why. Noah had been sensing cosmic disturbances all around him.

In addition, he'd been trying to improve another difficult situation. Recently he had made diplomatic overtures to Doge Anton, his nephew who had never formally resigned from the Guardians. So far Anton had not responded, but Noah wondered if it might be possible for the two of them, at long last, to reform the Merchant Prince Alliance into a more environmentally-aware entity. That would not be easy, because of the influence Francella seemed to have over her son, whom she had brought to power. Noah was sick of the politics, the constant small-minded maneuvering and jockeying for position when much larger issues were at stake.

As he entered a dimly lit tunnel, Noah saw Thinker approaching.

"The boys have given me important information," the robot said. He described the successful wild podship hunts.

"At least that's some good news," Noah said.

"There's more, Master Noah. As you know, the Parviis have a vast galactic network of pilots who are in control of podships, and they're the ones who cut off podship travel to Human and Mutati worlds."

Noah nodded. He had learned this previously from Tesh.

"Master, their transportation network is in complete disarray. At the Tulyan Starcloud, the Tulyans mounted a surprise attack against the Parvii swarms and scattered them into the galaxy. Many Parviis died, and the powerful morphic field that keeps their race together has fallen apart. Their leader withdrew the entire podship fleet to a secret place, the Parvii Fold."

"So that's what Tesh wanted to tell me," Noah said. He thought for a moment. "And Eshaz. Where is he?"

"Still at the starcloud, with the podships they captured."

"The boys say that Tesh came here to discuss using diplomacy on the Parviis. She couldn't convince Woldn on her own, and wants your help. Tesh thinks the entire podship fleet should be used to transport Timeweb repair teams around the galaxy."

"We'd better find her right away," Noah said.

"Exactly what I was thinking," the robot said.

Chapter Sixty-Seven

For every life form that is declining, another is in its ascension. It is one of the eternal balances of galactic ecology, and an engine by which the system continues to advance.

—Master Noah Watanabe

Acey Zelk lay awake in an agitated state, staring into the shadows of the barracks building, one of several inside the largest subterranean chamber. He heard Dux sleeping on the bunk just above his, and through a high window he saw a faint glow of indirect lighting on the ceiling of the natural cavern. Before retiring for the night, Acey had gone off on his own and asked a few questions of a pretty young woman, pretending to be Giovanni Nehr's friend. Now he knew exactly where Gio was in another chamber, inside one of the robot-assembly buildings.

Gio, wearing his foolish body armor, had his own private quarters there; he was receiving favorable treatment as if he were a general in Noah's forces instead of a supervisor of robotic assemblies. Even that position irked Acey, because it showed that Gio was gaining undeserved respect in the Guardian organization.

Acey knew he had given his word to Dux to stay away from the man, and that meant something. But other things were more important. He could not ignore what Gio had done to them.

Silently, Acey slipped out of bed and grabbed his shoes and

clothing, which he put on when he was outside the barracks. Like a shadow, he hurried through a tunnel toward the robot section, following the directions that the young woman had provided. On the way he passed sentient machines as they went about their sleepless work, carrying materials and blinking and beeping with their electronic communication systems. Acey felt a slight current of cool air in the passageway, which he attributed to all of the activity around him. The robots hardly gave him any notice.

Reaching the designated structure, which had been painted Guardian colors, Acey opened a door and slipped inside. Just as the young woman had described, it was an assembly area and an inspection facility for former Red Beret robots, which were disassembled there and checked in detail. Robot parts lay in neat groupings, and work was continuing under the supervision of a small, blinking robot.

It was quite noisy in the building, and Acey wondered how anyone could sleep through it. He got his answer when he opened the door to Gio's quarters and slipped inside.

The windowless room was filled with white noise like the steady pulse of an ocean, or the inside of a seashell, a continuous sound that drowned out all of the activity outside. In dim light coming through cracks around the door, Acey saw body armor on the floor and Gio on a bed, fast asleep. Leaning down, Acey removed a puissant gun from its holster, and set the charge. A yellow energy chamber on top of the barrel glowed.

Finding the white-noise transmitter on a bed table, Acey adjusted the background murmur, making it go up and down. With the glowing weapon behind him to keep the light low, he stood at the head of the bed and watched as Gio began to toss and turn, his sleep disturbed.

With his eyes still closed, Gio reached for the noise transmitter, but could not find it on the side table. He opened his eyes, and at first did not see the intruder.

"Looking for this?" Acey asked, tossing the transmitter on the table. "Or this?" He shoved the glowing barrel of the gun in Gio's face.

Startled, Gio tried to pull back, but the agile teenager jumped on the bed and straddled him, with the gun jammed against his forehead.

"What are *you* doing here?" Gio asked, recognizing his attacker.

"That's my question for you," Acey said. "I'm here to stop you from pulling off your next nasty little scheme." He saw fear in the man's eyes.

"Please don't kill me," Gio whimpered.

In disgust, Acey swung the gun and hit him hard on the side of the head.

Dazed for a moment, Gio lashed out and threw the teenager off, causing Acey to tumble to the floor. At the same time Gio set off an alarm, and klaxons sounded.

In Noah's office, the Master of the Guardians and Thinker had been holding a late night meeting with Tesh, discussing the surprising new information about podships—those under Tulyan control and those at the Parvii Fold—and the apparent breakdown of Parvii power.

As Tesh spoke about her own people and all of the tragic deaths, her eyes misted over, but she seemed able to overcome it and find an inner strength. Newly impressed, Noah felt his anger subsiding. She had come in and landed like a hot-rodder, but her flying skills were superb and she did have important things to tell him. Things that were better said in person than over communication links that could have been intercepted or compromised. For the moment Noah and Tesh set aside their differences, though he felt the residual tension between them, and knew from her demeanor that she did, too.

"Acey and Dux say you tried to convince the Parviis to allow their podship fleet to be used by the Tulyans for repair work on the galactic infrastructure . . . Timeweb. Apparently, Woldn didn't like your proposal."

"That's right, but I still consider myself one of your Guardians, and I'm here seeking your leadership on this critical matter involving galactic ecology . . . the phrase you coined, Master Noah."

"What do the Tulyan leaders think of your idea? I assume you discussed it with them?"

"Of course, but they don't think Parviis and Tulyans can ever work cooperatively on a project of that scale. They say they don't need Parviis to pilot podships, that Tulyans can do that, and the web repairs, too."

"That sounds short-sighted," Noah said. "But I suppose it's the result of millennia of hatred and loathing between the two races."

"The Tulyan Elders think I'm a wild card, and since I'm a Parvii they don't trust me. But Noah, if I work with you and the Guardians—offering solutions for the huge ecological crisis—maybe they'll take me seriously. Maybe they'll take *us* seriously." She paused. "The Tulyans are an ancient people, with a history of pacifism. They scattered Woldn's swarms this time, but I don't think the Tulyans should try to go against the Parviis again without help, not even with the weakened state of my people."

"So that's where Humans come in, eh?" Noah said. "We're much more warlike, and can stand up to your tough brothers and sisters."

She shook her head. "I came to you, Noah, because the Tulyans respect you—and because Humans can convince them of the need for diplomacy in this matter. If we send a joint Human-

Tulyan diplomatic mission to the Parviis, maybe Woldn will finally listen."

He nodded, but hesitantly. "Maybe."

She went on to tell him what she had related earlier to Eshaz, that the ancient Parviis had used powerful telepathic weapons against their enemies, and that Woldn had obviously gone back to the Parvii Fold to resurrect those powers.

"But Woldn said most of the breedmasters and war priests were killed when the Tulyans disrupted his morphic field, thus slowing down the regeneration of Parvii telepathic power." She paused. "I feel we must move quickly with diplomatic overtures, before my people find a way to regenerate their destructive powers. As a species we are survivors, and as bad as it looks for Parviis now, I think they will find a way."

"Diplomatic overtures, you say, and not a military strike?"

"I would never cooperate with an attack against my people. For their sake, and for that of everyone else, diplomacy is the only way."

"But couldn't it come with military might reinforcing it?"

Folding her arms across her chest, Tesh stared at him. "I will not discuss such matters. If you keep pressing me, we shall have nothing more to discuss."

"I wouldn't say that, Tesh. Actually, you showed good sense coming here, providing us with reconnaissance about what happened to the Parviis and verifying that they still control thousands of podships. I also want to meet with the Tulyan Elders, and I would like you to take me there."

She was about to say something when the alarm klaxons went off, with the pattern of sound indicating the location of trouble.

"Robot section!" Thinker said, heading for the door.

Noah ran around the slower robot, followed by Tesh.

★ ★ ★ ★ ★

Human and robot Guardians were hurrying ahead of Noah, and he ran after them, just ahead of his two companions. Reaching one of the robot-assembly buildings, Noah saw that the doors were wide open. Inside, sentient machines and Human Guardians were gathered at the interior door that led to Giovanni Nehr's private quarters.

Pushing his way through and entering the room, Noah saw Gio and Acey rolling on the floor, fighting for control of a puissant pistol. The weapon glowed yellow. A shot rang out, and one of the robots fell. Then the gun fell, and one of the Guardian women kicked it away.

Two Guardian men grabbed Gio to restrain him, while a pair of robots took hold of Acey.

Noah demanded to know what they were quarreling about, but both Acey and Gio sulked without saying anything.

"Dux and Acey told you about the prison moon quarrel," Tesh said, "when they claimed that Gio tried to push Dux out of an airvator, but it's gone beyond that. Now the boys think Gio drugged them and shipped them into space."

"Is that so?" Noah said to Acey.

The young man nodded.

"Well?" Noah said, looking hard at Giovanni Nehr. "Did you do it?"

Standing up straight, the chisel-featured man said, "None of it. The boys are liars."

"Acey, what proof do you have?" Noah asked, waving off the Guardian robots. They released their hold on the teenager.

"Dux and I saw what he did on the airvator, and we tried to set aside our anger about that. Then he drugged us and put us in a spacebox. We could have been killed, and he didn't care. He just wanted to get rid of us."

"Tell me more about this alleged drugging," Noah said. "Start at the beginning."

"To be honest," Acey said, glaring over at Gio, "we didn't actually see him do anything, but he's the only one who *could* have done it. For some reason, he wanted to get rid of us."

"Earlier, you promised me that you would set your differences aside," Noah said. "Now you've decided to break your word based upon a mere suspicion?"

"I'm sorry," the boy said, hanging his head, "but I know he did it to us. No one can ever change my mind about that."

"Gio is in charge of new robot recruits from the Red Berets," Noah said, "making sure they are all torn down and thoroughly checked. He's been doing a great job, and I trust him completely."

"Well we don't," Acey said. "You'd better tear him down like one of those robots and find out what's going on inside his brain, because he has a really dark side."

Noah shook his head. "I find that impossible to believe."

"His brother is the Supreme General of the Merchant Prince Alliance," Acey said. "Jacopo Nehr is your enemy, so how can you trust his brother?"

"I don't consider the MPA my enemy," Noah said. "It's Lorenzo and Francella I oppose, not the new Doge. As for Jacopo Nehr, I've always respected him, since he raised himself up by his own bootstraps, unlike most of the noble-born princes. In any event, Gio never got along with his brother. We have good evidence of that."

"Dux and I didn't leave here on our own. That bastard drugged us and packed us in spaceboxes."

"You're still a Guardian," Noah said, "and I expect you to rise above personal conflicts for the sake of our cause. There are too many important problems to be dealt with for all of you to be squabbling like kids in a schoolyard."

Acey and Gio exchanged hateful stares.

"I don't want to see you within fifty meters of each other. Stay apart. Do you both understand?"

They nodded.

"If Eshaz were only here, he could discover the truth," Tesh said, moving to Noah's side. "Tulyans can touch your skin and read your thoughts. Are there are any other Tulyans here at the headquarters?"

"Zigzia," Noah said. "She sends messages for us to the starcloud."

"We could do that," Tesh said, glaring at Gio, "but I believe Acey and his cousin."

"I may be able to solve this right now," Thinker said. A tentacle snaked out of his head and hovered over Giovanni, the robot's organic interface. "Shall I?" Thinker asked, looking at Noah.

Pursing his lips, Noah said, "I've always resisted using that, or the Tulyan method for lie detection. I refuse to run a police state around me. Instead, I prefer to look into the hearts of people, and in that way I sense if they are loyal to me or not. I try to inspire people to follow me, to believe in my ideals."

Looking at Gio, however, Noah noticed him sigh in relief. This gave the Guardian leader pause, but still he did not give Thinker the go-ahead. "I must say, Gio," Noah said, "that I have always sensed you are troubled, but I never sensed any betrayal of me or the Guardian organization."

"I'm totally loyal to you," Gio said.

"That may be true," Noah said, "and I won't force you to undergo lie detection. However, if you want to clear this matter up, there is an easy way to do it."

"A painless way," Thinker said to Gio. "In only a few seconds, I can download the contents of your mind and analyze them."

Gio struggled against the men who were holding him.

"I don't like what I'm seeing here," Noah said. "Why would

you want to harm those boys?"

"I didn't want to harm them. That was an accident in the air-vator, and I took steps to make sure they could breathe inside the spaceboxes."

"So you *did* do that," Noah said.

"I told you!" Acey exclaimed.

"Only because I knew they would never let up on me," Gio said. "I had to get rid of them before they got rid of me."

"We're not like you," Acey said. "We don't sneak around pulling dirty tricks."

"Take Gio away," Noah said to the men holding him. "Lock him up until I decide what to do with him."

"No!" Gio shouted, struggling unsuccessfully to get free.

Disgusted, Noah turned his back on him.

The cell had an electronic code, which the two Guardians activated with a touch pad to lock Gio inside. The prisoner didn't bother to sit on the bed, since he didn't plan to stay that long.

A week ago, he had supervised robots as they repaired the locks on the cells, so he knew the codes. Now, after the Guardians left him alone, he uttered the eight digits aloud to voice-activate the lock. The metalloy door slid open with a soft squeal.

Gio ran out into the corridor, and made his way to a secondary entrance to the headquarters. Again, he knew the codes to get out, since he had been one of the most trusted Guardians, and had been sent on several reconnaissance missions into the nearby towns.

But as he worked the codes, he heard something behind him and whirled.

Thinker stood there, with orange lights glowing and blinking around his face plate. "My probability program brought me here," the robot said.

"You predicted I would be here?" Gio asked.

"Probabilities are not the same as prescient-based predictions. Machine programs are not the same as organic brains. Nonetheless, my system works rather efficiently."

Expecting Thinker to detain him, Gio hesitated and considered his options. The door was not responding.

He repeated the codes. This time the door to the secondary entrance opened, sliding into the wall.

Gio stepped through the doorway, not feeling the electronic signal that the robot fired into his brain, erasing all knowledge of the headquarters location. For Thinker, the safety of Noah and the Guardians was paramount, and he had decided it was time for Gio and the organization to part. This man who had worn armor and had served in Thinker's own army could not cause trouble any longer. . . .

As Gio ran through the moonlit woods, he felt confused and lost. Why couldn't he tell which direction to go? His brain whirled, making him dizzy. Sitting on the ground to gather his thoughts, he saw the trees whirling around him. Every direction looked the same to Gio, and he had no idea where he was, though part of him knew that he had been here many times before.

Back in the headquarters, Thinker had been behaving strangely. But where had that been, and what had the facility looked like? He had no images of the place, only of the people and robots he had been with there.

Thinker did something to me, Gio realized.

Feeling a wave of sadness, he knew he had not betrayed Noah at all. Though Gio's motives had been complex and he had a penchant for promoting his own interests, he had genuinely liked and respected Noah, and had hoped to advance his own career in the Guardian organization. Admittedly Gio had taken shortcuts to get ahead, but he wasn't the only one who'd ever done that.

Now all of his hopes were dashed. The Guardians thought he was a bad person, but that wasn't the case at all. He had always been loyal to Noah, and had done a good job for him.

He just couldn't get along with those meddlesome teenagers.

Chapter Sixty-Eight

Such an odd pairing, Princess Meghina and Lorenzo del Velli. She is known to show compassion, and has a love for exotic animals, while he has revealed himself to be the opposite, a cruel and scheming man. It suggests that our perceptions of both of them may not be entirely accurate.

—Subi Danvar, security briefing at Guardian headquarters

The young Doge was not sure how to respond to the conciliatory messages from Noah Watanabe, which he had been receiving in the form of personal letters delivered by an intermediary. To Anton, it seemed as if he himself had lived two lives. In the first one, Noah had been his beloved uncle and much-admired Master of the Guardians. But in Anton's second incarnation, Noah had been the most wanted criminal in the Merchant Prince Alliance, accused of murdering his own father and of guerrilla attacks against corporate and governmental interests.

Dressed in a golden cloak over a jerkin and leggings, Anton paced the perimeter of a rooftop garden connected to his private office suite. Across the square he saw the Hall of Princes, with its red-and-gold banners fluttering in the breeze, each emblazoned with the golden tigerhorse crest of the del-Velli royal house.

My house, and my father's, he thought.

Even with the change in his own position, and the resultant metamorphosis in his relationship with the Guardians, Anton didn't think he could ever hate Noah. Now, in his official capacity as the most powerful of all merchant princes, Anton might be forced to put him to death, but he could never hate him.

Anton held the latest letter now, written in Noah's own hand. The paper crackled in a gust of wind. He had delayed answering the earlier communications, which must have made Noah think he was ignoring him. But that was not his intent.

It occurred to the Doge that Noah might very well guess what was going through his mind at that very moment, that Anton had never intended any disrespect by not answering. Noah must know that his own sister would interfere and prevent answers, but in this case that had not occurred. The letters had been delivered to him directly, and Francella did not know about them. Somehow, Noah had used his contacts to arrange that.

The young leader found himself in a difficult political position, feeling conflicting pressures and loyalties. The letter in his hands mentioned setting priorities, and placed the Mutati threat near the top. Noah wanted a cease-fire, so that the Guardians and merchant prince forces might work together for a common good.

Anton re-read the letter's provocative last sentence: *"I have recently obtained access to a podship, with a pilot for it."*

This intrigued Anton immensely, but he was politically aligned with his own mother Francella, who hated her brother. In addition, Anton was now married to the daughter of General Jacopo Nehr, a man who was still on friendly terms with Lorenzo del Velli—who had recently instituted a program to find Noah's elusive Guardians and annihilate them. The former Doge was doing that with his own private forces, in alliance with various corporations who opposed Noah's guerrilla environmental activities.

So far Anton had used his own influence to keep his forces

and other government resources out of such operations, asserting that they were needed elsewhere. In reality he still admired his uncle, and could never envision taking overt action against him. Anton had also resisted making any contact with him, thinking it was best to remain essentially neutral and let the warring factions fight it out among themselves.

I must not allow personal feelings to interfere, Anton thought as he went back into his office. *I must make the right decision for the Alliance.*

From youthful inexperience, he was not certain whom to consult about this situation. As time passed, he had come to the realization that he would need to make the decision on his own.

He added the letter to the others, locked away in a cabinet.

Chapter Sixty-Nine

It is one thing to know you are going to die someday, at an indeterminate moment. It is quite another to see the process accelerate in front of your eyes.

—Francella Watanabe

With money, all things are possible, she thought. *What a lie that is, what a cruel lie.*

Money could not buy love or happiness, or the salvation of Francella's life, which continued to dwindle away while she suffered helplessly. For weeks, the wealthiest woman in the Merchant Prince Alliance had been holed up on the lower floors of her cliffside villa, avoiding all Human contact. She took her food through slots in the door like a prisoner, and she wasn't much different from that, because she was trapped inside her ever-weakening body. She looked like an old lady now, like her own grandmother. The elixir that had been prepared from Noah's blood was not working on her at all, though she had been trying it in all conceivable doses, taking care to space them out (as Bichette had recommended) so that she did not overdose.

Enraged, she hobbled through the villa, even going to the top floor that was still leased to Lorenzo, though he had not been there in months. She smashed every mirror in the elegant home, even breaking anything that showed the slightest reflection of her aging face. Hardly any piece of glax survived, and she had every window covered on the inside (and many on the outside) with shutters. She even ordered that every serving robot be painted in dull colors, and that their synthetic eyes and other forms of visual sensors have no sheens whatsoever. Everything in the villa had to be either modified or replaced, to meet her demands. Even the smallest item that could cast a reflection.

Throughout Francella's increasing madness, money rolled in. Much of it amounted to paper profits, since she received regular nehrcom-transmitted statements on how her holdings continued to mount around the galaxy. But a lot of it was real and tangible, profits that she could get her hands on from her extensive Canopan operations, and from her generous share of her son's tax collection revenues, much of which came in from the many companies that had their galactic headquarters on Canopa. This planet, home to Prince Saito Watanabe, had been second in its wealth only to Timian One. And now, with the obliteration of the capital world, Canopa was preeminent.

She had enough money to keep CorpOne's expensive medical laboratories and other industries going strong for a long time, facilities that were now heavily guarded by her own corporate military forces, along with contingents of Red Berets that Anton had assigned to her. With money, it should be possible to find a cure for her malady. But how long would it take? She was running out of time.

In her rising despair, she had considered hurling herself off the cliff by her villa, shooting herself in the head (or having someone do it), taking poison or having it injected, and even getting into a vacuum rocket and flying far away into space, bound for unknown regions. How romantic that last option sounded, and how utterly foolish. If she did that, or decided on any of the other options, it would amount to giving up. And she wasn't about to do that. As long as she could manage one breath from her lungs, she would struggle to have a second, and a third.

Each mouthful of air and each moment had become precious to her, but the effort to sustain herself was hellish. She wished she could just rest and stop thinking about her problems, but knew she had to keep trying. Something would turn up, a medical procedure or even a miracle that had seemed impossible before. If her brother could have his miracle, she deserved her own, too.

Her thoughts ranged from philosophy to the pits of gloom, from hope and light to dark, homicidal rage. Her medical researchers lived in terror of her, and well they should, for their inexcusable failures. Periodically she had been getting rid of the people she felt were incompetent, or getting in the way of progress. All of her medical laboratories had been fitted with video-recording devices, enabling her to watch the progress of each experiment closely, listen in on the conversations, and send out her killers. All while never leaving her villa. Thus far she had spared Dr. Bichette, but with her own increasing medical knowledge—from observing and from her studies of technical holobooks—she had been selecting the doctors to work with him.

Bichette had been recommending that she broaden the scientific study of the elixir by bringing in more test subjects than just herself and the handful of others they had been using. She was coming around to agreeing with him. By seeing how the elixir worked on different people, it would surely reveal more information, and might open up new, critical avenues of research.

So it was that one day Francella transmitted her orders directly to Dr. Bichette, who had been ordered to never go out of range. "I want you to immediately distribute elixir to a broad spectrum of Canopa's population," she said. "Charge a price for it, but not too high, so that we pick up a variety of social strata and genetic types. Don't put any limitations on it. I want all galactic races—at least those on the planet now—to have access to the elixir. Include a sampling from Lorenzo's space station, too."

Francella could not see Bichette on any screen at the moment, but she heard him muttering angrily, followed by the suction sound of a toilet. She smiled to herself.

Presently, she saw him in the hallway outside the restroom, staring up into an electronic eye. "Did I hear you right?" he asked.

She saw two robots with dull silver patinas pass by him and continue on their way.

"You did, and I want it instituted immediately. My lawyers will form a new subsidiary of CorpOne to handle the sales. Mmm, we'll call it LifeCorp, and its product will be the Elixir of Life. How does that sound?"

"Excellent, ma'am, but I must tell you something we have discovered. We can produce millions of capsules, but we must be careful not to use up all of Noah's blood plasma in the manufacturing process. Until we locate him, the blood supplies we have are irreplaceable."

"Of course, of course."

"Very well then, ma'am. I'll take care of it right away."

"I know you will."

Everything in Francella Watanabe's life was on the fast track, including her bodily decay and the commands she issued in a desperate attempt to stave off the end.

In a matter of days, LifeCorp salesmen spread out to the major cities of Canopa, using old-fashioned hucksterism and showmanship to draw crowds and sell the product. In this manner, they sold more than two hundred thousand capsules of elixir, as many as they had been allotted, while leaving plenty of Noah's plasma for Francella herself and for other studies.

Even in the face of mounting military and political tensions, her new profits were substantial. But she didn't care a whit about the money. Concurrent with the marketing program, she dispatched an army of medical researchers to study the path of each capsule of elixir after it was sold, analyzing how it affected those who took it. Each purchaser had to sign a holodocument, agreeing to cooperate with the research program. Offered the prospect of eternal life, no one argued with that.

Out of all the elixir capsules that were sold, the product did enhance the DNA of a small number of people . . . but only six. This was in line with a computer projection that Francella discovered Dr. Bichette had withheld from her. Against what have been expected, she actually forgave him for that, as she came to realize he had not wanted to discourage her, and she would not have wanted him to. Even if the odds were pitiful, and they were close to that, she wanted every chance she could get. Every straw of hope.

The sales and research program became like a lottery, with the prize going to only a few. But what a prize it was! The winners emerged under widespread publicity and then tried to continue their lives and vocations, envied by all who knew them.

One of the lucky winners was Princess Meghina, the infamous Mutati who wanted to be Human, and who had remained in that shape for so long that she could not change back. She lived in her own private apartments on Lorenzo's orbital Pleasure Palace.

Far across the galaxy, at the Tulyan Starcloud, Eshaz was summoned to the private office of the First Elder. As Eshaz entered, he saw Kre'n standing at her central work table, with Dabiggio sitting in a sling chair on one side. Uncharacteristically, the big

Tulyan Elder had a smile on his bronze-scaled face, which surprised Eshaz.

"And where is your Parvii friend and her vast fleet of podships?" Dabiggio asked.

"She'll be back," Eshaz said.

"With the ships?" Dabiggio's large body caused the sling chair to sag low, just above the floor.

"If anyone can do it, she can."

"So, she's a super Parvii, just as Noah Watanabe is a super-Human. Is that it? My, you certainly have influential friends. But has she even sent a message? Any word at all?"

"Not to my knowledge," Eshaz admitted.

"We should never have let her go," Dabiggio said. He hefted himself out of the chair and stood by Eshaz, at least a head taller than him. "She admitted having information beyond the reach of our truthing touch . . . all that stuff about breedmasters, war priests, and unstoppable telepathic weapons. She was probably a spy, and has given military intelligence about us to the Parviis."

"After millions of years, the Parviis have a lot of dirty tricks," another Elder said, a thin male who was one of the followers of Dabiggio. "The way they magnify themselves should tell us something. They never are what they appear to be. How do we know they even resemble Humans in their appearance? Maybe they're something else entirely, something they don't want us to know about. Think about the way their swarms move, too, defying physics and even the imagination. They breathe without air? What are we to believe about such a race?"

"Even if Tesh Kori brings the ships," Dabiggio said, "we shouldn't let her back into the starcloud. I say we keep the mindlink barrier up and strike the fleet the way we hit the swarms."

"If she brings the ships, we're going to let her in," Kre'n said, interrupting the exchange between the Elders. "Bringing them here would be a feat never seen in the annals of history."

"And you would sacrifice our race just to see it?" Dabiggio asked. "There is no limit to the tricks they could pull on us if we let them in. These are *Parviis* we're dealing with, remember, not innocent children."

"We're all in trouble anyway," Kre'n said. "Even if she brings us half that many, or a hundredth, we have to take the chance."

"OK," Dabiggio said, grudgingly. "But if she doesn't get back soon we need to embark on repair missions with what we have, making a last-ditch effort to save what's left of the galaxy."

"Agreed," Kre'n said.

"She'll be back," Eshaz repeated. "I know she will."

At that moment, thousands and thousands of Tulyan repair teams were being assembled on the three worlds of the starcloud, along with the potions and other supplies they needed for their work. As it looked now, there would be many more teams than ships, a reality that would restrict the efforts considerably.

To deal with this serious limitation, the Elders were assembling reports from all of their web caretakers. The trouble spots were being prioritized on a triage basis, like injuries on an immense galactic battlefield. . . .

Chapter Seventy

We have discovered six immortals—the Mutati princess, four Humans, and a Salducian diplomat. It is not too early to declare all of them immortal. Their cellular structures have changed dramatically, with the addition of what we are calling 'warrior antibodies'—proteins in their bodies that annihilate all disease pathogens, both overt and latent. As stipulated in the contracts they have signed, we are now drawing their blood and flash freezing it. This offers the potential that much more of the elixir can be produced, and that we will not need to worry so much about using up the plasma of Noah Watanabe.

—Dr. Hurk Bichette, report to Francella Watanabe

Whenever Lorenzo gambled in his magnificent orbital casino, he did not relax, not even when he was winning, which was virtually all of the time, due to the unregulated programming of the games and machines. He always had a lot on his mind, and as the revenues poured in, he was not much happier than Francella.

One glittering evening he stood in front of his elegantly dressed patrons to promote his newest game, which featured a smiling Mutati simulation. Behind him an oversized mechanical creature changed smoothly into a variety of alien and animal shapes, while the patrons oohed, aahed, and hissed good-naturedly.

"The players sit at those stations," Lorenzo said, pointing to chairs and screens that ringed the faux Mutati, which continued to metamorphose. "When the bell rings, you have one minute to place your bets and select from the shapes on the screen, as you guess which shape the monster will take when it stops."

"Like a roulette wheel?" a woman asked.

Lorenzo laughed. "Certainly not. It's like a *Mutati!* Can't you see that?"

The crowd laughed, and people moved forward to take seats at the play stations.

At a gesture from Lorenzo, the large mechanical creature stopped metamorphosing, and became what looked like a flesh-fat Mutati, in its hideous natural state.

Leering at the creature, a drunken nobleman asked loudly, "Is that what Princess Meghina looks like when she takes off her makeup?"

Some people laughed nervously, while others gasped in shock, since it was known that Lorenzo had stood steadfastly by his courtesan wife, and had even given her private apartments on the orbiter.

"I shall consider that the liquor talking," Lorenzo said with a hard stare. "Otherwise, I would have to create a new game just for you, based upon the torture chambers in the Gaol of Brim-rock."

This elicited hearty laughter among the nobles and ladies.

"It's nice to see all of you enjoying yourselves," Lorenzo said, "but keep this in mind. My lovely wife will get the last laugh on all of us. She has not only changed her appearance to that of a Human, but she may have become immortal, enabling her to dance on our graves."

This dampened the amusement somewhat, but Lorenzo knew these foolish people would soon be back at the games, transfer-ring their assets to him. He only had to make their losses amusing, and even verbal jousts served that purpose. The gamblers would keep coming back.

In the midst of the throng, Lorenzo recognized a tall, sharp-featured man and nodded to him. It was Jacopo Nehr's younger brother, Giovanni. Lorenzo heard he had been traveling, so he must have made it back to Canopa just before the cessation of podship travel.

As the Mutati game got underway, Lorenzo slipped into an office to discuss the events of the day with his attaché, Pimyt. The Doge Emeritus greatly appreciated the loyalty of this aging Hibbil, and had raised his salary to even more than he had earned as a government employee.

"What are you doing with all of your money?" Lorenzo asked. He and his aide sat at a table where cups of steaming mocaba juice had just been set out for them.

"Hiring bounty hunters," the Hibbil said, as he took a sip of the beverage without waiting for it to cool. High temperatures never seemed to bother him, though this was not reportedly a Hibbil characteristic.

"Eh?"

"To bring Noah in." Pimyt had wet fur on his upper lip, from the drink.

"Oh, but you don't have to pay for that personally. Just pay it out of my accounts."

"I'd like to bring Number One in with my own money. Somehow, it sounds more special."

"Ah, nice idea. I'll raise your salary to make up for the payments. Come to think of it, maybe I'll pay for some bounty hunters myself, making it like one of my gambling ventures. I am a lucky man, you know. Despite my recent political challenges."

"You are, indeed. Now, onto business. So far, even with the help of our powerful corporate friends on Canopa, we cannot locate Noah's hidden headquarters. We could use help from the new Doge, but to get to your son we have to go through Francella, and she's gone into seclusion."

"So much for her promises of access to Anton. Well, we'll have to get Noah without him. I want him more than anything."

"We'll get him anyway. I have a devious move in mind. Since Anton's ascension to power, Noah has gone to ground and is no longer attacking government facilities, perhaps under some secret arrangement that we don't know about. Even so, we can make it look like he's still operating."

Pimyt laid out an intriguing plan, causing Lorenzo's eyes to narrow in concern.

"We can penetrate some of the corporate guard forces on Canopa and destroy assets, making it look like the Guardians did it."

"Which corporate assets?"

"NehrGem. They have a jewelry-manufacturing operation in the Valley of the Princes."

"But Jacopo Nehr is one of our friends."

"And he hasn't been helping enough, not as much as some of our other friends. I have incontrovertible evidence, if you want to review it."

"No, that's your job. I trust you."

"Thank you. Maybe Jacopo has been distracted by his military duties, but—as you know—we don't accept excuses."

Lorenzo nodded.

"We won't do major damage to his facility," Pimyt said, "only wrecking a small percentage of it. Just enough to anger Jacopo and get him working harder to find our bad guy. We'll use some of your backup Red Berets, the ones stationed down on Canopa."

"Go ahead and set it up."

The little Hibbil nodded. "One more thing, Your Magnificence. This just came in from the government." He activated a telebeam unit on the table, causing a black-and-white message to flash on, floating in the air. The words were backwards to Lorenzo, so he touched a pad to spin it around his way.

"Interesting, wouldn't you say?" Pimyt said.

"To say the least."

Truly, this was startling news, and Lorenzo was not sure what to make of it. The shutdown of podships had enlarged. No longer confined to Human and Mutati worlds, it now encompassed the entire galaxy . . . and neither he nor Pimyt could imagine why.

CHAPTER SEVENTY-ONE

Princess Meghina is expressing a desire to come out of seclusion and mingle with the patrons of the orbital casino. Polls show that much of the public is willing to assume the best about her, asserting that she should never have been born a Mutati in the first place.

—Telebeam report to Francella Watanabe,
read just before one of her ranting tirades

Ostensibly, the damage to NehrGem's industrial complex appeared minor, as only a small section of one jewelry-manufacturing building had been destroyed by the remote-guided rocket, and fire suppression systems had prevented further damage. But that section had contained the rarest gemstones in Jacopo Nehr's collection, garnered from mining operations around the galaxy. If podship travel did not resume, he could not hope to replace these losses. Even some piezoelectric emeralds of the type used in nehrcom transceivers had been destroyed, making it an Alliance security matter and a subject of utmost military importance.

In a matter of hours, forensic evidence revealed that the perpetrators had been Noah Watanabe's Guardians, based upon tracking records that turned up on fragments of the rocket. And, with a brashness that made Jacopo's blood boil, Noah even sent a telebeam message to Jacopo's offices afterward, claiming full responsibility for the attack.

Feverish with anger, Jacopo ordered immediate retaliation, and he began searching for a place to strike. This proved to be a challenge, since the perpetrators could not be located. They were like wisps of wind, gusting up here and there and then disappearing into thin air. As a consequence, the targets were limited . . . but not non-existent.

Within two days he set his sights on a warehouse and storage yard where the confiscated assets of Noah Watanabe were held under government seal. These were items that had been removed from the Ecological Demonstration Project and from the orbital EcoStation.

Seeking no approval from Doge Anton or the Hall of Princes, Jacopo launched a full-scale bombing attack on the warehouse and storage yard, using one of the merchant prince aerial squadrons. Not surprisingly, since there were no defensive weapons at the facility, he succeeded in completely destroying the target.

That evening, he was confronted at his office by one of Doge Anton's Red Beret officers, Lieutenant Colonel Erry Pont. Sputtering in protestation while the officer read a list of charges against him, Jacopo summoned his own security personnel to prevent the man from arresting him. Six uniformed NehrCorp guards rushed into the office and surrounded the red-uniformed officer.

"You cannot hope to resist the power of the Doge," the officer said calmly. Jacopo recognized him as the son of Gilforth Pont, one of the leading noble-born princes. In an obviously intended slight, Lieutenant Colonel Pont had not removed his red cap, and gazed at Jacopo with an arrogant expression.

"Take off your hat in my presence," Nehr demanded.

The officer glanced around, then did so. But his arrogant expression did not change and he said, "In your vengeful zeal, General Nehr, you overlooked some rather important legal details, which I would be happy to explain while I take you into custody."

"I will *not* be taken into custody!"

"Even though you are in command of the Merchant Prince Armed Forces," Pont explained, "you carried out an unauthorized and illegal course of action. Those were no longer Guardian assets you destroyed. They were the assets of the Merchant Prince Alliance, since they had been officially confiscated and placed under seal."

"Mere technicalities. I'll explain it all to Doge Anton myself."

"He has authorized me to tell you that he is not interested in any explanations. He is quite upset."

"Why? Is he a puppet of Noah Watanabe as rumors suggest, protecting Guardian assets and refusing to bring the little worm to justice?"

"The Doge will not be pleased to hear you said that, General."

"Or is he a puppet of his mother, who is coddling noble-born brats like you and your father?"

"General!"

"Tell Anton I refuse to be arrested, and I refuse to listen to any charges!" Nehr thundered. He waved a hand. "Now go, before I place you in one of my brigs!"

"I'm afraid he's gone too far," Doge Anton said to Nirella, as they prepared for bed. "I know he's your father and I respect him, but he can't go around half-cocked, attacking whatever he wants, using MPA forces."

"You're right," she said, "but your mother is pushing to have him removed since he is not noble-born, and you must be your own man."

"With you at my side, I will be," the youthful leader said, with a soft smile. He kissed her and added, "I'm sorry I'm not a better lover, but the stresses of the job are taking their toll."

"I adore you anyway," she said.

It saddened him to notice disappointment in her eyes. During the months that they had been married, Anton was growing to love Nirella. Time was healing the wounds he suffered when he lost Tesh, and now he only wanted to please his wife.

"I have to at least fire him," Anton said, at last. "Our highest military officer is still subject to the laws of the MPA."

"I know." She fluffed her pillows and climbed into the large bed they shared.

"What is your rank in the Red Berets?" he asked, even though he already knew the answer.

"Why, I'm a reserve colonel," she said.

"I'm giving you a promotion, to Supreme General of the Merchant Prince Armed Forces."

Her eyes widened. "What?"

"We'll put the word out that it's only an interim appointment, until we decide on a permanent replacement. Don't worry about making a mistake. The Mutati war is on suspension anyway."

"But I'll need to be in touch by nehrcom with our forces all over the galaxy, to make certain everything is in readiness. I'm not sure if I'm qualified for that."

"You're as qualified as your father, since you co-manage the galactic operations of Nehrcom Industries with him, and I know you have extensive military knowledge. I've seen the holobooks you read. You're a student of military tactics and strategies."

"True, but I do not have anywhere near the prestige of my father."

"I have to admit, Jacopo was doing well as Supreme General until this lapse. Maybe he will recover his senses with rest, and again qualify for the job." Anton scratched his head. "Mmm. Instead of firing your father or taking him into custody, I'll put him on a leave of absence for an indeterminate period. That's the political way to handle it. He still has powerful friends and allies, and I don't want to lose their support."

"You're learning fast," she said.

The following afternoon, upon learning of the Doge's decision, Jacopo Nehr took his wife, Lady Amila, and a few men who were loyal to him and joined Lorenzo on the space station. There he conferred with two men whom he thought had remained loyal to him, Lorenzo and Pimyt.

But in this time of galactic chaos and tension, relationships were not always what they appeared to be.

After the six Elixir of Life winners were announced, Princess Meghina began to socialize with the other five, and they formed an exclusive club. Under continuing medical observation, the small group arranged regular get-togethers in Meghina's royal apartments on Lorenzo's orbiter. All the while, Francella and her researchers eavesdropped electronically on everything they said.

In the cities and towns of Canopa there were philosophical debates about the elixir, as people considered whether or not they would like to become immortal, if CorpOne ever offered more of the precious substance for sale. They considered it like a lottery.

One evening on board the orbital gambling casino, Lorenzo announced that he would like to become immortal himself so that he could spend the rest of eternity with his pretty wife. The Doge Emeritus revealed that he was at the top of a waiting list for the elixir, and would take it himself as soon as it again became available.

In Noah's camp there were also debates, with his Guardians lining up on both sides of the issue. The outspoken Acey Zelk, having heard how apparent immortality had changed Master

Noah, did not want it for himself.

"What fun would there be if I knew I could not be killed?" the teenager asked one afternoon while taking a break with Dux. "The risk of death makes life worth living."

"It does give things an edge, doesn't it?" Dux said. "As for myself, I think I agree with you. Maybe if everyone I cared about, such as yourself, could be made immortal I would accept it for myself, but the odds are slim that the elixir will work on any of us."

Overhearing this exchange, Noah saw a certain wisdom in their opinions, but for himself he did not entirely agree. He wanted to accomplish so much that he didn't see how one lifetime could possibly be enough for him. From an early age Noah had always seen broad horizons, had always felt that he could make important contributions. Now, the longer his allotted lifetime, the more he could achieve.

Admittedly Noah had felt trapped at times by his own enhanced existence, as if it were—paradoxically—yet another prison confining him. But if he could ever regain access to Timeweb it might open wondrous possibilities for humankind and new glories for all of the galactic races . . . if only they could see the wisdom of working together instead of at cross purposes.

Thus far Noah was presuming that he still had his own immortality, since he had been feeling physically strong, without any hint of the aches or pains that his friend Eshaz had complained of . . . a Tulyan who had lived for nearly a million years.

But Timeweb continued to reject every attempt Noah made to reenter it, and this disappointed him deeply.

Chapter Seventy-Two

The immortal Mutati courtesan presents us with difficult questions. Out of the thousands of doses of elixir that were distributed, Princess Meghina is the only Mutati known to have consumed any, and the cellular effects on her were dramatic. Mutatis typically have lifespans similar to those of Humans, so the possibility of immortality for every shapeshifter who consumes the Elixir of Life is frightening. Maybe this is not the case and it is only a coincidence, but it presents obvious security concerns, as it could result in the ultimate domination of that race over humankind. I would strongly recommend two courses of action: We must only distribute additional doses under strictly controlled conditions, and you need to notify your son of the situation. After all, he is the Doge, responsible for the welfare of all of us.

—Dr. Hurk Bichette, telebeam to Francella Watanabe

A week passed.

Despite his inexperience on the job, Doge Anton had already developed a routine. Each morning he arose early and had breakfast brought to him in his office. If the weather was nice, he ate in the adjacent rooftop garden, as he was doing now.

He flipped on a telebeam projector beside his plate and read the messages as he ate, letting an electronic fork automatically lift morsels of omelet to his mouth. It freed up his hands to continue working.

As usual there were several messages from his mother, listing the most important appointments he had that day, and how to handle each of them. She was not pleased that he had appointed Nirella Nehr as interim Supreme General, and for days she had been pressing to have him not to make the appointment permanent. In Nirella's place she had been touting her own candidate, Gilforth Pont, providing reasons why he would make a great general.

The trouble was, Anton knew the man, and he didn't have the first idea about what it took to lead the Merchant Prince Armed Forces. Neither did his spoiled son, who had manipulated the system to obtain an appointment as a lieutenant colonel in the Red Berets. Anton didn't like people who worked their connections to get ahead. Instead, he liked those who advanced through the sweat of their own brows.

The fork continued its passage from the plate to his mouth, using sensors to keep from missing or stabbing him. He paused to take a sip of tangy juice, and turned the fork off. He didn't feel like finishing the omelet.

Consistent with his opinion of others, Anton felt some embarrassment for his own appointment to the highest position in the Alliance. He was the son of a noble-born prince himself (albeit out of matrimony), and in danger of becoming one of the very dandies he loathed. Still, he had high hopes of proving that he deserved the job. Already he was asserting himself, showing his mother that he could make important decisions on his own.

He knew she could not really do anything about that, because she held her own lofty social position in large part due to her relationship with him, her bragging rights as the mother of the Doge. She tried to act like she was in charge, in tacit control, but he really held the more important cards. He just needed to figure out how to play them.

His feelings for her were evolving. Anton was beginning to see Francella as a complete person, with strengths and weaknesses. He didn't think he could ever forgive her for abandoning him at birth, but at least she had paid a family to raise him. That showed some modicum of concern, and suggested that she wasn't nearly as bad as she seemed to be.

Yet the stories of her raw rage were terrifying, the things she allegedly did to Noah, or tried to do to him, as well as the rumors that she may have killed her own father and blamed it on her brother. Her actions in the laboratory may have been controlled experiments; at least that was what she claimed. In addition, she insisted that she had nothing to do with old Prince Saito's death, and Anton wanted to believe her. He also worried about her health, and hoped a way could be found to slow or reverse the accelerated aging she had been suffering.

A robot servant removed the dishes, and he continued reading the telebeam images that floated in front of his eyes. One of the messages—from an investigator he respected—cited proof that Noah was not responsible for the attack on Jacopo Nehr's jewelry-manufacturing complex after all, and that Lorenzo del Velli had actually been the perpetrator.

Interesting. So Uncle Noah is not guilty of everything after all.

Anton considered sending the information to Jacopo Nehr himself, then reconsidered and forwarded it to Nirella instead. It was her father, and she would want to do whatever she could to ensure his safety. But why had Lorenzo done such a thing? The plots among merchant princes seemed endless.

After forwarding the message to Nirella, along with his own cover note, Anton paused to consider who else should know. His mother? Eventually, yes. But first, he wanted to do something he had been delaying for too long.

Because of Lorenzo's deception, the young Doge finally

decided to meet with Noah, and he responded to his uncle's diplomatic overtures.

Reading the telebeam message in his underground office, Noah felt a rush of elation. Anton said he looked forward to resuming their close relationship, and suggested a neutral meeting place—in a canyon on the far side of Canopa. That sounded all right to Noah, but he would check with Subi before answering, to make certain that the necessary security measures were taken.

Touching his sapphire signet ring, Noah closed the transceiver. The message disappeared into his ring in a wisp of gray smoke.

Just then he heard a thunderous explosion, and the shouts of men. As he ran out into the main chamber, he saw men, women, and robots heading toward a breach in the entrance, carrying weapons. Subi Danvar hurried up to him, and shouted, "Cameras show soldiers and heavy vehicles outside! We can't hold them off for long."

Subi guided Noah toward a side tunnel, which they entered at a full run.

"MPA?" Noah asked.

"No, paramilitary. They're wearing Red Beret uniforms."

"I didn't think Anton would do this to me," Noah said.

"Maybe he didn't. As the Doge Emeritus, Lorenzo has Red Berets, too."

Noah cursed, and as he ran with Subi, he wondered how his enemies had found him. At the adjutant's suggestion, Noah had beefed up the energy-field security system and metalloy barricades at the main entrance, so that—along with the brave Guardians who were facing the attackers—should slow them down.

Reaching a rear chamber, Noah and Subi assembled fighters and equipment. From all tunnels around them, fully armed

Guardians streamed in and received their orders.

More explosions sounded. Looking at a portable security screen, Subi reported: “They’re at all of the entrances. We only have one way to get out and try to hit them from another side.”

He pointed to a Digger machine.

High in the enclosed operators’ cabin of the vehicle sat Acey Zelk and Dux Hannah, side by side. “Let’s go!” Acey shouted. He shut the door and fired up the big machine. Its engines made a deafening roar.

In the face of the overwhelming onslaught, Noah and a force of Guardians used the Digger to tunnel an escape route for them. Following a compass, they set a course toward the northeast, his old ecological compound.

With Acey at the controls the machine hummed, throwing dirt and rocks behind it, which robots pushed back with smaller machines, allowing the fighters to surge forward into the earth. The Digger was fast, and the robots had to work hard to keep up behind it.

Noah smelled the dust and dirt, and he coughed, as did the Humans with him. He saw an opening ahead, and heard what sounded like running water.

Abruptly the Digger coughed too, and the engines shut down. On top of the machine, Acey spat expletives.

Part of the tunnel collapsed overhead, trapping Acey and Dux and many of Noah’s loyal followers. At a command from Noah, robots rushed in and began digging furiously, trying to rescue people before they stopped breathing. Noah and Subi climbed on top of the partially buried Digger, and used a puissant pistol to knock dirt away, causing it to cascade harmlessly to the ground. They saw the teenagers now, inside the sealed cabin. The boys pushed the door open and climbed out.

From the rooftop, Noah surveyed the machine. A large rock

had crushed the engine compartment, and the Digger would need repairs before it could be used again. As a security measure, to prevent the units from repairing themselves and going on burrowing rampages, as they had done in the past, Subi had disconnected the sentient features. It was just a dumb machine now, totally useless.

At the front of the Digger, Noah saw through the large opening it had cut, revealing a cavern and a subterranean stream. Guardians were climbing down an embankment to the water, gathering along the edge.

"Now what?" Dux asked.

"Where does this stream lead?" Acey asked. "Does anybody know how far it is to an outlet?"

Tapping buttons on his security computer, Subi tried to get information. "Nothing here," he said.

Acey repeated his questions, scrambling down the embankment and shouting them to the Human and robotic Guardians around him. No one seemed to have any answers.

Noah, Subi, and Dux went down to the stream, too. Noah dipped a hand in the water. It was not that cold.

"I've done some swimming in my life," Acey said, testing the temperature himself. "Extreme sports where I had to hold my breath for a long time." He waded into the water.

Figuring out what Acey had in mind—an underwater swim—Noah shouted: "Hold it! You don't know how far it is to an outlet."

"What choices do we have?" Acey asked, with a wide grin.

"I'll do it, then," Noah said. "I can't die, remember?"

"And let you have all the fun?" Acey shouted. "Wish me luck!" He swam away downstream, taking powerful strokes.

Noah dove in and swam after him, but Acey was a faster swimmer.

The brave teenager went under, followed by Noah.

Just when Acey felt as if his lungs would burst, he went over a waterfall into a pool of deep, cold water—outside. Noah, who aspirated a great deal of water and should have drowned, joined him moments later. Both of them took several moments to recuperate.

Then Noah made out shapes on the shore, surrounding the water. Humans and robots. They drew closer, and he saw Guardian uniforms and colors on them. One of his subcommanders shouted to him, "We got out a secondary entrance. It's just you two?"

"No!" Noah shouted. "Subi and others are back there, hundreds of Guardians." He pointed in the direction of the waterfall. "We need to break through rock and get them out."

"You mean with a Digger?" the subcommander asked.

"Exactly."

Noah heard the roar of another Digger, and saw its hulking shape appear.

In only a few minutes, with Noah directing, they dug back to the stranded Digger, and Noah's squad of followers.

Noah and Subi then led a counterattack and drove away the Red Beret forces—which outnumbered them—with hardly any resistance.

As the battle turned, the two men watched on a remote videocam as the attackers hurried into military vehicles and drove off.

"That was too easy," Subi said. "Did you notice? Just before running, they were talking feverishly on com units."

"I saw that," Noah said. "We'd better get under cover and regroup."

Chapter Seventy-Three

No motivation is more powerful than the desire to annihilate your historical mortal enemies. It is one of the dark forces, which invariably seem to be stronger among the races than the forces of good. This does not bode well for the balance of the galaxy, which is connected to all activity and continues to erode . . . while the undergalaxy does the exact opposite. Our loss is their gain.

—Report of web caretakers to the Council of Elders

Noah and Thinker surveyed the rubble of the battle, watching as Subi, the teenage boys, Tesh, and others quickly retrieved usable weapons and took them inside the shelter of the headquarters. Medical robots tended to the injured, with most of the bots having been custom programmed a short while before by Thinker.

As the sentient machines performed their work they transmitted signals to Thinker, reporting on the conditions of the patients.

When their tasks were complete, Thinker passed the information on to Noah. "Fifteen dead Red Berets," the robot leader said.

"How many did we lose?" Noah asked.

"Fifty-four."

"That many?" He thought back. "But I only saw a few."

"Aren't robots as important as Humans?" Thinker asked.

"Of course. Your contributions are tremendous. We couldn't do it without you."

"There are six Human dead, and forty-eight seriously damaged robots."

"Fifty-four in all, then."

"Right."

Noah felt considerable relief, but didn't want to offend Thinker by showing it, or pointing out that dead machines could be repaired, while Humans could not. Except for himself. And half a dozen others, from what he'd heard.

Soon additional information came in, this time from Subi, who rushed over and interrupted Noah and Thinker. "We took prisoners," the adjutant said breathlessly, "and they confirmed our suspicions about Lorenzo. The attack force was under his command from the orbiter, using Red Berets stationed on Canopa."

"So EcoStation is more than a gambling casino," Noah said, bitterly. "We built it and that idiot turned it against us."

"How did they find out where we are?" Dux asked.

"It was only a matter of time," Thinker said, "and probabilities. They have been searching for us intensely."

"This headquarters is no longer safe," Subi said. "They'll hit us with a massive force next."

Noah noticed that his signet ring was flashing colors, and shifting from sapphire to gold. The color change and pattern of flashes told him the source of a telebeam message that had just arrived for him: Doge Anton.

Opening the connection, he saw words floating in the air: *"Hello, Uncle Noah. For the sake of the MPA, I'm declaring a formal cease-fire with the Guardians, while you and I discuss ways of ending the hostilities. For your part, you must discontinue all guerrilla attacks against corporate assets, including those owned by my mother and my father. I found out about Lorenzo's attack on you, and put a stop to it. Not that you needed my help. I just made it easier for you."*

Speaking into a recording mechanism, Noah transmitted a response: "Much appreciated. All right, I'll keep my end of the cease-fire. I assume you'll see that Lorenzo does the same."

Moments later, he saw the Doge's response in front of his eyes: *"I'll do my best, but watch out for his tricks. He and your sister are always plotting against you."*

When the exchange was complete, Subi said to Noah, "We should still dig in and open up as many escape tunnels as possible. Let's take new precautions, lay traps, and do the unexpected. I think we should also send a recon team to the orbiter and see what Lorenzo is doing there. Obviously he's using it as a command center against us, but maybe we can get through and find out what he's up to."

"The best defense is a good offense," Noah said, nodding. Tesh approached him, a look of sadness on her face. She stood by him, listening as he and the robot continued their conversation.

"Wearable surveillance cameras would be handy on such a mission," Thinker said. "I've done repairs to a hibbamatic machine that Subi brought in some time ago, and it can produce as many cameras as you need, tiny units that look like buttons and are totally undetectable to scanners. They'll project images from the space station back here."

"As I recall," Subi said, scratching his head, "you were less than impressed by the quality of products produced by that machine."

"I improved it," the cerebral robot said. "The thing is not perfect, but it should serve our needs, especially on short notice. The cameras will project images back here just fine; they're a simple enough mechanism."

Noah nodded. "All right, Subi, set up the recon mission. How many people do you want to send?"

"Eh?" Subi was staring at Dux, then at Acey, who were only a few meters away. "I'm thinking three," he replied. "Say, these boys have the look of Sirikan nobility. Isn't that where you're from?"

"From Siriki, yes," Dux said, "but from the back country. Our families are dirt poor."

"Well, I'd say a nobleman or two passed your way on vacation, and spent the night. You two have just the look I want for this mission. If you're game for it, I want you to act like young nobles and wander around, seeing how much you can transmit back to us."

"Right," Dux said, exchanging nods with Acey. "Our own little casino game."

Looking at Thinker, Noah said, "After you produce the cameras, I want you to have tunnels dug to the clearing where our podship is, so that we can get as many Guardians on board the craft as possible for a mass escape, if necessary. Human *and robot* Guardians."

Then to Tesh he said, "Supervise new construction inside the podship, racks to stack robots, and vertical structures to accommodate as many people as possible."

"That is a fine idea, Master," the robot said, with orange lights blinking around his face plate.

"Sounds good to me, too," Tesh agreed.

"As for me," Noah said, "I'm going to meet with Anton, at the place he designated. There's no point taking security with me. He's proven himself by intercepting Lorenzo's attack. Besides, I'm invulnerable, in case some of you haven't heard yet." He grinned. "And if I get captured, you guys can just break me out again."

Thinker made an odd mechanical noise. Then: "Don't get overconfident, Master. The last time you were caught, your sister cut you up into little pieces. Don't forget: She's Anton's mother, and his benefactor."

"Perhaps you're right. Maybe I am being overly optimistic."

"At least take a squad of robots with you," Thinker said, "to make it harder for them to capture you. We have our own longevity, because we can always be repaired."

"Not always," Noah said, "not if the damage is too great. And perhaps it is the same with me." He chewed at his lower lip. "Very well, I'll tell Anton I want fifty of my guards, and he can bring the same number."

Across the galaxy, about as far as anyone could go, Woldn felt much better, and was working to regenerate an entire galactic race. He dispatched cleanup teams to remove the floating bodies from the Parvii Fold and the connecting tunnels, and separated his surviving people into groups, with special attention to the most healthy.

Of those who were in the best condition, he instituted an intense Parvii reproduction program under the supervision of two surviving breedmasters, to generate as many offspring as possible, as fast as possible. With a short gestation period of only a few days, the population began to increase, and reached adulthood in a matter of weeks.

Soon Woldn was culling the best of the offspring and combining them with the best of the older adults, selecting who would be future podship pilots, and who would be trained for other important professions.

He had the historic goal of his galactic race firmly in his mind, and it would never leave his thoughts. Maintain full control of the podships.

One major problem existed, but he would do the best he could despite it. While he had managed to save two breedmasters, only one war priest had survived, carrying with him the secret of the ancient telepathic weapons. Throughout their long military tradition, war priests had always worked in groups of twenty or more, forming among them a telepathic seed weapon, which was then passed on to the swarms. Over the millennia there had been no need for such a powerful weapon, but the war priests had practiced their craft anyway, generation after generation, awaiting the moment when they might be called to duty.

Now, after all of that preparation, only one of them remained, but he was the most skillful of his group, and the unspoken leader among them. This one, who went by his ancestral name of Ryall, had risen from his deathbed and gone immediately to work. "I can do it anyway," he promised Woldn. "It will take longer, but there are still Parviis with substantial telepathic powers. I will teach them the ancient arts, and we will have the weapons again. . . ."

Addressing a gathering of future pilots, the best of the best, Woldn announced, vocally and telepathically at the same time: "We're not going to resume our podship routes until we take care of other chores first. The Tulyans will pay for what they did to us!"

The din of buzzing and applause filled Woldn's brain, and lifted him to a state of euphoria.

"Soon!" he told them. "We avenge our dead!"

Chapter Seventy-Four

Some people should never have been born, while others should never die.

—Ancient Saying

Acey knew his cousin was uncomfortable in the bright, variegated cape, leggings, and liripipe hat, as Acey was himself, dressed in his own gold-and-white outfit. But the two of them looked perfect for the reconnaissance mission, like typical young lords out squandering their inherited wealth. And their companion Subi, even though he was actually a rough-and-tumble type, looked suitably magnificent himself, like a no-nonsense corporate head, or a front-line military officer with many Mutati kills to his credit.

Disembarking from the shuttle, they stepped through an air-lock onto the space station. Following a throng of gamblers, they bypassed inattentive security officers and swept into the large central chamber of the casino. Acey heard the tinkling of coins, the voices of card dealers, and the squeals of anticipation and delight as nobles and their ladies played the games. Robotic waiters passed between the patrons, plying them with gratis exotic drinks and reducing their inhibitions.

The three Guardians split up and explored side chambers and corridors, transmitting images of their surroundings back to headquarters with the cameras concealed in the buttons of their clothing. By prearrangement, they would meet again in an hour.

Acey was surprised by the lax security. Perhaps it was due to the gaiety of this section of the space station, or some of the guards had quaffed those exotic drinks themselves, but any red-uniformed men and women he saw seemed unconcerned and chatted casually with passersby. Waving cheerfully to one of the guards, as Acey had seen others do, he continued on his way into a corridor.

There were restrooms down there, along with a gourmet restaurant, and numerous other rooms, many of which were unlocked. He saw gambling patrons peeking into rooms curiously and either entering, or closing the doors and leaving. He did the same. Poking his head into a small private dining room he was surprised to see Giovanni Nehr in a black waiter's uniform, serving a well-dressed Hibbil. They had not seen him yet. The center of the red-and-gold dining table had been inlaid with the golden tigerhorse crest of Lorenzo's House del Velli, as had all of the chair backs.

Inside Acey's pocket, he carried an unusual weapon that looked like a billfold full of money. Silently, slowly, he pulled it out and activated an internal pressure pad, causing the device to metamorphose into a powerful little laser pistol, with a silencer attachment.

Feeling uncontrollable anger, Acey burst into the dining room with his weapon drawn, not noticing Subi and Dux come up from behind and try to stop him.

In a blur of movement the Hibbil drew his own projectile weapon and fired, sending darts through the air with little pinging sounds. The diminutive, bearlike man was surprisingly fast, but not very accurate in his aim.

Ducking and running, the Guardians took cover behind the ornate chairs and fired laser bursts, an eerily silent battle that filled the room with blue light. Acey expected an alarm to go off at any moment, but it didn't happen. Then he noticed signs of ongoing construction activities in the room—a couple of open junction boxes and a wire on the floor at the base of a wall. The alarm system might be inoperable in here.

Hurling chairs along one side of the table, Gio used their cover to leap into a hatch by the window, and slammed the door shut behind him.

"Emergency-escape route," Acey said to Dux, firing in that direction.

The laser bursts had no effect on the hatch. Through thick clearplax, Acey saw Gio don a spacesuit with a manned maneuvering pack attached. In only a few seconds, he leaped out into space. Firing red flames from the thruster on the MMP, he propelled himself around the outside of the space station.

The Hibbil tried to sound an alarm, but Subi fired a laser beam into his shoulder, causing him to fall on the deck, moaning in pain. Acey ran for another escape hatch but the Hibbil started firing again, forcing Acey to duck for cover behind the overturned chairs. Subi, bleeding from a wound on one arm, crept around the other side of the table, making his way quietly toward the Hibbil.

Seeing another escape hatch nearer to him than to Acey, Dux considered running for it. But he didn't have Acey's skills with mechanical objects or weapons. Acey should be the one to go.

"Acey, look!" Dux shouted. He pointed at the hatch.

"Go!" Acey shouted to Dux. "If you can get him, do it!"

Coming around behind the Hibbil, Subi made a rude noise. The Hibbil whirled, but before he could fire, Acey leaped on him and hit him with a fist, causing the alien to drop his weapon. The furry little man fell back with a curse, but came straight at Acey and pummeled him with surprisingly hard blows.

"We're trying not to kill you," Acey grunted, "but you're not making it easy."

Subi joined in trying to subdue the Hibbil, who fought back with ferocity.

Dux wanted to help them, but decided he'd better go after Gio, to keep him from further compromising their security. He wished Acey hadn't been so impulsive, but now they were committed and their choices were limited.

Climbing inside the escape hatch, Dux slammed the door shut behind him. Dux was not the fighter that Acey was, and didn't think he was anywhere near as brave, but Gio was trying to get away, and Dux did not want to waste any time. Putting on his own suit and maneuvering pack, the teenager shot out into space, steering with controls on his belt. He held his laser pistol in a gloved hand.

Ahead he saw Gio trying to connect to the space station, on a windowless section where there was another hatch. He was having some trouble making the connection, and looked back nervously at his pursuer. Dux fired a warning shot that flashed blue against the hatch, causing Gio to recoil.

Logic told Dux that he should try to kill Gio, since it would not be possible to take him back to Noah alive. But he hesitated. Gio did not appear to be armed, and he couldn't just murder him in cold blood. Looking back at the modules of the space station, Dux did not see many windows on this side, except for those on the private dining room he had just left. So far, he and Gio didn't seem to have attracted any attention.

But Dux—with limited mechanical abilities—had not noticed the weapons on his own maneuvering pack, and on Gio's. The man activated a high-powered projectile gun and fired a dart that grazed Dux on one side, not hitting his skin but penetrating the life-support system of the suit, causing oxygen to leak out.

Gasping for air, the young man propelled himself directly toward Gio and spun away from two more shots, which sent him several hundred meters away from the station. He put the jet on full thruster, trying to get back in time.

Now Gio had time to make the connection to the space station. As he pulled open the hatch, however, Dux hit him in the helmet with a laser blast, blowing his head off. Blood gushed into the vacuum of space, and the body floated away.

The hatch was open, and Dux—nearly passing out from low oxygen—tumbled inside, then closed the hatch behind him. Finding himself in what looked like a food storage room, he caught his breath. Then a door opened, and Dux expected to be captured, or worse.

Instead, it was Acey and Subi. "We followed your emergency locator," Subi said. "You got him?"

Dux nodded. He felt relieved to be alive, but not particularly proud of killing his first man. But if anyone deserved to be his first, it had been Giovanni Nehr.

Regaining their composure and smoothing their clothes as much as possible, the trio walked calmly down a corridor and out into the gambling casino. They passed a Mutati game where patrons were thronging around, and continued on to the shuttle station, in another module.

Through the windows they saw that a shuttle was just unloading, and other patrons were lined up to board it. Hurrying through an airlock, the three Guardians joined the line.

Noticing a little blood on Subi's arm, a female guard asked him what had happened.

"It's nothing," Subi assured her, faking a slur to make it look like he had been drinking. “Just a little too much fun.”

With a smile, she waved him and the teenagers onto the shuttle.

Chapter Seventy-Five

Understanding the weak points of your enemy—and of yourself—can be the difference between victory and defeat.

—Teaching of the HibAdu War College

On the space station, Pimyt lay on a medical bed, receiving treatment from a nurse for the injury he received when three strangers attacked him and killed the waiter, Giovanni Nehr. His injured shoulder ached, but something else concerned him much more, and he was impatient to get back to his office.

All of the violence had occurred in a new section that did not yet have security cameras, but he did have images of the three men from the moment they arrived at the orbiter, and afterward when they wandered through public rooms, and later when they boarded a shuttle to leave. The way they split up on arrival troubled him. It suggested that they were doing reconnaissance work, perhaps in advance of a military attack.

"This will hurt a little," the nurse said, as she cleaned bloody fur out of the wound.

In his mind, the Hibbil ran through a list of suspects who might have perpetrated this intrusion. It could be Doge Anton or Francella Watanabe who sent them, or the noble-born princes who still hated Lorenzo for his policies when he was Doge. It might even be Noah's troublesome Guardians, who had fought back so tenaciously against Lorenzo's forces. The attackers could have been Mutatis, though he didn't think so, since they were Pimyt's secret allies and would not want to do him harm.

But paranoid thoughts darted through his mind. In his own long career, he had developed enemies, too, perhaps even more than Lorenzo.

"Hurry it up," Pimyt said, in an agitated, squeaky voice. "I have work to do, and this is costing me valuable time."

"If an infection sets in," she snapped, "it will cost you a lot more than that."

"Okay, okay. But pick it up, pick it up! You're as slow as a nursing student."

"What an unkind thing to say." Her hands shook with anger, but she did speed up, and slapped a healing patch over the wound, a little too hard.

Pimyt didn't say anything about the bolt of pain her mishandling caused. He just sat up and hurried off, glad to get out of there.

Alone in his office, the Hibbil considered the grand plan that he and his people had set up, in cooperation with their Adurian allies. Doge Lorenzo del Velli was no longer in control of the Merchant Prince Alliance, but during his time in that position, Pimyt—as his Royal Attaché—had been in a key position to set things up on behalf of the secret HibAdu Coalition, designed to overthrow both the Humans and the Mutatis.

More work needed to be done, and Jacopo Nehr's foolish loss of his position as Supreme General was presenting new obstacles. But Pimyt prided himself on his own craftiness, and thought he might come up with some clever way to replace the loss. Perhaps he could get to Nirella Nehr and influence her in the same way he had her father. After all, the business interests of father and daughter ran parallel. But it was not so easy for him to get to her in his present position. Even with this obstacle, and others, the die was cast. Victory would just take a little longer to achieve.

At least that mad shapeshifter, Zultan Abal Meshdi, had been prevented from foolishly destroying any more merchant prince planets. The intervention of Noah Watanabe had been most helpful, when he recommended to Lorenzo that they establish sensor-guns on all pod stations, to keep podships from arriving and potentially bringing in more Mutati planet-buster bombs. Following Noah Watanabe's fortuitous suggestion, the Hibbils had been only too happy to set up defensive perimeters on all pod stations that orbited Human-controlled worlds, thus preventing wayward Mutati outriders from coming in and torpedoing another valuable planet.

But not before key worlds were destroyed by the hell-bent shapeshifters, including the merchant prince capital of Timian One. Valuable resources that might have been spoils of war had been destroyed.

For decades, the Hibbils and Adurians had been fostering disorder in their intended victims, enabling the imminent conquerors to divide the spoils between themselves. As a result of this wide-scale sabotage, it would be a diminished war between Humans and Mutatis if it ever resumed—which it most certainly would if podship travel ever started again. Such an unexpected problem for the HibAdu Coalition, and a mystery as to how or why the galactic transportation system had been cut off—another unexplained occurrence to add to the litany of them concerning the sentient spaceships that had wandered the cosmos since time immemorial.

But the inventive HibAdus had come up with a solution. After undermining the Mutati lab-pod production program, they had used Hibbil machine expertise to develop an excellent navigation system for the vessels, a secret that had been kept from the Mutatis. Now, on Adurian and Hibbil worlds, the Hib-Adu Coalition was mounting a military offensive of massive proportions.

While Pimyt's people had known about an alternate galactic dimension for some time, they had never previously been able to capitalize on it. Centuries ago, using the viewing skills of captured, drugged Tulyans and projecting images from their minds, the Hibbils had been able to see the galaxy's weblike connective tissue on screens. Now the HibAdu Coalition had their own burgeoning lab-pod fleet. Using Hibbil manufacturing expertise combined with Adurian biotechnology, their factories were working around the clock.

The Coalition had a Hibbil method of guiding lab-pods, a nav-unit that caused the vessels to travel along selected podways. Initially the lab-pods had been considerably slower than traditional podship travel, taking more than three days to get across the galaxy, along the longest routes. This had been more time-consuming than traditional podship travel, but had still been remarkably fast in comparison with Mutati solar sailers and the hydion-powered vacuum rockets of the merchant princes. Gradually, the Hibbils had discovered ways of improving the speed of lab-pods, but they had not been able to attain the optimal speeds that should have been reached, according to hull-speed engineering calculations. One of the long-lived, captive Tulyans had revealed the reason for this: increasingly frayed podways that caused all podships traveling over them to slow down.

Still, the lab-pods functioned as well as could be expected, under the circumstances. On both Hibbil and Adurian worlds, the cloned spacecraft were being put into military service. Some of the fully-functional lab-pods had already been used to land clandestine Coalition military operatives directly on Human and Mutati worlds, after bypassing pod stations and defeating planetary security systems, so that no one knew they had gotten past.

Now, thousands of lab-pods fitted with nav-units had been

built, and more were on the way.

They were aided in their efforts by another Hibbil innovation. Some time ago the Adurian Ambassador VV Uncel had passed interesting technology on to them, information that the Mutatis had obtained on the workings of the famous nehrcom cross-space communication system. While the Mutatis struggled to perfect it, with their research efforts inhibited by gyros provided to them by the Adurians, the HibAdu Coalition had no such impediments. They had perfected a working nehrcom system that linked their growing military enterprise . . . and through a system of complex, secure relays they were in contact with conspirators such as Pimyt on merchant prince worlds.

Chapter Seventy-Six

Pitfalls are always around you . . . sometimes visible, but more often not. Survival frequently depends upon seeing them with your inner eye.

—Noah Watanabe, *Drifting in the Ether*
(unpublished notes)

The large, unmarked grid-plane circled a remote canyon, with Noah and fifty robots in the passenger compartment. At the controls of the vessel, Subi Danvar used infrared and other electronics to survey the conditions below. With his naked eye, Noah saw a transport vessel on the ground, bearing the red-and-gold colors of Doge Anton. It was midday, with fast-moving clouds overhead that cast scattered shadows on the landscape.

The house colors demonstrated that Noah's nephew was a del Velli now, and confirmed what he had heard, that Anton was no longer using his foster name of Glavine. This gave Noah pause, since this was the son of the man who had just launched a sneak attack against Guardian headquarters. Were the two of them working closely together now, and were soldiers hiding in the surrounding terrain, ready to pounce and capture Noah again?

Noah wanted to think the best of Anton, for he had known the young man for years, and hoped he had not changed for the worst since becoming Doge. In his high position, Anton might have inherited certain political necessities, but Noah had always trusted him . . . and Anton had never let him down before. He could not have lost his sense of honor so quickly.

But Noah recalled only too well his own wounds from having trusted Giovanni Nehr, of thinking he had seen goodness and loyalty in Gio's heart, and how wrong he had been. Still, he had a feeling about Anton, that this was an important, even essential, relationship to be developed even further. Noah did not see any benefit in fleeing on Tesh's podship to another world, because what would he do there? He didn't want to raise an army to attack the merchant princes; instead, he wanted to work with them against the Mutatis and the Parviis, who were causing so much damage to everything they touched.

Today was a necessary step. He *had* to risk it.

The grid-plane went into its vertical landing mode and dropped slowly toward the shore of a river at the bottom of the gorge, passing billions of years of sedimentation and rock formations on the sheer canyon walls, in all the shades of brown he could imagine. Gusts of wind buffeted the craft, but Subi kept it under control.

Around Noah the robots were entirely silent, because they had been packed compactly and programmed to sleep. All of them were boxy in shape, which made them easier to pack in tight quarters.

Robots had certain advantages, Noah realized, and this was only one of them. The primary reason he had brought them was another—he didn't want to risk losing Guardians in case he was wrong about Anton. As for Subi, he was Noah's equal in many ways, and when the big man wanted to go someplace, it was hard to stop him. Subi, intensely loyal, wanted to make certain that every possible safety precaution was taken. He had even formulated a plan to take Anton hostage in a quick strike, if necessary. Assuming Anton was even there.

As the grid-plane settled onto a sandy beach, Noah got his answer. Doge Anton del Velli, looking elegant and rested, strode toward him across the glittering, silvery sand, leaving his own entourage behind. He wore a thick coat, to protect against the unseasonably cold weather. His blond mustache looked freshly trimmed.

Subi disembarked first, followed by Noah, both wearing green-and-brown Guardian uniforms. Then the robots came to life, and began clattering down the ramp to the ground. As they did so, Anton showed no alarm, and left his own guards a considerable distance away, by his own plane.

As if in answer to Noah's unspoken question, Anton said, "I have nothing to fear from you, and you have nothing to fear from me."

Standing in sunlight, the two men clasped hands firmly, then embraced. For a moment, it seemed to Noah as if nothing had ever separated them.

"It seems like a long time since we saw each other at your wedding, doesn't it?" Noah said, as they separated. "It's only been a few months, but so much has happened."

"And not all for the best," the Doge said, scowling. Wind whipped his long hair. He gestured, "Come, Uncle, and accompany me on a walk."

Noah nodded, and followed Anton's lead as they strolled away from both aircraft onto a rocky section of beach.

"Speaking of uncles," Anton said with a sidelong glance, "my wife is grieving over what happened to Gio."

Noah nodded, and said, "An unfortunate incident."

"Yes, most unfortunate. But Gio was not like his brother, was he?"

"No, sadly he was not like Jacopo at all."

"Tragic situation. He'd fallen on hard times, was working as a waiter on the orbital casino."

Noah expected Anton to press for more information, voicing suspicions that Guardians might have killed Gio, but instead the young Doge dropped the subject and said, "You may have noticed that I made no real effort to find you, or mount my own attack. I, too, have had odd mental experiences. While I should know where your headquarters is, because I have been there, I cannot remember anything about the location. It is as if a portion of my memory has been erased." He stared hard at Noah, and added, "Did you do that to me?"

"Not consciously, but perhaps it is linked to the powers I received. The Supreme Being who gave me those powers may have wanted to protect me, so he did a little tap dance inside your brain."

"As good an explanation as any, I suppose." He smiled. "I never wanted to take action against you anyway, no matter how hard my mother pressed me. Now, why did you request this meeting?"

The Master of the Guardians closed his coat, to protect against the cool wind that was whipping through the canyon. "Undoubtedly you have heard things about me, how my cellular structure has taken on certain unusual propensities."

"Not only have I heard that, I was on the pod station when Mother fired a puissant blast through your chest. You're like a reptile that can grow back its lost body parts."

"On a much more advanced level than any reptile," Noah said, as they stepped over a log. "You heard what she did to me in the laboratory?"

"Yes." He smiled ruefully. "That wasn't very nice of her, was it?"

"She has certain—personality defects. Doge Anton, forgive me for insulting your mother, but I may be the only person who has the right."

"I don't dispute your right to say anything you please about your sister, but there are other sides to her as well, sides that have surprised me. I've seen compassion in her eyes when she looks at me, and she has done things for me that can only be interpreted as love. Of course, she always has her own personal ambitions and motivations, but she really has shown me love, in the only way she knows." He paused. "It's a distant sort of emotion with her, but it is still there, as if it's been suppressed for her entire life and is finally breaking free."

"It's not enough," Noah said, in a bitter voice. "I know her bad side only too well. Did you take the Elixir of Life?"

"No, for a couple of reasons. One, I don't know if I want to live forever. And two, look what it's done to her. It could do the same to me."

Noah nodded. He thought for a moment, and said, "Even when it works, it's no blessing."

They sat on a flat stone in a patch of sunlight, watching the clean mountain water flow swiftly by them. Noah related some of his incredible stories so that Anton could better understand the immensity of the challenges facing humankind and the entire galaxy. He told of his travels through a web of time and space, of signs of decay around the galaxy, of wild podships captured by the Tulyans, and of injured Parviis taking their entire podship fleet out of service in order to recuperate in a galactic fold. He also described the ancient caretaking duties of the Tulyan race, and how that had been diminished severely when they lost their podships to the Parviis.

Anton was astounded at what he heard, but did not question it. For several long minutes after Noah stopped talking, the younger man just sat there, absorbing the fantastic details. Presently he said, "It is common knowledge that podships are mysterious space travelers, and your account fills in missing elements. But tiny creatures piloting podships? If that is the case, why have the Parviis maintained podship service for so long throughout the galaxy, without ever charging for it?"

"They do not value money, in any form. Their entire existence is centered around controlling the sentient spaceships. It's all they want to do, all they have ever wanted to do, all they have known. The problem is enormous. I'm sure they are planning to do something big with those podships—more than a hundred thousand of them—and it might not be the resumption of podship routes."

"What do you think they'll do?"

"A surprisingly powerful Tulyan attack drove the Parviis into a frenzy and killed many of them. I have a Parvii friend, a female, and her guess is that they plan to get revenge on a genocidal scale. They're weakened now, but she doesn't think it is the end for them, since they are survivors. Their swarms may be able to regenerate powerful telepathic weapons that have not been used since ancient wars."

"And your Parvii friend has the podship you mentioned in one of your messages?"

"That's right." He hesitated. "You know her."

"Eh?"

"The Parvii female. Tesh Kori."

Anton's jaw dropped. "What?"

Noah went on to tell him about the magnification capabilities of her people, and how her amplified skin not only looked real, but seemed real to the touch.

Looking at his uncle in astonishment, Anton said, "I feel like my head is going to explode with all of this new information."

"Every word of it is true."

"I don't doubt it. I've never doubted anything about you, Noah. But why are you telling me all of this?"

"Because we need to work together, with all of our followers, instead of at cross purposes. Tesh came to me, asking for my help with a diplomatic mission to the Parvii Fold. She already went there on her own, trying to convince Parvii leadership to allow all of their podships to be used for web caretaking duties.

They turned her down, declared her an outcast. I'm willing to help Tesh, but the diplomatic mission must go first to the Tulyans, to convince them to join the effort. The Tulyans have captured almost four hundred wild podships in deep space, but they need more vessels for all the web repair work that is needed."

"They have that many ships?"

"It's a pittance, compared to what the Parviis control."

"But *four hundred* ships! We could fill them with military equipment and troops, and attack the Parviis in their nest!"

"Tesh would never consent to that."

"If only we had a way of getting around her."

"She has the only podship at our disposal and she knows how to seal its operations against intrusion. We have no choice. She's the only way we can get to the Tulyan Starcloud."

"So we tell her a few lies."

Noah scowled, shook his head. "I don't want any part of that."

"I'm afraid you're being naïve, Uncle."

"Perhaps you're right, but let's rethink this. There must be another way."

"As Doge, I shall take the responsibility. I like your suggestion that we work together, but I shall have to consider how best to accomplish that. Aside from how to handle Tesh, there are certain political hurdles to leap. My mother has many important allies, and they will be watching me closely."

"This is a matter of utmost urgency."

"I realize that."

"And Lorenzo? You can keep him from attacking me again?"

"Only if you discontinue all guerrilla attacks against corporate assets. I know, both my mother and father have caused you a lot of grief, but you need to be the good guy here. If you can do that, I can lean hard on Lorenzo. He's upset that I intervened to stop his attack against your headquarters, and I pulled every political string I have to do it. So far it's holding, but you need to keep your end of the bargain."

Noah nodded, and smiled. "You have my promise. Well, aren't you the master diplomat now."

As they sat there, Anton described the difficulties he had experienced in adjusting to his new position as leader of the Merchant Prince Alliance, and his frustration at trying to rule a fragmented, barely connected domain. He also admitted that his mother would continue to impede any alliance he might want with Noah—but she had been counseled by high officials that the MPA needed this cease-fire so that they could focus their assets on larger, galactic-scale matters.

Noah scowled. "Francella's concerns are petty and self-centered, but for the sake of larger issues I will try to overlook the enmity we have always felt for one another." He cleared his throat. "Sometimes I sense forces working to keep the entire galaxy in disarray. Why do Humans and Mutatis hate each other, anyway? Does anyone know?"

With a shrug, Anton said, "I only know that the mutual animosity goes back for thousands of years."

"And look how many competing camps we have on Canopa," Noah said, "at the heart of merchant prince rule. Your forces, mine, Francella's, and Lorenzo's, all splintered to one degree or another. Look at all of the corporate security forces on Canopa alone. I know for a fact that they've never been adequately coordinated with MPA forces, and this is true on other worlds as well. With greedy individuals and corporations looking out for their own interests, we're in no shape to fight anyone except ourselves."

A cold wind picked up as the sun disappeared behind clouds. "We'd better get going," Anton said, rising to his feet.

In deference, Noah rose afterward, and as they walked back

toward the aircraft, he marveled at how Anton was already showing leadership skills, including the way he led Noah around at their meeting place, deciding when to leave.

As they approached the landing sites, they heard excited shouts ahead, from their companions. Running in that direction, Noah and Anton saw a large, ragged rift along the river shore, with the Red Beret soldiers clinging to the edge of the hole, yelling for help. Noah's robots were setting up rescue equipment, but the hole widened and all of Anton's people disappeared in a great thunder of earth and rock, along with his grid-plane.

"My God!" Anton exclaimed.

While Noah hurried Anton aboard his own aircraft, along with Subi and the robots, the hole went in and out of focus, glowing red around the edges. A portion closed over, leaving a scabrous covering of ground and rock, but he saw more of the hole ripping the gorge open in the other direction.

Moments later the grid-plane lifted off, and rose above the danger area.

"Tesh told me there were strange things occurring on planetary surfaces," Noah said, looking back at the long rip in the planet as they cleared the tops of the cliff faces. "She and Eshaz talked for a long time about things that have been concealed from most galactic races for too long. Apparently the Tulyans call that a timehole, a rip in the fabric of time."

"No one can hope to stop such forces," Anton lamented. He sat with his head in his hands, almost unable to cope with the immensity of the crisis and all of the information that had been thrust into his young mind.

"Maybe not, but we have to try. We need to ensure that the Tulyans are dispersed as much as possible, to perform their ancient healing procedures."

Anton did not respond.

Looking back at the ragged, growing timehole, Noah shuddered. This one was much larger than anything the Tulyan had described to Tesh.

Aboard the space station, Pimyt received a coded nehrcom message, relayed to him from the receiving station on Canopa. According to the urgent transmittal, the HibAdu Coalition had noticed unusual geological activities on a number of planets around the galaxy. It was an unexplained, simultaneous phenomenon, which their scientists were investigating.

On Bilwer, one of the Mutati worlds, an entire battalion of Coalition soldiers had been landed secretly—but the ground opened up beneath them and took almost all of them, closing afterward like the mouth of a dragon swallowing a meal.

Chapter Seventy-Seven

Every moment is fresh and new, like the first breath of a child.

—Ancient Saying

What looked like a large hawk flew over the sparse, northern forest of Dij, extending its wings and soaring upward on the cool air currents and then drifting back down. It landed high in a tree at the edge of the janda woods, and gazed across the broken landscape, which sloped upward into the foothills of the mountains.

The aeromutati Parais d'Olor enjoyed long flights by herself to explore remote regions, looking for new places to take her lover, the Emir Hari'Adab. In the distance, she saw the high, craggy mountains of the Kindu Range, where Mutati religious hermits were said to live. She had seen pictures of the elusive people in the pages of holobooks, and had always found them intriguing. She wouldn't think of disturbing them in their retreats, however, for that would be like fouling the rugged beauty of the planet itself.

Over the peaks, an immense podship emerged from space in a flash of green light and approached, surprising her. It floated down like a dirigible and landed in the clearing. Wondering how this could possibly happen—since she thought podships could only dock at pod stations—she flew closer, and perched on top of a rock formation.

A hatch yawned open on the side of the mottled gray-and-black vessel, and uniformed soldiers marched down a ramp. They did not, however, wear the gold attire with black trim of the Mutati Kingdom. Instead it was a uniform she had never seen before—orange and gray—and this troubled her. Some of the soldiers were hairless Adurians, while others were short, bearlike Hibbils. They began setting up camp structures.

What are they doing here? she wondered, *and why are the two races mixing?* This was most unusual, and disturbing. The Adurians were Mutati allies, but not the Hibbils, who were instead aligned with the merchant princes.

A short time later, a second podship split the sky and drifted down to the ground. More alien soldiers streamed out. There were thousands of them, an army of Adurians and Hibbils.

Even more unusual, Parais saw what looked like gun ports open on one of the vessels. Hibbils brought in a portable scaffold, and raised it to the level of the ports. Zooming her vision, she saw that they were cannons, and the furry little soldiers were making adjustments or repairs to them.

Weapons on a podship? Parais had never heard of anything like that. Podships had only been known to transport the smaller vessels of the various galactic races. Never anything like this.

Deeply concerned, she flew away, to tell the Emir Hari'Adab what she had seen.

Chapter Seventy-Eight

"There can be no more lofty goal in life than the search for truth. It is the essence of nobility. It is the only air I want you to breathe."

—Eunicia Watanabe, to her son Noah
on the boy's ninth birthday

In the grid-plane, Noah and Anton sat at a table, engaged in animated conversation. They were covering a lot of important ground, going over the galactic web and podship crises, the suspended war, and what actions they might take together.

Since the Parviis were incapacitated, they agreed it might be possible for the entire Tulyan podship fleet—almost four hundred vessels, plus any additional ones they might have captured—to venture out onto the podways. Noah and Anton wondered if the Council of Elders had already decided to do that, as in the old days, filling the vessels with Tulyan web caretakers.

The proper course of action seemed clear, if only the Tulyans could be convinced of it . . . and Tesh, who had the only podship available to Noah. Based upon what he had learned about the Parviis and the remarkable things that his journeys into Timeweb had revealed to him, Noah didn't think Tesh's idea of diplomacy would work, since the Parviis were too entrenched in their ancient ways and peculiar power structure. Instead, a more drastic course of action was required: Using the

Tulyan fleet, Humans and Tulyans needed to make a military assault on the Parvii Fold and take control of every podship the Parviis had. After that, a massive web repair operation could be undertaken for the entire galaxy . . . if it was not too late.

They had to move quickly or risk complete galactic disaster, a collapse of the infrastructure in all sectors. There was also the problem of the Parviis. If they recovered, which could happen at any moment, they would surely swarm the pods and take them back, just as they had done for millions of years.

On every one of those points, Noah and Anton concurred wholeheartedly. But they had run into a stumbling block—whether or not to lie to Tesh—and for the past ten minutes their conversation had heated up, with neither one of them backing down. For Noah it was a matter of principle, while Anton was looking at a larger picture. All the while Noah saw the weakness in his own argument, and struggled to find a way to deal with the problem.

Subi landed the grid-plane near Anton's villa, overlooking the industrial centers and offices of the Valley of the Princes. It was sunset, with a violent splash of color across the western sky.

"We're there," the big man said.

Only half hearing him, Noah didn't move. He saw the anger on Anton's face and heard it in his voice.

"Clearly, we need to have Tesh take us to the Tulyan Starcloud for a meeting with the Elders," Anton said, "and it's imperative that we leave right away." He slammed his fist on the table. "But think man! We're talking about a military strike against her own people, so we can't let her in on it, especially not before getting her to take us to the starcloud."

"I won't deceive her," Noah insisted. "She deserves better."

"And what if she doesn't like our plan—which seems obvious—and won't take us to the starcloud?"

Hesitation. Then: "I might be able to take control of the ship away from her."

"And you might not. Isn't that right? The podships fear you, and you're still having trouble getting into Timeweb, right?"

"No one can carry on a conversation with a podship, and it doesn't help that I recommended the pod-killer sensor-guns, but I only did what was necessary to protect the galaxy, and humankind." He sighed. "You're right. There are complications."

Noah hung his head, knowing he could not win this argument, and that Anton was right. Too much was at stake for Noah to hang on a point of personal honor between him and Tesh. This was a matter affecting huge populations and countless star systems.

"Which means you can't pilot the ship telepathically," he said. "It sounds to me like your odds of wresting control away from her are slim."

"True, but I won't lie to her. There must be another way."

"Not that I can see. Think it over, and let me know what our options are."

That very day, Noah had again tried to gain access to the galactic web, but had failed. And even if he ever made it in, with circumstances being what they were, he wasn't at all certain if he could hold the connection. The galaxy was in a state of increasing chaos. It seemed safer for Tesh to pilot the podship by entering the sectoid chamber and taking direct control of it.

"I have a solution," Noah said, with a thin smile. "*You're* going to have to convince her . . . in your own way. I won't contribute one word to your argument."

"No problem," Anton said. "Let's get over there now."

Noah gave new flight instructions to Subi, and they lifted off.

Many changes were occurring in Nirella del Velli's life.

She had only been married to Doge Anton for a short time,

and for an even shorter time she had been the Supreme General of the Merchant Prince Armed Forces, succeeding her father. Events were going by her so rapidly that she could hardly figure out what to do. It was like trying to grab hold of the tail of a comet. But she was in a leadership position, and people needed to follow her direction.

But if they only knew how afraid she was, how unsure of herself. And if Anton only knew. Still, she didn't want to add to his burdens by saying anything to him. He already had too many problems to handle, and she didn't want to add to them.

Now another situation had surfaced. An anonymous telebeam message had arrived in the past hour, and she had been pacing her office ever since.

It was a tip that her father was being blackmailed by Lorenzo's attaché, Pimyt. She was not provided with any other details. *Her own father.* What could it possibly involve? As far as she knew, Jacopo Nehr had led an exemplary life, with only the one justifiable incident where he lost control and destroyed government assets. But if that event was already public, and he had lost his job over it, what more could there be?

Upset and confused, she decided to find her father and discuss it with him personally.

Chapter Seventy-Nine

Love comes in all variations. Ironically, it is as unpredictable as its opposite—war—never the same each time it is played out.

—Naj Nairb, a philosopher of Lost Earth

The Emir Hari'Adab always felt out of balance when his beautiful aeromutati girlfriend was out flying alone on one of her wilderness explorations. Parais loved those trips, connecting with remote and pristine beauty. He would never think of denying them to her, would never ask her not to go, or tell her how low and out of sorts it made him feel whenever she was away. If he decided to say anything to her about his innermost feelings, if he clipped the wings of his pretty bird, he knew she would remain at his side and try to be cheerful about it, but she would not be the same person. A part of her would be wounded, and it would make him feel even worse than he did at the moment.

So, he suffered through his quiet misery.

As the ruler of Dij, with the concomitant duties his father had assigned to him, Hari had countless matters on his mind. He remained busy when Parais was away, filling each day with work to keep from having to deal too much with his emotions. But these days, ever since the Zultan had started his psychotic Demolio program, Hari was having trouble focusing on much else.

While the young Emir had taken no part in leading his people into the mass insanity, which ran rampant on every Mutati planet except Dij, each day that passed without him rectifying the situation made him feel more and more culpable. He was, after all, the eldest son and heir of the Zultan of the Mutati Kingdom.

As the designated ruler of the planet Dij, he ran it like a fiefdom, deriving a substantial income for himself and sending taxes to his father on the capital world of Paradij. Bucking pressure from the Zultan, Hari had steadfastly refused to use Adurian gyrodomes or portable gyros, and had issued edicts on Dij making them off-limits to his subjects as well. Even though the Adurians were military allies, he had never trusted them, believing they were too smooth and always had answers that sounded as if they have been coached.

Now, after long contemplation and soul searching, Hari had decided upon a radical course of action. *I am a sane person, but I must do an insane thing,* he thought.

His plan would require the ultimate in security precautions as he dealt secretly with a brilliant Mutati scientist named Zad Qato. Ideally, Hari would have liked to have gotten together personally with Qato . . . which would have meant having the Paradijan take a solar sailer to Dij, since Hari could not go to him without calling unwanted attention to himself. Unfortunately Qato was under close scrutiny himself, and could not go flitting around the solar system on long journeys that took weeks in each direction.

Qato did, however, have the highest level of military security clearance in the Mutati Kingdom, which gave him access to the Mutati variation of nehrcom communication. It was by this method that the two sent coded messages back and forth. The quality of the transmissions was poor, since the Mutatis had not solved all of the problems of the system. But it did work, and they sent instantaneous transmittals to one another at prearranged times.

Zad Qato, long in years and wisdom, shared Hari's aversion to Adurian gyro units, and to the entire Demolio program that the Zultan had forced on his people. At Hari's urging, Qato had performed careful calculations of trajectory for the Demolio torpedoes, and had adjusted the projected route of a particular shot.

Only the two of them knew this, and Hari prayed that they would not be discovered before they could put their ambitious plan into effect. Everything had to go just right, and the guidance problems had proven to be very difficult. But for the particular target they had in mind, it just might be possible. . . .

Chapter Eighty

Life is not fair,
But death is,
The great and eternal equalizer.

—Noah Watanabe, *Galactic Insights*

Francella Watanabe, after all of her schemes and dark triumphs, had withdrawn from virtually everyone and everything. For months she had refused to allow anyone into her private quarters at the villa, and had received her food and other necessities through pass doors. The connected rooms smelled horrible, and bore evidence of her increasingly dismal moods, with furnishings overturned and broken, paintings ripped from the walls and smashed, and dirty clothing strewn about.

Periodically Francella hurled heavy objects off the balconies and loggias. Sometimes when she threw things out they went over the cliff, but once in a while she intentionally hurled heavy objects into the gardens and onto walkways when she saw people down there. More than once, she had struck servants, and had seriously injured two of them.

One evening a private investigator came to inquire about the injured servants. He stood on the loggia outside the entrance to the main floor, while Francella shouted at him through a closed door, refusing to open it. "I warned them to stay out of the way!" she screeched. "It's their own fault if they didn't listen!"

"Get yourself some psychological help," the man shouted back. "You're not well."

"Don't tell me what I need! I'll give you three minutes to leave, or I'll destroy your career!"

She heard low voices outside, and departing footsteps. Then, watching from a curtained window, she saw the investigator hurry along a walkway, looking back nervously, wary of getting hit by something. He climbed into a groundjet and sped off.

Satisfied for the moment, Francella turned a chair right-side up, and sat down, breathing hard.

She continued to rake in profits from her various corporate operations, but had stopped selling elixir, owing to the unpredictable and potentially dangerous nature of the product. As Dr. Bichette had so wisely pointed out, if it worked on the only Mutati known to have taken it—Princess Meghina—could it possibly work on *all* Mutatis if they got their hands on it, and render them indestructible as a race?

Francella had always considered her own interests above those of anyone else, but with her own death staring her in the face, she did not want to become the laughing stock of galactic history. No, she would rather give up her own life than risk being responsible for the elevation of the Mutatis to the immortal—rather than mortal—enemies of humankind.

On one level, she did not wear such an altruistic sentiment easily, for it ran counter to the narcissistic spine of her lifetime, and subjugated her to a footnote of history at best—without a chance of rising above the corporate legacy left by her father. But on another, deeper level, she was actually enjoying the new sentiments, and they felt right to her. Near the end of her existence now, when she was having trouble walking without a cane, when her own breathing was becoming labored and she looked a hundred years old, she was at least connecting with her inner self. It had not really taken her a century to achieve that, not in terms of elapsed years, but spiritually and emotionally she'd had at least that much experience.

No one would believe it if she revealed these innermost thoughts, so she felt it best to keep them to herself, not writing them down or recording them in any way. Many people found religion (or at least spirituality) at the end of life, and perhaps she was doing the same. In any event, it was private and personal, and she had nothing to prove to any other Human being, only to herself. Francella had set events in motion, and had attempted with all of her energy to destroy her hated brother, but it had all backfired on her.

Running parallel with that, even her attempt to bring Princess Meghina down were failing miserably. Francella had always disliked the attractive blond courtesan, since the two of them had been long-time competitors for the affections of Lorenzo del Velli. Francella had tried to ruin her by revealing her true identity as a Mutati, but that had not gone as she had envisioned. Through a cruel twist of fate, Meghina had gained the upper hand. She had become an exotic personality at the gambling casino and an attraction for the guests, going out and mixing with them, telling colorful anecdotes. Even worse, Meghina had received the precious gift of immortality, while Francella had suffered the exact opposite—a death sentence that was being carried out on her with tortuous certainty.

Ever since the discovery that Meghina and five others had achieved immortality from the elixir, Francella's medical laboratories had been taking samples of their blood and flash-freezing it. All the while, Francella had been pressing Dr. Bichette to make more elixir from these samples. But he had resisted, pointing out that it had only been a few months since their apparent transformations, and computer projections indicated that their bodies could eventually reject the elixir, setting in force a reaction like that suffered by Francella, or worse.

He didn't want to make any new product from them until he conducted more extensive studies. And in her decline, Francella was running out of the energy to argue with him.

She felt as if she had been chopped up mentally and spiritually, just as she had tried to hack apart Noah's body. On one level, Francella still wanted to destroy her enemies, principal among them her own twin brother. But on an entirely different level, she had been experiencing something new and surprising: altruistic feelings for all of humankind.

It occurred to her now that maybe she only *thought* she felt such benevolence. Maybe, subconsciously, she was really concerned about her own spiritual legacy, and didn't want to risk leaving herself out there as the consummate idiot of all time who had set loose a demonic elixir that led to the downfall of the entire Human race.

Francella could still risk that, widening the elixir studies, and maybe the worst would not come to pass. Maybe Princess Meghina had only achieved her apparent immortality because of some quirk in her body chemistry. She was, after all, unlike other Mutatis psychologically, and physically as well, now that her body would no longer change form. Francella had to admit that the courtesan had never acted like a Mutati, and investigators had never turned up any evidence against her to show that she was disloyal to the Merchant Prince Alliance or to Lorenzo.

She was too perfect to suit Francella, irritatingly so.

If only I wasn't so impulsive, she thought. *If only I hadn't injected Noah's blood into my body.*

With newfound clarity Francella wished she had waited for her laboratory to make elixir and that she had taken only that, without first contaminating her body, harming it with the raw primal energy that flowed through Noah's veins. But even if she had waited for the processed product, she reminded herself now, that would not have guaranteed the success of the elixir on her.

Still, the odds had not been *that* low: six in two hundred thousand . . . one in thirty-three thousand.

Through all the horrors that Francella had been through, her skin was not only wrinkling and drying out, it was also changing color to a sickly yellow-orange cast, as if an artificial tanning lotion had not mixed well with her body chemistry.

Across the room, a tabletop telebeam projector blinked, signifying the arrival of a message. If this communication did not please her, she would destroy the projector and open a new one, from those she had stacked in a closet, all in their original containers.

Opening the electronic message, she read the words that danced in front of her face, then changed her mind and touched a voice activation panel to listen instead. It was Dr. Hurk Bichette:

"Your troubles might have something to do with the fact that you are Noah's fraternal twin," Bichette said. "Perhaps there is a 'Janus Effect' at work here, with an opposite outcome for each twin. Noah is immortal, while you have become the opposite, and are suffering from a form of the aging disease progeria. We are following this line of research, and hope to provide you with an antidote."

Bichette went on to list, in his usual self-serving way, all the things he and his staff were doing for her benefit, how they were working around the clock, never relenting in their efforts to save her. She'd heard such drivel from him too many times.

In the midst of a sentence, Francella fired a puissant pistol at the projector, causing it to disintegrate.

But Francella had more telebeam projectors in storage, behind locked doors where she could not easily go on rampages and destroy things. She also had more than five thousand doses of the Elixir of Life, the same formula that had been sent out to the public. So far she had only consumed a few doses, and it had not gone well for her. Now she would try something different.

Shoving trash out of the way, the desperate, aging woman brought all of the elixir out and sat in the middle of the floor with it. Surrounded by laboratory boxes, she took dose after dose by squeezing the blood-red capsules between her fingers and feeling the prick of the injection needles. In a few minutes she felt no effect, only pain on the tips of her fingers, which were bloody from all the needles.

Dr. Bichette had warned about the danger of overdose, but at this point she could not see what she had to lose.

Chapter Eighty-One

> If something disappears entirely, with no trace remaining of it, how can anyone ever prove it was ever really there? Aren't memories notoriously unreliable?
>
> —From *Worlds and Stars,* one of the philosophical plays

The operators of a Mutati deep-space telescope saw a blinding flash of light, but it was not what they had hoped and prayed for, to God-On-High.

A fraction of a second later, the Mutati homeworld of Paradij—with billions of the Zultan's citizens—was obliterated. An armed lab-pod had gone off course and split open the core of the planet. The massive explosion had taken Paradij's three moons with it as well.

Receiving confirmation of the destruction by messenger from the communication station, Hari'Adab screamed, "It can't be! No!"

He could not hold back the flood of tears. It was late at night, with the cold darkness of an eternal shadow seeping into his soul. Trembling, he knelt in his family's private chapel, gripping the sheet of parchment that had just been handed to him. Behind him he heard the gently beating wings of the messenger as he flew away, and the opening and closing of the doors.

The ominous words had been etched on tigerhorse skin by the Mutati version of a nehrcom transceiver, and even contained—like the audio-video versions of other transmittals he had seen—gaps and static markings, reflecting the imperfect quality of the transmission. But enough remained to tell him what had occurred.

It was not supposed to have gone like this. He could not comprehend the immensity and error of the disaster . . . or his own part in it.

The old scientist Zad Qato had assured him that the Demolio would only hit one of the moons of Paradij—Uta—the location of the primary Demolio-manufacturing facility. Once the main factory had been on Hari's own world of Dij, but eventually the Zultan decided to move them to an automated facility on Uta, where he could visit the operation regularly.

In an engineering marvel that might have been one of the Wonders of the Galaxy if it had been widely publicized, the ancient moon Uta had been sealed with an Adurian-generated atmosphere, a living organism that cocooned the moon in an oxygen-rich enclosure that allowed Mutatis to breathe the air. Automatic gravity systems further enhanced the moon for habitation, enabling the shapeshifters to walk about normally on the surface.

After making hundreds of Demolio shots from Paradij, the Zultan had recently decided to move the launches to Uta. In a gala kickoff ceremony, Abal Meshdi went to Uta to broadcast the event to all the citizens of the Mutati Kingdom.

Infiltrating the Uta facility and gaining the trust of the Zultan, Zad Qato had calculated the trajectory carefully, and after Abal Meshdi's speech the lab-pod was supposed to have boomeranged around and hit Uta, killing the Zultan, a handful of Mutatis in his entourage, and a small number who supervised operations at the automated factory. In setting up the assassination, Hari'Adab had not liked the prospect of collateral damage, but under the plan it would have been a necessary sacrifice, saving trillions and trillions of war deaths—both Mutati and Human—at the hands of his insane father.

For some time, Hari had contemplated the unthinkable familial sin, the act of patricide. Sometimes, as he stood with his father, he had considered killing him on the spot, but always he had weakened. In close proximity, the old Zultan had intimidated him, and had prevented the movement of the younger Mutati. Hari had stood frozen, unable to go through with it. Even when he visualized making the attempt he worried that something might go wrong and he would fail. If that happened, he would never get a second opportunity.

He had considered countless other ways of accomplishing the dreaded task, such as sending an assassin after the old terramutati, or bombing the Citadel of Paradij. But his father had dramatically tightened the network of security around himself and all of his palaces, so Hari could not come up with any such plan that had the remotest chance of success.

That only left two workable options, doing it himself in close proximity or blowing up the Uta moon. Since he could not accomplish the first method, that left only the second. It was beyond unthinkable, especially for a Mutati who had always prided himself on his high morals. But it was the only way.

Zad Qato had assured Hari that the trajectory calculations and guidance system adjustments would be absolutely perfect. Now, Hari could not even yell at the old scientist, since Qato had been on Uta at the time of the launch, and the powerful detonation of Paradij had taken the moon with it.

Hari was deeply saddened at the tragic loss of his own father, as well as the old scientist and so many other shapeshifters. It had gone horribly wrong. By this horrendous act, Hari knew he had put a stop to his father's murderous aggressions. But that realization did not help assuage his conscience, not in the least.

There might be a few outriders still in deep space with the capability of firing torpedoes, and he could only hope that they were not on prearranged attack schedules. But he knew that the Demolio torpedo program could not continue on a large scale, since the Zultan had coordinated everything himself, and Mutatis would not do anything important without his blessing.

Now, in his private chapel, Hari went to a cabinet and removed a ceremonial sword. Unsheathing it, he pressed the tip of it against his fleshy midsection. And prepared to fall upon it.

At that moment, Parais d'Olor—hurrying to tell Hari about the podship landings—flew by the chapel window and looked through it. Seeing what he was about to do, the beautiful aeromutati crashed through the plax and knocked the sword away with one of her powerful wings.

"My darling, my darling!" she exclaimed, gathering her wings to pull him to her bosom.

Looking up at her gentle, compassionate face, Hari wished he had been faster with the sword. But that would have required bravery, which he did not have. He felt the deepest, most mournful sadness anyone could ever experience, for he knew with certainty that he would be condemned to the eternal damnation of the undergalaxy for this. He had indelibly blackened his soul.

There could be no redemption for what he had done.

"But why, why would you do this to yourself?" she asked.

After saving Hari's life, Parais escorted him into his palace and put him to bed. "You must rest," she said. "Everything will look better in the morning."

"That is not possible," he said.

"I will remain with you," she promised, "never taking trips away from you, never leaving your side. I love you so much, and you must believe me when I tell you that life is worth living."

Deeply despondent, Hari admitted what he did—the unimaginable, accidental destruction of Paradij in an attempt to stop his father's psychotic military program. As he told her he saw shock and horror register on her face. But she recovered quickly, and spoke to him in a soothing tone. "It's not your fault," she said. "It must have been the will of God-On-High."

"More likely, it was influenced by the demons of the under-galaxy."

"Forgive me for saying this, but your father was the most evil Mutati I've ever met. I was chilled to the bone in his presence. The galaxy is a better place with him gone."

He nodded, but did not brighten.

"Don't be sad, my darling. Wherever you're going, I'll be by your side."

"You would kill yourself?"

"Without you, I would have no reason to live."

Struggling to maintain his composure, Hari touched her face with one of his three hands, and followed her perfect contours with his fingertips, the exquisite bone structure and classic features. He could not imagine her dying, but knew of no way to keep her alive unless he remained among the living.

"With the Zultan dead," she said, "the victim of his own demented plan, the Mutati people need a strong, ethical leader to keep them on the proper path. And you—as Abal Meshdi's eldest son—are that leader. You shall be the new Zultan."

They placed their hands on a copy of *The Holy Writ,* and shared a prayer.

After Hari had rested, Parais told him of the strange podship landings on the other side of Dij, and of the Adurian and Hibbil soldiers that had disembarked. She expected him to say he already knew about it, but he looked shocked.

Immediately he dispatched his own military forces to the site, with orders to rout the intruders. In the operation, his fighters killed half of the aliens and captured the rest. They also took control of two podships. But these vessels, his scientists determined by tracking their DNA histories, proved to be of the laboratory-bred variety that his father had been cloning on a secondary world in the star system. And these two, unlike the others that had been so unreliable for cross-space shots, had navigation systems that worked perfectly, taking test pilots out into deep space and back.

None of the prisoners would reveal anything, but Hari's linguistic experts soon learned that the nav-units had Hibbil markings on them.

Chapter Eighty-Two

It should not be possible for a vast connective tissue to exist, touching every celestial body in the heavens, but this is, nonetheless, the galactic design. How do planets orbit suns when the webbing is intact, and fall out of orbit in sectors where the webbing has decayed? To comprehend, it is necessary to expand your mind, and when you believe comprehension is reached you must suspend it, because the true answer comes from a different portion of your brain.

—Noah Watanabe

Disembarking from the grid-plane, Noah led Anton and Subi along an electronic-camouflaged path to the main entrance of the subterranean headquarters. It was early evening, with stars twinkling faintly against a charcoal-gray backdrop. They walked inside a moving infrared bubble, which permitted them to see through the darkness in all directions.

"Are you taking me to the podship?" Anton asked. "Is that where Tesh is?"

"Possibly, but we don't want to alarm her by going directly there. It is best to act more casual, and broach the matter with her in my office, or over a meal."

"You're right. I'm just impatient to get on with it."

"So am I, but we need to be careful what we say to her."

"You mean, what *I* say to her," Anton said. "I have to

convince her on my own, remember?"

Noah shot him a rueful smile, and considered the situation. Despite the electronic camouflage, certain realities were apparent. Anton's father—Lorenzo del Velli—already knew the location of the facility, so Noah saw no point in concealing it from the young Doge. The information was out anyway, and besides, there was a cease-fire and Noah needed to work with Anton closely if the Human race—and every other race, for that matter—had any chance of surviving the growing galactic cataclysm. He even wished the Mutatis well, as long as it didn't come at the expense of humankind.

Though Noah had been indoctrinated from an early age to despise all Mutatis, he had never really understood the historical underpinnings of the conflict, and now he could not bring himself to wish extinction on them. There must be good and bad Mutatis, just as there were good and bad Humans.

Maybe Princess Meghina was one of the good shapeshifters. After all, she had tried to prevent Francella from shooting him on the Canopa pod station. Meghina was known as a courtesan, but she also had a reputation for being compassionate, and for donating funds to animal-welfare groups as well as to impoverished people on various MPA planets, especially those living in the back country of her own homeworld, Siriki. She had even been kind to Noah's father, Prince Saito Watanabe, caring for the old man more than any courtesan should.

In the red darkness, Noah saw a wide stone that marked one of the secondary entrances to the headquarters. Touching a button on his belt, the stone slid aside, revealing a metalloy door. From another control on his belt, Noah sent coded signals. The door did not open.

"I just changed the codes," Subi said.

"Yeah, I know," Noah said, "but I thought you programmed the new ones into my belt."

"I did."

"Don't worry," Noah said, as he transmitted more signals. "I still have other ways of getting in, an access override."

"We shouldn't have to use the overrides," Subi said, watching as Noah transmitted an alternate code. "Okay, there it goes."

The large door irised open, revealing a dark tunnel beyond. Subi led his companions inside, and closed the entrance behind them. Lights flashed on in the tunnel, and they hurried through it.

"In all the excitement," Anton said, walking beside Noah, "I forgot that I need to maintain contact with my own office, or they will worry about me. Can you get a message to them, under my seal?"

"Of course."

"You want to help with my diplomatic mission?" Tesh asked, staring at Doge Anton. Glancing over at Noah, she said, "Did you tell him everything?"

"Yes." Noah sat beside the merchant prince leader, sipping a glass of redicio wine. They were inside a large subterranean cafeteria, serviced by robot waiters. Noah saw Tesh's green eyes flash at him, and he felt the emotional charge between himself and her. He also noticed the interaction between her and Anton, the remnants of what once had been an intimate relationship.

"But how can you trust this man?" she demanded. "He's the Doge now, the leader of the Merchant Prince Alliance. Your enemies! How could you do such a thing?"

"You trusted me once," Anton said. On the tabletop, he touched her hand.

She pulled away.

"I want you to take me to the Tulyan Starcloud," Anton said. "It's essential to begin the diplomatic mission there. Your idea about going to the Parviis is a fine one, but it can't be done casually, not the way you did it the first time. No, I'm going to advocate that it must be a full-fledged mission, led by the finest diplomats, both Human and Tulyan."

Glaring at Doge Anton, she kept her thoughts to herself.

"For something this important, I need to go myself," Anton said, as if anticipating a question she might have.

"And your entourage?" she said.

"Not needed for this initial trip. Though the Tulyans respect Noah, they do not generally trust Humans. I must take this gradually." He smiled stiffly at his former girlfriend.

Tesh swished the wine in her glass, didn't drink it. "Something doesn't feel right here," she said. Looking at Noah, she asked, "What do you have to say about this?"

"I'm outranked by my nephew. He's doing the talking."

"Are you being deceptive? I'm sensing something else going on here."

"This is an important matter with far-reaching consequences," Anton said. "We don't have time for *feelings.*"

Wrong way to put it, Noah thought, shaking his head.

Flashing an angry look at Anton, Tesh rose. "You're in no position to be condescending." She walked away.

"Tesh, wait," Anton said.

But she kept going, and didn't look back.

"That went well," Noah said to Anton, when she was out of earshot. "She's not stupid, you know."

"I remember," Anton said. "She always was difficult for me to handle, and that hasn't changed. What do we do now?"

"Wait for her to cool off," Noah said.

After reducing herself in size, Tesh entered the sectoid chamber of the podship. Scurrying up a wall, she attached herself to the green flesh, where she felt the gentle, soothing pulse of the creature. Bathed in the lambent green light, she heard the faint background hum that had historically linked all of these creatures in the galaxy. Holding on to the thick flesh was no effort for Tesh at all. Through the connection, she peered through the eyes of the podship into the darkness, and up to the vault of stars.

Closing her eyes, she let her mind drift.

It was so peaceful here, and seemed to Tesh like the safest place in the universe, where she could gather her thoughts and sort through problems. Since landing near the Guardian headquarters, Tesh went to the sentient spaceship a couple of times a day, just to be by herself. Now she pressed her tiny face against the flesh, and felt the creature's warmth, and the subtle changes in its pulse. Each day that she was with the alien organism she felt closer to it . . . as if it was becoming part of her, and she was becoming part of it.

"I dub thee Webdancer," she whispered, on impulse.

It was an appellation that brought to her mind romantic images of podships skittering along the web, from star to star. She sometimes wondered if these simple, beautiful creatures should be left free and wild, to roam the galaxy on their own.

It had agitated her seeing Anton again, since it reminded her of some of the arguments they'd had after she met Noah, when Anton accused her falsely of not being faithful to him. She'd been with possessive men before, and had never liked it. Anton had taken it relatively well when she broke up with him, though he had seemed genuinely sad.

Sifting through her thoughts, she realized that she felt gloomy just sitting at the same table with him. Once there had been strong feelings between them, almost love, and she still cared about him. She also knew him well enough to sense when he was not telling the truth, or when he was concealing something from her.

But what could it be?

Anton wanted to travel to the Tulyan Starcloud very badly, to see the Council of Elders. Supposedly to make sure they performed caretaking operations for MPA sectors. In truth, that might be part of it.

Or. . . .

She didn't want to think about the alternative.

Abruptly, Tesh detected an increasingly strong tugging at her mind, something trying to break her mental and physical link with the podship, trying to take Webdancer away from her.

Her serenity broken, Tesh came to sharp awareness and fought back.

Deeply fatigued, Noah had been drifting off to sleep, just beginning to peer into a dream world of alpine lakes and canopa fir trees, with gnarled rocks above . . . formations that looked like living, fairy tale creatures. The rocks moved slightly, as if they were talking to each other, but they did not seem threatening to him. They were like sentinels, protecting the realm of his reverie.

But an odd, intrusive sensation began to come over Noah, as if two dimensions were rubbing together, grating on the tranquility of his dream. In a violent jerk, he had suddenly been ripped away from slumber and thrust out into the cosmos.

He found himself spinning along the vast, curving strands of the web. From what he'd heard, he'd expected to see only a few podships out there, occasional wild ones. But there were hundreds of gray creatures flying one direction and another, maybe more of them than that, taking courses that seemed different from those he had seen before. These ships were going slower, skipping along the web for a distance, slipping off, and getting back on again. Still, they were making their way across the galaxy at much higher speeds than conventional solar sailers or vacuum rockets.

To his dismay, Noah noticed great rips in sections of the web, ragged holes in the fabric of the galaxy and regions where planets and stars slid and tumbled out of orbit, with no web tissue connecting them at all. The podships went around those problem sectors, but even where the web looked normal the sentient vessels could not go as fast or as efficiently as the podships he had seen previously.

These vessels were most peculiar. Stretching his mind and peering into them, he saw that they were piloted by Hibbils, sitting inside navigation units that were unlike anything he had seen before. Surrounding the furry little men were arrays of computers and servo machines, blinking lights and panels. He saw no Parviis on board any of the ships. And in the cargo holds he found something very troubling, transport ships full of Adurian and Hibbil soldiers.

What does this mean?

With each podship that he viewed, he sensed increasing agitation, as if the creatures were sending signals to each other, warning one another about him. Gradually he felt his connection to the podships slipping, and the interiors began to flicker in and out of view. Soon he could not view the interiors at all, and the sentient spacefarers began to veer away from him, like frightened fish in a cosmic sea. Focusing his energy, Noah tried to take command of one podship, and then another, but to no avail. They sped away from him, in all directions.

As I suspected, they fear me, he thought. *They know about the sensor-guns I recommended.*

Their continuing reaction against Noah suggested to him that they had a means of sensing danger, but only at a primitive level. If they had been more intelligent, they would realize that he had actually saved many more of their kind than he killed by preventing the Mutatis from using their planet-buster weapons . . . weapons that destroyed podships as well as merchant prince worlds.

Breaking away, Noah found that he could expand his mind again. With a rediscovered measure of control, he tried to locate the Parvii Fold where Tesh said one hundred thousand podships were, and where he presumed that the Parviis were attempting to recover. But he could not locate the region, not in any of the sectors in the galaxy. She had told him it was in the most out of the way place, so perhaps he just needed to look harder. Discontinuing the effort for a moment, he tried to see another assemblage of podships, at the Tulyan Starcloud. He made out the milky star system, but could not get close to it, could not penetrate the powerful mindlink security veil of the Tulyans.

His mind arced involuntarily, and he sped across the galaxy, back to Canopa. To his surprise, he surged into the podship and saw Tesh inside the sectoid chamber. Somehow he had gotten past the defenses of the creature. Was that because he had been more closely associated with this one in the past than with any other? Did it trust him more?

Almost immediately, Noah sensed the uneasiness of the creature, but his own mind pressed forward, trying to overcome the resistance. He had not intended to fight her for control of the vessel, but found himself doing so anyway, without his volition. He struggled to break away and leave Tesh and the podship alone, but the more he tried, the harder another side of his psyche fought for dominance . . . over him, and over them.

Against the powerful mental onslaught, Tesh lost her hold and tumbled to the floor of the sectoid chamber. But she fought back ferociously, aided by the podship, and Noah was glad they did, because it seemed to him that Tesh had more of a right to control this creature than he did.

Gradually Noah found himself losing the battle, and presently he peered into the alpine dream world again, as he drifted off to slumber. The sentinel rocks were larger now, and more powerful.

They set up a defensive perimeter, letting him sleep.

As he continued dreaming, Noah found himself viewing the interior of the podship, but his hold was tenuous, with only flickering images coming to him. Tesh had just emerged from the sectoid chamber, and had switched on her magnification system. The images shifted, and abruptly Noah stood with her inside the passenger compartment, gazing at her while she glared at him. Looking down, Noah saw that his feet seemed to float in space, with swirling nebulas and speeding comets below him. He sensed the uneasiness of the podship around him, and saw the interior skin of the vessel trembling.

"My mind scanned Timeweb," Noah said, his voice remote. "I don't mean to be here. I didn't do it on purpose."

"You tried to take control of this ship again," she replied, a scolding tone.

"Not consciously. I didn't even enter the web consciously."

"Just as you are not here consciously now?" Tesh said.

"Yes. When I was out in space, I saw strange podships, filled with Hibbil and Adurian soldiers. The ships were piloted by Hibbils inside computerized navigation units. So strange, and troubling."

"There is a disturbance in the web," she said.

"Most peculiar. Thinking back now, I do not think those podships are normal. I suspect they have been created artificially, perhaps cloned for military purposes. The Hibbils and Adurians are not to be trusted."

"You must tell Doge Anton what you saw."

"When I awaken. So odd," Noah repeated. "Those strange podships veered away from me and fled in fear. Even this podship does not accept me. I sense its fear."

"I know," she said, softly.

"Why can't the podships understand that I don't want to hurt them?"

"Don't you know?" she responded. "After you recommended the establishment of pod station defense mechanisms all over the Merchant Prince Alliance, three podships were destroyed at the Canopa station. Podships, even cloned ones, know your part in the destruction of their kind. They sense it, smell it on you."

"I know that, of course, but I only did what I had to do, because of the terrible Mutati military threat. That's what I mean, that they should be able the sense the truth, the unavoidable actions I took."

"On some level this podship might realize that," Tesh said. "Perhaps that is why it permits you this close."

As Noah touched the interior skin of the creature, it recoiled and shuddered. "This is most distressing to me," he said.

"I understand," she said, "and perhaps in time they will, too. I don't blame you for the podships. You only did what you thought was necessary."

He smiled winsomely, and saw its disarming effect on her.

"Noah, I still care about you, despite all that has occurred." She smiled gently. "Since you have come to me in this manner, does that mean I'm your dream girl?"

"No question about that. I knew it the moment I set eyes on you, though I tried to deny it, tried to stay away from you. Look at this! I can't seem to get away from your charms, even when I sleep."

They drew together, and kissed. . . .

On the podship, Noah and Tesh had their first sexual encounter. For both of them it was astounding, but Noah wondered how it could have possibly occurred, since she was actually so tiny in her physique, a creature the size of a Human finger. Previously she had explained that the magnification system around her was so complete that it processed physical acts—in all of their intimate details—as if her body was really much larger.

But now, experiencing the spectacular sensuality with her, Noah could hardly believe it.

Chapter Eighty-Three

We have not yet seen all of the life forms that can be created in this universe.

—Tulyan Warning, a common finding of the timeseers

"I hate him as much as Francella does," Lorenzo muttered.

He stomped around The Pleasure Palace, where robots and other workers were preparing for the evening's gambling activities, carrying immense trays of food and setting up the finest wines and other liquors. Even with the cessation of podship travel, Lorenzo still had his valuable wines, especially old growth redicios and vintage champañas from around the galaxy, having accumulated them during his two-decade tenure as Doge. Keeping all of that was part of the deal when he abdicated. He also kept the del Velli corporate operations and his own Red Beret forces, stationed on the ground near two shuttle stations and on the orbiter.

Maintaining pace with the aged but still spry man, Pimyt moved his little legs rapidly. "It is too bad we didn't kill him," the Hibbil said. "Now Noah is making important political advances, aligning himself with the new Doge."

"My foolish son Anton," Lorenzo grumbled. "I'd disown him, but he has his own wealth now and wouldn't care. My options are badly diminished. Why isn't Francella keeping them apart? And what about her promise to give me access to the Office of the Doge? She must be dying. It can't be good that we haven't heard from her."

"Noah still has our prisoners," Pimyt said. "Shouldn't we negotiate with him for their return?"

"I don't negotiate, unless I have the upper hand. You should know that by now. You taught it to me."

"True enough, but it's embarrassing to linger like this."

"Hang embarrassment. It can't be worse than our failed attack, or having to abdicate." Lorenzo gestured with his hands as he spoke, and accidentally slammed into a tray carried by a young waitress, spilling food on all three of them and sending dishes crashing to the floor.

"Oh, excuse me, Your Magnificence!" she said.

Workers hurried to clean up the mess while the flustered woman used a towel to wipe Lorenzo's billowing white tunic, where a crepe had soiled the fabric.

"You're only making it worse!" he thundered. "Get away from me!"

She burst into tears and hurried away.

Kicking the tray out of his way, Lorenzo continued his angry march around the casino, ignoring the soiled white shirt and the food on his shoes.

"Do you think the Doge might attack me?" Lorenzo asked.

"Unthinkable. That would cause an uproar against him by the merchant princes."

"Still, I want more protection up here. I want you to order more of my soldiers onto the orbiter."

"But that would require reducing our forces at the shuttle stations, where they perform screening operations to keep undesirables from coming up here."

"Then put in a requisition and get me more troops. Raise a stink about it."

"Yes, Sire. Right away."

"We'll pay for it . . . or some of it . . . if we have to, but only as a last resort. Don't offer anything. Just make demands. I want more powerful gunships patrolling the space around us, too."

"All right. I'll take care of it." As if afraid that Lorenzo would give him a longer list, the little attaché hurried away, leaving almost as rapidly as the waitress.

Pimyt would prefer to have Lorenzo still in charge of the Merchant Prince Alliance, since it gave the HibAdu Coalition more opportunities to set up their military plans. But the coded nehrcom messages he had received told him that things were going well enough anyway, with Hibbil and Adurian troops stationed strategically on merchant prince and shapeshifter worlds, ready for major, simultaneous attacks.

For his own personal safety, and for the benefit of the clandestine military operations, Pimyt did not want the orbiter to fall under attack. Conceivably, Noah Watanabe could convince Doge Anton to mount an offensive against Lorenzo. It was not likely, but he wanted to eliminate the possibility.

Purporting to operate under the authority of Lorenzo, Pimyt dispatched a priority telebeam transmission to Doge Anton, asking him to broker a peace conference between Lorenzo and Noah. The Doge Emeritus would not be pleased to learn what he was doing, but Pimyt didn't care. It would protect the orbiter, and would give the Hibbil the additional time he needed to accomplish the goals of the Coalition.

Pimyt was stalling for time, but didn't need very much more now. The Adurians had discovered a way to speed up the process of growing cloned podships. As a result, the fleet was expanding rapidly, and the ships were filling with troops and military materiel.

Within the hour, Pimyt received a response from Anton's office, saying the Doge was away on important business, and would attend to the matter upon his return. There were other things as well—referred to in the communication, but not explained—that needed to be taken care of before any arrangements could be made for a peace conference.

Chapter Eighty-Four

The universe is a treasure chest filled with mysteries.
—A Saying of Lost Earth

As Tesh emerged from the sleeping quarters that she shared with female Guardians, she found Doge Anton del Velli awaiting her. He stood at the top of a stairway that led down to the cavern floor from the barracks building, with his arms folded across his chest.

"I thought we might have breakfast together," he said.

"We can talk here," she said, scuffing her foot on the deck. "I don't feel like getting indigestion, with you at the table pressing me for what you want."

"I need to get to the Tulyan Starcloud right away. It's very important. Look, you're the one who suggested a diplomatic mission to the Parvii Fold."

"I suggested it to Noah, not to you. As far as I'm concerned, you're not needed." She paused. "In any way."

"It isn't going to help the situation if you and I can't be on cordial terms. That's the least we should do, after the feelings we shared in the past. Besides, I never did anything to hurt you. Why are you taking this attitude with me?"

"Because I sense something, that you aren't telling me the whole truth."

He sighed. "I just think the diplomatic mission needs to be

undertaken with more preparation. I'm willing to throw my full efforts into the enterprise, and we need high-level Tulyan involvement, too. You can't just go to the Parvii Fold with Noah Watanabe, only the two of you. Is that what you have in mind?"

"I assume he might bring some of his top Guardians, such as Subi Danvar and Thinker. I know he has others, too, who have negotiating skills."

"Well, we need a lot more than that."

"How much more?"

"That's what I want to discuss with the Tulyan Elders."

"Is military force part of your plan?"

"The Tulyans are pacifists."

"Throughout most of their history, they were. But their mind-link attack with comets changed all of that. I'm afraid they aren't in the right frame of mind to talk with Woldn. And Woldn isn't going to feel favorably toward them."

"We can't just go to the Parvii Fold in one ship, with a few people. No matter the high office I hold, we need more of a show than that. If the Tulyans pitch in and we fill their podships with a diplomatic delegation, that will carry more weight with Woldn."

She eyed him skeptically. "You're still not telling me everything, are you?"

He grimaced. "You know me too well. But please understand that in my position, I cannot provide all of the details. This is a matter between Human and Tulyan governments, at the highest levels."

"And I'm a mere pilot, you mean?"

"No, it's just that certain matters of galactic security must remain confidential. I am the Doge, and you must respect that."

"You're not *my* Doge. I am a Parvii, not a Human." She paused. "So, you admit wanting to discuss additional, unspecified matters with the Council of Elders?"

"They involve sensitive diplomatic issues."

"And Tulyan caretaking operations for MPA planets?"

"Perhaps," he said.

She kept her eyes narrow. "They will do that even if you don't ask for their help. I know them, and understand their motives. MPA sectors will get the same treatment as other sectors, according to priorities. Are you going to ask them for favoritism? Is that it?"

"Of course not. I only expect what we deserve."

Shaking her head so that her long black hair made a snapping sound, she asked, "Why don't you send a message through Zigzia, the Tulyan female who works with Noah's Guardians? Through her, he is in regular contact with the Council of Elders, sending messages across Timeweb."

"We tried that, but there are transmission problems, and we haven't been able to get clear signals through. It's patchy at best; signals keep breaking up. Zigzia and Noah think it has something to do with the galactic infrastructure failing."

She was about to say something, but instead glowered and took a deep breath.

"For this mission, I can only do it in person," he said. "Maybe it's meant to be. There can be no intermediaries, no couriers or messaging technology. I must look in their eyes, and they must look in mine."

"Then you're not in any position to ignore me, are you? Not if you want to hitch a ride."

He reddened. "You're absolutely impossible!"

"And you're not?"

"This matter can't be delayed," Anton said. "Don't you understand? The galactic infrastructure is failing, and we need to leave right away!"

"And if I say no, the whole damned galaxy falls apart?"

"Something like that. Yeah."

"Why is it all on my shoulders?" Her eyes smoldered.

"It's not. We're in this together."

"Well, I don't feel that way."

"This goes way beyond feelings, Tesh. It goes beyond emotions."

"You just said the wrong thing again, *Mister.* As usual."

Before Anton could recover, she whirled and left.

Too upset to eat, Tesh headed for her podship. Nearing the tunnel that led to the vessel she ran straight into Noah Watanabe, as he rounded a corner.

"Oh, I'm sorry," he said, as he stumbled trying to avoid her. The two of them remained on their feet, and stood looking at each other awkwardly.

"That's all right," she said with a smile. "I have a lot of insulation in my energy field. It acts like an airbag, reducing any impact on my body."

"I was just looking in on our newest robot recruits," he said. "Gio Nehr was responsible for tearing them down and inspecting their programs, so to play it safe we've been checking all of his work."

"I'm heading for Webdancer. Oh, that's what I call my . . . *the* podship."

"I like it. Do you want company?"

"To pick up where we left off?"

He frowned in confusion as they began to walk together. "Kind of. I was going to ask you what you decided to do about Anton's request. He's young and doesn't always put things very well, especially to you, it seems."

"We just had an ex-lovers' spat," she said.

"Oh, so you turned him down?"

"It wasn't about that. But even if it had been, I'd turn him down. But never you. I enjoyed last night."

"What?"

"In the podship." She tossed her long hair over one shoulder. "We made love, in case you've forgotten so soon."

"That really happened?"

With a smile, she said, "I'd say so."

They reached the end of the tunnel, and passed through the electronic security.

"I thought it was a dream," he said. "My physical body wasn't with you."

"Sure seemed like it to me. It was terrific, like supernatural sex."

Noah thought about this and finally said, "Maybe it's a projection of some sort—like your magnification system makes touching your projected skin seem real. Maybe I locked onto something like that while I was dreaming."

"I can't think of a better explanation."

"Actually it seemed like more than a dream before I was with you. I was out in the galaxy, taking a telepathic trip through Timeweb. I didn't try to get out there, either. I was pulled out of my dream."

"Strange."

Ahead, beneath a shimmering veil of electronic security, the gray-and-black podship waited. They mounted a platform next to it, and a side hatch yawned open.

"Will Webdancer allow me to board?" Noah asked.

Tesh touched the mottled skin of the creature, and stroked it gently. "I think so," she said. "The podship knows I'm in full control now, and that you pose no threat."

With trepidation, Noah followed her. As in his dream, he saw the trembling of the vessel's interior skin, and he moved forward quietly, as non-threateningly as he could. He had heard of podships reacting to intruders by sealing themselves up and closing off all sections, suffocating the passengers.

Gradually, the trembling of the thick skin ceased, and Noah breathed a sigh of relief. But he had no illusions about regenerating his past piloting abilities. He thought that Tesh's presence, and her feelings of support for him, were calming influences on the creature. On a level that he didn't understand, these podships were able to sense danger, and he was pleased that he seemed to be making some small progress in convincing one of them that he was not a danger to their race.

"How does your magnification system work?" Noah asked, keeping his voice down. "That might give us a clue as to what happened between us last night."

"I don't know how the system works," she said, "only that it does." They paused in the middle of the passenger compartment, and the hatch shut behind them, a compression of cellular material over the opening. "Just as we don't understand how podships work, but we use them anyway."

"How do you activate your magnification feature?"

Pushing the collar of her blouse aside a little, she pointed to a tiny, dark mark on the skin of her neck. "I rub that spot for a moment. It's an implanted device."

"Med tech?"

"Enhanced. It creates an energy field all around me that makes me look much larger than I really am."

"But what happened with us last night wasn't technological. Unless. . . ."

"Unless what?"

"Unless there really is an area of overlap between the scientific and the spiritual. I've never been devoutly religious, have considered myself more of an agnostic about such matters. But the *Scienscroll* of the merchant princes says there is an overlap, a theoscientific universe of the heavens."

"Maybe the explanation lies in the holy scriptures of your race," Tesh said. "In fact, the more I think about it, maybe that isn't as odd as it sounds. After all, there is a distant genetic link between Humans and Parviis."

"Perhaps, though I'm not a student of religion. Or, the answer lies in a combination of truths from the Parviis, from Humans, and from all of the other galactic races, including the Tulyans."

"I hate to think that Mutatis are part of God's sacred design," Tesh said. "They're more like something out of the undergalaxy, something that should have never been allowed to escape." She shuddered at the thought. Then, as if to calm herself, she ran a hand along a bulkhead wall, and felt the faint pulse of Webdancer.

"Sometimes it's hard to envision the truth."

"At least you have eternal life now," she pointed out. "That gives you enough time to investigate the greatest questions in the universe and discover the answers."

"You mean like, 'What is the meaning of life?' "

She nodded. "Maybe it's even bigger than that. Maybe the question should be, 'What is the meaning of the universe?' "

Looking around the compartment, Tesh stared at the place on the floor where they had made love the night before.

Noah saw where she was looking, and smiled. She kissed him on his lips, and drew him against her body. But he pulled away.

"Did Anton ever tell you the truth?" he asked.

"Going back how far?"

Showing no amusement, he said, "I don't mean when you were lovers. I mean about why he wants to go to the Tulyan Starcloud."

She shook her head. "Just political doubletalk."

Pursing his lips, Noah said, "Anton wants the Tulyans to help him mount a military operation against your people. He wants to capture the huge Parvii podship fleet—all those thousands of ships—and prevent Woldn from using it to take revenge on the Tulyans."

"I thought so. That occurred to me, and I even asked him if he wanted to use military power. He lied to me, and I didn't want to believe that could be the reason." Tesh felt anger rising. "Does he expect me to turn against my own kind?"

"I understand why you're hesitant, Tesh, because he's talking about going after Parviis. I don't want to admit it, but I agree with Anton. He should not have lied to you, but he is right. I hate to put it this way to you, but we need to attack the Parvii nest. For the sake of the entire galaxy, you must be a Guardian before you're a Parvii, before anything else. It's that critical, my darling, and we don't have much time."

"I'll give you an answer when I'm ready," she said. "As for our little rendezvous, I'm no longer in the mood."

"Neither am I," he admitted.

They talked stiffly for a while longer. Then the Parvii woman opened the hatch for Noah and he went to his office, where he found the Doge awaiting him.

"Subi said he saw you with her," Anton said.

"I told her the truth. You weren't getting anywhere, so I tried a different tack."

The young Doge covered his eyes with one hand, then peered through his fingers at the older man. "What did she say?"

Noah told him.

Unable to sleep that night, wondering what Tesh's answer would be, Noah tossed and turned. Finally, he began to drift off.

And as before, Noah was sent spinning on another mental journey into Timeweb. This time he discovered a new aspect, and saw the web in curving layers that peeled away before him like those of an onion, showing some familiar aspects and some that were new to him. Each layer, he realized to his amazement, was an entire, huge galaxy. How many were there? He couldn't tell, and couldn't gauge the full scope of what was seeing. The images compressed, and again he beheld the familiar, faint green web lines of the cosmic filigree, with very few pods flying along it. He was surprised to see that the Mutati homeworld Paradij did not exist anymore.

Only a debris field remained.

Curiously, the less Noah tried to enter Timeweb, the more he was able to go into it. Two nights in a row. The sensation terrified and excited him simultaneously. He wanted to see these things and learn the secrets of the heavens, but didn't want to at the same time. He thought he might be several different entities at once, and that his life was like an umbrella for all of the creatures living under it, including the Human aspect of Noah, as well as his spiritual form that ventured into the universe, and much more. But details eluded him.

Suddenly he felt himself sucked far across the web, and he was speeding through space at multiples of tachyon speed, covering vast distances. Gradually, as if he was on a machine in the process of shutting down, he stopped spinning, but felt a sharp, sudden pain in the middle of his back. Something had just struck him from behind, penetrating the skin.

Whirling, he saw the image of his sister Francella—looking haggard and old but with a fanatical energy and the fierce gleam of madness in her eyes. Screaming soundless epithets, she flew at him across space, firing lightning bolts from her fingertips—eerie, noiseless lances of light in rapid succession.

He dodged them and fought back in the same manner—as if the two of them were mythological beings battling one another in the heavens. Moment by moment, Noah felt Timeweb suffusing him with power, and he drove the crazed apparition back, hitting her with so many energy bolts that her entire form lit up in flames that should not have been possible in the oxygenless void.

She screamed, again without making a sound, and disappeared into a ragged rip in the web of time.

Chapter Eighty-Five

> Think of secrets, small and large. Secrets within each individual's mind and expanding outward into the cosmos, until the entire universe is filled with them. Based largely on selfishness and narcissism, they have become an unhealthy, dangerous energy.
>
> —Master Noah Watanabe

Unknown to Doge Anton or Lorenzo del Velli, two laboratory-bred podships filled with HibAdu soldiers had slipped through Canopa's security network and landed on a desolate, remote prairie. Activating an electronic veil over them, they made themselves—and their new military camp—invisible to satellites or aircraft.

After the soldiers were set up with their assault aircraft and other equipment, Pimyt made arrangements to use one of the lab-pods, along with its crew. At shortly past midnight, the lab-pod flew to a prearranged rendezvous point north of Rainbow City, where the scheming attaché boarded it, taking with him a bound, drugged man. The prisoner, carried by a bulky robot, was Jacopo Nehr. . . .

The subsequent journey across space took more than an hour, a very slow passage that Pimyt learned was due to deterioration of the galactic infrastructure on which they traveled. The sections they had to traverse for this trip were especially rough.

A few minutes into the flight, Nehr stirred from his bench in the passenger compartment and struggled with the electronic cuffs securing his wrists, then tumbled onto the deck. Unknown to him, a Hibbil sat in a comfortable VIP chair at the rear.

"What is this?" the inventor demanded. "I'm on a podship? Who's back there?" Craning his neck, he tried to see across the compartment to the rear, where he seemed to sense another passenger. His voice was slow and slurred, the residual effects of the drug.

Pimyt muttered to himself. Without replying, he transmitted a signal to release the electronic restraints.

He heard Nehr walking around the compartment, and in a few moments he saw the enraged, confused man. The eyes were red and bleary, the graying hair tousled. Watching him, Pimyt sat calmly on his padded chair, so short that he couldn't be seen until now.

"You did this to me," the enraged inventor said, holding onto the back of a chair to keep from falling. He looked around at the mottled gray-and-black walls, which to him must look like a standard podship. "But how? Podships are operating again?"

"In a sense," Pimyt said, bouncing off his chair.

"What do you mean?"

The Hibbil shrugged, and smiled enigmatically.

"Shouldn't we be somewhere by now?" Jacopo asked, going over to a porthole and peering out.

Gazing calmly past him, Pimyt saw stars, nebulas, and brilliant suns flash by. "We're taking the long way," he said.

"The long way? I didn't know there was such a thing. I've never heard of a podship trip longer than a few minutes. Eleven or twelve at most. Where is my wife? Where is Lady Amila?"

"She's back on the orbiter. Now just sit back and relax," Pimyt said. "We'll be there in due course."

Pacing nervously around the cabin, Jacopo opened cabinets

and inspected vending machines and mechanical gaming stations. "What kind of a podship is this?" he asked, standing in front of a plax-fronted mechanical galley. "I've never seen amenities like these. Have they been custom fitted into the compartment? How did they get the podship to accept all this stuff?"

"You ask a lot of dull questions," Pimyt said, with no intention of telling him that this was a lab-pod.

The secretive Hibbil saw it as a game, fending questions and not providing any answers. He was not happy with Jacopo Nehr for losing his position as Supreme General of the Merchant Prince Armed Forces, punishment for the foolish attack on a sealed government warehouse and storage yard. The resulting fallout made Nehr less useful to the HibAdu Coalition, since he could no longer be used as a conduit for coded military messages. Most of the important military communications had already been sent through Jacopo, but a number of details remained, and Nehr's blunder was hampering their operations.

Even so, his firing did not make him entirely useless. He was still the father of Nirella Nehr, who was now the supreme Human military commander. Having the inventor-prince as a hostage might give Pimyt some leverage with her, to make her the new conduit. If he could ever get through to her and make the additional threat to reveal the secret of her company's nehrcom units. So far, she had been too busy to see him.

Finally, the agitated Jacopo took a seat near the front of the compartment. Several times, he got up and walked around, looking increasingly nervous and upset. At last he laid down on a bench and closed his eyes.

A short while later, Pimyt shook him.

"Whah?" Jacopo said. He seemed to have dozed off.

"We've arrived."

Pimyt climbed on a bench and looked through a porthole.

Below, he saw the largest of the Hibbil Cluster Worlds, and shivered with pleasure. He always felt this way when returning to the planet where he was born, the place where he had happy memories of long ago, before he began to work with the irritating merchant princes.

Glancing to one side, he saw Jacopo looking through another window. "You will be permitted to oversee your robot manufacturing operations on the Cluster Worlds," Pimyt said. "You will not, however, be allowed to contact anyone back home, and you will have no access to your own nehrcom transmitting system."

"Why have you done this to me?"

"Patience, and you will find out."

Ipsy had been on the Hibbil planets for several weeks, and had survived surprisingly well—largely because he was viewed by the furry little people as a novelty, with his patched-together body and free-spirited ways. After initially earning money by telling stories on street corners, Ipsy had talked his way into a job at Jacopo Nehr's largest machine manufacturing plant. A facility that used to export huge numbers of robots to the Merchant Prince Alliance, it was now getting by on much lower sales to other galactic races. Ipsy, with his marketing success at the Inn of the White Sun, had boasted that he could build this business, too.

When Jacopo arrived and entered his own office, he found Ipsy there, sitting at the factory owner's own desk. Knowing that the wealthy man was due to arrive, the little robot had positioned himself boldly, in order to get the most attention.

Remaining in his boss's chair, the fast-talking robot spewed forth a steady stream of marketing ideas. "The Adurians need to replace their delivery robots," he said, "and the Salducians are complaining about getting thousands of bad machines from one of your competitors. *Lemons.* And I can give you a whole list of additional opportunities. I've been doing my research, you know."

Feeling angry and irritated, Jacopo lifted the robot out of the chair and placed him roughly in a side chair. "Let's get one thing straight in the beginning," the former general said, slipping into his own chair. "I sit here, and you only take a seat if I give you permission."

"Of course, of course," the robot said. "You like my ideas, I assume."

"Do you know why I'm here?" Jacopo asked.

After a moment of processing data and blinking lights, the robot said, "To supervise your business operations here?"

"No. I could have done that from Canopa. Do you have any idea why I was brought to this planet?"

More blinking lights. "Not known."

"Can you find out for me?"

"You are the boss. But do you like my sales ideas? I worked very hard on them, and I wish to please you."

"Nothing pleases me at the moment."

"I will work hard to rectify that."

Jacopo nodded.

In the days that followed, Jacopo overcame his initial irritation and began to institute some of Ipsy's suggestions, many of which had excellent prospects of success. But the robot failed in one important respect, because he could not obtain information that Jacopo wanted. The reason he had been brought to the Hibbil worlds.

Chapter Eighty-Six

> Francella's moral fabric ripped open and she plunged through, into something entirely unexpected.
>
> —Secret notes of Dr. Hurk Bichette

For the better part of a day Noah had been using an intermediary in an attempt to find out about Francella, but no one at her villa or at her offices provided any information. The supernatural battle with her had seemed so real to him, and there had been the strange sexual encounter before that with Tesh—an event that she insisted had actually occurred. Could that possibly mean that Francella was dead? In the fight, she had fallen through a rip in Timeweb.

Hesitant to discuss the situation with Anton, Noah decided to say nothing about it to him. The two of them got together for breakfast and lunch, and both times they discussed Tesh, speculating what she was thinking and what her answer might be. Once they saw her walking briskly through a tunnel with other Guardians, but she strode right past them without speaking or making eye contact.

Every couple of hours, Noah went alone to his office to check status reports on his wicked sister. Just after dinner he received a telebeam response, ostensibly from Francella's house manager, a Mr. Vanda. Floating in the air, the words said, "I regret to inform you that Ms. Watanabe is deceased. She died here peacefully within the hour."

Noah felt an unexpected surge of pain and grief. Tears flowed onto his cheeks. Angry at this display of weakness, he brushed them away. He shouldn't have such feelings for her.

Now he had to talk with Anton. Inviting him to his office, Noah sat at his own desk, waiting. When the door opened and the young Doge walked in, Noah saw a mask of grief on his face.

"You know about her?" Noah asked.

"For most of my life I hated my mother for abandoning me," Anton said, "without knowing who she was. When I finally met her, I hated her even more. Then, when I spoke with her and her feelings opened up to me, I began to sympathize with her."

"I always felt sympathy for Francella," Noah said. "Even when I loathed her the most, I tried to be understanding." He paused to reflect. "It wasn't always easy, because of her mental illness."

"You've been a good brother and a good uncle," Anton said.

"I'd like to pay your mother my last respects," Noah said. "It's the least I can do, and I'd like to do it right now."

His blond eyebrows arched. "Now?"

"Yes. I don't want to attend any funeral service for her, not with crowds of mourners. She was a famous, powerful lady, and the mother of Doge Anton. They'll come in droves. I just want to say a few last words to her. Do you want to go with me?"

"What about security?"

"I can arrange it. We know from reconnaissance how she guarded the villa. Under merchant prince tradition, her body will remain there for at least a day."

"This could be a trap laid for you," Anton said. "I'll go with you, and you can use me as a hostage if anything goes wrong."

"I wouldn't think of it, *Sire!*"

"I understand more about politics than you do, Uncle. I'm

going with you, and you can't stop me."

Noah bowed his head.

In short order, Noah put together a security squadron led by Jimu, and went to the villa in a groundtruck. It was a clear night, with stars sparkling overhead like diamonds. The vehicle didn't stop at the front gate; with the robots firing their weapons, it burst through. Against superior firepower, the guards ducked for cover, not shooting back.

Disembarking at the great house, a hundred robots stormed the building, followed by Noah and Anton. They met no resistance, as the guards fled into the darkness.

Jimu set up a perimeter around the villa, then accompanied Noah and Doge Anton into the lobby. There, Noah spoke with the balding house manager, Nigel Vanda, a short, dark-skinned man who couldn't seem to stand still.

"Sorry I didn't give you advance notice," Noah said. "You know who we are?"

The man nodded. "Though I am surprised to see you together." He bowed to Anton.

"Where is she?" Noah demanded.

Looking dismal, Vanda gestured to the right, constantly twitching. "Mistress is in the master suite."

Noah had come on impulse, wanting to say his final, respectful good-bye to a woman he had always loathed and always loved, in his own private way. He felt recurring waves of sadness, more than he had expected. She was not only his sister; she was his fraternal twin. In the natural order of things they should have been very close, but it hadn't been that way and never would be. Their ill-fated relationship seemed symptomatic of the chaos in the universe.

He wanted a few moments alone with her body, but to play it safe he had brought the robots along, to prevent falling victim to one of Francella's schemes. Considering the possibilities, Noah had an odd, overcommitted feeling. Though he had brought along considerable firepower, something prickled the hairs on the back of his neck. He glanced around, met Anton's equally concerned gaze, and then looked back at the house manager, who stood shaking in front of him.

The nervous little man looked cheerless, with sadness filling his eyes and his mouth downturned. He looked as if his mistress might very well have died, and he had cared about her. Anton said he had seen her good side, and Noah had heard about some of her kindnesses from others as well. She just never showed that side to him.

And now she was gone.

"Take us to her," Noah said to Vanda.

"We haven't moved her yet," the house manager said. "I have sent for the proper attendants. Procedures must be followed."

"I understand," Noah said. . . .

Francella's body lay on the marbleine floor, surrounded by expended elixir capsules. She looked very dead, with her eyes staring into nothingness. Jimu checked the suite first, dispatching twenty robots into all of the connecting rooms. Presently, the dented little robot announced, "All clear, Master. I'll check the body now."

"No," Noah said, leaning down and feeling her neck for a pulse. There was none. "She's gone." Then, to Anton, he asked, "Could I have a few moments alone with her?"

"Of course."

Doge Anton, the house manager, and the robots left.

As Noah leaned over Francella he picked up her unwashed odor, and nearly gagged. The rooms were a cyclone, with furnishings and food scattered everywhere. She wore a filthy blue robe and lay in a fetal position, with her face turned to one side.

Out of the corner of his eye Noah saw something move, and he jerked in reaction. A black roachrat scampered over the garbage, ignoring him. Shuddering at the conditions under which his sister had been living, and in which she had died, Noah threw a holobook at the rodent. The creature ran off.

Feeling a wave of sadness Noah reached out and gently massaged Francella's high forehead. The wrinkled skin was still warm, so perhaps she had not died when he had the cosmic confrontation with her. She must have passed away sometime afterward. He felt his own heart skip a beat. She looked like a very old woman, one that had not aged well.

Why did she look this way?

All of a sudden Francella came to life and struck out at him with a dermex, stabbing it into his stomach. He stumbled backward, grabbed at the medical device, and finally hurled it aside.

"Too late," she said. The face was cadaverous, the eyes dark and hellish cesspools. "I injected you with my own blood. Now let's see if you are truly immortal after all."

"But how? You had no pulse!"

"Either I'm a zombie or CorpOne has a medical division, and there are drugs to simulate death." She cackled with fiendish delight.

Noah struggled to his feet, trying to assess how he felt.

Laughing cruelly, Francella then brought a knife out of her robe and held it to her throat. She paused, and her expression saddened. For a moment, Noah saw a softer side to his sister. "I'm so tired," she said.

"Hand me the knife." Noah tried to sound calm, but heard his own voice crack.

"So you can kill me with it?"

"Don't talk that way, Francella. Let me help you. Give me a chance. *Please.*"

Madness overtook her face, especially in the gleaming eyes. "I'd rather do it myself," she said. With an efficient move, she slashed her own throat. Blood spurted from the wound, and she slumped to the floor.

Noah hurried to her and tried to stem the flow of blood by pressing his fingers against an artery. It wouldn't seal, and sprayed in his face. "Jimu!" he shouted. "Get in here!"

The door exploded inward, and a dozen robots surged into the room, followed by Doge Anton.

"Master!" Jimu said.

The house manager ran forward. He looked confused, and in apparent disbelief. A good performance, if that's what it was.

"She wasn't dead," Noah said, glaring at the little man. In his arms, he felt her go limp and lifeless. He cradled her and rocked her, but refused to cry.

Jimu sent for reinforcements, and in a matter of minutes a small army of Guardians surrounded the villa.

On the second level, Noah took a shower and changed into clothes that were brought for him. Then, in the dining hall, a medical team led by Dr. Bichette performed a battery of tests on him.

Finally Bichette met privately with Noah, in an anteroom. "There seems to be no injury or adverse effect on you," the doctor announced.

But in Noah's private thoughts he was not so certain. Returning to his headquarters at shortly past dawn, he slumped into a soft, oversized chair in his private sleeping quarters.

He had never expected to be with Francella when she died, not like that. It was as if she had perished twice, first in the paranormal space battle and later in the villa. Somehow she had entered Timeweb with him in the earlier encounter, and she should not have been there. But it really had happened. One aspect of her, the spiritual one, had fallen through a timehole and vanished into another realm.

Then the rest of her, all that was left of her demented, anguished existence, finished herself off.

Chapter Eighty-Seven

Enhancements and extensions are always possible, but only within certain frameworks, which can be quite large. Ultimately, when the eye has seen as far as it can see and the mind has stretched to its farthest reaches, eternity and infinity only exist in the imagination. The paired concepts are artificial constructions, and not reality.

—Tulyan Wisdom

At first the knocking sounded distant, as from many kilometers away, or from a nearly forgotten memory. Noah straightened in the big chair, and blinked his eyes open. The louvers were drawn over the two windows in his room, and across the large sheet of glax in the door. Under the circumstances, with the perpetual darkness of living underground, he had tried to bring as much outside light into his quarters as possible through the glax, albeit the artificial illumination of the chamber that contained the barracks and his own private section.

Most peculiar, though. He saw blue light around the edges of the door. Rubbing his eyes, he stared, and heard the knocking again.

"Noah, are you up?" *Tesh.*

He shuffled over to the door and opened it. She wore a blouse and slacks, and her entire body glowed blue, as did the clothing.

"Oh, I'm sorry," she said, looking him over. "Did I wake you?"

"That's okay," he mumbled. "I had to get up and answer the door anyway."

She smiled thinly at the witticism. "I suppose you're wondering why I'm blue this morning."

"The thought did occur to me." He felt concerned for her. "Something wrong with your magnification system? It's not dangerous to you?"

"It's just a color I selected for my energy field," she said. "We Parviis can do that, and blue is the way I feel."

"Melancholy, you mean?"

She nodded and said, "You look terrible, Noah. Your eyes are sunken and tired, and you have dark shadows under your eyes. Out all night drinking?"

"Hardly, but I didn't get any sleep. Long story."

"I'd better go, and let you rest."

"Don't. I'm all right."

With a gesture and a yawn, Noah invited her into the compact room, which had been designed in the manner of a ship's compartment where space was at a premium. High walls were filled with shelves and cabinets, and some of the furnishings served dual purposes, with fold-down tables and a settee that converted into a bed. Too tired to even hit a button when he got back to the room, he had not activated the bed.

As Tesh entered and took a seat at a small table, she said, "I'm blue because I've made a difficult decision, one I don't feel entirely good about."

He felt his pulse jump. "The starcloud trip?"

"Good guess." She chewed nervously at her upper lip, couldn't seem to come up with the proper words. The blueness vanished, and she sat there dressed in white.

Watching the Parvii woman, seeing the turmoil on her lovely

face, Noah's mind spun. Her words could mean two things. Either she didn't feel good about having to reject the request from Anton and Noah, or. . . .

He didn't dare hope, almost didn't want to know the answer.

Looking away, Tesh acted as if she could not bear to utter the words herself, as if she didn't want to hear them from her own lips.

Shambling over to the table, Noah touched a brown button on one edge, tapping it twice. A mocaba-juice processor popped out of the wall and within seconds it started brewing and filling two cups with steaming, dark beverage. He smelled the rich aroma.

Feeling the need to fill the air with words, Noah changed the subject. While talking, he handed the mocaba to her and sat down beside her at the table. He told her of his second dream trip into Timeweb, and of all of the layers he saw out there, the wondrous galaxies.

"They are like the pages of a great book," she said, "the Story of the Galaxy. My people have a saying: 'Each layer is like a different version of the same reality, like the colors of a sunset shifting slightly, moment by moment.' "

"So many mysteries," he said.

"No Parvii I have ever heard of, and no Tulyan, has ever mastered all the mysteries of the cosmos. Perhaps if you gain control of the ability to come and go in Timeweb, you will see more than we ever have. Some things cannot be taught; they must be experienced."

Lapsing into a long silence she sipped her coffee, didn't seem ready to say whatever was really on her mind.

"Unfortunately there is much more," Noah said. He told her of his cosmic battle against Francella and the later bloody, final confrontation. "It was as if she died twice," Noah said. "First her spiritual self and then the physical, one after the other."

Several minutes had passed since he had poured the mocaba juice. He dipped a finger in the cup to test the temperature, then took a long drink of the lukewarm beverage.

"How awful," she said. She kissed the reddish stubble on his cheek. "I'm so glad that you're all right."

"I'm not really all right," he said. "Part of me didn't want her to die. I . . . I hoped we could be like a real brother and sister some day, despite all that had occurred between us. With Anton's involvement, and what he was telling me about the nice things she did for him, I thought she might be changing. It was like the way I felt about my father. He and I had been estranged for so long, and then there was a glimmer of hope. But he died." Noah hung his head. "Now I've lost both of them."

"I'm so sorry."

"I appreciate that." With what must be a pained expression, he looked at her.

"We're both a mess this morning," she said. From the sharp glint in her eyes, he thought she might be ready to tell him.

In a husky whisper, hardly able to get the words out, she said, "I will take you and Anton to see the Tulyans."

He felt elation but suppressed it, out of concern for her. The reason for her own sadness was obvious. She had made a courageous and momentous decision, choosing the Guardians and the welfare of the galaxy over the interests of her own people. It must be the hardest choice she had ever made.

"You are destined for greatness," she said, "and I will not stand in your way."

"But you are not a timeseer," he protested. How can you say that about me?"

"You are destined for greatness," she repeated, this time in an eerie, almost synthesized voice that sent a reverberating shudder through Noah's body. Deep in her eyes, he could almost see the entire universe cast in an emerald tint, galaxies on top of galaxies, stretching all the way back to the beginning of time.

Chapter Eighty-Eight

It is the most important thing I have ever done. On this event, the entire future hinges.

—Doge Anton del Velli, private notes

As Webdancer split space and emerged into the Starcloud Solar System, Tesh guided the podship toward the globular pod station floating in the milky void. Sunlight filtered through the mist. She judged it was the middle of the day in this region.

It had taken her almost thirty minutes to negotiate the journey across space, at least three times the normal duration. Suddenly the way was blocked by many podships with large Tulyan faces on their prows. At the same moment she sensed something inside the sectoid chamber with her. Looking around, she noticed a faint vapor that sparkled a little in the air, like tiny metallic particles. It dissipated quickly.

Ahead, the vessels parted and permitted Tesh to steer through their midst, into the main docking bay of the station. As Noah, Anton, Tesh, and an entourage of Human and robotic Red Berets disembarked and passed through an airlock onto the walkway, they were approached by a group of Tulyans.

Another podship pulled into the docking bay and moored. Noah recognized Eshaz's face on the craft, but in a matter of seconds the flesh of the podship morphed and smoothed over. Presently Eshaz walked out of the vessel, emerging from a hatch in the side of the hull.

The web caretaker first greeted Tesh, and the two of them spoke cordially for a moment. "I saw you in the sectoid chamber," he said, "and told my friends to let you through."

"I sensed something there. A faint metallic vapor. That was you?"

He nodded.

"We have different powers, you and I," she said. Gesturing toward Anton, she added, "The Doge has urgent business with your Council of Elders. He could not send you a nehrcom because your people don't have them, and he didn't want to use Zigzia and the web."

"It is too important," Anton said, "so I wanted to come here personally."

"What business do you have?" Eshaz asked.

"I prefer to only say it once," the merchant prince leader said. "Can you take us there directly? It is most urgent."

"As you wish."

During the shuttle ride, Eshaz told them that the Tulyans had been busy, and had wrangled an additional five hundred wild podships, giving them more than nine hundred in all. Eshaz reported that no Parvii-piloted ships had been seen out on the web thoroughfares at all, and he theorized that Tesh's people must still be holed up in the galactic fold, not coming out for any reason.

"Your fleet is growing," Anton said.

"Hunting has been made easier by the absence of competitors," Eshaz said, "though we don't know how long that will last."

"I'm not a Parvii anymore," Tesh announced. "I'm a Guardian."

Noah smiled gently. His brown eyes were filled with appreciation and compassion. He and Tesh exchanged slight smiles.

Showing his own appreciation, Eshaz nodded to her. He went on to say that Tulyans had recently seen other mysterious podships out in space, traveling much slower than regular Aopoddae. "They must be defectives," he said, "mutants of some sort, and a large number of them. My people, piloting our own podships, cannot form any kind of telepathic link with the unusual creatures and cannot see inside, even though we have always been able to do so with other podships, while piloting one of them."

"They may be clones," Tesh said, glancing over at Noah.

"I had a paranormal experience and saw inside them," Noah said. "The vessels are operated by Hibbils."

"*Hibbils?* But why?"

"Perhaps we can sort it out together," Anton said. "The sooner we pool our resources against whatever forces are at work out there, the better."

Later in the day the Council of Elders gathered to hear the important visitors, inside the floating, inverted dome of the Council Chamber. Looking around as he entered the large central room, Noah noted that the audience seats were packed with Tulyans, murmuring to each other in low, excited tones. Robed Elders began to take their seats at the high bench.

The floor beneath Noah was a clear material, through which he saw filtered sunlight, with podships tethered in the mist. He took a seat at the front with Eshaz, Anton, and Tesh.

"Who will speak first?" one of the Elders said.

"That's First Elder Kre'n," Eshaz said to Noah. "Some say she's as old as the galaxy itself."

Rising to his feet and stepping into a designated circle on the floor in front of the bench, Doge Anton del Velli wore a formal dark-blue cape and suit that he had brought along for the occasion. He held a liripipe hat in his hands. "I'm going to get right to the point," he said, in a firm voice that was carried throughout the chamber by the enhanced acoustics of the circle. "On behalf of the Merchant Prince Alliance, I propose a military joint venture between my people and yours, to attack the Parviis in their nest. I know you have traditionally been a non-violent people, but I am told that you did mount an attack against Parvii swarms who were gathering against you, and you scattered them in disarray."

"An unfortunate situation," Kre'n said, scowling.

"But necessary," Anton said. "Now help us finish the job. My military forces are the finest in the galaxy. With your fleet and the telekinetic ability to control comets and meteors. . . ."

"Our telekinesis works best in the starcloud," the old Tulyan said, leaning forward and looking down sternly. "Mindlink still functions away from the starcloud, but in a much diminished form."

"All the more reason to join forces with me. I can fill your ships with soldiers and war materiel."

"It is one thing to defend our sacred starcloud, and quite another to mount an aggressive military campaign far across the galaxy."

"Your ancient enemies are regrouping," Anton said, "and they'll be back, trying to accomplish what they could not before."

"Then we will drive them off again."

"Maybe, and maybe not. In any event, why wait for them to come, and why take the chance that they might succeed, using ancient, more powerful weapons? We need to annihilate them in their galactic fold, preventing them from causing more harm."

"These ideas trouble me," the First Elder said.

"We live in troubled times," Anton said. "But I ask you most urgently to consider the merits of my proposal." The young Doge bowed and swept across his knees with the hat, then returned to his seat.

By prearrangement Noah followed him to the speaking circle. Standing tall, with his voice strong, he said, "I have had a number of remarkable experiences, spinning across the cosmos in my mind, taking incredible mental journeys. It is all impossible, of course, but seemed real to me each time. Later I came to realize how authentic the cosmic experiences actually were, on a level unknown to any other person of my race."

As he spoke, Noah noticed all of the Elders leaning forward, listening to his every word.

Taking a deep breath, Noah continued, "Something highly unusual has happened to me, but I have never considered it power, not in any sense of the word. Perhaps it is an ability, or a talent, or just a freak cosmic connection. Whatever it is, comes and goes. No matter what, even if I had full control of myself in Timeweb and I could accomplish meaningful things in that realm, I would consider it a *responsibility* to the entire galaxy, not something I do for selfish reasons."

He met Kre'n's gaze, and added, "Just as your people consider it a responsibility to take care of the web."

"We have heard many stories about you," said the largest Elder on the bench, looking very intense and severe as he sat beside Kre'n. Earlier, Eshaz had said his name was Dabiggio.

"I am here to second the request of Doge Anton," Noah said, "and to tell you this. For the sake of the galaxy, all podships must be returned to their rightful custodians, your people. It is not a matter for diplomacy, though we have considered this option at length. Since time immemorial, Parviis have controlled a vast fleet of podships. It is what they do, and what they think they were born to do. I don't think they will move aside for the sake of anyone, and certainly not where their mortal enemies are taking a central role in using the podships. Instead, we need to strike the Parviis hard and recover the Aopoddae. Tesh says the Parviis are ill and weak, but may be recovering. And—they have more than a hundred thousand vessels."

As Noah spoke, some of the Elders stepped down from the bench and walked around him, looking down at him closely. The large aliens made him uneasy. Even the shortest of them was still half a meter taller than he was, and all of them weighed several times what he did. Finally he asked, "What is it?"

For more than a minute, the old Tulyans said nothing, and a hush fell over the entire chamber. Looking around, Noah noticed a certain deference toward him on the faces of some Elders . . . but Dabiggio and others seemed to regard him with suspicion.

"There are many legends among my people," Kre'n said, "and one of them concerns a Savior." She placed a large hand gently on Noah's shoulder. He felt her rough, scaly skin against the side of his neck, touching bare skin. "You may be the one," she added.

Noah did not particularly like what she had just said. Tesh's earlier comment bore some similarity: *'You are destined for greatness.'* First from a Parvii and now from a Tulyan . . . to his knowledge, these were the only two galactic races that had ever dominated podships.

Am I really the first of my race who has been able to do it, too? he wondered. *I think I am, but what if I am not? What if there have been others in the past. . . .* He paused in his thought process, when it occurred to him that he might be a genetic mutation that would continue into the future, from his own offspring. Yet another galactic race, or subrace.

If the galaxy survives.

But he thought his special ability might be gone, since he could no longer enter Timeweb voluntarily, and of late had only been able to gain entrance through his dreams. It was as if two dimensions were rubbing together at the time-and-space nexus of his life, sliding him into and out of each realm.

Still, Noah sensed that he had not entirely lost the ability, and that it lay dormant somewhere deep inside, verified by the dreams. One day, the skill would resurface again, but only when he was ready to receive it.

But the suggestion that he might be a Savior was an aspect that terrified him, one that he did not feel equipped to handle. Gazing up at the rugged, ancient faces of the Elders and at the audience around the chamber, he wanted to announce that he was not anyone's messiah, that he was just one man, and he would do the best he could.

As Noah considered this, he noticed that most of the Elders had returned to their seats, but First Elder Kre'n remained behind. Now she said to him, in a husky whisper, "I just read your thoughts." He had almost forgotten that she was still touching his neck, but now he became aware of it, and remembered what Eshaz had once told him, that Tulyans could read minds this way.

When she withdrew her hand, Noah felt sudden panic, and a swooning sensation.

"Don't say what you're thinking to them," the Tulyan leader urged, still whispering. "Let those who think you are the Savior continue to believe. It makes them more likely to authorize the military venture. Only time will tell if you really are the one. You don't even know yourself."

Reluctantly, Noah nodded. Kre'n returned to her own position on the bench.

Noah continued, speaking passionately. "At this moment in galactic history, there is a critical need for unity between Tulyans and Humans and cooperation on an unprecedented scale." The great chamber had fallen silent, while everyone listened to his words.

"I don't know the full extent of my abilities, or why I've been placed here at this time of terrible crisis." He paused and looked around the chamber with a determined expression. "Truly, I can only tell you what is in my heart, something your First Elder has ascertained with her touch. We must move forward together and survive . . . or die together. Doge Anton is right. We must form a military joint venture and attack the Parvii Fold."

Whispering filled the chamber, and Noah concluded his remarks.

After he resumed his seat between Eshaz and Anton, the Council engaged in a brief debate among themselves, speaking in low tones on the other side of the bench. There was a good deal of whispering, and periods when the Tulyans read each other's minds by touching hands.

Finally, the Elders resumed their places at the bench, but this time they remained standing.

In a somber tone, the First Elder looked at Doge Anton del Velli and announced, "We agree to form a military partnership with you. Due to the pressing need to regain our relationship with the sacred Aopoddae fleet, we see no viable alternative." She cleared her throat. "We will provide podships and pilots for the enterprise, while the merchant princes will provide weapons, fighters, and the military commander in chief."

"That is satisfactory," Doge Anton said, rising as he spoke.

"I must emphasize that we were never masters of the sacred fleet," Kre'n said. "Instead, it was a cooperative arrangement between two sentient races for the well-being of the entire galaxy."

"May I propose a name for our joint assault force?" Noah asked, standing beside Anton.

Kre'n nodded.

"The Liberators," Noah said. "It will be our mission to rescue podships and return them to you, for the stewardship and maintenance of galactic infrastructures."

"We are not inspired by such designations," Kre'n said, with a slight smile, "but it is known that you Humans are. Very well, for the purposes of this mission, we shall be known as the Liberators."

Chapter Eighty-Nine

The endings and beginnings of life perpetually feed into one another, in infinite and fascinating variations.

—Master Noah Watanabe, unpublished interview

While Tesh no longer wanted Anton as a lover, she had been impressed by a number of decisions he had made recently, all surprising in view of his youth and political inexperience. According to stories circulating while his demented mother was still alive, he had emerged quickly from behind her skirts to carve his own identity as a leader. Now he was working closely with Noah Watanabe, a man Tesh looked up to more than any other.

The aggressive plan that the two men had conceived for the Tulyan Starcloud trip had irritated her at first, but in the end she had seen the wisdom of their views, and the absolute necessity of carrying them out. The way Noah and Anton were setting aside political animosities between the government and the Guardians was admirable, and she liked their decision to bring a nehrcom relay unit along on the voyage. While it was of no use at the starcloud, since it was out of range of land-based installations, they had foreseen how it would be employed elsewhere.

As Tesh approached Canopa, piloting Webdancer at the head of the Tulyan fleet, Doge Anton used the relay unit to send a coded transmission ahead, ordering the shutdown of the pod station defense system. This was done, and the podships arrived en masse, surrounding the facility. A few of the ships took turns to disembark passengers. The vessels were unlike any others seen in that sector, at least in modern times. They had large reptilian faces on their prows, giving them a hybrid appearance, like the strangest race in the entire galaxy.

At the pod station, Anton's wife, General Nirella Nehr, greeted the Doge and his entourage, bringing with her a contingent of Red Beret and MPA soldiers. She wore a red uniform with gold epaulets and braids, the first time Tesh had ever seen her in it. The impressive garb suited her. This woman of impeccable reputation looked very official and comfortable in her position. She saluted the Doge, then stood rigidly at attention as he spoke to her.

"Begin loading our specialized military personnel and hardware onto the podships," Anton said. "Exactly as I told you to prepare before I left, except now we have a larger fleet than I anticipated . . . more than nine hundred ships. We will make stops all over the Merchant Prince Alliance, gathering the largest possible strike force."

"So it's really going to happen," Nirella said. "An assault on the Parvii Fold!" The female officer glanced at Tesh, then back to Anton. "As you ordered, we've been getting everything ready in your absence, including our most powerful space-artillery pieces."

He plans well, Tesh thought, looking at her former boyfriend. *Let's hope this leads to a good result.*

Although he struggled to conceal it, Pimyt was alarmed to see Human military activity on Canopa, with hundreds of podships setting down on the surface of the planet. Where did Doge Anton and Noah Watanabe get all of those vessels, and why did they have reptilian faces on their prows, giving them the appearance of odd Aopoddae-Tulyan hybrids? The Hibbil wanted to relay nehrcom messages to his people, but since Lorenzo's fall from power he was being denied access to a transceiver.

Using his remaining connections, Pimyt traveled around the planet to see more of what was going on. Through the payment of bribes, he learned what was happening: a major military venture to the Parvii Fold, with Tulyan pilots operating the ships. He felt his spirits lifting. There were persistent rumors that the Parviis had powerful telepathic weapons, so with any luck at all, the task force would be wiped out and never make it back to Canopa.

On the third day of military preparations, the door to Pimyt's office on the orbiter slammed open, and Nirella Nehr marched in, wearing her uniform and cap. Just before the door closed behind her, he saw her soldiers crowding into the corridor outside.

"Where is my father?" she demanded, leaning on the desk and glaring at the Hibbil, only centimeters from his furry face.

"I don't know," Pimyt said, indignantly. "How dare you come in here like this?" Actually he'd been trying to arrange an appointment with her to work his wiles on her, but she had either been too busy to respond or had her own reasons for avoiding him. This was not what he had in mind.

"Some of the people you've been paying off are talking, and we have established a pattern. You've been blackmailing my father, haven't you?" She was so angry that spittle sprayed on his face.

Wiping off his cheek, the attaché responded in a syrupy tone, "You and I might come to an understanding, in exchange for certain . . . cooperation."

With a sudden motion, she grabbed him by the neck and shouted, "I'll hook you up to the same Hibbil torture machine that Lorenzo used on General Sajak, melting his body piece by piece, from the feet up!"

"And what a galactic scandal that would cause," Pimyt countered, with a sly, ostensibly fearless smile. "Especially when embarrassing information about your father is released at the same time. Let's call it an industrial secret about how your precious nehrcom works. It's not quite as complex as you've let on, is it?"

When she reddened, he grinned and added, "The disclosure is all set up, an automatic reaction if anything happens to me."

Her eyes narrowed dangerously, and for a moment he thought she might murder him on the spot. Then she whirled and stalked off, without another word.

As she left, angry and frustrated, Pimyt realized he had only won a skirmish with this female general, and there would be additional confrontations. Maybe he should have told her more, everything he knew about the internal workings of the nehrcom. But she had caught him off guard, and he'd wanted more time to consider what to tell her.

Just then the door burst open again, and a squad of red-uniformed soldiers marched in. A young officer slapped a document onto the desk. "We are placing you into protective custody," he announced.

"But I don't need any *protection!*" the little Hibbil protested, as he was lifted into the air, with his feet kicking. "I can take care of myself!"

"Orders directly from the Doge," the officer said, showing him an oval red seal on the document. He snapped electronic cuffs around Pimyt's wrists and ankles.

"But Lorenzo would never. . . ." Pimyt caught himself, having gotten so flustered that he had forgotten political realities. "Why would Doge Anton do this?"

"Gee," the officer said, "I'd ask him, but I think he's kind of busy."

"Lorenzo will not like this!"

"The two of you can discuss it at length," the officer said. "He's being taken into custody, too."

The following morning the Liberator fleet departed, bound for Siriki, the second wealthiest planet in the Merchant Prince Alliance. As the warships left Canopa, the pod station defenses were reactivated, while ahead, at Siriki, they were temporarily shut down, for the least possible amount of time.

Noah, Anton, and Nirella rode in the flagship Webdancer, which was piloted by Tesh. Her vessel was the only craft not piloted by a Tulyan, and as a consequence it was the sole one that did not have a reptilian face on its prow. All of the ships (including hers) had a useful new feature: gun ports that opened and closed in the thick flesh of the hulls at the command of the various pilots, so that weapons could be fired through them. Intriguingly, the podships had done this en masse when weapons were being loaded aboard them, so they obviously had a collective way of understanding the lofty purpose and magnitude of the mission.

Many Guardians rode in the warships, including Subi Danvar, Acey Zelk, and Dux Hannah. All of them would fight side by side with Red Berets and MPA soldiers against a common enemy. But by far the most numerous of the passengers on board the spacecraft were Tulyan pilots, more than one hundred thousand of them in transport vessels inside the cargo holds, waiting for the opportunity to regain control of the huge podship fleet.

During the preparations for this ambitious undertaking, Master Noah had been at Anton's side, giving him advice and marveling as he saw his young nephew assume the reins of power and gain the respect of his troops. He was exactly the sort of doge that a venture of this magnitude required.

As one of the leaders of the desperate military effort, Noah felt strong and very much in contact with this dimension of reality, which was inhabited by his physical body and its conscious memories. In recent days he had not dreamed at all when he slept, and perhaps this had something to do with how tired he was when his head hit the pillow, causing him to go deeper into unconsciousness than the REM level of dreams.

At Siriki, specialized military personnel and space weapons were loaded aboard the ships, and the fleet moved on. This procedure was repeated at the seventeen largest Alliance planets, until they had what they needed. In the process, Noah and Anton discovered that Human military assets on all of the planets were not as extensive as shown in the records left behind by ex-Doge Lorenzo. The bases were smaller, and even seemed to be positioned in non-strategic locations. The two men vowed to look into it further upon returning to Canopa.

Having earlier discovered deficiencies in the military installations on Canopa, Anton had ordered the arrests of Lorenzo and Pimyt, along with their top associates. Even if they proved innocent of wrongdoing, Anton said he did not want to leave that group in charge of anything, not even the orbital gambling facility. He didn't intend to leave a power vacuum that Lorenzo could exploit.

With minimal fanfare, the task force set course for the galactic fold of the Parviis. Speeding ahead, Webdancer seemed anxious to join the battle. Not far behind the sentient flagship, in the midst of other Tulyan-piloted vessels, flew one under the guidance of Eshaz, bearing his determined face on the prow.

It was the most important military operation in the history of the galaxy.

ABOUT THE AUTHOR

Brian Herbert, the son of Frank Herbert, has won several literary honors, and has been nominated for the highest awards in science fiction. In 2003, he published *Dreamer of Dune,* the Hugo Award–nominated biography of his father. His earlier acclaimed novels include *Timeweb*; *Sidney's Comet*; *Sudanna, Sudanna*; *The Race for God*; and *Man of Two Worlds* (written with Frank Herbert). Since 1999, he has written eight Dune series novels with Kevin J. Anderson, all of which have been major international bestsellers. Their 2006 novel, *Hunters of Dune,* reached number three on the *New York Times* hardcover bestseller list. In 2004, Brian published *The Forgotten Heroes,* a powerful tribute to the U.S. Merchant Marine. He has been interviewed by media all over the world.

For more information, visit www.dunenovels.com.

ABOUT THE AUTHOR